Praise for *Simon's Dream*

A psychological and paranormal crime thriller, *Simon's Dream* by Jeremy Howe is a gripping hunt for long-overdue justice. Surreal, spiritual, and undeniably creative, this slow-burning novel digs into powerful themes of unfulfilled purpose, vengeful justice, and the casual violence of our modern world.

Simon Verner is still figuring out his future in the waking world, but once he falls asleep, he has begun occupying the life and memories of John Stinson, a heroic Chicago police officer whose brutal murder has become a cold case. Compelled to find the cop-killers, if only to get a good night's sleep, Simon enlists the help of a mystic healer, who catapults his consciousness into a kaleidoscope of past lives, revealing his rare and powerful gift. However, navigating the timeless space between waking and dreams is dangerous, and an ominous Void villain warns Simon to abandon his search for Stinson's killer, or face his own doom.

Unexpectedly emotional and inspirational, Howe has crafted a gritty and supernatural escape set boldly against an iconic Chicago backdrop, for an original visionary crime novel. —Self-Publishing Review

Simon's Dream

A Novel

Jeremy Howe

ISBN: 979-8-218-22257-4

Printed in the United States of America

Special Thanks

Thank you to my wife, Galixie, for her encouragement and support throughout this entire process. You're truly an inspiration and my best friend.

My parents, I love and appreciate you for everything you've done for me over the years. I'm forever thankful for you both.

To my friends Talmadge, Nick, Michael and Andrew, I appreciate you guys for always having my back.

Feel free to check out Michael's blog page at: https://medium.com/@mbronson

Megan, your hard work and time spent editing this manuscript is greatly appreciated.

Thank you to Garth von Ahnen for your time and effort with the cover art.

And thank you to the reader picking up this book to read. I hope you enjoy it!

Prelude

Present day Zimbabwe, roughly 15,000 BC

He kneeled alone in the mud for three hours straight, praying to their God, Mwari. He begged and pleaded for a second chance to prove himself to his father, Zooberi, the Tribal Chief. His last several hunts have proven scarce for the Tribe, with little to show for his efforts. Meanwhile, his brother, Magdoo, had brought back bountiful wild game to feed the Tribe. Their father had shamed and humiliated him in front of the entire Tribe, telling him that he was a poor hunter and provider to his people. But most hurtful of all, he had called him a lesser son than Magdoo. That is what brought him here to the Altar of Mwari.

His hands coated in mud, he smeared his cheeks and raised his arms skyward. He pleaded with the small statue of Mwari to make him a better hunter than his brother. He asked for more respect within the Tribe. But most importantly, he asked to be in better graces with his father.

"What are you doing, Mubiru?" Magdoo's voice startled him, and he quickly stood up and turned around to face his brother. "You know it's against customs to pray directly to Mwari without the Oracle present. Have you strayed so far from the Path to do this?"

"I must prove myself."

"Not like this," Magdoo said and approached his brother, placing a hand upon Mubiru's shoulder. "I will help you hunt. I will show you how to catch game like I do. Together, we can bring bountiful food back to the Tribe."

"I cannot bear the shame," Mubiru said, matching his brother's stare. "I will not allow you to pity me. I will prove that I'm a better hunter than you."

"Then you leave me no choice," Magdoo said reluctantly, lowering his hands to his sides. "I must tell Father. You ignore our customs. You must learn respect." He turned from his brother and walked away.

Mubiru spat in the mud as his brother left and resumed his prayer. Suddenly, a deep voice called to him from the Altar, and he leaned forward to listen.

"I will make you a great hunter," the voice said, beckoning the man to come closer to the clay statue. Deep, sinister feelings that Mubiru had kept hidden for years were beginning to bubble to the surface. "Break me, Mubiru. Destroy this clay entity your Tribal Elders have trapped me in, so I may be free once more, and I will help you be a great hunter. Break me. Break me."

Mubiru picked up a nearby stone, raised it over his head, and brought it down repeatedly with all his might upon the clay statue until it was smashed to nothing, reduced to bits and pieces.

A pair of hands grabbed his shoulders from behind and forced him onto his back in the mud, looking up at his father's face.

"What is the meaning of this?" Zooberi asked. "What have you done, Mubiru?"

The Oracle approached the Altar of Mwari, wailing. "You have destroyed us! Why? Why have you done such a thing?" She began to cry deeply as she picked up pieces of the smashed statue in her hands, shards of clay falling between her fingers.

Zooberi looked at his son with great shame in his eyes. Not able to bear the pain any longer, he turned his back on Mubiru.

An hour later, after a quick meeting between the Tribal Elders, Mubiru was banished from the Tribe. He was blindfolded, hands bound behind his back, and led far away from camp, into the Unknown under the cover of a darkened, moonless night. After an hour of walking, he was shoved down to the ground, his blindfold removed, and his hands cut free. Before he could stand up, the boys assigned to the task of leading him out into the Unknown were long gone, and the sound of their feet shuffling through the dry weeds had grown distant. Mubiru was not sure of the way back to the camp. It was too dark, and he could barely see anything. Hyenas cackled in the distance.

His heart raced as he tried to find shelter, or a weapon to protect himself. The Tribe had stripped him of his weapon, and he was defenseless. He cursed his Tribe. He cursed his father. But most of all, he cursed his brother Magdoo. He couldn't just keep his mouth shut. He had to go and tell Father what Mubiru had done, like a good little soldier.

Another hyena scream close by, almost sounding of laughter, made the hair on his skin stand on end. Goosebumps rippled across his bare arms. The only clothing covering his skinny body was a piece of cloth tied around his narrow hips.

Before he was banished, Father had told him that he wasn't to return until he brought back a special kind of herb for one of the sick women in the Tribe. She was with child, but she wasn't feeling well, and apparently this herb would help her. Despite the task he was given, he couldn't help but feel that he had been made an example of by the Tribe for something so small. His older brother was always making fun of him, mocking him, for how slow he was when hunting.

The lack of food with each passing season had become increasingly worrisome. The watering hole was drying up, and soon they would need to find a new place to set up camp. Water was scarce in this dry, arid landscape, but he had hope that he would be the one to find a new, bigger watering hole to save the Tribe. That was why he always brought back so little food on his hunts; he was exploring to find a new home for the Tribe. Or so he told himself. Despite his repeated attempts to tell his brother this, Magdoo refused to listen. He just wanted all the glory and recognition for himself, while Mubiru was ridiculed and rejected.

He crouched low in some tall grass behind a large boulder. The sound of rustling in the grass behind him, and he turned around to see what was making the noise. A brief growl, and the beast was on him quickly, clawing and biting at his neck and bare chest. Teeth sunk deep into the flesh of his shoulder, and he cried out in pain. He reached for a nearby rock and smashed it against the side of the animal's head, causing its body to go limp instantly. He threw the carcass off him and stood up, clutching at his bleeding shoulder. Two more hyenas attacked him from behind; one jumped on his back, the other chewed on his ankles. Three more. Four more. His fate was sealed. The ravenous beasts gnawed away at his flesh, exposing tendon and bone in his arms. A loud whistle nearby, and they immediately jumped off him, lowering their heads.

Emerging from the tall grass, a large, muscular man emerged, carrying a walking stick with fire licking the top point of it. He looked down at Mubiru with an expression of pity.

"You poor soul," he said in a deep voice, bending down to gently touch Mubiru's bleeding chest. "My apologies for this."

"Are you Mwari?" Mubiru asked, struggling to catch his breath.

The man chuckled, shaking his head. "No. I am Popobawa."

Mubiru's eyes grew wide, and the blood remaining in his veins turned to ice. He recognized that name. A name that brought immense terror to the Tribe. Popobawa was a great and ancient demon. Legend stated that this demon could taint a human's soul for the rest of eternity.

"Before you die, I will grant you one wish," Popobawa said. "In return, your soul will be mine until the end of time."

"My brother," Mubiru said, his ability to speak and breathe becoming increasingly difficult with each passing second, "I want my brother to be cursed. In every life. And… I want to be there. I want… to watch him suffer for doing this to me." Staring up at the demon Mubiru cried in pain.

"Shhh," Popobawa said gently, and he withdrew a knife seemingly from thin air. "Your death will be remembered, young one. I will make your wish come true, Mubiru."

A smile began to spread across Mubiru's face. The smile turned to laughter. It hurt so much, but he couldn't stop himself. This was all he ever wanted, to see his brother Magdoo suffer. For always being better than him. For betraying him. His laughter was quickly silenced by the knife that plunged into his heart, killing him instantly. Popobowa picked up Mubiru's lifeless body, carried him back into the tall grass and disappeared into a spinning black vortex.

Chapter 1

Chicago, Illinois. Present day.

The beeping of the alarm clock was the first thing I heard this morning, just like every weekday morning. Well, almost every weekday morning. Sometimes I wake up to my neighbors arguing, or the garbage truck below my window outside, emptying the dumpster behind the apartment building. But on most mornings, such as this one, it was the alarm clock, the most reliable thing in my life. I reach over and shut it off, ready to start another workday.

I examine myself in the bathroom mirror. My scraggly, curly brown hair has grown longer than I usually allow it to. Blue eyes and a short, yet pointy nose fill out the rest of my average features. I'm not ugly, but I doubt most women would consider me cute or handsome either. The best word to describe me would be average. The type of an average man that would be a perfect candidate for a police lineup, the victim of a crime taking their time on the other side of the glass, passing over me, knowing I'm innocent.

I take a shower, shave, then get dressed, all the while shaking off the cobwebs of last night's dream, which were becoming increasingly vivid every passing night. Dreams of being a police officer in Chicago, but they make no sense. Every night they're jumbled and disjointed, until eventually the dream fades away and I forget about what happened. Until I have another similar dream.

"Morning Hank," I mumble while sprinkling food in his small tank.

I just cleaned the tank last night, and it's immaculate. A small pirate ship is front-and-center on the floor of the tank, resting on tiny, bluish green pebbles. Bending down to watch my buddy Hank, I can see my reflection in the glass. The little goldfish, my only roommate, swims toward the food eagerly and begins to gobble up his breakfast. Good boy. I'll do the same.

I pour myself a bowl of cereal then check the fridge for milk. Opening the carton and taking a rancid sniff, I toss it into the sink and take a step back, shaking my head. That's not good. The cereal will just have to be dry this morning. That's just wonderful. Now my routine is already out of whack. I hate it when my routine gets disrupted.

When I get down to my car, it won't start. I turn the key in the ignition several times, pumping the gas pedal. This car is on its last legs, which I've known for quite some time.

"C'mon," I growl. "Don't do this to me now. C'mon."

I keep turning the key, the engine cranking without starting. Finally, after several more tries, it finally starts. As I exit the parking lot, the car backfires, scattering a flock of birds.

The morning commute to Lowland Woods Golf Course is uneventful. Just the usual, dealing with people that either want to go twenty over or ten under the speed limit. It's a race to some, as if they're in a life-or-death situation, swimming frantically toward the egg. To others, it seems to be a frightening experience, like they haven't left the house in a few weeks and the speed of the world is just too much for them to handle. I just try to make it to where I'm going without getting killed. If there's one thing I've discovered in my twenty-three years of life so far, it's that it doesn't matter how fast I drive; eventually there'll be a red light up ahead and we'll all be waiting there together.

I clock onto my shift on time, as always. Punctuality is one of my few specialties, a trait taught to me by my stepfather, Doug. A man that I don't much care for, but he did serve our country and community with decorated honors. Respect is something that he commands, more than deserves, in my humble opinion. I may not be the fastest, or most accurate worker at the golf course, but at least I can show up on time. It's the least I can do for this company that's given me a sense of purpose in a life that, five years ago, had little purpose.

"Good morning, Simon!" The cheerful, cute young front desk attendant Brittany waves happily at me.

"Good morning, Brittany."

She's a beautiful young woman, around my age, with jet black hair and heavy mascara around her brown eyes. Today is Friday, and this will complete her third week on the job. The rest of her is a total mystery to me, and I'm fine with keeping it that way.

For the next eight hours I serve the Chicago community by driving around in a golf cart with a metal cage around it, referred to as a "range picker," scooping up golf balls on the driving range. Rich businessmen, who either take the day off or are on an extended lunch, enjoy coming to the Lowland Woods course to blow off some steam and whack a bucket of golf balls around for hours on end. Golf isn't exactly my favorite sport. As a matter of fact, I don't like any sort of organized sports. Hitting a small ball into a hole with a stick is about as simple a game as I can think of, and I don't even really consider golf to be a sport. I don't dare say that around here, though.

A loud clank hits the side of the metal cage, followed by hoots of laughter off in the distance from a couple hundred yards away. The men high five one another, and another man takes his turn, intentionally aiming the golf ball at the cart. At first, I found this type of behavior to be immature, and the sound of the golf ball striking the side of the cage to be jarring. But after four years on the job, I've become used to it.

My co-workers don't talk to me while on the clock, probably because I typically have my headphones on while driving around the caged cart, or while in the breakroom, or anywhere that I'm not associating with customers. The job is simple, enjoyable, and most importantly follows a routine. Every day is typically the same as the last, and that's exactly how I like it. Unexpected excitement is not something that I particularly enjoy, and I'd much rather be back at my apartment spending time with Hank, listening to a podcast or reading a good book. Having a job that follows an uneventful, basic routine, is very therapeutic and has helped me immensely with trying to find out who it is that I really am.

I often wonder if I was meant for more, like serving the country as Doug did, or serving the community as a police officer, like I do in my hazy dreams. As a kid growing up, I wanted to be a police officer. Laws are essentially rules for a society to abide by, and I love rules because they follow a form of structure. If you stay within the specified guidelines, then you're okay. However, if you deviate from the written procedures in order to gain some sort of an advantage, or harm another person maliciously in some way, then you've broken a rule and need to be put in a timeout. It makes sense, when broken down in a way that a small child can understand. Enforcement of laws are something that I've always felt to be necessary in order for society to stay functional, otherwise there would be chaos and anarchy.

That being said, I'm not a cop, enforcing the laws of the land. Instead, I'm picking up golf balls in a motorized steel cage and serving as a form of target practice for rich men in sportswear.

While on my afternoon break in the cramped and dusty breakroom, I check my phone and see I have one missed text from my friend, Jess, asking if I'll still be meeting up with her and Ron at Moretti's tonight.

"*Yes, see you at seven.*" I reply. Friday night is my friends' get together night at our favorite restaurant and I look forward to it every week.

Steve, the company owner and my direct boss, enters the breakroom. He tries to get my attention by waving at me and motioning for me to remove my headphones, which I do courteously for him, giving him a friendly head nod.

"Hey there, Simon. Just making sure everything's going smoothly today?" he asks while eagerly clapping and rubbing his hands together. He's owned the golf course for over three decades, and he takes good care of the greens as well as his staff.

"Everything's going good," I say, taking a sip of water. "Well, I better get back to it."

As I stand up, he gives me a big smile and two thumbs up. I return his enthusiasm with one thumb up of my own, then walk past him, leaving the breakroom.

After my shift is over, I meet with my counselor Angela. Her office, located in a high-rise building downtown, is nice and plush with dark blue carpeting and pictures of flowers and happy children on the walls. I've been seeing Angela for about four years now. I really don't think I need a shrink, but my mom suggested I check her out, and Jess encourages me to keep going, saying that she's seen a big improvement in my attitude. Jess says it's good to let it out every now and then. I guess talking to someone about what's going on in my life can't really hurt, especially if the two most important women in my life are encouraging me to go.

"So, tell me, Simon, any changes since our last visit?" She always starts each session with the same question while crossing her legs. She sits in her high-backed leather chair, and I sit in my designated comfy seat. Today she's wearing a red skirt, slightly shorter than usual. It must be date night. She's always very genuine in her positive attitude toward me, and I can tell she cares about my problems, if you want to call them that.

"No, nothing too crazy," I say, then chuckle. "Although, last Tuesday at work, I did have a customer get a little upset about his tee time getting mixed up. But I was able to handle it, thanks to your prior advice about dealing with difficult situations."

She writes this down in her notepad, nodding slowly as I speak, giving the usual "mmhmm" after I finish talking.

"That's very good, Simon. Very good." She pauses and puts her pen up to her lips. "Anything new with your stepdad? Last time we met you were having another difficult time in regards to a recent argument you two had."

I close my eyes and shake my head side to side slowly. When I open my eyes again, I can see tears forming.

"Nothing's changed there." I say, then reach for the box of tissues. "Sorry." I say as I'm wiping my eyes.

"You have nothing to be sorry about." Angela puts the notepad down on the table and looks me in the eyes. "You two have had your differences over the years. That's why Jill recommended that you come see me all those years ago. After Doug kicked you out, you were lost and confused. But most of all, you were angry. I'm proud of the progress you've made. You've got a place of your own, you got that little fish, Hank. You've still kept your friends from school, Jess and Ron, and have a steady job. You were in a much different position when we first met. Both spiritually, socially and economically. Wouldn't you agree?"

She always knows how to make me feel better. She gives me an assignment to try and smooth things over with Doug when I go over to their house Sunday afternoon for lunch. I tell her that I'll try, but I make no promises. That doesn't seem to sit well with Angela, but I'm not going to lie to her. Honesty is something that I find to be the most important thing in a relationship. I expect those I trust to be straight with me, as I feel honesty is a sign of mutual respect amongst two individuals.

A couple hours later I'm sitting with Jess and Ron at Moretti's. It's a family friendly pizza restaurant and bar, with good drinks on tap, and an overall fun atmosphere. I'm glad we didn't choose some corner dive bar to host our weekly hangouts. The upbeat music and bright lighting help to lift our spirits after a long week at work. Our Friday night routine is to grab some food and drinks, and just have a good time in one another's company.

"So, how's that goldfish of yours?" Ron asks after taking a large gulp of his drink.

"Hank," I say, and take a drink of my own. "Hank's doing good, man. He just, you know, swims around a lot and eats and poops and sleeps."

"Sounds like you," Jess says to Ron, elbowing him playfully.

Jessica Williams, or "Jess" as she prefers to be called, has been my best friend since elementary school. She's been my go-to person to talk to whenever something difficult comes up, and I feel confident she'd say the same about me. Her mom passed away last year, and I was there to help her during that time. She's also been there for me during some recent tough times in my life.

Ronald Douglas and I met back in high school. His short black hair with some hair gel in the front, combined with his above average physique, make me pale in comparison whenever we're next to one another. Especially in a crowd of females. We didn't care much for each other at first. I thought he was cocky and full of himself, but after a while we grew to like each other, and now I'm proud to call him my friend. He also lives in the apartment directly across the hall from mine. He had put in a good word for me to the landlord to help me get the place a few years ago.

"How's that new promotion working out, Jess?" I ask. She recently got bumped up to a lead position at the call center where she works.

"More duty, more hours, slightly more pay," she says. "But I'll make it work. It's okay so far."

"Yeah, don't let the man bring you down," Ron says in his thick Brooklyn accent. His family moved to Chicago when he was ten. "My dad got put on salary once at his old job, and we barely saw him for a couple years when I was a kid. It was like he was a totally different person."

Jess is what many would call "beautiful." Her long, blond hair is in a tight ponytail tonight. Her blue eyes, which are like looking at two separate small ponds on a sunny day, are especially bright and reflective with the fluorescent lighting of the restaurant. Compared to my average looks, she's like an angel. But there's never been a spark of romance between us as we grow older together. Boys were after her all through high school. Even now, there's a couple of guys eyeing her from the bar, whispering to one another. I stare at them until they got the message and turn around. My mom always asks me, "Simon why don't you and Jess date?" And I tell her the same thing: we're just friends. I've always been alright with that, or at least that's what I tell myself. I don't want anything to change our friendship, and I'm happy with the way things are between us. The last thing I would want is to lose her by acting on feelings that she might not share.

I have a suspicion that Ron, on the other hand, has had feelings for Jess for years, but hasn't acted on it. At least not to my knowledge. It wouldn't really bother me if they did decide to date. After all, they're my best friends.

"You're still going over to your folks this weekend?" Ron asks.

I take a big drink, then slam my glass down on the wooded counter much harder than I was meaning to. "Yes," I say, and leave it at that.

"Will you tell Doug something for me? Tell him that Ron tells him to go f–" Jess elbows Ron in the ribs, sending some of his drink splashing.

"Please try and behave yourself this time, Simon," Jess says, then gives me a smile. Her eyes look like she's in some kind of pain.

When I get back home, I toss the key on the table next to the front door, then shuffle into the bedroom, lying face down on my bed. Sleep overtakes me instantly.

I know that I'm dreaming, but I'm looking through the eyes of another man. The Chicago cop that I've been having dreams of lately, all of which have taken place in a first person setting, just like this one. I'm looking through a car windshield toward a fast-food restaurant. The taste of the hamburger that I'm chewing is so realistic, and the breeze blowing through the open side window of the car is refreshing. It's as if I'm in a virtual reality game and am just along for the ride. I can see, smell, touch and hear everything this man can, but I can't control his movements. I have no control over what he says or does.

He pulls down the sunshade and flips up the mirror. His eyes are brown, his hair is short and black, gelled up in the front, and he has a prominent mustache.

Who is this person? I wonder to myself. *It's like I'm actually him, but this is not me. How is this possible?*

He's sitting in the cop car with the engine running. His long-time partner, Mike, has just told him the bad news. The man they arrested last week on domestic violence charges, Travis Daniels, has been released from jail. Butterflies flutter up in his stomach, then they're instantly squashed down by a heatwave of anger.

"This is such bull," he says to Mike. "After all we did to bust that guy. He was beating on his old lady, everyone could see that. How can they let him out already?"

"Between you and me John, the system's broken. Has been for years." Mike unwraps his hamburger and takes a bite. "Heck, I don't care who you tell. That's no secret." Spittle from the hamburger make their way onto the dashboard of the police cruiser. Mike always talks with his mouth full, something that's bothered John for years, but he's learned to just let it go.

Despite his receding hairline, Mike's always had that happy-go-lucky attitude to him, and a face that always looks like he's on the verge of breaking out in a gigantic smile. Everyone at the station loves Mike.

"We have a commercial burglary on North Halsted Street," a female voice crackles over the police scanner. "James & Sons. We need all nearby officers to respond. Over."

John picks up the radio. "This is officer John Stinson, badge 40092. We're in the area and on our way. Over."

He flips on the siren and peels out of the parking lot. Mike quickly finishes his hamburger and crumples up the wrapper, tossing it out the passenger window.

By the time they arrive at James & Sons, the thieves have already smashed the front glass window display of the jewelry store and are inside. John and Mike are the first officers to respond, but sirens can be heard faintly in the distance. They both exit the vehicle and draw their pistols, sprinting through the front door.

"Freeze!" Mike yells. "Hands up where I can see them! Now!"

Four men in black clothes and black ski masks put their hands up. One of them reaches behind his back, and Mike fires a shot. The bullet hits the man in the kneecap, sending him to the ground, jewelry raining down around him. The other three men drop the paper bags they're holding and put their hands up.

"On your knees!" John commands.

Two other police cars arrive, the Chicago P.D. emblem on the side of the cruisers. Four officers enter the store now, their weapons drawn as well. A woman can be heard wailing erratically from the back room.

"It's okay ma'am, you can come out now," one of the new arriving officers says. He takes one look at the man on the ground clutching his knee, blood soaking through his black pants. "Jesus, which one of you shot this one?"

"I did," Mike grumbles while holstering his weapon.

When they get back to the police station, Sergeant Doug Lewis calls Mike and John into his office.

"What happened in there?" Doug asked. "We got a traumatized store owner claiming you opened fire in her store."

Oh my God that's Doug! He looks so much younger, and with a full head of hair. This is so crazy! Why am I dreaming of a younger version of my stepdad?

"He was reaching for a weapon," Mike says. "I took the shot. It was self-defense, sir."

Doug turns his attention to John. "Is that true?"

"Yes, sir" John says. He clears his throat. "Self-defense. It appeared he was reaching for a weapon."

"Make sure that's in your report." Doug tells the both of them. "While I've got you two in here, I just wanted to let you both know that your applications have both been received and are being reviewed for the open detective position. Try and be patient, as it'll take us several months to select the best candidate for the job. You two go home and get some rest. Dismissed."

John and Mike look at one another briefly, then get up to leave.

Doug clears his throat. "Actually, John, why don't you hang back a bit. There's something I need to discuss with you before you go."

John nods his head to Mike before he leaves and shuts the door, then takes a seat at Doug's desk again.

"Between you and me, you're my favorite when it comes to this promotion," Doug says. "You've got the guts and the brains to get the job done. Something which is sorely lacking in this precinct. I've got an assignment for you to get started on. A form of on-the-job training, if you will. You interested?"

John clears his throat and leans forward. "Yes, sir. Very much so. But I don't want there to be any animosity between me and Mike. He's an outstanding officer, and I'm proud to call him my partner. He's a good friend to me."

Doug waves his hand dismissively. "If he can't holster his weapon during a simple robbery, he's no good to me. You're the right man for the job. Prove me right, and the promotion is yours."

"Understood. Thank you, sir."

"Don't thank me yet, son. This case is going to test you. I'll give you a brief overview. A couple days ago, the mayor's brother, Tony Alvarez, was murdered. I don't want Mike on this case. He's too much of a loose cannon, and I don't want him stirring up a hornet's nest." Doug slides two photographs along the wooden desk in front of John, and points at one of them. "This here is our main person to interrogate, Rafael Chavez. I need you to press this man for information. And when I say press him, I mean it. He's hiding the truth, and he needs to be broken."

Doug takes a breath and continues. "As chance may have it, this is also the same man that Mike shot in the leg today. He's the right hand to this man, William Marcini." Doug points to a photo of the second man, a well-known figure around the city. "Marcini's crime family is strengthening its hold on this city. But as you know, we walk a fine line with him. He's one of the biggest supporters of the police in this town, so we need to tread lightly. I don't want you going all gangbusters on this, Stinson. Keep a low profile. Our best detectives haven't been able to solve this thing, so I figured a fresh set of eyes might do the trick. But you have to keep this discreet, understood? Nobody's to know you're investigating Alvarez's murder."

He hands John a thick file to read over and study.

Later that evening John's at home eating dinner with his lovely wife, Samantha. They own a small two-bedroom home in the suburbs.

"Hon, I have some news," Samantha says, resting her hands in her lap.

Once he's done chewing, John gives Samantha his full, undivided attention and puts down his fork.

She smiles at him, her dimples showing. "You're going to be a father, John."

He stares at Samantha. Suddenly, he scoots his chair back, the legs of the chair grinding against the linoleum floor and walks over to his wife. Putting his arms around her, he begins laughing and kissing her cheek repeatedly. She joins in his laughter. Holding each other's hands, they each quiet down and stare at one another, keeping a sharp focus on their partner.

"That's the best news I've heard all day," he says, a tear streaking down his cheek. "I'm so proud of you, hon."

She rests her hand over his right hand. John's the happiest he's been in his whole life. He's going to be a father. Someday, another human will be calling him Dad.

Suddenly, the kitchen walls and table begin to fade away, and morning sunlight hits me in the face. It's Saturday morning.

Chapter 2

I finish signing the paperwork shoved in front of me, and the salesman walks me over to the brand new, shiny blue sports car. She has a big spoiler sticking off the back, and chrome wheels. It's a dream come true.

"Congratulations, sir," the salesman says, and holds the keys out in front of me. I snatch them eagerly and unlock the car. "Might I say, I'm a bit jealous," he continues, leaning against the hood as I open the door and hop in. "Now, Mr. Verner, drive safely. Come back if you need anything. Give me a call if you're in the market for–"

"Thanks, Josh. Great job," I abruptly say and shut the door. The car starts right up with a boisterous roar. She drives beautifully. I've had my eye on this vehicle for several weeks, and I had come in after work on Monday to start the application process. Sure, the asking price was a bit high, but I was able to negotiate Josh down to a more reasonable deal and traded in my old clunker. I've always been what Jess calls a bit careless with my money. It's one of the few issues she and I have ever disagreed on. What she calls careless, I call carefree. It's my money after all.

Clouds are populating the early afternoon sky as I get on the interstate, picking up speed faster than I ever could in my old ride. The vehicle even comes with a sunroof, and I pop it open to let a fresh breeze roll through. This is what's it's all about. Work hard and play harder. Doug's going to be so jealous when he sees me roll up in this baby tomorrow, and Mom's going to flip a lid. In excitement, I hope.

I'm passing cars like they're standing still as I make my way north on Highway 41 with Lake Michigan to my right. This is the happiest I've been in a long time. The power of the vehicle, the plush leather steering wheel in my hands and my curly hair flapping in the wind through the open sunroof; all of these new feelings give me a sense of freedom that I haven't felt in quite some time. I let out a rebel yell as I push the pedal down, begging the car to go faster and she responds immediately by giving me more and more speed. The rush of adrenaline overtakes me and I yell louder. It's out of character for me to drive so far above the speed limit, but darn it, this is a once in a lifetime experience for me. Finally, I have a car that I won't have to struggle to get started every morning. I have a car that actually goes faster than other cars. This is what freedom feels like!

For several hours I drive around the area, until eventually I'm heading East on Interstate 90 going through the old, nearly abandoned city of Gary, Indiana. Passing through Gary has always brought me back to reality some, seeing a once great American city turned over to criminals and great big, beautiful buildings left abandoned and rotting away to the mercy of time.

A short time later, I head back toward Chicago and drive to Jess' apartment. I text her from the parking lot, asking if she's available to hang out. She responds back that she is and buzzes me up.

"So, what brings you by?" Jess asks while toweling off her wet hair.

"I just bought a new car!" I exclaim, slightly out of breath, and lead her to the window looking down at the parking lot. "You see it? It's that blue one right down there."

"Wow," she says, cautious excitement in her voice. "What made you decide to get a new car?"

"Well, let's just say it was time. My old ride…she was running rough, and bless her heart, she gave it all she had to get me to work and back. But I needed an upgrade, so I went out and did just that."

"Well, I'm happy for you," she says. "Give me a few minutes to get ready and you can take me for a ride, if you want?"

"Sounds good," I say.

Jess is a very talented artist, working exclusively with oil paintings. Her primary focus is on still life and portraits of others. Paintings of bowls filled with fruit, vases filled with flowers, and an assortment of others line the walls of her apartment. Several months ago, she had sold me some paintings, which I turned around and sold to a local art collector. The money I got from that sale is what I used for the down payment on my new car. Deep down, I feel guilty about doing that, and I haven't been able to bring myself to tell Jess that I sold her art, but I'm sure she would understand.

A few minutes later, Jess and I are walking out to my car. She takes a few minutes to admire the vehicle and pretends to pose in front of it like a model on The Price is Right. I open the door for her and drive us down to the mall for an afternoon of shopping.

We browse around the various stores, and I buy a pair of shorts after trying them on. Afterwards, we go to the food court and grab some lunch.

"Does Ron work tonight?" Jess asks.

"Yeah, I think so. I didn't bother to knock on his door before I left this morning. Figured he wanted to crash after working last night."

She grabs a fry and chews off half of it, the other half dangling in her hand. She stares off into the distance, deep in thought. Then she turns her focus back to me, a look of exhaustion on her face.

"My job's just got me so mentally worn down lately," she sighs, then smiles. "Did you want to watch a movie?"

"Sure. Sounds good."

After we finish our lunch, which mostly consisted of a debate of which movie to go see, we walk into the cinema connected to the mall. I concede to her wishes and agree to watch the movie that she'd chosen, which turns out to be a chick-flick.

Sitting next to her in the theater, her arm placed on our adjoining arm rest, a sudden urge comes over me to place my hand on top of hers. I stare at her smooth skin, wondering what it would be like to have her fingers laced between mine. My heartbeat quickens, and I snap my attention back to the screen, shaking my head. Why would I even think of wanting to hold her hand? Grow up, Simon.

Jess laughs at something that happened in the movie, and I chuckle with her, not sure what it was that had happened. Her laugh is contagious. Every time I hear that genuine belly laugh, the urge to laugh with her always overtakes me. She has a wonderful sense of humor, something that I find to be one of her most endearing qualities, to go along with her smarts and kindness. I look back down at her hand, but my arms remain firmly planted in my lap.

Whether or not I should hold my friend's hand in the movie is so immature, isn't it? Why would I want to potentially damage a healthy relationship with her? These are thoughts that should be going through a fifteen-year-old, not someone eight years further along in life.

Ignoring all the warning signals and red flags, I pick up my right hand, and force myself to move my arm in her direction. This is it, the moment to test the boundaries of our relationship, to see if she's feeling the same way that I am. We're both adults, after all.

Sure, some may call me a sicko for wanting to tamper with the infamous "friend zone" that females seem to box some of their male friends into. While it's true that my friendship with Jess matters more to me than anything in my life right now, deep down I want this friendship to be more. Subconsciously, I've known for years that I wanted our relationship to take the next step. But something has been preventing me from taking the leap. A reluctance, perhaps, to be rejected, and have Jess tell Ron and all of her friends what a loser I am is for trying to put the moves on her for no reason.

I can picture it now, Jess telling her girlfriends that men are insufferable pigs, that they only want one thing out of a relationship, while women want so much more. She would tell her friends that she thought Simon was a good friend, not someone who ignored the friend zone. The shame. The hurt. I can't do it. I pull my hand back and put it back in my lap.

"I'm going to the bathroom," Jess whispers in my ear, and gets up to leave.

My face is flushed, my palms are sweaty, and my heart's beating like I've just ran a marathon. That was a close call. Thankfully, her call to nature saved me from making a monumental mistake. I take a deep breath, and attempt to get back into the movie.

I seize my opportunity and gain control of the arm rest.

When Jess returns to her seat a few minutes later, she keeps her hands in her lap for the rest of the movie. That feels much better now. I smile, a wave of relief and satisfaction washing over me, melting away my previously overwhelming sense of anxiety.

Toward the end of the movie, out of my peripheral vision, I get the feeling that she's staring at me, her head slightly tilted in my direction. However, when I look over at her, she's staring straight at the screen. It must've just been my imagination.

Later that night after dropping her off at her apartment, I relax in my own place. Bringing a wooden chair over from my computer to Hank's fish tank, I sit and watch my little buddy swim around. Time just seems to stand still as I watch him meander back and forth in his little home. I prop my elbow on my knee, resting my chin on my fist, viewing the show. Bubbles are released from a small plastic scuba diver in the bottom of the tank, one of the added features I've recently installed in Hank's aquatic paradise, and I watch as they dance and float up to the surface.

Almost four years ago, I remember when my mom, Jill, bought little Hank when I had first moved into this place. He was much smaller back then, probably about half the size he is now, and she was holding him in a little plastic bag of water. My apartment, on the other hand, felt much bigger when I first moved in. I was so excited to have found this place, with the help of Ron. I'm still very much content and lucky to have lived here for so long, and I'll always be thankful to have a roof over my head. Nothing really beats the feeling of having a place to call home after not having one for over a year.

Back at that time, with baby Hank in his bag, my hair was much longer, down past my shoulders. Mom was examining the apartment, ducking her head into the bathroom, then making her way back into the bedroom. The apartment is very narrow. The entry way immediately leads into the kitchen, and behind the kitchen is the bathroom off to the right. Across the hallway from the bathroom is Hank's fish tank. Further on is the bedroom off to the right, and straight ahead is a small living room area with a window. When I had first moved in, the only furniture I had was the chair I'm sitting in now and the same bed I still own.

I remember as Jill had set Hank's bag down on the table, which at the time was placed where Hank's tank is now, she had looked at me with a sad sort of expression on her face. A look almost of pity.

"Are you going to be safe here?" she asked with a heightened level of concern. "Is this neighborhood really the best to be living in?"

"Like you care," I said, not able to bring myself to look at the woman who had the audacity to call herself a mother.

She looked at me, her car keys dangling in one hand, and nodded her head.

"I suppose that was deserved. I won't keep you for long. I just wanted to bring you a housewarming present."

"Wow, a goldfish," I said, looking at the plastic bag with baby Hank staring at me. "What in the hell am I going to do with a goldfish? Eat it? Is that supposed to be dinner or something? You're the best, Mom."

"Doug's down in the car. I better get going."

She bent down to give me a kiss on my forehead, then turned to leave. She stopped at the door and turned around. "I know you blame me for what happened, and I hope one day you can find it in your heart to forgive me."

"I don't blame you, I blame Doug," I said, raising my voice. "That guy treated me like I was some kind of soldier, not the 'son he always wanted.' You remember that crap he always used to say when you two started going out?"

Jill looked down at the ground and sniffed. "He just wanted you to–"

"To what? Huh, Jill? To follow in his footsteps? I just wanted peace and space, and you couldn't even give me that!"

"That's only half the story, and you know it."

"Go on, get out!" I yelled. "Go back to Doug!"

The sound of pounding came from the other side of the wall next to me, followed by a man yelling "keep it down!" I looked over at the wall, and by the time I look back at Jill, she'd left, and the door was closed. Looking up at the ceiling with paint peeling away, my vision became momentarily clouded with tears. I wiped my face with the back of my hand, and looked back down at the plastic bag, the little fish still swimming in place, staring at me.

"What are you looking at?"

I stood up and walked to the window, staring out at the dark parking lot. I could see Jill getting into Doug's car, and she shut the passenger door. Police sirens could be heard nearby, and two cop cars were speeding down the road behind the parking lot. I can still remember the neighbors above me stomping around like they were having tryouts for a dance team. The neighbors in the apartment next to me, where the pounding came from, were also making noise. A loud, rhythmic thumping against the wall, followed by the sound of a woman's screaming. Whether from pain or pleasure, or both, I wasn't sure. Putting my back against the cold wall, I slid down it, sitting on the hardwood floor, and placed my head in my hands, weeping.

A few minutes later when I looked back up, the plastic bag was still sitting on the table, the little orange fish staring straight ahead at me. And then I smiled. I filled up a bowl of water, and plopped him in there, where he stayed for our first night together. Ron had helped me pick out a fish tank and set it up with me the following day.

I now look at Hank in his tank, swimming around gracefully. He doesn't stare at me that much anymore. But when he does, I think back to our first night together.

My stomach tightens knowing that I have to visit Mom and Doug tomorrow.

Chapter 3

Mike's chasing after another guy that had jumped out of the backseat of the vehicle they were pursuing. Officer John Stinson wasn't prepared for this evening. Not at all. What started as a reported kidnapping has become a true test of endurance, as well as patience. With his pregnant wife at home, John wishes for this night to be over so he can be at home taking care of what really matters. His family. Instead, he's climbing up nine flights of stairs in one of the most rundown apartments in the city, chasing one of the suspects.

"I said stop!" John shouts. The suspect continues running up the stairs, laughing. Sweat streaming down his face, his neck, pretty much everywhere a man could sweat and he pauses to take a breath. "I'm not cut out for this."

He starts climbing the steps again, slower than before. His legs are burning. Muscles that he hasn't used in who knows how long scream in agony for him to stop and sit down. But he knows he can't. The punk he's chasing has a gun, and the screaming child they've kidnapped.

"Catch us if you can!" the criminal yells down. John looks up at the zigzagging stairs above. The building is fifteen stories tall, and there are five floors remaining.

A loud thud from above and shouting. John quickens his pace up the steps, a sudden surge of adrenaline forcing him to see what's going on now. One of the doors on the eleventh floor is open, and voices could be heard inside the apartment. John unholsters his gun and enters.

The place is a mess with dirty diapers, discarded candy bar wrappers, beer bottles and magazines strewn all over the soiled carpet in the living room. Dishes are piled high in the kitchen sink. The place smells of beer and mildew.

John approaches the bedroom and pounds his fist on the closed door loudly. "Come out with your hands up!"

With his pistol in one hand, he reaches for the doorknob. Suddenly the door bursts outward and smacks John in the face, causing him to stumble backwards and land on the carpet. He loses control of the gun and it drops to the carpet. His vision is blurred, unable to focus on his surroundings. He hears a small mouse squeak and skitter away under the living room couch. A pair of strong hands grabs him by the collar, lifting him to his feet, pulling his arms behind his back.

"Well, well, you did good after all," a man's muffled voice says in front of him.

"I told ya boss. We led him here just like ya told us to."

"Don't speak. Did I ask you to speak?" The first man says. John assumes this first man is the leader of this operation. "Shut up. I'm not paying you to talk."

The stench of strong alcohol from the leader's breath. Bourbon?

"Do you know who I am?" The leader says to John.

"My name's Officer Stinson with the Chicago Police Dep–" Solid steel smacks John in the mouth. He tastes iron on his teeth.

John's vision slowly begins to return. A pair of dark brown eyes are all that he can see beneath the leader's black ski mask, hiding his face.

"I know who you are, Officer Stinson." The way he pronounces "Stinson" had an air of loathing and hatred. "I had you brought here for a purpose tonight, John. Tonight, you will die."

The leader swiftly punches John in the gut, knocking the wind out of him.

"Stinson, we meet again," the second man says breathes into John's ear, still holding his wrists behind his back. "Soon, you'll get what's coming to you."

The leader snags John's pistol up off the floor.

"I guess you won't be needing this much longer," he says while pointing the gun at John.

A loud bang, and an immense stab of pain erupts in John's knee cap. He immediately reaches for his knee, screaming. A pair of cold hands grab the side of John's face, applying duct tape over his mouth. Hands yank him off the floor and lead him to a chair by the window. He can see out at the neighborhood below where it's begun raining. The basketball court below is lit up in bright lights.

Hands roughly sit him down in the wooden chair, and he can feel rope being tied around his wrists and ankles. He tries to talk, but all that comes out are muffled noises behind the duct tape. The hands behind him forcefully turn the chair around so that the window is at John's back. The leader hands the gun to the second man, who approaches him slowly with the pistol pointed at his face.

"You won't be missed, John," the man says, aiming the pistol at John's head.

He pulls the trigger, and the gun fires.

BANG

I wake up, soaked in sweat, screaming. Throwing the covers off frantically, I stand up, and stumble forward, catching myself on my nightstand. The neighbors pound on the wall, yelling at me to shut up. The clock on the nightstand says 10:37 AM.

My head's throbbing in pain, and I place my hands on my temples, trying desperately to massage some relief and comfort. A wave of nausea overwhelms me, and I run into the bathroom, violently vomiting into the toilet. I collapse against the side of the bathtub, puke staining the front of my shirt.

There's something seriously wrong with these dreams I'm having. This isn't normal. I feel like I'm actually the police officer, John Stinson. The scariest part of all is that I remember what happened, down to the very last detail. My dreams are no longer hazy. I remember him chasing the alleged criminals up the stairs, and I remember the gun in his face. These aren't normal dreams anymore. They feel like they're something much more powerful and personal.

I clean myself up and try to eat some breakfast as I sit next to Hank. I stare blankly at the fish tank, deep in thought about what these dreams could possibly mean. Hank swims into my vision and stares at me. I place my hand gently against the glass, and he presses his face against the side of the tank on the other side.

Grabbing my phone, I do a quick online search of "John Stinson." Various news articles come up, and I click on a story from the Chicago Tribune. Reading the article, I nearly lose control of the glass bowl in my other hand. I look up at Hank.

"He was a real person."

Hank keeps staring at me, not blinking.

"I'm having dreams of someone who was really alive, and..." my voice trails off as I continue to read the different headlines.

"Chicago police officer murdered in a crime that was never solved."

"Local police baffled by death of local officer."

"Grieving widow of slain officer gives birth to son."

"Death of Officer Stinson goes cold."

I keep browsing online, reading several articles from different news outlets, explaining how his murder has gone unsolved since 1986. The more I read, the more I feel like I understand who this man was. Like I have some sort of a connection with him, but I can't quite put my finger on it. Waves of déjà vu wash over me, and I begin to feel nauseous again.

Hank has since gone to explore another area of his little tank, leaving me alone with my thoughts. It feels like the walls of the apartment are closing in around me. The foundation of this new life I've tried to build for myself has begun to wobble on its axis. None of this makes any sense. I shake my head and take my half-eaten bowl of cereal into the kitchen, scraping the discarded food into the trash. Shaking my head, I go back into my bedroom to finish getting ready to go see Mom and Doug.

On the drive over to their house, I reminisce on the past, and of Doug. When I was a teenager still living at home, he had asked me what my plans in life were going to be. He asked if I was going to stop "mooching" off him and his wife. I reminded Doug that his wife is my mother, and I do have plans, I just haven't figured them out yet.

The Army made Doug's plans for him when he was my age by sending him off to fight in the jungles of Vietnam. I, on the other hand, was starting from the ground up. My true life's ambition while growing up was to be a cop, or to work in some sort of a position within the Chicago police force. That was when Doug laughed at me, telling me I didn't have what it took to be a cop. He was a police chief in Chicago for 35 years before retiring last August. Doug continued to mock me, telling me the force would eat me alive, saying things like "Being a cop is much tougher than the superhero comic books you have your head glued to."

Now that I know that Doug was John's boss, I've decided to test the waters today and ask him what he remembers about Officer Stinson, and what light he can shed on the death of the former fallen officer while in the line of duty.

The grass has been freshly mowed, and the large maple tree in the front yard has been trimmed since I was over last. I rev the engine a couple times in the driveway for good measure before I shut it off. Jill comes running out of the house and clasps her hands over her mouth. I give her a hug once I get out of the car.

"What do you think, Mom?" I ask.

"How…it's great, Simon. It really is." She's smiling from ear to ear and shaking her head. "I know that old car wasn't very reliable anymore. When were you going to tell me about this?"

"I wanted to surprise you," I say, laughing. "Surprise!"

Doug's standing on the front porch, holding the door open. "You two get in here before it starts to rain."

Mom goes inside first, and Doug places his hand on my chest as I'm about to go inside. "You forget something, genius?" he asks.

"What? Did you want a hug too, Doug?"

He stares at me for a moment, then lifts his chin toward the car. "You might want to close your sunroof. Unless you like getting your upholstery damp. Your choice."

After I close the sunroof, I go inside and sit down on the living room couch. It's the same couch that I used to sit on as a kid, watching TV with my parents before bed. It's always fascinated me how certain smells can take you back to another time, and that's exactly what this couch does to me almost every time I come over now. Doug's already seated in his recliner as Mom emerges from the kitchen holding a tray of homemade lemonade.

"Thanks, Mom." I grab a glass and take a couple sips. "It's delicious."

I put the glass down on the designated coffee table coaster. Doug eyes me the entire time, examining me as if I'm one of his suspects about to be interrogated. I clear my throat as Mom goes back into the kitchen.

"So," I say, clapping my hands on my knees. I can't force myself to look at him yet. "How's it going, Doug?"

He sniffs and places his glass down. "How in the world are you going to afford that car? What, are you off robbing gas stations like your old man used to in order to pay for that?"

"Doug!" Jill is standing at the entry way into the kitchen. She gives him the look. I know the look, but apparently Doug doesn't. Or he doesn't care. Probably the latter.

The house is a traditional rancher style with new cream-colored carpeting. I grew up in a different part of town in a split-level home, but I could've seen myself growing up in something like this.

"What, hon?" Doug asks in a snarky tone. "I'm just trying to figure out how the kid's supposed to pay for that car working at a golf course."

Jill clears her throat and looks at me. "Honey, I'm sure you've done your research before buying this car, right? This is a big investment, and I'm sure what Doug's trying to say is that we just want you to be careful."

"Yeah, I'm good. I've been saving up some money for the down payment, and I don't have to pay anything for 90 days because of this special promotion they got me on. I can make the payments if that's what you're worried about."

"Please, for the love of God, tell me you didn't make Jess co-sign for you," Doug says.

Now I stare at him. I look him directly in the eyes, but the man doesn't flinch. He's like a lion. Clearly, he's not intimidated by me, and why would he be? He's dealt with his fair share of scum over the years, and I'm not exactly the scariest man in town.

"Nobody co-signed for me, Doug." I keep staring at him. "Sorry that it's so painful for you to be happy for me that I have a car that actually starts."

"Come on you two," Jill says. "You both promised to be good. Can we just enjoy lunch and each other's company? I made a nice roast for us today, since it's been so long." I can see her eyes getting a bit watery.

Doug and I are both civil to one another throughout lunch. Actually, civil wouldn't be the right word, since he stayed quiet, focusing on the meal in front of him. Mom and I catch up, and she tells me about her friend Beverly, and her trip to the mall last week. Mom's been retired for ten years now, shortly after she married Doug. We talk a little bit about Dad, which elicits no response from Doug. Mom laughs when I tell her the story of Dad taking me sledding when I was nine, a story that sends her into fits of giggles every time I tell it. Most people probably wouldn't find a story of a little boy crashing into a tree and being rushed to the hospital very funny, but the way I tell it to Mom always gets her going.

Throughout the meal, the thought of John Stinson keeps nagging at the back of my mind.

"Doug, when you were on the police force, did you know of an officer named John Stinson?"

I figured it best to start off slow, like easing into a cold pool. Or a very hot tub, whichever situation suits this one best. My question results in Doug momentarily choking on his mouthful of roast beef, and he wipes his mouth with a cloth napkin. He gently places it down.

"Yeah, I knew John. Why?"

His forehead is beginning to sweat as he takes a drink of water. Nothing rattles Doug this much, or at least not that I've ever seen. Clearly, the subject of John has hit a nerve. I was expecting him to either say no, or to ignore me. I'm caught off guard with his open honesty. As I'm trying to think of a response to why I asked that question, without him thinking I'm crazier than he already thinks I am, he asks again, rougher in tone this time.

"Why do you want to know about John?"

"I was reading up on his death the other day. Did they ever catch the man who killed him?"

Doug gives me that same icy stare. "No." He looks down at his plate, then back at me. He's still perspiring. "We never could find who killed John. I was still working that case until the day I retired. I'm surprised it's still being covered by the media. There were so few leads, it makes me upset to even think about. What makes you say it was a man that did it?"

"Well, it's just a guess," I say, thinking fast. "I mean, most murderers are men, right?"

"Yeah, I suppose so," he says after a brief pause. "Whoever killed him was a sick son of a bitch, though. His body washed ashore a few days after someone put a single bullet in his head, as well as his knee. There were no fingerprints at the crime scene, which we concluded was some rundown apartment several miles away. Whoever did this was damn good. They were clean, methodical and thorough. The worse kind of criminals, if you ask me."

Mom sits there patiently while we talk, apparently enjoying the bonding session between her only son and husband. Eventually, she speaks up.

"Pie, anyone?"

After dessert, Mom leads me into the spare bedroom where several photo albums are kept up on a high shelf in the closet. She has me reach up to grab the one she's pointing at, and we open it up, one half in each of our laps while sitting next to each other on the bed.

My relationship with Mom has definitely improved over the last few years. It took me months to want to talk to her again, until she had apologized for making me move out with nowhere to go. Angela was the one that helped me realize that nobody is perfect, and whether what Mom did was right or wrong, it's best in life to forgive and move on, rather than holding grudges. She says that holding grudges only leads to hurt feelings, anger and resentment, and over time a dam of sorts is built between two people that can be too much of an obstacle to overcome. Angela says that it may be easier to be mad and stay mad at someone over something, but it's easier to cope with forgiveness.

Be that as it may, I just tell myself that one day, we'll all be dead, and I would much rather die knowing I've pissed off as few people as possible. If Mom passed away and I was still mad at her, and never had the opportunity to forgive her, to let her know that I'd forgiven her, I know I would have a difficult time dealing with that. So, in a way, forgiving my mom was done for my own selfish reasons.

We look at the photo album together, and we each point at certain pictures and share a chuckle. Mom has a brief story behind every picture that was taken, down to the year and the month, and whatever important event was taking place at the time. One picture was for my second birthday, another was my first day of school, then another was Dad's birthday.

I stop at one of the pictures of my dad, taken during Father's Day, and it suddenly hits me how much I look like my old man. He had the same light brown, curly hair, the same looking nose and chin. We turn the page and there he is again, sitting in a golf cart.

"Wow, I really did follow in Dad's footsteps, didn't I?"

Mom giggles, and points at another picture of dad with a young boy holding a blue balloon standing in front of Wrigley Field.

"That's you with your dad before your first Cubs game," Mom says, sniffing. "This was right around the time that we found out he had cancer. Oh, Simon, he talked about this day for years, even before you were born. He always wanted to take his son to a Cubs game. This day had meant so much to him. And you had a fun time. Look, you even got a balloon."

I remember being there, standing next to Dad, holding that blue balloon. The memory, hazy at first, clears up as I think back on it now. The picture definitely brings back memories, with my dad wearing a Cubs jersey, and me in a little Cubs shirt and baseball cap.

We walked for what felt like miles around that stadium. The loud sounds, people everywhere talking louder than normal, laughing louder than they should, but it was an overall positive energy from the adults everywhere. Even little kids, some younger than me, walked by with smiles on their faces. The smell of hot dogs cooking, popcorn and donuts wafted into my nostrils, causing me to salivate.

Dad bought me cotton candy, which felt like it was almost as big as I was. He held the balloon while I carried the treat with both hands, following him up to our seats. We climbed up to our seats which were near the back of the upper deck, way up at the top. I could barely see the miniature-sized men down on the field, throwing a white dot back and forth to one another.

"What're they doing?" I asked, still holding the big cotton candy with both hands.

"They're warming up, Son," he said, leaning forward and clapping his hands.

"I'm hot. It's July, Dad," I said, causing him to bust up laughing.

For the next three and a half hours we sat up in those seats, watching a game that I understood very little of, but Dad was there to explain the rules the entire time. He would point down at the field, and I would try to see exactly what he was looking at. At one point everyone stood up and sang a song, which I wasn't expecting.

"You know, I think I remember just about everything about that day except for who won the game," I say, and laugh. "But, looking back, it didn't really matter then, and it matters so much less now. That was one of my favorite days with him."

Chapter 4

John holds the door open for the pretty young woman carrying two textbooks. She smiles at him, and he smiles in return. He's been trying to build up the nerve for weeks now to talk to her, to say anything, other than just smiling and gawking at her like an idiot.

How do I know he's been trying for weeks now? I know he has feelings for her, I can just…sense what emotions he's going through. How?

He follows her from a distance at first, then he picks up speed. She abruptly turns around mid-stride, and John walks into her, knocking the textbooks out of her arms. He apologizes profusely while helping her pick up the books, and they lock eyes.

"Going to class I take it?" John asks.

Man, this guy's worse than I am.

She chuckles and smiles up at him. Her jet-black hair shines against the fluorescent lightbulbs above. His heart flutters as she smiles at him. She's the most beautiful thing he's ever seen, and he's still in shock that he actually said something to her.

"Yeah, math class," she says, and clutches the textbooks tight against her chest. "How about you?"

"Yeah, same. Math class," he says. "I'm in your class. I sit a few rows behind you. My name's John, by the way."

"Samantha," she says, smiling softly. "Sorry, I didn't know we had the same class."

They both sit in their usual spots. John pays little attention during class, as his mind wanders off, thinking of what else to say to Samantha next time they have a chance to talk.

Afterwards, he goes to the lunchroom and pulls out a paper bag from his backpack. Peanut butter and jelly sandwich, a bag of chips and an orange. The usual meal during lunch. Someone sits next to him at the cafeteria table, and John is shocked when he looks up to see that it's Samantha.

"Hey, did you understand that homework assignment?" she asks, and opens up the textbook.

They sit at the cafeteria table for the next hour, talking about who they are, their interests, their likes and dislikes, what brought them to Northwestern University, and what degree they're going for. Very little is discussed regarding the math homework.

John learns that Samantha wants to be an elementary school teacher, and she needs to pass this math class to continue with her program, and in turn John tells Samantha that he's thinking about getting into Criminal Law.

Two more classes during the afternoon, then he works the evening shift as a campus security guard. It's only his second week on the job, but he tells Samantha he feels like he's found something he likes and understands. They promise to meet up before class tomorrow and work on the math homework together.

Which is exactly what they do the next day. And the day after. By the end of the week, Samantha decides to sit next to John in their math class. She lives on campus and one day invites John over after class to study at her place. John's heart begins pounding, and he's sent into a cold sweat. Invited over to a girl's house? This is a first.

His heart is racing as he knocks on her apartment door. Snow is falling, and steam is coming off his breath like an exhausted bull about to charge at a red flag. The door opens and he's greeted with her wide smile; her big brown eyes draw him in like the world's most powerful magnet.

"Come in, it's freezing." He steps inside, not realizing he was probably standing there, staring at her like a crazy person.

They sit on the couch in the small apartment for hours, talking about anything and everything. Throughout the afternoon and into the evening they share stories, leading to laughter. The math homework gets shoved aside as they talk, and Samantha prepares a meal that they eat together.

"Well, I better get to bed," Samantha says a couple hours later. "I have a biology lab in the morning, which I unfortunately have to get up early for."

John looks up at the clock and realizes it's already ten. They talked all night, and it feels like he just got there. He gets up to leave and says his goodbyes. As he's about to leave, she grabs his arm and turns him around.

"Aren't you going to kiss me goodnight, John?"

The scene fades away and I wake up to the beeping of my alarm clock. It's Friday morning, and every night over the past two weeks I've had dreams about John Stinson. Dreams about his days while working for the Chicago P.D., dreams about being married to an older version of Samantha, about John as a kid, then later in life attending his mother's funeral. Different snapshots of this man's life, all laid out like sections of a quilt. The dreams, or visions as I prefer to call them, come to me in no particular order. I have no control over what happens during the vision, nor what vision I see. It's all so random, yet I have a feeling in my gut that I'm being shown all of this for a reason. But why me? And why now?

Twice now I've had the dream about his murder in the dirty high-rise apartment. The men wearing ski masks, one of them shooting John with his own police issued pistol. I've begun to keep a journal, writing down a summary of each dream in the hopes of trying to piece this man's life together.

Later that day after work, I'm sitting in Angela's office.

"Is something else…troubling you?" Angela asks, leaning forward.

I unfold my hands and put them back on the arm rests. "Yeah, well…" I look her in the eyes. Lots of mascara tonight. Good for her. Another date night. "This stays, you know, between us, right?"

Angela smiles. "Of course, like always. Unless you plan on harming someone else or yourself, what you say in here is always strictly confidential."

I take a deep breath. "Alright, well, after all that talk about 'progress', you might be regretting saying that. But here I go. I've been having some really bizarre…dreams lately. Like, super realistic dreams. It's as if I'm seeing everything from the viewpoint of a police officer, and everything in his life, from childhood until the moment he's…murdered."

Angela gives her usual "mmhmm" and begins to take down notes.

"His name is….no, it was, John Stinson." I take another deep breath. "I'm seeing everything from his eyes. I feel everything he felt. What he touches, smells, hears, all of it. I'm sensing it like I'm actually him. But I can't control anything he says or does. I'm just, like, along for the ride, if that makes any sense."

"You're having vivid dreams that you're someone else. I see." She puts the pen up to her mouth. "How long have these dreams been going on for?"

"A few weeks now. At first, I thought they were just crazy realistic dreams. But I kept having them. Over and over, of the same guy, but at different times in his life. But here's where it gets weird. I researched him, and he really existed. Here, check this out." I pull out my phone and open up an article about his unsolved murder. Angela takes the phone with great care and reads the article.

"Did you research this man before?" she asks, handing me back the phone. "Maybe for a school project, or was there a story on the news that you saw? You know, studies have been conducted which say that even if we're not totally invested in a news story, our brain is always tuned in and listening. It can bury deep down in our subconsciousness things that we might not have been paying attention to at the time, but the information is stored there for later."

Heat rushes to my face. She's just not getting it. She doesn't believe me. I was afraid this would happen.

I put the phone back in my pocket and glance up at the clock.

"It's time for me to go."

Angela looks at the clock. "Simon, don't shut me out. We have another 20 minutes."

"Just forget about it." I leave her office and slam the door roughly behind me. Angela's calling my name as I go out the front door, begging me to come back.

I drive down to Moretti's to hang out with my friends and blow off some steam. The place is incredibly loud tonight thanks to the Bulls game on TV, making it challenging for us to talk. Ron had to miss last week's hangout time due to work, so this is the first time I've seen him in a couple weeks.

"Did you see my car coming in?" I ask excitedly to Ron.

"Yeah, that blue sports car? Very nice ride." Ron pumps his fist at the TV, then looks at me. "How's about tomorrow I come over, then you drive us down to the beach in your fancy sports car. What do you say?"

"Sounds like a plan, man," I say.

Ron turns his attention to Jess. "You've been awfully quiet tonight, Jess. What's up? Is work going okay?"

She's been staring at her drink most of the night, barely touching it. She looks up. "Work? Work's kicking my butt." She shakes her head, then takes a big drink.

"Sorry to hear that." I keep raising my voice, practically to a shout because of the noise in the bar. "Did you want to hang out with us tomorrow and go to the beach?"

She nods her head and smiles. "Yeah, I'd like that."

Chapter 5

Flashes of lightning can be seen as they pull up to the home of the domestic disturbance call. John keeps the flashing lights going on the police cruiser and kills the siren. Shouts can be heard from inside the run-down one-story house, which are drowned out by the loud rumble of thunder galloping across the blackened sky. Mike pounds on the front door, asking for the husband of the household, Travis Daniels, to come to the door. He refuses.

John opens the metal gated fence as he makes his way around to the backyard. The trash can is overflowing with beer bottles and diapers. Hail begins to pelt his brimmed cap as he approaches the back sliding door, where he can see a small child in his diapers looking up at him through the other side of the glass. He turns on the flashlight, pointing the white beam of light inside the darkened home.

The first thing that catches his eyes is the thick layer of mold on the linoleum floor. The carpeting leading into the living room is heavily soiled, and the husband is peering through the peephole of the front door with a shotgun in his hands. The wife is strapped down to the couch with duct tape around her mouth; her wrists are zip tied together. If this little boy wasn't in the way, it would make it so much easier for John to grab this wacko and save the wife and kid.

He realizes the child isn't moving. He's just standing there, staring at John. Looking down at the toddler's feet, he sees that a shimmering substance of some kind is oozing around his bare feet. Superglue.

John has to think fast. If he's careless and attracts the armed man's attention, he risks the kid being hurt, or worse, by the dad firing the shotgun at the sliding glass door. If he doesn't act quickly enough, the man may hurt the wife even more.

Crouching down in front of the toddler, John covers his face with his hands, playing peekaboo. He quickly moves his hands away and makes a silly face. The little guy smiles, thankfully not laughing loud enough to attract his father's attention. John points at the child and covers his eyes. The little boy catches on quickly and covers his eyes as well, just as John was hoping he would. The thunderstorm is now directly overhead; booms of thunder are getting louder and closer together with the flashes of lightning.

Taking the baton out, John waits for a flash of lightning, and slams it against the glass sliding door just as a crash of thunder deafens the sky, causing the entire door to shatter. Within an instant, John crouches down and shields the toddler from the glass raining down from above. Shards of glass land on John's back, and one shard slices the back of his neck. He crawls over to the kitchen bar, using it as a shield between himself and the living room where the armed husband is still waiting at the front door. He can hear the man more clearly now. The little boy, his feet still superglued to the floor, stands silently, twisting his head around to watch John crouch for cover.

"I'm not coming out there, you hear me! I'll kill her! Now, get off my property!"

The child begins wailing at the top of his lungs. Footsteps can be heard on the linoleum floor, and John sees a cowboy boot and the muzzle of a shotgun. John shuffles off his stomach into a crouching position and waits for the man to walk over to the little boy.

"Shut up you little–"

John tackles the man from behind, sending them both flying through the empty sliding door. They roll together onto the back patio, then into the backyard, and John attempts to grab the shotgun away from the man. He's strong, and begins to wrestle it back, the double barrel pointed up at the sky. With an earsplitting blast, the shotgun fires, causing both men to lose their grip on the gun, falling to the grass. John reaches for his baton, but the man is on him instantly, pressing the stock end of the shotgun down on his windpipe, cutting off his oxygen. White flashes fill his vision from above, and a streak of lightning appears over the man's shoulder. His face is a snarl, saliva oozing out of the corner of his mouth.

"You think you can break into my house, pig?" Travis Daniels says, drooling into John's face.

Something strikes the man on the side of his head with a loud thud, and John begins gasping for air, the pressure on his windpipe now relieved. Mike is now rolling around the grass with Daniels, both of them shouting and grunting. The toddler is still screaming from the doorway of the house.

Daniels punches Mike in the face twice, and is now on top of him, choking him with his bare hands.

Scrambling up off the ground, John grabs the shotgun off the grass, and forces the barrel directly to the back of the man's head.

"Freeze!" John shouts. "Place your hands behind your head!"

The man stops choking Mike, raising his hands to the sky, slowly following John's instructions.

"Oh, you're making a big mistake," Daniels says, chuckling.

"Put your face on the ground and keep your hands behind your head." John reaches for his handcuffs. Mike struggles up and grabs the man's wrists, bringing his hands down behind his back. "You have the right to remain silent..."

The dream washes away as sunlight streams through the bedroom curtain. I roll over on my back, and sigh.

The man was a hero. He saved the wife and that little kid. I shake my head and look over at my alarm clock. Jess and Ron will be here in a few minutes, giving me just enough time to clean up.

After I do my usual morning routine and feed Hank, I go back to my bedroom and make another journal entry from last night's dream. On the back page, I've begun a timeline of sorts, going back to John's childhood, all the way to the night he's killed.

The sound of knocking on the apartment door scatters my thoughts.

I open the door for Jess and Ron, and they enter the apartment with cheerful smiles, each wearing a backpack and sunglasses. It's nice seeing my friends so excited to spend their day off at the beach with me. Ron gives me a handshake and brushes past me to take a look at the fish tank.

"Where is he?" Ron asks while bending down to look inside Hank's aquatic domain.

"He's in the back hiding behind that scuba diver," I say while helping Jess take off her backpack. "I fed him breakfast already so he might be taking a nap."

Jess giggles while peering into the tank next to Ron. "I think I get it now. His name's Hank because it rhymes with tank. Hank in a tank. Right?"

I look up at the ceiling. I guess I never really thought of it like that. Jess begins to take herself on a self-guided tour around my humble abode, nodding to herself.

"What?" I ask. "You've been here a dozen times. I try my best to keep it clean."

"No, no, it's nothing," she says. "It's just… where are those paintings I sold you?"

"Honestly, Jess…" I begin rubbing the back of my neck. Should I tell her the truth, or lie and spare her feelings? "I put them in storage. I love them, I really do. They're too good for this place, though. I mean, look, the walls are crumbling. I made sure they're covered up and safe for when I get a new coat of paint on the walls."

She smiles. "No worries. I'm glad you like them."

I look over at Ron, who is still amazed with the fish tank.

We make it down to the beach along the shores of Lake Michigan a little before noon. Thankfully, the weather is unusually warm for this early in spring, and people have come out from hibernating in their homes to enjoy the first warm day of the year after a long, cold winter. Jess has packed a picnic blanket that we lay upon the sand, and Ron has brought his signature homemade sub sandwiches, complete with turkey, ham and smoked provolone. We enjoy lunch and each other's company under the clear blue sky and take in the sights of the water.

"Jess, you seemed a bit down last night. Is everything alright?" I ask.

She clears some rogue hairs out of her face. Her hair has gotten so long.

"Yeah, I'm alright," she says, looking out at the water. "I'm just really mentally drained from this job. For a couple years, I've been eying this promotion, like I really thought I would do a great job with it. And now that I have it, I don't know, I feel like it's been a huge mistake accepting the job. The pay is only like an extra $40 on each paycheck, but the toll it's taken on me emotionally…it's just not worth it."

Ron and I look at each other. This is usually where he excels, knowing just the right thing to say to cheer someone up. Myself, on the other hand, I've always struggled with finding the right thing to say at the right time. I usually come up with something clever to say way after the moment has passed. Today, however, I'm the one that seems to have the right answer, while Ron is grasping at straws.

"Jess, if you were still in your old position, not knowing what you know now, and you hadn't applied for this new job. When someone else had gotten it, what would you have felt?"

"Not knowing what I know now, I…I would've been jealous, I suppose. Deep down, I don't know, I would've been a bit spiteful. Not against that person, but because I've been working there for so long and I know what to do."

Ron nods his head. "You could probably own that company."

"I don't think I can own one of the biggest banks in the country, Ron," she says, chuckling. "But thanks anyway."

"When I was twelve, I made it to the spelling bee finals," I say, looking down at the sand. "Spelling was something that I was always good at, or so I thought. But when I made it to the final stage, standing in front of the whole school in the auditorium, do you remember what word I got, Jess?"

She shakes her head.

"The word I had gotten was 'antiseptic.' And I remember being so nervous, I was sweating like crazy, and I ended up spelling the word wrong, right in front of the whole school. I spelled it with a 'c' instead of an 's' and lost the contest. For several days, I was so bummed and upset with myself. Most of all, I think I was embarrassed, because the one thing I thought I was good at, it turned out I wasn't even the best at it in our school."

I take a deep breath and close my eyes. "I remember you came and sat next to me at lunch one day, probably about a week after that all happened, and I'll never forget it, you said to me 'Simon, I was very proud of you up on that stage. Only two percent of the students tried out, meaning the other ninety-eight percent didn't.'"

I open my eyes and Jess is smiling, her cute dimples showing.

"I think what Simon is trying to say is at least you tried," Ron says proudly. "And we're proud of you."

"Yeah, I got that," Jess says, laughing. She looks at Ron, then at me. "Thank you. Both of you."

"Ultimately, we just want you to be happy," I say. "We're here if you need to talk. Or vent."

"Always," Ron says.

We hang out together on the beach for another couple of hours, and Jess' mood is brightened. She laughs at both of our stupid jokes, and even builds up the courage to get into the water, up to her ankles. The water must be freezing, but she's laughing and playfully splashes some water up to Ron and me. I don't dare enter the lake any time before June. Her long blond hair flaps behind her like a small, bright cape. She's the most beautiful woman on the beach. Probably the most beautiful woman in the city. I look over at Ron, and he's laughing too, the sun reflecting off his sunglasses.

I drop Ron off at our apartment first because he has to work early in the morning. Jess remains in the front seat as I drive to her place. She asks that we stop for some ice cream on the way, which sounds great to me after a day at the beach.

She gets her favorite flavor, mint chocolate chunk, and I get vanilla. We sit down at one of the small tables and enjoy our tiny cups of ice cream. We're the only people in the shop besides the two girls working.

"You know, I've always found it funny that you enjoy just plain vanilla ice cream. They have more exotic flavors here, you know."

"I'm a simple man with simple tastes."

"I know you are. You've always got to have everything just so. You've got your standard routine every day. Which I think is great. You're very organized, neat and clean and you like plain vanilla ice cream. Yet I still can't figure out what on Earth possessed you to buy that sports car. Don't get me wrong, it's a nice car. It's really nice, Simon. It just seems… I don't know, you don't seem like someone who would impulse buy something like that. You strike me as more of a compact car kind of guy."

"Well, here's the thing," I say, taking a small bite of ice cream. "I saw that car every day for two weeks at the car lot on my way to and from work. If I hadn't seized the opportunity to buy it, someone else would have. And one day, that someone else would have driven past me, and I would've been filled with regret for not taking a chance and ”

"Oh my God, shut up," she says, laughing. "I see where this is going."

After a few moments of silence pass, I take a deep breath.

"I'm a complete mess right now," I say, running my hand through my hair.

"What?"

"You're going to think I'm crazy."

"Yeah, well I've always had my suspicions." She smirks. I look her in the eyes, and the smirk fades away. "You're freaking me out. What's going on?"

"I'm going to tell you something. Something that's super weird, and I need you to promise not to laugh."

"What is it?"

"Promise me you won't laugh."

"You're a serial killer, aren't you?"

"What?" I ask. "No. What the hell, cut it out. I'm being serious here, Jess. Promise me you won't laugh."

"Alright, fine. Whatever, I won't laugh. Just spill it, what's going on?"

I take a deep breath, then look over at the counter with the cash register. The employees have gone into the back room. "I've been having dreams lately."

She keeps staring at me, nodding her head slowly. "Okay? What kind of dreams?"

I tell her about my dreams of Officer Stinson, in as much detail that I can. She listens intently, and doesn't laugh, nibbling away at her ice cream.

"It's so real Jess. I don't know if it's like an out of body experience, or some kind of emotional transference, I really don't know. But all that I really do know for sure is that I want to solve this crime. It's still a cold case, after all these years, and nobody could find who killed him. I feel like I'm being called upon to find his killer. I'm not sure why me, and why now. But I do believe that everything happens for a reason, and it's my destiny, or whatever, to bring whoever pulled the trigger that night to justice."

I stop to catch my breath, and Jess is waiting for me to continue. "What do you think?" I ask.

She nods her head, looks out the window, then looks back at me, an intense look on her face. "I think I know who you should see about this."

Chapter 6

Officer John Stinson slowly cracks his knuckles before entering the interrogation room, where Mike has just finished with the suspect. The door opens and Mike walks out, puffing out his chest.

"I warmed him up good for ya, Johnny boy," Mike says, slapping John on the back. "But he's hiding something. I can…I don't know. I can feel it or something. He's holding back on us."

John stares at the suspect through the two-way mirror and sighs.

"It feels like we're swimming upstream here, Mike." John places the coffee cup down. "How many times have we questioned this guy? Four? Five?"

"Something like that," Mike says. "But I feel like we're on the verge of breaking this thing wide open. Look, we already know he's connected to the boss. I guarantee you he was a witness to the Alvarez murder. My good cop routine wasn't working out. Now it's your turn. Go get 'em."

He slaps John on the shoulder as he enters the interrogation room and the door slams behind him, an extra measure from Mike to add effect to John's grand entrance. John's kept his word with Doug, keeping this case a sworn secret from everyone except for one person. Mike, being the better investigator among the two of them, agreed to help and take a deeper look into the Alvarez case. Not wanting to hurt his partner's feelings, and honestly needing Mike's help after being on the case for some time with no leads, John's requested to question Rafael Chavez again.

The man has a pair of handcuffs on; his hands stained with grease. He's a bald Hispanic man, with a thick mustache and a tattoo of a dragon encircling his neck. He's wearing an orange jumper, issued by the Cook County Department of Corrections. John approaches the table with his arms crossed, and stares down at Rafael Chavez.

"Can we cut the show already?" Chavez asks. "Look, you caught me robbing the jewelry store, alright? Your buddy already shot me in the knee, and you're lucky I'm not pressing charges for that."

John keeps staring at the man.

"What?" Chavez asks. "Are you going to say something, or are you some kind of a mute? They hire a bunch of mutes around–"

John slams his hands down on the steel table, causing the man to give a brief "yip."

"Enough! Stop toying with us, Chavez. I know you're holding back. Now, tell me what I want to know before I shoot your other kneecap!"

Chavez gulps, sweat glistening off his forehead. "Look man, like I already told your buddy, I don't know anything about nothing. He kept saying something about 67th. I haven't been on 67th in months, man, you know that. I've been in here." He innocently shows John his handcuffs.

John takes a seat at the table and stares at Chavez. He pulls out a pack of gum from his back pocket and takes out a piece. "You know what I think? I think that robbery was a distraction. Yeah, I think you were a decoy sent by your boss. That's what I think."

Chavez doesn't answer. John continues. "I think you know who tied up this man for unpaid debts, you know who attached cement blocks to his ankles, and your crew dumped him in the lake. Not you, obviously, but someone from your crew." Chavez remains silent.

"Nothing to say now, huh?" John pops the gum into his mouth. "I'll tell you what. You help us catch whoever committed this crime, it'll look good for you. I'm talkin' reduced time. I can guarantee you'll be out of here in a few months tops, if you just tell me who killed this man."

John pulls out three photographs from his coat pocket and slides them across the table in front of Chavez. Keeping his attention only on Rafael, he intently studies the man's expression for some sort of reaction or telltale clue. Nothing. Chavez's face remains deadpan.

"This guy look familiar?" John asks, then blows a bubble. "Take a good look, Chavez. Be smart about this. Let's start with a name."

"Tony Alvarez," Chavez says, rolling his eyes. "You keep asking me these same damn questions. But if it makes you happy, I'll play along. Tony was new to the crew. But he messed up too often, so the boss had to cut him loose. He was a lost cause. I had nothing to do with it."

"I know you had nothing to do with it. We've established that." John takes a fourth photo out and slides it onto the table. "This is your boss, William Marcini. He's the kingpin of your whole operation. Am I right?"

"Right."

"And Marcini wanted Alvarez dead, right?"

"Right," Chavez says, then sighs, his leg shaking up and down, rattling the shackles. "I'm a dead man. Even if I get out of here, I'm a dead man."

"Then find somewhere else to live. Try moving out west. Go to Hollywood and be in movies. I don't care." John stands up, spits his gum on the floor, and walks around the table behind Chavez. "Don't clam up on me now. Who did Marcini hire to kill Alvarez?"

Chavez silently stares at the photographs for several moments. "Lawyer."

John grabs Chavez around his dragon-tattooed throat and lifts him up out of the chair, throwing him against the wall. "Who did Marcini hire to kill Alvarez? Give me a name!" John yells.

He's not sure how much longer he has before other officers come in to break this up. He lifts Chavez up by the collar and pins him up against the wall, pushing his forearm against the man's throat. Chavez looks John in the eyes and begins laughing.

"You're loco, ese. I'm not telling you anything." Chavez spits in John's face.

John stares at the bald Hispanic man for a moment, then punches him twice in the face. Chavez's lip has busted open, blood running down his chin.

"Tell me who Marcini hired! Now!"

"Lawyer," Chavez says, smiling, displaying a set of gold teeth.

Pounding can be heard on the interrogation room door, and four police officers pile into the room, pulling John off the still laughing Rafael Chavez. The front of his orange jumper is soaked in blood.

Two of the police officers grab Chavez to take him out of the room. "I like you," Chavez says to John, smiling.

The two remaining officers help John to his feet and lead him out of the interrogation room. Doug is standing beside Mike, his arms crossed.

"What in the hell were you thinking, Stinson?" Doug asks.

"I almost had him, Sergeant Lewis," John says. "We need to stop wasting time and bring Marcini in for questioning!"

"Get him out of here," Doug says in disgust to the two young policemen, his steely glare following John out of the room.

Later that night, John's eating dinner with Samantha. She keeps staring at his bruised knuckles and has remained silent throughout the dinner. John hasn't said a word since he got home.

Samantha takes a sip of her water, then gently sets down the glass. "What happened?"

"This punk..." John shakes his head. "There's a big-time mafia family trying to take over this city, and I intend to take it down. I will take it all down. With or without Doug Lewis' support."

"Whatever happens, we'll get through this." Samantha puts her hand on top of John's. "I believe in you. I'll always have your back. And pretty soon, this little one will have your back too." Samantha places her other hand over her stomach.

John stares at his beautiful wife, her jet-black hair cascading over her shoulders. Her eyes are staring intently at him, as if burrowing into his heart.

"And I'll be here for the both of you," John says, tears beginning to well up in his eyes. "Once I'm done with this case, I'm going into private security. Something much safer. But I have to find this killer, Sam. I feel...I don't know. I feel like it's my destiny to catch whoever did this."

"I know." She stands up and grabs their plates from the table. He stares at his wife. The most precious person in his life, the most amazing thing that's ever happened to him. He wishes he could just walk away from this case, just hand it off to Mike or Doug and tell them he's out, he has a family to take care of now. But he's compelled to see it through. The Marcini crime family is like a virus to this city, and he can feel their roots strengthening.

He also wants to prove himself to Doug and show that he's the right man for the promotion to detective. Despite the two-week unpaid suspension, he got for his actions today, he knows he'll do everything in his power to get this promotion. For Samantha, and their unborn child.

As he's lying in bed next to Samantha, he stares up at the ceiling. The bedroom is pitch black, and his wife is sound asleep, but he's not tired. He knows he can't sleep until he catches whoever killed Tony Alvarez.

Chapter 7

I wake up to the sound of my alarm clock beeping. Sluggishly, I roll over to see what time it is. The clock says 9:45 AM. My eyes open wide, and I'm sent into a state of panic. Jumping out of bed, I scramble to put my clothes on. My shift started 45 minutes ago, and I've clearly slept through my alarm. I've never been late to work. Not a single day.

Steve's waiting at the front door as soon as I get to work, his arms crossed over his chest, tapping his foot.

"Where have you been, Simon?" he asks.

"Steve, I'm so sorry," I say, sprinting to the time clock. I punch in at 10:17 AM. "I'll make it up, I promise. I'll stay late, work through my lunch, and come in early tomorrow. Please, let me make this up to you."

"Step into my office."

I follow Steve to his office. Posters of Tiger Woods, Phil Mickelson, and other golfers cover the wooden walls.

"I'm very disappointed in you," Steve says, and grabs a pink sheet of paper from his desk drawer. "Tardiness is my biggest pet peeve, and you know this."

"Sir, I do. I really do. I'm so sorry. I overslept." I run my hand through my greasy hair. I skipped my morning shower. "I've been here almost four years now, and I've never been late. Please, let me make this up."

"You will make it up," Steve says. "But I also need to write you up."

"Write me up? Steve, this is the first time I've ever been late."

"You didn't call. You didn't text. You have my number."

"You're right, I should have called. I messed up, and I accept that."

I sign his stupid pink document and start my shift. The day is already out of order, I can't even remember where to start. Spending the rest of the morning picking up golf balls in the range picker, I should be furious about being written up, worried about losing my job, or feeling bad about letting Steve down. Except none of those emotions are going through my head.

As I operate the range picker, all that goes through my mind is the mystery surrounding this man I keep having visions about. Did he ever catch who killed Tony Alvarez? Was this linked to his death? I was in such a hurry to leave the apartment this morning, I forgot to write down the dream in my journal. There are so many holes in this case, and the visions are all out of order. It feels like once some questions are answered to this mystery, more answers are questioned.

I eat lunch by myself, wearing my headphones as usual. Finally, something is back to normal today. Until someone taps me on the shoulder. I look up to see that it's Brittany, the pretty front-end receptionist. She motions for me to take off my headphones.

"What's up?" I ask as she pulls up a chair.

"Are you alright?" she asks, concerned. "I know Steve can be kind of tough sometimes."

"I just slept through my alarm, and I'm not sure why. I just hope it doesn't happen again."

She has black hair and brown eyes. She's wearing some sort of perfume that I find very…alluring.

My God, what's up with me? One day I'm attracted to Jess, my best friend since grade school, now I'm lusting over this other woman. Plus, I bought a sports car I'm not sure I can even afford. Now I'm showing up late to work? Look out Chicago, you've got yourself a real rebel on the loose here.

She giggles and pulls out her cell phone. "What's your number?"

I give her my number, and she sends me a text of several emojis of a kiss and a heart, causing my heart to skip a beat, then speed up. What is with today? Nothing is going as it should.

"I think you're really cute, Simon. How about we go out tomorrow tonight?" she asks giving me a wink.

Am I still dreaming?

"Th-thanks," I stutter, and put down my phone. "Ditto."

She winks at me again and stands up. "You can pick me up at seven in your nice new car. I'll text you my address." Her deep, smoky sounding voice doesn't really fit in with her young face, but I'm not one to complain.

'Ditto?' Why in the world did I say that? I never openly flirt like that to girls. And what a stupid thing to say…I should just go back to bed.

After work, I meet Jess downtown for dinner.

"You're late," she says as I sit across the table from her.

"I know, I'm sorry. I was late for work this morning, and the whole day's been goofed up ever since. I had to stay late to make up time, and I forgot to text you."

"You poor thing. That must've been quite stressful," she says, giving me a cheeky smile.

"You kid because you care," I tell her, and give her a fake smile in return. "So, tell me about this person who can solve my dream situation."

"Her name's Loretta," Jess says, taking a sip of her drink. "You'll like her. She's really into more natural, herbal stuff. And something you'll like is that she's really in tune with nature."

I stare at her, and discover she's being serious. "What, you're taking me to some sort of a…fortune teller? A tarot reader? What does she do?"

"Nothing like that," Jess says, dismissively waving her hand. "She's able to get in touch with your heart, body, mind and soul."

I shake my head. I don't press the issue further as I don't want to hurt her feelings. Her help is greatly appreciated, but I'm not sure if this is what I'm really looking for.

After dinner, we walk six blocks to Loretta's shop, which is named "Sweet Loretta's". I open the door for Jess, and a bell placed above the door announces our entrance. The interior is dark, dusty, and smells heavily of incense. Candles are burning all throughout the shop, where several shelves containing items ranging from crystal balls, mood rings, more incense, and different shapes and colors of rocks are randomly arranged. The place is eerily quiet, with no music playing and no other customers browsing. The only sounds come from a trickling fountain behind the glass counter, and a black cat meowing on top of the counter.

A black woman emerges from the backroom, walking through a tapestry of colorful beads.

"Jess, darling." The woman, who I assume to be Loretta, greets Jess with a warm smile and a big hug. "And this must be Simon. Pleasure to meet you again, child." She limply extends her right hand to me, which I take and shake. Her fingers are incredibly long, and her hand envelopes mine easily.

"Nice to meet you, Sweet Loretta," I say. "Have we met before?"

"Loretta, just Loretta," she says, and takes back her hand gently, dismissing my question. "Please, follow me."

Jess and I follow Loretta around the counter. The black cat stares at me with bright green eyes, and hisses. "Ignore him." Loretta's voice can be heard faintly from somewhere behind the beaded curtain, where Jess and I follow.

The back room appears disorganized at first, with several cardboard boxes stacked against the walls, one single flickering fluorescent light illuminating them so we don't trip.

We enter a room off to the left, behind another beaded curtain. This room has one black light hanging over a black table with green carvings drawn on it. Jess smiles at me, her teeth brightened by the black light. I look down at my white tennis shoes, which are glowing.

"Come, children. Sit." Loretta is already seated at the round table.

Jess and I sit across the table from her. "So, Simon, tell me what's ailing you. And please, be open, honest, and don't hold anything back. I will believe whatever you tell me, child."

"Well, it all started a few weeks ago. I've been having…dreams."

"Keep going, child. Don't stop. Loretta's all ears."

I clear my throat and look down at the black table with green artwork. After looking closer, it's not artwork but some sort of letters in a foreign language, presumably a form of Asian.

I proceed to tell Loretta about my dreams as John Stinson, being as detailed as I can remember.

Loretta reaches across the table, and I take her hand. "Now, child, I want you to take a deep breath and relax."

I do as she asks. She releases my hand and gets up to rummage through a box behind her. After she finds what she was looking for, she comes around the table and places a purple pill in my hand.

"Now, I want you to drink this…" she places a water bottle on the table filled with a yellow liquid, "…and on your last sip, I want you to swallow this pill."

Loretta begins to puffing some kind of fruity scented air fragrance around the room, and chanting in a strange language. I look over at Jess, who is watching Loretta calmly.

"Jess, can I see you outside, please?" She follows me through the beaded curtain.

"What is it?" she asks. "She charges by the hour. On my dime, I might add."

"Are you sure about…all of this?" I ask, motioning inside the dark room with the woman still puffing and chanting. "Are you just pulling my chain here, or what? This woman's out of her mind."

She takes my hands in hers, and steps closer to me. "She's the sanest person I know. After my mom died, I came here once a week for a couple months, and she healed me." She looks directly at me, her blue eyes glowing with a level of intensity that I've never seen from her before. "Do you trust me, Simon?"

"Yes."

"Then you can trust her. You want to know who killed this John Stinson guy, right?"

"Yes, I do, but I don't want to get drugged in the process."

"They're all natural. It helps her to open a chasm into your soul." She presses her hand against my chest. "Come on." She grabs me by the hand and leads me back into the dark room. I take my place back at the table.

"Are you ready, child?" Loretta asks.

"Whatever. Let's do this," I say reluctantly, and drink the liquid, which tastes like grape juice. I take the pill as instructed, and swallow that with the last of the liquid. I sit and stare ahead blankly. Several minutes pass with nothing happening. The three of us just sit there, staring at one another in silence.

Loretta has a twin sister that I wasn't aware was in the room before. I look over at Jess, and she has a twin sister too. Two women with two twins in the same room. What are the odds? The room smells fruity. I look down at the table, and can read what's written in bright green.

Share your thoughts, and the Father of Time will reveal all. Welcome to the Void.

My head begins to feel too heavy for my neck to support it, and I lay my head down upon the table, closing my eyes.

Loud, grunting noises can be heard behind me. I stand up, and a black man wearing nothing but a small piece of cloth is staring at me, holding a large wooden club. A bonfire separates the two of us.

The other man across the fire begins grunting, attempting to speak to me in a language I don't understand. I look down and realize that I'm only wearing a small piece of some kind of cloth as well. My wooden staff, the weapon, is leaning up against a large rock behind our campfire.

I'm suddenly sent back into the man's subconscious, and he resumes control. His name is Magdoo, and this is his home.

Chapter 8

Hyenas can be heard howling close by. The temperature has dropped significantly over the last half hour as Magdoo sits around the campfire with the Tribe. His younger brother, Mubiru, has been exiled from the Tribe, cast out by himself with nothing, not even allowed to take his weapon. Magdoo is concerned for his brother's safety. A tribal member begins grunting at Magdoo and giving him random hand gestures. He responds back to the other man and gives some hand signals in return, and the entire tribe begins laughing along with him. He must've told a funny joke, as the tribal leader, his father Zooberi, gets up and pats Magdoo on the back.

Suddenly, a hyena emerges through one of the bushes surrounding the camp, followed closely by three others. The first animal gives a loud howl, and charges at one of the young women. Chaos ensues, with tribal members scrambling for their weapons, swinging randomly at the charging animals. Magdoo is an even better warrior than he is a storyteller. He leaps on the back of the animal that has attacked the young woman, it's mouth firmly gripping her neck. Magdoo also has a strong hold on the hyena's neck, and he gives it a strong twist, followed closely by the sound of a loud "crack." The animal drops limp on top of the woman's body. It's too late for her, and he searches for the next animal to kill.

Within minutes, all four of the wild hyenas are killed, three of them at the hands of Magdoo. His father is badly wounded. More howls can be heard in the distance. He lifts Zooberi up over his shoulders, and together with the rest of the Tribe, they enter the nearby cave for protection and hopefully some rest. The campfire continues to burn as Magdoo looks back. He knows it is too late for his younger brother. He is on his own now. He wishes the best for Mubiru, whom he loves with all his heart. He is filled with regret and remorse, wishing he would have given Mubiru another chance. One day, he knows he'll be with his brother again. He closes his eyes.

When his eyes open again, it's daytime, and he's looking up at a large pyramid surrounded by sand. He hears a crack and feels the sharp sting of a whip on his shirtless back. He's pulling on a large rope, dragging a heavy object behind him. He is no longer Magdoo, but a man in his later years with slightly lighter skin. He pulls harder on the rope, and the heavy concrete square slab drags through the desert sand behind him. He's so tired, physically exhausted from the burning sun and the grueling labor of dragging these square stones for hours with no rest or water. He collapses face first in the hot sand.

The man feels immense guilt. He had traded his family for some drinking water several months ago. He hasn't seen them since. The water only lasted him a day, but the suffering he's endured has been much longer.

One of the guards, presumably the one cracking the whip, kicks him in the side, breaking a rib. He feels a hand on the back of his head, shoving his face deeper into the hot sand. He's fighting for oxygen, but instead takes in a mouthful of dirty sand. If only he could see his wife and daughter again, he would be a better father. If only, if only…

She opens her eyes, and she's sitting in a royal palace. The grapes are especially sweet today, and she giggles with delight at the performance of their jester, Roland Le Fartere. The large, open hall is well lit by several torches along the cement walls, which stretch high to the ceiling.

"Can I get you anything else, your Highness?" a young female servant asks.

"No," she says flatly, while popping the last grape into her mouth. She begins laughing more excitedly at Roland's last act and claps her hands loudly.

A young male knight approaches Queen Eleanor's throne, and stoops down on one knee.

"My Lady, I come bearing news," he says in a somber tone.

"Speak it!" she commands.

"It's King Henry, your Majesty. He knows what you're planning."

Her heart sinks. All of her planning and preparation against her husband; there's no way he could've found out. Impossible! She'd been conspiring with their eldest son, also named Henry, to overthrow her husband, King Henry II.

It was times like these that Eleanor wished she was back home in Aquitaine. With a heavy heart, tears form in her eyes, and she blinks.

Who are all of these people? Why am I only seeing glimpses of their lives?

He opens his eyes and aims down the sights of his musket. He fires the weapon, killing the man wearing a blue uniform. He crouches down and begins to reload. Surrounded by other men in red coats, their bunker has turned to a pit of mud. A cannon fires off to his right, and more musket fire erupts toward the left.

"Pull back!" his general shouts. "The Patriot rebels are flanking us! Pull back!"

He grabs the musket and puts his head down, running as fast as he can with the other soldiers. He's been fighting against the Rebel army for several months now in the colony known as Virginia, and he's hated every second of it here. He wishes he could just leave this war with no purpose so he can be back with his wife and three boys. He had built a homestead, a log cabin, with his bare hands in the foothills of the Blue Ridge Mountains months prior. Unfortunately, his duty to the Crown has proved to prevail his time as of late. He fears that if caught, he'll be sent back to England in chains, the fate of his family unknown, left to the barbarity of the Patriots.

The ground explodes directly in front of him, knocking him back, sucking all air out of his lungs. Rebels begin pouring into their dungy barracks.

"Say goodnight, Redcoat," says a Rebel soldier standing over him, pointing the barrel of a musket directly into his face. He pulls the trigger.

Where is Jess? Where is Loretta? Are we still in her shop? Did she drug me? I knew this would happen. Jess, if these visions ever stop, I swear…

Laura awakens from a short night's rest to the sound of her daughter's coughing. She's caught the flu, and Laura's husband has ridden their horse into town to get more medicine.

"Momma, when's pa coming home?" young Arnie asks.

"He'll be back soon, hon," she says comfortingly. "Can you fetch some cold water in a bucket, with a rag please, dear?"

Arnie runs off in pursuit of the requested items, and she places the back of her hand on her daughter's damp forehead.

"Oh, hon, you're burning up."

Her daughter coughs several times, then moans. Arnie returns with a bucket of cold water and a wash rag. She takes the rag, dunks it into the cold water, wrings it out and gently places it on her daughter's forehead.

The front door is violently kicked open, and two men wearing black cowboy hats enter, letting the cold night air into the small wooden home. The spurs on the heels of their boots can be heard, and one of them swipes aside his long red scarf to reveal the six-shooter on his hip.

"I ain't takin' no for an answer, Laura!" one of the men says. He has a full beard and is filthy from head to toe.

"Get out of here, Jacob!" she yells. "Can't you see I'm with my children? My daughter is sick!"

"Yeah, and?" Jacob asks, annoyed. "Your husband ain't here to protect you, woman."

Jacob and his partner reach for Laura, and she screams. Two loud gunshots ring out from beside Laura, and the two men drop to the wooden floor, their black hats sliding off their heads. She looks up to see young Arnie holding a revolver, a slight hint of smoke still spewing from the barrel of the gun.

"Oh, Arnie!" Laura yells, grabbing her son. The gun falls harmlessly to the floor. Tears form in her eyes, and she closes them against her son's chest.

He opens his eyes and sees the enemy aircraft straight ahead. He fires the guns on the P-38 Lightning, striking the Japanese aircraft several times until it explodes in a ball of flames, careening down to the Pacific Ocean below. Two more Japanese planes can be seen coming from the South, and he banks the plane's right wing down in order to flank them.

He slowly sinks below the enemy aircraft, then elevates back over the top of them in order to gain an advantageous position on their six. Within 30 seconds, he's behind the Japanese planes, and takes them both out of the sky.

Gunfire is heard behind him, striking his left engine. Fire and smoke envelope the engine, and he loses altitude. The blue ocean is in his line of sight, and the last thing he sees is a picture of his wife and son. He kisses his fingers, placing them over the photograph as a final goodbye to his family in St. Louis. He closes his eyes, bracing for the final impact.

He's naked, being carried through the air by an older female. She hands him over to a young woman. She's crying and smiling. Holding him up close, her arms enveloping him, she kisses his small forehead.

"He's a beautiful baby boy," the nurse says. "Have you decided on a name?"

"Johnathan," his mom says. "His name is Johnathan Stinson."

All of a sudden, it feels as if I'm being dragged out of baby John's subconscious, driven down into a deep, dark, empty chasm where life has never existed before, and was never meant to thrive. I'm sitting down on what feels like dark nothingness.

Suddenly, all the lives that I've just witnessed and several more begin flooding past me, like individual prints on a large quilt. Individual memories, the happy moments, sadness, doubt, elation, all their emotions. All of their feelings and memories. These people, who I've never known, yet it feels as if I've known them all before, all too well.

All sight goes dark again, and the sound of footsteps can be heard behind me. I stand up and turn around. A man is standing in front of me dressed in an all-white suit with thick, dark eyebrows, brown hair in a bowl cut, and no facial hair. His eyes appear sunken in, like he hasn't slept in weeks.

"Hello, Simon," he says. "It seems to me that you've been seeing quite a lot recently, haven't you?"

I briefly hesitate, my breath catching in my throat. "Who are you?" I ask. "Where am I? And how do you know my name?"

He begins to chew on his inner lip, shaking his head. "For the time being, you can call me 'X,'" he says, then gently grabs my shoulder. "This is called the Void. It's the space between the waking and spiritual world. This is where your mind goes when sleeping, but not yet dreaming." He steps closer, less than a couple inches from my face. "I know all about you, Mr. Verner. Your past. Your present. Even bits of your future. I've been there. And I will always be there, for better or worse. But right now, I need to ask you a favor. Stop looking into who killed John Stinson. Do you follow me?"

I stare at him, unmoving. Worried that if I blink my eyes again, I'll wind up somewhere else.

"Why?" I ask.

"Because I'm politely asking you to," X says patiently. "Consider this your one and only warning. You can have a long, happy life ahead of you with your friends. You can grow old and die in peace. Just let the Stinson murder go unsolved. Now, enjoy your time with Sweet Loretta."

He shoves me down on the ground, and I begin falling again, tumbling down head over heels deeper into the endless black Void. Memories of my own life flood past me now, thoughts of Jess and Mom and Doug. My childhood. Sitting next to Dad's hospital bed just before he passed away. Images flash in front of me that I don't remember. Ancient looking staffs shooting out violent flashes of yellow and blue, colliding head on, sending sparks in every direction. An armored man sitting on a throne of skulls, surrounded by an endless sea of red lava, smiling wickedly. An immensely tall building, towering high up above into the clouds and beyond. Visions of an older version of myself, with people I know, but they look much older. Ron and Jess lay dead next to me in a pool of their own blood, their unmoving eyes staring up at me. I scream as I continue to fall, plummeting towards nothing, with no ground or sky in sight.

I open my eyes, still screaming, with my face down on the black table in Loretta's shop, drenched in sweat.

Chapter 9

Jess and Loretta each have a strong hold on my shoulders, trying to prevent me from falling back in the chair.

"Calm yourself, dear child," Loretta says softly in my ear. "Hold him still, Jess. Hold tight. I'll be right back."

My feet are pressed hard against the carpeted floor, my face still flat on the table. I begin to breathe in and out, fast at first, then slower until my heart rate begins to return to a normal rhythm.

"I'm alright," I say. "You can ease up. I'm not going anywhere. I'm back."

Jess' hold on my shoulder eases up and I sit back against the chair, just as Loretta enters the room, spraying more of her strange substance around the room.

I take a deep breath, staring at Loretta. My face feels flushed, and my heart rate spikes again, this time in anger.

"Speak your mind, Simon," she says, putting down the bottle and taking her seat across from me at the table. Jess sits next to me.

The room is still dark, and the black table still has the glowing green letters on it, unreadable once more. The black light illuminates the white scarf around Loretta's head, and the beads in her long dreadlocks.

"What was that?" I ask, my voice shaky. "What did you drug me with? LSD? Some new mushroom? What, are you some pharmaceutical scientist testing a new hallucinogenic? Is that what this was, an experiment? I can't believe…" I turn my attention to Jess. "This woman is dangerous. All I wanted to know was who killed that police officer. Not…whatever that was. We need to get out of here. Right now!"

I stand up to leave, but the room begins to spin around me, faster and faster. Losing my balance, my feet feel like microwaved butter, and I fall face first onto the carpet. Jess and Loretta once again rush over to aid me back into the chair.

"Tell me what you saw, child."

"Stop calling me a child!"

Loretta sighs and sits back down in her seat. She takes a drink out of another bottle she had hiding beneath the table.

A few moments pass in silence, and the room finally stops spinning around me. I chug a bottle of water provided by Jess and take several deep breaths.

"I'm sorry," I say, squeezing the bridge of my nose between my fingers. "I just wasn't expecting to be drugged tonight, that's all. I was late to work this morning, so this has been a pretty messed up day all around even before this. The new girl at work started hitting on me for some reason." Jess sits back in her chair, arms crossed. "I've been having these crazy dreams, then I come in here and have you send me down into some damn rabbit hole like I'm Alice. I don't know what's happening."

I wipe my face and look up expectantly at Loretta for an answer. Jess remains silent, her hands now in her lap.

"Simon, tell Loretta what you saw," Jess pleads.

"I…I don't know what I saw." I take a deep breath. "I was in an African tribe or something, and then I was an Egyptian slave. At one point I was the freaking Queen of England. There were lots of people who I…I guess I *was* them somehow, but I wasn't able to control anything they said or did, just like with John Stinson." I shake my head and tell them in greater detail what I saw.

"I see," Loretta says. I instantly get the feeling that I'm sitting across from my counselor Angela again. "I think I know what you saw." Loretta takes a deep breath, furrowing her eyebrows and not breaking eye contact from me. "Now, what I'm about to tell you may sound a bit…out there to you. But, Simon, what you have is a very unique gift. And for some reason, this gift is beginning to blossom and develop for you at a pivotal moment in your life."

"Why me?" I ask, still shaking my head. "I'm…I'm a nobody. I work at a golf course for crying out loud. I've got nothing to contribute to society."

Loretta clicks her tongue. "Child, you're lying to yourself. What you just said, that's flat-out not true. But if you're going to sit there and have a pity party, you've come to the wrong place. I'm here to open up your mind and spirit, not have you cry on my shoulder for mommy."

"You don't know me."

"No, I don't," Loretta continues. "But I have a gift too, you see. I can sense people's auras. And your aura, what I can see at least, tells me the opposite of the way you feel about yourself. You're special. You've got a big heart, but you're afraid to open it up because you're afraid of getting hurt. That's understandable. I'm similar in that way. But you're far more valuable than what you're giving yourself credit for."

"I don't see how I'm special. What supposed 'gift' do you think I have?"

"Your ability to dream into past lives," Loretta says, sitting forward. "Every dream, for everybody, is a window to somewhere else. For most people, it's just a window to an alternate reality. A reality that's temporarily created, then that window closes when they wake up, and the reality ceases to exist. What you have, though, is the ability to open an entire doorway into another person's mind. Someone who actually lived and experienced the world before. This gift is entirely new to you, and you don't know how to navigate it yet. But in time, you will."

"Well, I was sort of figuring that with John Stinson," I say. "Not to be rude or anything, but I had a feeling I was getting those dreams to solve his murder mystery."

"That's true. You are," Loretta says. "But your gift is much, much more than that. When I was able to tap into your aura, I got an accurate reading. You also have the ability to dream into other people's past lives. People that you were connected to."

"Like, what, I'm able to tap into my family tree or something? Those people were my ancestors?"

"No," she says dismissively. "Those past lives were *your* past lives. Lives that *you* lived." When she says 'you,' she points directly at my chest from across the table.

"I'm sorry, I'm not following," I say. "So, all of those people, including John Stinson, are my past lives, and when I dream, I see their greatest hits or something?"

"*Your* greatest hits," she says, raising her voice. "You're seeing key moments from *your* past lives through your past eyes. Don't think of them as separate people, because for you, they aren't. They're actually *you.* You're witnessing key moments that you've already lived and experienced, you just can't remember them yet. When a soul transfers bodies from death to birth, we lose those associated memories. Except for you!"

I stare blankly at the woman. She's now smiling, which is made brighter by the black light.

"That's nuts," I say. "How can I possibly be dreaming of my past lives?"

"I don't know!" she says, her voice still elevated. "It's absolutely incredible. In my experience, you're only the fourth person who could tap into their past Soul Beams." She shakes her head, her dreadlocks flapping around her cheeks.

"Soul Beams?" Jess speaks up, finally. "What's a Soul Beam, Loretta?"

"Soul Beams, that's just kind of a name we came up with a few years back, my old group and I," Loretta says, waving Jess off. "Basically, we all have souls, right? When we die, our soul will go into a kind of limbo status for an unknown period of time. It's different for everyone. We don't know why. Best guess is that's they're…recharging, for lack of a better term. Anyways, your soul will then transfer itself into your next body, and you live out another life. The number of lives a soul can live is unknown. Some say it's unlimited. Some say twelve. Nobody really knows for certain. However, I believe that in the end, we're judged by our overall service in our combined lives, and our souls are sent to either a good or bad resting place, depending on how we grade out."

Jess and I stare at one another, then back at Loretta.

"Well, thank you for your time," I say, standing up again. "But it's getting pretty late and I need to get some sleep so that I'm not late again for work tomorrow."

Loretta gets up and rushes around the table, grabbing my arm. "Simon, I know that this sounds crazy to an outsider, to someone not as experienced in studying the human spirit. But please, you have to believe me, child. Your gift is blossoming into fruition for a reason. My best guess is that you're being sent these memories from Beyond for a reason. Only one person can solve the mystery of John Stinson's murder, and it's you. It can only be you."

"Loretta, I do have one more question," I say quietly. "Do you know someone named 'X'?"

She releases my arm and takes a step back. "Did you see him?"

"Yes, at the very end, after I went through my Soul Train."

"Beam. Soul Beam," Loretta says. She pauses and looks down at the floor. "Whatever he said to you, you must ignore him."

"Who is he?"

"He'll try to corrupt you. He's a manipulator who wears many different faces and will use any means necessary to burn you down. You must resist him, no matter what he says."

Jess is quiet on the drive back to her place, her arms crossed.

"Are you cold?" I ask.

"No, I'm alright," she says softly. "I'm so sorry. I thought she was just going to give you some herbs to take home and help you relax. With all that you've been through…I just wanted to help you loosen up a bit, that's all. Just to calm yourself. She'd given me some stuff that helped me after Mom passed. I wasn't expecting anything like that to happen."

I look over at Jess, and gently place my hand on her shoulder. "You have nothing to be sorry about," I say. "Actually, I'm going to think about what she said. Believe it or not, I didn't think what she said sounded so crazy once she explained it. At least I've got some sort of an answer to go off of, now. I'll sleep on it."

When we get to Jess' apartment, I walk her up to her building in the dark. We give each other a hug.

"So, who's this girl at work hitting on you?"

"Her name's Brittany," I say. "We have a date tomorrow night. She seems pretty nice, actually."

"Well, I hope you have a good time. Goodnight, Simon." She pinches my cheek, a bit roughly, then scrunches up her nose. "Sweet dreams."

She turns and walks into her building.

When I get back home, I put my keys into the little dish by the front door, then walk over to Hank's tank. I feed him dinner, far later than I had intended.

After changing into my pajamas, I lay in bed, watching the nightly news on the small TV on top of the dresser. Three fatal shootings tonight. Corrupt politicians. Bad news, and more bad news. I drown out the old man reading his teleprompter and start to think back on what Loretta had said. I look over on the nightstand and reach for the business card she handed me on the way out the door. If I have any more issues, I'll make sure to give her a call.

Why am I suddenly being given these visions of my own past life? I guess I'll worry about the "why" some other time. What matters now is piecing together the memories I've been shown in order to catch my prior killer. Doug had mentioned that he still thought about the cold case to this day. Maybe, just maybe, if I could help Doug solve this cold case, he would finally warm up to me. Maybe he would accept me, in a world where I never really felt accepted. Maybe…

He's fishing in a small lake with his dad. Upper Red Lake, Minnesota. June, 1960. The sky is clear and blue. Birds fly between the trees off in the distance. The water's incredibly clear, with barely a ripple on the surface.

Now I can remember the where and when. This is good. Maybe I can start to piece this puzzle together a little more efficiently now.

He feels a tug on the end of his fishing line, and he begins reeling in. For being a little boy, John's surprisingly strong.

"You got one?" his father asks him, shifting his weight steadily in their small rowboat.

"I got one, Dad!" John says excitedly, continuing to frantically reel in his catch. Finally, a small fish emerges from the water, its mouth around the hook. Dad reaches over and gently grabs the fishing line in one hand, the fish in the other, and brings them both into the boat. "I thought he'd be a lot bigger than that. He was putting up such a fight."

Dad laughs, and John feels so proud for catching his first fish.

I remember catching this fish with Dad. We took it home and he grilled it on the backyard barbeque. It tasted amazing, but I felt guilty afterwards for taking that little fish from his home. Dad was so proud. Dad was proud…

Five years later, on September 13th, 1965, Dad strides over to John as he's sitting on the family couch, watching *Leave it to Beaver* in black and white on their brand-new TV. Dad turns around, shouting back toward the kitchen.

"I said I'll be back in ten minutes! Shut your mouth, woman!" His booming voice vibrates John's chest like a nearby bomb going off. He slams the door on the way out, another explosion of sound. John looks out the window as dad gets into the red 1958 Chevrolet. Mom's crying in the kitchen, but he just sits on the couch, tears forming in his eyes.

I remember this day so vividly. This was the last time I ever saw Dad. He just drove away and left us. Like he didn't even care.

The weight of the couch shifts next to John, but he doesn't turn to see who's sitting next to him.

"What do you think, Simon? Pretty sad, isn't it?"

That's the voice of X! Turn your head and look at him, John!

X puts his hand on John's shoulder but gets no reaction from the fourteen-year-old whose attention is squarely on the TV, trying desperately to hold back a wave of emotions. He hated it when his parents fought like this.

"It's okay, Simon. You can talk to me. I can hear your thoughts. Dreams are my domain. Go ahead, speak to me."

What do you want?

"I want you to see some of the other… moments in John's life," X says, chuckling. "Oh, Simon. You're going to be so disappointed in dear old John. You probably think he's some kind of a hero, don't you? Think again. Any other questions before we continue the tour?"

How did you know John?

X sighs, his deep exhale blowing a rush of warm air on the side of John's face "Everyone always thought he was such a Saint. If people would've just looked beneath the surface, they would've seen what a coward he truly was."

Did you kill him?

"Sheesh, relax a minute, will ya? Although, that would make your little investigation so much easier though, wouldn't it? Alright, I'll show you some more."

John's out on evening patrol by himself. His sweaty palms tightly grip the steering wheel. It had rained earlier but was tapering off now. Pools of yellow reflection from the building's neon signs glow off the puddles of water in the asphalt. Flashing signs on both sides of the street, inviting desperate men to enter and give their last dollar for a night of empty love.

A voice crackles over the police scanner, and John immediately mutes the radio.

Why is he on patrol by himself? Isn't Mike supposed to be with him?

"Hey, look at you Simon! You've seen enough cop shows on the ol' boob-tube that you're an expert on the police now, is that it?" X says from the backseat, grabbing the passenger side head rest. "Hey, before you start complaining, I'll be quiet. I just want you to pay attention to what you…er… I mean what John does here."

John pulls the police car over in front of a warehouse, kills the engine and steps out. He walks briskly through a side door of an old, abandoned warehouse where a large, bald man with a beard is holding the door open for him. They nod at one another. Mike's standing inside the small office with a man sitting in a small wooden chair. His wrists are bound behind him by rope and a heavy layer of bonding tape is over his mouth. His muffled shouts are quickly silenced when Mike pistol whips the man across the face. The man stares at Mike for a moment, then slowly turns to look at John, an intense look of hatred in his eyes. The familiar dragon tattoo is visible on his neck.

John knows that what he's doing isn't right, but he's been left with no choice. In order to solve this case, he needs to break Chavez and get the information he needs. Mike has continued to insist on helping with the investigation and has convinced John that this is the best method to break the enemy.

"Chavez," John says, then chuckles. "Let's pick up where we left off last month. How did we end up in this situation? Oh, I remember, you have information, and you're going to give that to me. Right now." He bends down so that he's looking directly into Chavez's face. "Tell me what I want to know, or I dump your body into the lake still breathing. Just like Marcini did to Alvarez."

John rips the duct tape off Chavez's mouth. "Like I told you last time, I don't know who Marcini sent to kill Alvarez." Chavez says, his voice quivering.

John points the pistol at Chavez's forehead. "Last chance. Who killed Alvarez?"

"I don't know!" Chavez shouts. "Look man, I told you, I don't kn–"

John punches Chavez in the face. "You want to die?" John screams in his face. "Tell me who Marcini sent to kill Alvarez!"

"Sizzle, pig!" Chavez says, blood trickling down his chin. "I'm tired of your games. You just don't get it, do you? Why don't you go question Marcini? You flaunt your badge, but you don't deserve to wear it. Protect and serve my ass. You're a coward, Stinson!"

John eyes the man for a moment, then turns to leave. Mike's waiting outside with the bearded man, hands in his pockets. "Keep him tied up and take him somewhere secure. Duct tape his lying mouth shut." John tells them.

As he leaves the warehouse, he kicks a tire on the car and screams, holding his hands behind his head. He gets back into his patrol car and drives away.

"See, what did I tell you?" X says smugly from the backseat. "The dude's a bad cop."

How did you know about this?

"Because I saw this in John's dreams." X says. "He lets this moment linger with him, and many more to come. He feels guilty, sure. But you know what's sick, Simon? He's dreamt about killing Chavez for quite some time before this moment. He just hasn't done it yet. No, let me rephrase that. *You* haven't done it. Yet."

I can't control what I dream, any more than I can control my past life.

"Sure, keep telling yourself that. Anyways, I just wanted to show up in case I wasn't clear earlier this evening. *Do not pursue this case further*. You were a bad cop in your past life. It's not worth your time pursuing who killed you. It's over with. Pretty soon, these dreams will go away, and you'll go back to picking up golf balls and talking to your little goldfish."

I've never dreamt about work. Not once. How do you know what I do for a living?

Silence. X doesn't respond. John keeps his hands tightly gripped to the steering wheel, a look of fury on his face.

Chapter 10

At work the next day, all I can think about is John. What drove this good man to kidnap Chavez and lock him up in an abandoned warehouse? There seem to be other, more ethical ways to get information.

As I drive the rattling range picker around, picking up an endless stream of golf balls, an idea strikes me. Actually, several ideas, just like the golf balls that are striking this rickety machine I'm sitting in. I should press Doug for more information, since he was John's boss, and while he may not know who killed him, he may know more about the Marcini/Chavez/Alvarez connection. Heck, he might even know who killed Alvarez. Maybe that will get that ball rolling.

I should also try to find a chance to talk to William Marcini. I did some research last night and discovered he's still alive, and owns a fine dining Italian Restaurant in town, aptly named "Marcini's." After that, I should try to find out if Mike is still alive. If so, he's probably a gold mine of information. From the memories I've seen, Mike always had John's back. I should also try to track down his wife Samantha and their child.

Another golf ball clanks off the rattled cage, and I turn the machine around, beginning another sweep of the driving range.

Later, while on break, Brittany bounces into the employee breakroom area. She's wearing an incredibly low-cut black top, and her hair is in pigtails. She comes over to my table, motioning for me to remove my headphones.

"Can I help you?" I ask.

"Are you excited for our date tonight, silly?" she asks flirtatiously, raising her voice up an octave, and pressing her shoulders together, giving me a free show of some kind.

Honestly, I'd completely forgotten. It was only 24 hours ago that she had asked me out, but it feels like it's been at least a week. My mind truly has been someplace else.

I clear my throat and give her a warm smile. "Yes, I'm looking forward to it. What time did you want me to pick you up?"

"Pick me up at seven," she says. "Where are you taking me?"

"How do you feel about Italian?"

At 6:50 that evening, I'm parked in the last available parking space in front of Brittany's apartment. Her building's much nicer than mine, and in a better neighborhood. A tinge of jealousy hits me momentarily, but I shake it off. I know how lucky I am to be in my current place, and I'll always be grateful to Ron for helping put a roof over my head. I flip down the mirror in the visor to get a better look at myself. For a brief instant, I see X in the backseat, smiling at me. I quickly turn around, but the backseat is empty.

I close my eyes and take several deep breaths, then turn back around in my seat to resume my work in the mirror. Spongy would be the word I would use to describe my full head of curly hair. My eyes look fine. What am I even looking for? Forget it, this is good enough. Quit stalling, and go up to your date, Simon.

I'm not sure what Brittany sees in me, but I'll take her out for a nice dinner and see where this goes. She seemed so excited earlier at work, I would hate to let her down.

Grabbing the flowers off the passenger seat, I walk up to her building. Surprisingly, the front entrance is unlocked, and I go in and take the elevator up to the seventh floor.

Red carpet with intricate patterns in the hallway leads to her door. Several black and white photographs of historical Chicago line the walls. Moments of a past time captured and preserved for future generations to gawk at and wonder about. People in fine clothes, going about their busy days in the dusty streets of the town, old cars driving on brick roads. Men hard at work, erecting large steel beams that have stood tall far after the builders passed on, and will likely remain standing far after I've passed into my next life.

Next to her door is a small wooden table with a vase full of marbles sitting on top of a white doily. She opens the door as soon as I knock, and the sight of her takes my breath away. Squeezed into a skintight black dress, her hair is no longer in pigtails, but down past her shoulders. A purple ribbon is placed with care on top of her hair. Her full lips are tinted with red lipstick, and her eyes are heavy with mascara. Not too much, but just enough to make me stare, and make my knees buckle.

"Come in, silly," she says, giggling. "You're right on time."

I awkwardly stretch my arms out, handing her the flowers. She graciously takes them and rushes ahead into the apartment to find something to put them in. I follow her into the dimly lit and incredibly clean apartment.

"Go ahead and make yourself comfortable on the couch. I'm almost done." Her voice trails off down the hallway.

I do as she asks and sit on the couch, where a gray cat is waiting for me on one of the cushions.

"Hey there, kitty," I say, reaching my hand out to pet it. The cat hisses furiously, and I recoil my hand back into my lap.

Her apartment is spotless. In front of the couch is a glass coffee table with one book on it, *Of Mice and Men*. Perpendicular to the couch is a small love seat which faces out toward the back balcony. Her view is amazing, with the Chicago skyline perfectly front and center. Behind the love seat is a marble-topped bar, with the kitchen on the other side. The smell of lilacs becomes stronger, and a pair of hands begin to gently massage my shoulders.

"First dates are always exciting, aren't they?" Her voice has dropped an octave since our brief conversation at work into a more smoky, late-night radio show personality.

"Yeah, for sure," I say, my voice squeaking.

"Don't be nervous, Simon," she says, laughing.

"Well, I'm ready to eat. How about you?" I stand up from the couch, clapping my hands together.

"Yes, I'm ready. Where are we going? Italian, you said?"

"Right. Have you ever been to Marcini's?"

We walk down to my car, and I rush ahead to open the passenger side door for her.

"Such a gentleman," she says while getting into the vehicle.

We make it to the restaurant at 7:30. They seat us in a booth, and the waiter, complete with bowtie, offers us the wine menu. I decline and choose to stick with water, which is received with an eyeroll from Brittany.

"I'll do a glass of your *Bolgheri Superiore*," she says, handing the menu back to the younger waiter.

After he leaves, Brittany keeps staring at me intently.

"You know, I just try to stay away from alcohol on work nights, but on Friday and Saturday, lock your liquor cabinets!" I chuckle and take a gulp of water.

"Tell me about yourself," Brittany says, and rests her chin up on the backs of her fingers, her elbows placed on the table.

"Alright. I'm twenty-three and single. I work with you at the golf course, where I primarily pick up golf balls on the driving range."

"You know, I've been curious about that," she says. "Golfing is a seasonal sport. What do you do when the weather cools down and there's snow? The course isn't open year-round."

"Steve also owns an indoor computer simulated driving range downtown off Wicker Park. Actually, I've worked there longer than at Lowland Woods, and Steve liked me enough to hire me for both, thankfully."

"I see," she says inquisitively. "And I'm assuming you're an avid golfer yourself?"

"No, not at all," I say. "I've tried it, and I'm alright. It's just not my thing. I'm more interested in picking up the golf balls than hitting them, I suppose. I find golf to be incredibly…boring. Also, it's a game for rich people, which I am not." I wait for a response but get nothing in return. "How about you? Tell me about yourself, Brittany."

"Well, I'm twenty-five, also single," she says. "I like long walks on the beach. My cat Chester, whom I'm assuming you've made acquaintances with, is my best friend at the moment. I just moved to Chicago last July."

"From where?"

"San Francisco."

The waiter arrives with Brittany's wine and refills my water. We ask him to give us another few minutes with the menu. Neither of us have even glanced at it yet.

"Chicago is a long way from San Francisco," I say, more as a question than a statement, encouraging her to go on.

"Yes, it is," she says, taking a sip of her wine. "My husband passed away early last year. It was a freak accident, and I just had to pack up and get out of there."

"Oh, I'm so sorry to hear that."

She waves me off. "I've grieved long enough, and he'll always be with me, but I know he would want me to move on with my life."

I sit there silently for a moment, trying to think of something to say.

"What do you do for fun?" I ask.

"I like camping."

"Hey, that's cool. My friends, Jess and Ron, we've been talking about going camping for the last few months. We've been waiting for the weather to warm up some. Maybe we could all go together sometime? We could use someone with some experience. You know, to set up the tent. Catch us a rabbit. Stuff like that."

She begins to laugh again. That deep, sexy laugh. It makes the hair on my arms stand up. Her laugh mixed with that intoxicating scent she's got on is driving me bonkers.

"That sounds like fun," she says. "Who's Jess?"

"Jess is my best friend," I say. "We've always just been…friends. We've been there for each other during some darker times over the years. I'm hoping you two can meet. I've got a feeling you'd hit it off quick."

The waiter arrives to take our order. After he leaves, I excuse myself to "powder my nose" which gets a roar of laughter from Brittany. Either she thinks I'm the next great comedian, or that wine is really kicking in fast.

Along the way to the bathroom, framed pictures of the previous owners are hanging on the wall. The restaurant is currently on its fourth owner, from 1992 to present, William Marcini. I stand there and admire the picture. He's an older man with balding hair wearing a black tuxedo with a red bow tie, but it's apparent that he used to be very handsome when he was younger. I look over to my right as the same man emerges from the men's restroom, wiping his wet hands on the pants of his gray suit. He looks me in the eyes and nods his head. I nod my head in return. An overwhelming sense of anger takes over me for some reason, and I have to close my eyes for a moment to regain my composure. It's rare for me to feel such a sense of rage and hate, and I'm not sure why. As much as I try to swallow down this bile of anger, it forces its way up, and I'm unable to stop it.

"Marcini!" I shout.

He stops and turns around, apparently startled by a stranger yelling his name. "Yes? What can I do for you, sir?"

My heart's beating like crazy, about to leap out of my chest. I freeze, unable to think clearly. Thankfully, an idea comes to me from nowhere. I reach out my right hand and step toward him, placing my left hand over my chest.

"Mr. Marcini, my name is…Samuel, and I'm working on a story for our school newspaper at The Daily Northwestern. May I have a moment of your time?"

He takes my hand, shakes it quickly, then stiffens his back. He flashes me a cheesy smile, one that's good for photographs, but cringey in real life situations. "Of course, young man. Anything for the youth of our nation."

"Thank you, sir, that's great," I say, sweat beginning to form on my forehead. I pretend to search my pockets for a piece of paper to write on, which yields nothing. "We're doing an article on the unsolved murder of a Chicago police officer from 1986. His name was John Stinson. After all these years have passed, is there anything you can say to shed some light on the story, maybe help put this case to rest?"

Marcini's stare turns cold, and he lowers his chin. "I'm sorry, who's that?"

"John Stinson, a former member of the Chicago police. It's known that you were a suspect in a murder investigation he was working on right around the time that he disappeared. Some say that it may be more than a coincidence. Tell me, Mr. Marcini, what was your relationship with Rafael Chavez?"

"Young man, if you weren't a paying customer…" he grabs my shirt collar, pulling me close, and lowers his voice. "How do you know all of this? Huh? Are you working with the Balazar's? Did they put you up to this?"

"No, sir. Like I said, I'm with The Daily Northwestern. The criminal justice department at the university has teamed up with our journalism department to dive into the John Stinson case."

"Is that so?" he glowers, tightening his firm grip on my collar.

"Yes, sir."

My heart rate has somehow slowed down, despite being downstream of Marcini's breath, the scent of alcohol spouting through his nostrils. I match his stare, looking back into his brown eyes, an unusual surge of confidence coursing through my body.

"I know you had Alvarez killed," I continue. "I know you're involved in Stinson's death. I don't know how, but you're involved. And I intend to bring you and your entire enterprise to justice. Stinson's wife was pregnant when you had him killed, did you know that?"

"You've got a real set on you, kid," Marcini says, shoving me roughly against the wall. "I had nothing to do with Stinson's death. You want answers about him, go talk to Doug Lewis, his old boss." He looks down at the ground for a moment, then releases his grip on my collar as two women walk past. Returning his stare to me, he continues. "I run this city, you understand me? Now, I suggest you finish eating your meal with your little girlfriend, then get the hell out of here and never return. You got that?"

I nod my head. Marcini turns around and walks away angrily, his shoulders twitching.

When I return to the dinner table, our food has already arrived.

"Long line at the bathroom, sorry about that." I say. "Bon appétit."

Throughout dinner, we talk about work, her cat Chester, my fish Hank, my car, her apartment, her car, and what she wants to do "when she grows up." She wants to be an airline flight attendant because she thinks she could handle unruly passengers and serve drinks while thirty thousand feet in the air.

I tell her that for one of my final assignments in a career class I took in high school, I wanted to be a cop, but my stepfather convinced me I wasn't cut out for the force.

"I think you'd make a great cop," she says.

"Yeah, in my dreams."

After dinner, I drive her back to her apartment and walk her up to the building.

"I had a really great time tonight, Simon. Thank you."

I reach out to shake her hand, and she takes it. Her hands are awfully sweaty. Then she stretches out her neck and gives me a gentle kiss on the cheek.

"See you in the morning," I say, and watch her go inside the building.

Chapter 11

John and Mike are out on evening patrol on the tough downtown streets, cruising past seedy bars and night clubs. Street walkers turn their backs when they see the patrol car rolling down the street. From the passenger seat, Mike looks out the window, scanning the nightlife. John isn't interested in the nightlife. Instead, he's focused on one man.

They pull up to one of the local strip clubs, and walk past the line of people waiting outside, flashing their badges to the bouncer at the front door. Once inside, the two cops sit next to each other at the bar and order drinks. The interior is dark. Strobe lights pulsate from the stage in the center of the room, and loud music thumps rhythmically. John isn't a fan of loud, obnoxious places like these, but this is where he was told to be this evening.

One of the strippers walks up behind John and props herself up against the bar on an elbow.

"Which one of you handsome men is John?" she asks, her voice high pitched and nasally.

John stands up. "Take me to him."

He follows the dancer through the club, watching as girls gyrate up on the stage. Men in business suits throw money at their feet, leaning forward intently.

Through a beaded curtain and into the backroom, John follows the young woman until he sees William Marcini sitting at a crescent booth with two men on either side of him. She pulls a chair away from another table and places it at the table for John. He takes a seat, directly opposite Marcini.

He looks so much younger with a full head of hair. He looks a lot healthier, too.

"So, I hear you've got one of my men, is that right?" Marcini demands, his arms crossed over his broad chest.

"You've heard correctly," John says. "We can make a clean swap. I'll give you back Chavez, and you tell me who killed Alvarez."

Marcini is looking down at the table, chewing the side of his lip. Suddenly, he looks back up at John, a fiery look on his face. "Fine, you got me Stinson. I admit that I had Alvarez killed. He was a whiny little brat and kept screwing up every little job I gave him. The kid was a thorn in my side. Being the mayor's little brother gave him a sense of...entitlement, I suppose. He learned the hard way with me that respect is earned, not given." Marcini sighs and takes another drink. "However, I'm going to need some proof that Chavez is still alive before I spill the beans on who I hired to do the hit."

John reaches into his coat pocket and grabs a few date-stamped photographs of Chavez, tied up. His eyes are bruised and swollen shut. Marcini takes several deep breaths looking over the photos. He raps his knuckles on the table, then turns to the man to his left, whispering in his ear.

"So, what's it going to be?" John asks. "Just tell me what I want to know, and I'll be on my way."

"You see, that's not how this is going to work," Marcini says. "You're in no position to bargain with me. I *own* this city. Half of the police force is in my back pocket. So, I'll give you one last chance. Tell me where Chavez is located, or we're going to have...problems."

"Is that a threat?"

"It's a promise."

Marcini nods his head, and a sharp wire begins to press against John's neck from behind. Instinctively, John grabs the wire with both hands, preventing the tension of the wire from compressing his windpipe, and slams his head backwards, smacking the man behind him directly in the nose.

The men on either side of Marcini both reach inside the inner pocket of their coats and pull pistols out, aiming them at John. Meanwhile, he's already gotten up from his chair and immediately flips a table on its side, jumping over it and crouching for cover. The man who had attempted to strangle John is lying unconscious on the floor with a bloody nose. Reaching inside the man's coat pocket, John finds a pistol. Shots are fired by the two men, bullets lodging in the wooden table and ricocheting off the steel legs beneath.

Silverware is strewn about the floor, as well as plastic cups from the overturned table. Keeping the pistol in one hand, John picks up several discarded pieces of silverware in one hand, heaving them over his shoulder in the direction of Marcini's booth. The armed men are still firing their weapons. John grabs the man lying on the floor and hefts him up, holding him up like a shield and aiming the pistol at the two men. Marcini has a revolver of his own now.

As John begins shuffling his feet toward the beaded curtain, the three men hold their fire, making sure not to kill the man that John's taken as a temporary hostage. The sound of bass heavy music grows louder, until eventually he's back in the club, the curtain sliding over the back of his head, as well as the man he's holding. A dancer is directly to John's left. He lets go of the man and turns to run, letting him drop to the floor with a thud.

Gunshots erupt from the backroom, and everyone near the back of the club screams. Dancers run off the stage, abandoning their positions at their poles. One businessman, struggling to regain his balance, reaches onto the stage and grabs handfuls of cash, stuffing it into his pockets. Apparently, people in the front section of the club haven't heard a thing, as the shots were drowned out by the loud music.

"Mike, we got to go. Now!"

John grabs the back of Mike's collar, yanking him off his stool as he's in mid-sentence with a beautiful young woman at the bar. The glass that Mike was drinking out of explodes, sending glass and whiskey flying. Bullets hit large bottles of alcohol behind the bartender, creating a cascading waterfall of broken glass and expensive liquor which falls to the floor.

The two officers run outside and quickly jump into the police cruiser. John puts the key in the ignition, but the vehicle doesn't start.

"C'mon, c'mon!" John shouts, turning the key as hard as he can.

Marcini and his two men aggressively walk out the front of the club, looking in every direction. One man runs to the left, the other to the right, following their leader's commands. Mike ducks down, just as Marcini sees the cop car parked down the road. He raises his pistol, and fires off three rounds, shattering the passenger side window and sending glass spraying onto Mike. Two other bullets hit the windshield, causing the glass to crack, but not break.

Finally, the car starts with a roar of the engine, and John shifts into drive, burning rubber as they enter the roadway, causing several cars to begin honking at them. John turns on the police siren, and cars in front pull to the side of the road, making a path for them to escape.

"What happened back there?" Mike screams.

"Marcini's a nut job, that's what happened!" John yells back, his voice shaking. "Jesus Christ, the guy's a total lunatic! I mean, I knew he had a couple of screws loose, but he's gone completely off the reservation, man. He needs to be locked up!"

"What did you think was going to happen, huh? You, what, thought he was just going to spill the beans on the case in exchange for Chavez?"

"Chavez means a lot to him!" John exclaims. "He totally changed when I showed him those pictures of Chavez tied up. He completely lost it in there."

"That's just great, John," Mike says, calming down. "Now what?"

John clutches the steering wheel tightly, still trying to catch his breath.

Later that night, John sits in the basement of their home. An empty shoebox sits in front of him on a wooden workbench. Next to the shoebox is a small black safe. Reaching inside his coat pocket, he pulls out a tape recorder. He ejects the cassette tape, places it in the shoebox, and shuts the lid.

"Gotcha," John says.

The safe is a perfect size for the shoebox, as it fits snugly inside. Shutting the little door and twisting the dial, he picks up the little safe and carries it further into the basement, placing it on the floor. He steps back, wiping his hands, admiring his work.

Against the far back wall of the basement, construction is almost complete on a small panic room that he's built entirely by himself, which will be unnoticeable to anyone not paying attention to the exact square footage of the home, as it's only three feet by three feet. It won't be on any blueprints with the house. Due to her pregnancy, Samantha hasn't been downstairs in several weeks. The only person who knows of this room will be John, and he plans on keeping it that way.

I WAKE UP feeling exhausted, like I've been running a marathon all night. Crawling out of bed, I proceed to do my usual morning routine. As I pass by Hank's tank on the way out of the bathroom, I peer down into his rectangular home, and he swims out from his little pirate ship of a bedroom, greeting me with his big eyes, puffing his little cheeks out. I mimic his expression, puffing my own cheeks out.

Arriving at work ten minutes early, I make sure to swing by Brittany's reception area.

"Good morning," I say enthusiastically.

"Good morning yourself, handsome." she says, back to her high-pitched voice. I figure this must be her "work" voice, as opposed to her deeper "date night" voice.

We chat with each other on break and agree to go out again Saturday night after I get back from my family dinner with Mom and Doug. I ask her if she's free Friday to meet Jess and Ron, but she's already made other plans.

After work, I drive home, change my clothes, and go across the hall to Ron's apartment. He had texted me earlier in the afternoon and invited me over to watch the Bulls game and hang out. I do my best to support the local ball throwing teams and enjoy hanging out with my buddy.

"Yo, Simon, you should bring Hank over sometime," he says while lying down on one of the couches.

Even after all these years living here, he still uses that Brooklyn accent. I'm not sure if it's by choice, or if it's just stuck with him, but I find it entertaining.

"He lives in a tank, man," I say. "It would be kind of an ordeal to bring him across the hall. You should come to visit more often. He asks about you all the time."

"He does?" Ron asks distractedly, taking a big swig of beer, finishing off his third one already. The game isn't even to halftime yet.

We sit in silence for over thirty minutes and watch the sporting event. Ron occasionally cheers when a player does something spectacular with the basketball, and I cheer with him for moral support.

"Are you getting hungry?" I ask, hands folded in my lap. "You want me to call and order us a pizza?"

"Yeah, man, that'll be great," he says, and pulls out his wallet, throwing me a $5 bill.

Shortly after getting off the phone with the pizza company, where I'm told it'll take an hour to deliver, someone knocks on the door.

"You expecting company?" I ask.

"No," he says, getting up from the couch. "Not unless the pizza is here in record time."

Ron opens the door and I can see Jess standing in the hallway with Loretta. I stand up in a hurry to meet them at the door.

"We've been knocking at your door for five minutes, then I remembered this is your boys' basketball night," Jess says. "Simon, can we speak to you for a few minutes?"

I step into the hall and shut the door behind me.

"What's going on?" I ask.

"Can we go inside your apartment, please?" Jess asks anxiously.

I lead the women into my apartment and shut the door behind us. The three of us walk into the small living room area. Jess and Loretta take a seat on the small love seat while I sit in the wooden chair next to Hank's tank.

"Simon, child, has the one who goes by the name X visited you in your dreams recently?" Loretta asks, her forehead creased in a concerned look.

"Yeah, Tuesday night after we left, I came home and had another round of dreams, and he was guiding me through more of John's memories," I say, leading them into my small living room area by the window. "Why, what's going on?"

Loretta looks at Jess expectantly.

"Simon, X entered my dream last night," Jess says solemnly. "He told me that you're not who I think you are, and I should stay away from you." Jess is sitting forward on the couch, her hands clasped together.

"Yeah, so?" I ask. "The guy's a total nut job. He claimed that dreams are his domain and told me to stop looking into the mystery of who killed John."

"That's why I wanted to come over and see you, Simon," Loretta says. "I'm not sure if I was very clear with you the other night, and I was worried I might've scared you off."

"No, not at all," I say. "You actually helped explain a lot of what was going on. It makes more sense now. The visions are opening a window into my past life. And I believe that I'm being shown these particular memories of mine to teach me, or to guide me, in order to solve the mystery of John's death."

"Do you believe you've been reincarnated?" Loretta asks hesitantly. "Some people are very resistant to that belief."

"Well, I believe it now. Honestly, it's the only thing that makes sense. After John was killed, I was born several years later. Those few people that I saw while having those hallucinations in your shop, those were my past lives, too. I'm not the most religious person in the world, Loretta. I went to church a little bit when I was a kid with my parents. And I want to believe there's a God, or some bigger entity, but who knows."

"And who says there isn't?" Loretta says. "After all, someone had to create the souls, and designate where they go in this world, right?"

I nod my head, and look over at Jess, who has continued to sit there quietly.

"Are you alright, Jess?" I ask. "Listen, I don't care about this 'X' person, and you shouldn't either. He's got some axe to grind with me, not you."

She nods her head, and slowly looks up at me. "There's something I want to get off my chest. I didn't believe you when you first told me about your dreams," she says quietly, keeping her eyes to the floor. "When we were having ice cream together. I was just going along with it because, well, you're my best friend and I wanted to support you."

I stare at Jess for a moment before I speak. "Was there something else X said to you in the dream?"

Jess digs through her purse, and pulls out a piece of paper, handing it to me.

"What's this?" I ask.

"When I woke up this morning, I had this…feeling, an overwhelming, unstoppable urge to write down this note. The need and desire to write the note was intolerable and intoxicating all at once. I'm not sure how else to put it."

"One of X's main abilities," Loretta says with confidence. "When he enters your dream, he can plant an idea in your mind like a seed that grows and flourishes quickly. Once you re-enter the real world, you have no choice but to carry out this idea. It can be incredibly dangerous and destructive to most. Simon, the fact that you've been able to resist him in the real world so far tells me that you're strong. Your powers can counter-balance his."

I nod my head slowly, folding the letter in my lap without reading it. "I still believe this murder needs to be solved. I'm going to dig into this, despite what X says. He can go kick sand. I don't care. I'll solve who killed John. It'd be easier with help, but I understand if you want to stay out of this."

Jess gets up quickly from the couch, and I stand up with her. She wraps her arms around me.

"Of course I'll help you," she says reassuringly.

"I'll try to assist anyway I can as well," Loretta says.

"You guys want to come over to Ron's and watch the basketball game?" I ask to break the awkward silence among us. "We got some pizza on the way."

"You kids go on ahead," Loretta says. "I just wanted to stop by and make sure that we're good. Keep in touch Simon, won't you?"

"I will. I promise."

I tell Jess to head over to Ron's, as I need to wash up first. After both women leave the apartment, I go back into my bedroom and pull out the notebook I've been keeping of my dreams. Unfolding the paper, I take a deep breath, staring at the page in front of me, my hands beginning to tremble.

The note reads:

> Simon, I've entered Jess' dreams now. I can turn her, and everyone you care about against you. The power of thoughts is the pinnacle, and eventual de-evolution, of mankind. Consider this your last warning. Do not pursue Marcini. Do not attempt to solve this crime. I strongly considered having your precious Jess wake up and slit her wrists this morning, but I figured that would send the wrong message. I hope this message will be strong enough.
>
> XOXO - X

I crumple up the note, briefly considering ripping it in half. Instead, I place it into the Stinson notebook, and put it back in the nightstand, slamming the drawer a little too hard by accident.

Suddenly, a thought occurs to me. I bolt out of the bedroom, run out of the apartment and down the hall. Loretta's standing at the elevator door, waiting for it to arrive.

"Is there a way to stop him from entering people's dreams?" I ask urgently.

She looks past me for a few moments, her eyebrows drawn down in concentration.

"Yes, I do believe I have just the thing. Just give me a few days. I'll call Jess when they're ready."

I give her a big hug. The strong smell of incense wafts off her clothes.

"Thank you, Loretta." I say, letting her go.

"Of course, child. You've got a very special gift. And I fear X is only going to try to prevent you from solving the crime. Or worse."

I go back to Ron's apartment, where he and Jess are watching the game.

Shortly later, the pizza arrives, and the three of us enjoy a nice, warm, greasy pizza and a basketball game in each other's company.

Chapter 12

After work the next day, I keep my appointment with Angela. As I sit in the waiting room, I thumb through the magazines on the glass corner table. *Better Homes and Gardens, Oprah, Sports Illustrated.* The staples of any modern American medical office's waiting room. Finally, Angela emerges from her office, followed by her patient, a balding middle-aged man. He keeps looking down at the floor, and she gives him a reassuring pat on the back as he lumbers past her. Angela looks up at me and takes a deep breath before calling me into her office.

The blinds are drawn, creating a dark, somber mood for today's session. Angela takes a seat and crosses her legs, as usual. Still heavy on the makeup; I'm encouraged that her relationship is taking off. Good for her.

"Simon, last time you were here, you cut our session short. May I ask why?" Her glare is piercing.

"Well, I wasn't expecting you to treat me as if I've lost my mind," I say defensively, crossing my arms. "And from the sounds of it, you're still a bit hostile. Now, this appointment can go one of two ways. Either you change your tone, and start treating me like a patient, or I walk out of here and never return. The choice is yours."

She clicks her pen, and writes in her little notebook, then looks back up at me. "I see. So, my…diagnosis of your issue, about having dreams of being another man, had offended you. And you're still upset about that."

"That's right."

"Well, then I'm sorry. Do you forgive me?"

"Yes, I forgive you."

"Great. Now, are you still having those same dreams?" she asks, her pen and notepad at the ready.

I only tell her about the dreams of John. I don't mention the appointment with Loretta and the visions of my other multiple past lives. I don't tell her that I've been reincarnated dozens of times. Angela, bless her heart, has been there for me during difficult parts of my life. I don't resent her at all, but I also don't want her to try and push more pills at me or try to lock me away in a padded cell.

The more I explain the dreams I had of John, and the extreme detail that I felt in those dreams, simply being a passenger in his subconscious but unable to control what's going on, Angela comes to her diagnosis.

"I think I see what's going on here, Simon," she says. "You have dissociative identity disorder. You see, deep in your own mind, you wish that you were a police officer. You crave some form of control; you desire a sense of law and order. Something that was stripped away from you when you were kicked out of your mom's house. By dreaming about being a cop, you now have that power to control the situation, and you abide by a code of conduct."

Seemingly satisfied with her incorrect and irrational diagnosis, she quickly scribbles down a prescription for me. I have no intention of having it filled at my local pharmacy. What a quack. That's fine, I've outgrown her. My problems are far too complex for her expertise. I'll keep coming back only because it's nice to have someone else to talk to about this, along with Jess. My biggest disappointment, however, was not getting a chance to tell Angela about my new girlfriend.

I stop mid-stride on my way out to my car. Girlfriend? Is that what Brittany and I are, boyfriend and girlfriend? We only went out on one date, maybe I need to relax. I shake my head. Only time will tell if she's really that into me, or if she's just after me for my good looks and nice car. I start laughing out loud as I open the car door, then quickly look around to make sure that Angela or one of her staff members didn't just witness me doing that. She'll have me locked away by the end of the night for sure.

On the way to Moretti's Pub, where I've agreed to meet up with Jess and Ron for our traditional Friday night out, I stop by a local park to clear my head. With everything that's been going on lately, I haven't really stopped to relax for a while. I take a walk around the park on the freshly paved trail. Kids are playing on a nearby jungle gym, complete with a swing set and a long metal slide. Their carefree laughter carries throughout the park; a sound so innocent that an overwhelming sense of longing takes me over. As a child, my dad would push me on the swings, and I would beg him to push me higher and higher, and I would scream with delight as the sky would get closer and the ground further away. I had wished I could grow wings and fly away, soaring through the clouds like a peaceful hawk, gliding above the ground.

Then the sky would fall away and the ground would come rushing back, only to feel my dad's reassuring push on my back as I flew upwards again.

Parents are sitting at the edge of the playground area, conversing with one another, some of them staring at their phone screens while their children have the time of their lives. I remember as a kid how the days would seem so much longer than they do now. It felt like a single day would stretch on and on. First there was school, which felt like it would take forever. After school, I was enrolled in soccer during the fall, basketball during the winter, and baseball during the spring. Soccer and basketball were by far my favorites. Baseball, on the other hand, was my enemy. I couldn't hit the ball, I couldn't catch the ball, and the coach would yell at me during nearly every practice. He would scream at me during the games, telling me to concentrate more. He would yell at me if I struck out, and I would usually spend most of the games on the edge of the bench, my eyes burning from tears.

I remember one game in particular, after I had struck out for the second time during the game and Coach had finished having one of his meltdowns with me, I had my head down and went over to the end of the bench, tears in my eyes. I was too embarrassed to wipe them away, because I wanted to look tough in front of the other boys. Even though none of them ever came over to cheer me up or encourage me, at least they didn't yell at me like Coach. I had wiped the back of my hand across my nose, cleaning up my sniffles, when a girl my age had come over and sat down next to me. She wasn't on the team, and I'd never seen her before, but when I looked up at her, she was the prettiest girl I'd ever laid my eyes on. Her eyes were a bright blue that I'd never seen before, and her long blond hair was in a ponytail which went about halfway down her back. She was wearing a yellow tank top and shorts, and just sat there, not saying a word.

I was nine at this time, old enough to know that girls were different than boys, but she didn't make me feel uncomfortable or different in the slightest. Actually, just the opposite. A sense of warmth radiated off of her, and I was drawn to her like a mosquito toward a blue light on a hot, damp summer's evening. But when I looked into her blue eyes, I wasn't zapped. I felt a wave of confidence and acceptance that I hadn't felt before with other kids my age.

On my next turn up to bat, I hit that baseball so hard it flew over the heads of the outfielders on the other team, and I took off running. I touched first base, then I rounded second base, and made my way to third, standing up.

Coach started screaming at me, telling me to slide. Why didn't I slide? I just ignored him. For the first time that season, it was as if his screaming voice was drowned out by a singing chorus of angels, and I looked over at the blond-haired girl on the bench. Her legs too short to touch the ground, they kicked lazily, her arms at her sides, and she smiled at me.

After my lap around the park, I get back to my car and drive to Moretti's Pub. Once inside, I sit down with my buddy Ron and that same girl, now a grown adult woman, just as beautiful, loving and caring as the day I met her.

"Hey, you!" Jess says as I sit down in the booth.

"We got a booth today?" I ask, surprised.

"Yeah, boss, what'dya think of this?" Ron asks, grabbing a mozzarella stick from the basket. "I just walked in here and boom, I saw this baby open and took it."

I bring up the idea of going camping next weekend, and they both agree. When I begin to talk about Brittany however, Jess suddenly goes silent for a few minutes. I didn't notice it at the time, as Ron kept asking questions, the first of which was "is she hot?"

After I got back home, I think back and wonder why Jess had gone silent. The only thing I can think of was that she's worried about X.

Chapter 13

The next morning, I drive over to Mom and Doug's for lunch. Mom called first thing in the morning, wanting to make sure I'm still going to make it over and that I bring an appetite, because she's making club sandwiches. She was assured that I'll be there at noon sharp, and I will indeed be looking forward to her homemade club sandwiches.

On the drive over, I stretch my car's legs, pushing 90 MPH on the Interstate, passing cars like they're standing still. Red and blue flashing lights creep up behind me, and I pull over. The cop issues me the first speeding ticket in my life. Well, this life anyway. I thank the officer for all that he does for our community, and he looks back, arching an eyebrow as if I've just insulted his mother. I reassure him that I meant what I said, he's doing a great job. He just shakes his head and gets back into his police cruiser.

When I pull into the driveway, Mom is waiting on the porch. She quickly flicks out her cigarette and stands up. I give her a warm hug, and she compliments my car again. She asks to go for a test ride, and I oblige. She tells me that Doug went out to run some errands and he'll be a little bit, so I tell Mom I'm taking her down to the beach.

It's a pleasantly warm, mostly sunny afternoon, and traffic is beginning to pick up. Mom laughs when I step on the accelerator. I don't dare tell her about my speeding ticket; she'll tell me to slow down, and that I need to be more careful.

When we arrive at the public beach along the shores of Lake Michigan, Mom gets out and stretches her back, then heads down to the closest picnic table and takes a seat. As I approach the table, it suddenly hits me how much older she's gotten in recent years, and a lump forms in my throat.

I still remember when I was a little boy, shortly after Dad passed away, and we had come to a similar beach to this. Heck, it might even have been the same beach. Mom and I had picked up some fast food at a local drive thru. We were eating lunch at a wooden picnic table, just the two of us. It was a much colder, breezier day. My hamburger wrapper blew off the table halfway through my meal, and I had run after it, not wanting to be a litterbug. It kept blowing down the rocky beach, closer to the water. The faster I ran, the faster that dang wrapper blew away. Out of nowhere, a man walking his dog stomped his foot on it, flattening the wrapper. When I looked up from his foot to his leg, then to his face, he smiled at me. He bent down and picked up the crumpled wrapper, walking it over to me.

"It's awfully windy out today, little guy. Wouldn't want you chasing this and falling into the water." He chuckled and outstretched his arm for me to take the wrapper, which I snatched away.

"Thank you," I said sheepishly, keeping my eyes on his dog.

"This is Rocky," the man said, smiling. "He's harmless. It's okay, you can pet him. He won't bite."

I reach my hand out to pet the Golden Retriever, who was almost as big as me. He licked my hand, causing me to laugh. Mom laid her hand on my shoulder and introduced herself to the man.

"I'm Jill. And this is my son Simon."

"Nice to meet you both. My name's Doug."

I walk over to where Mom is now sitting at a wooden picnic table. Her head is turned toward the water, the gentle breeze blowing back her long, mostly gray hair. She usually keeps her hair down, without any restrictions, allowing it to blow freely and do what it wants.

She turns toward me and rests her hand on top of mine, and smiles.

"Thanks for getting me out of the house, sweetheart," she says. "Doug's been spending most of his time in the garage pouring over his old files lately. After you came over last, he's been obsessed with some old case he had been working on. Stinson, I think the name was."

I nod my head, and swallow. I'm not sure how I feel about Doug getting involved in this case again. Only because I don't want Mom getting mixed up and hurt by X, William Marcini, or whatever other nonsense this case could stir up.

"I'm glad we could do this," I say contentedly. "I loved when you would take me down to the beach when I was a kid."

"You sure loved the water," she says, smiling. "I still remember taking you for your first swimming lessons. You were so adorable with your little floaties on your arms. And you were so serious about it, too. You treated it like some sort of mission to swim." She shakes her head. "You were always such a driven boy. I'm sorry I couldn't give you more when you were growing up."

"What're you talking about, Mom? You worked your butt off to make sure we had food on the table and a roof over our heads. Who knows where I would be without you?"

She wipes a tear out of her eye. "Thanks. But you and I both know that I wasn't a perfect mother. Far from it."

I drive us back to her home, taking the back way to get there through the familiar wooded area. Birds fly carelessly in front of the car. Rays of sunshine seep down through the trees, still mostly bare of leaves. It was a long winter. The sun plays dancing games around Mom's face as she looks out the side window. A deer, followed by two small fawns, stride up to the side of the road, patiently waiting for us to pass.

The adult deer, now leading the two fawns across the road behind us, is probably out looking for some afternoon lunch. In ten years' time, maybe less, this whole area will be covered in pavement, apartments and houses as mankind spreads into that deer's home. Other animals hide out of eyesight, seemingly unaware that mankind's crept closer into their habitat, less than a mile away. Man's structures and machines invade their backyard. Even driving the car on this stretch of roadway brings me a momentary feeling of guilt, knowing that I'm making noise and polluting their air. Even inconveniencing that mother deer and her two kids.

'Tree-hugger' is a term that might come to mind for some when they hear me talk this way, but I've always tried to be in touch with nature. It's not the animal's fault that the animal I happen to be, the human being, likes to spread out and devour the land and its resources like some kind of a virus. Do humans even belong on Earth? Did we even originate on this planet? Are our "Soul Beams" some alien origin, so that our ancestors could cheat death and live forever? Are Soul Beams some sort of artificial manifestation, created by machines to keep humans as pets and slaves, and they launched the first humans into space in a tiny capsule toward Earth so that we could terraform this planet to their liking in preparation for them? So that one day the machines come here and take over after they've exhausted all resources on the other planet?

There I go again, letting my imagination wander.

"What're you thinking about?" Mom asks, eyeing me quizzically. "I know that look you get when you're thinking about something. I'm your mother, after all."

"I'm fine."

"I know you. First, you get quiet. Then, you purse your little lips together. I can practically see the gears spinning around in your head, a little puff of smoke coming out right here." She tickled my cheek next to my ear.

"Quit it, Mom," I say, laughing.

We pull into the driveway and go inside the house.

"Doug still must be out running his errands," Mom says. "You make yourself comfortable, I'll be in the kitchen."

Remembering that Doug used to keep any case files he was working on in the garage, I go in there, quietly shutting the door behind me. Looking up on the top shelf in the garage where Doug keeps random newspaper articles, sports memorabilia and other miscellaneous items, I see one unmarked box. Grabbing a step stool, I bring the box down and place it on top of a wooden workbench. Inside are numerous tabbed file folders with various names on them. Near the back of the box, one name catches my eye: *Stinson.*

"Doug texted, he's on his way home," Mom yells from the kitchen, her voice muffled behind the closed door connecting the garage to the house.

She usually doesn't check her phone that often, so that text could've been sent anywhere from five seconds to five minutes ago. I need to work fast.

I pull the Stinson file out and open it on the workbench. Not wanting to turn on the overhead light and attract Doug's attention in case he pulls up in the driveway, I use my cellphone flashlight, casting the bright LED light on the documents. Several papers and photographs are placed haphazardly in the file, in no particular order that I can make out. As much as I want to just tuck this file under my arm and run out to my car, the thought of Doug catching me in the act stops me from doing so. If Marcini says that Doug knows more about this case, I'm not sure what he would do if he caught me. Doug's the type of man who lets his fists do the talking.

The photographs are labeled with names. The first picture is of a younger William Marcini. A muscular, handsome man with a mane of black hair, he's wearing a suit that looks similar to the gray suit he was wearing at the nightclub in my dream last night. The next photo is of a bald Hispanic man with a familiar dragon tattoo on his neck. Chavez.

The last photograph is of a young man with short, blond hair and an earring in his left ear. I pick up the picture, holding it closer to my face, not believing what I'm seeing. The bottom of the photo has the name "Tony Alvarez," but there's no mistaking who this man really is.

A trickle of sweat begins to make its way down my spine. With my hands beginning to tremble, I blink several times to make sure what I'm seeing is real.

The man in the picture is my boss Steve, the owner of the Lowland Woods Golf Course.

Chapter 14

Several minutes later, Doug, Mom and I are at the dining room table enjoying the homemade club sandwiches prepared from scratch.

"These are great sandwiches, Jill," Doug says between bites. "Is this sourdough?"

"Yes, it is!" Mom exclaims, wiggling around in her chair. "Good job, hon. I'm impressed with your sense of taste."

They really are delicious sandwiches. She managed to make a perfectly balanced ratio of bread, cheese, meat and mayonnaise in every bite. Mom really went all out. She has a very satisfied look on her face, knowing she's done well to please the two most important men in her life. After dinner, we all head back into the living room. I sit on my usual place on the couch, Doug in his recliner, and Mom in her wooden rocking chair that Doug made by hand several years ago. She's picked up knitting recently, and resumes working on a red and blue scarf.

"Who are you making that for, Mom?" I ask.

"This is for Joey," she says with pride. "They just moved to Minnesota last October. Did I tell you that?" I shake my head. "Anyways, your Aunt Beth tells me it got down to fifty below last winter! I just want to make sure they're warm for this upcoming winter, so I bought all this stuff and I've been getting better at making other things, too, like mittens and stocking caps and socks. After I'm done with this scarf, I'm going to try a blanket. I've got all summer."

I smile, a feeling of contentment washing over me knowing that Mom picked up a calming and sensible hobby. And to top it off, she's doing something to help my cousin's family, who have lived in poverty for years.

"That's great," I say. "I'm sure they'll really appreciate that."

Doug's remained very quiet during my visit today, barely saying a word. I seize the opportunity to ask him some more questions while I have the chance.

I look at him, squinting my eyes, and take a deep breath. "Doug, I've got some questions about the Stinson case. From my research, I understand he had a longtime partner named 'Mike.' What can you tell me about him?"

"Mike was a great officer," Doug says quietly. "He was very thorough, very loyal, and always wanted to do what was right. He and John were practically joined at the hip. There was an opening within the department for a new detective. A promotion, so to speak. A significant pay bump, more normal hours, you name it. They both applied for it, and I would've given them both the job if I could. But in the end, I gave the job to Mike, simply because he was better qualified."

"Interesting," I say calmly. That's not what my visions have shown me so far, but I remind myself to stay calm and keep pressing the issue. "Is Mike still a detective?"

"No, he retired a few years back. He's living on a ranch down in Indiana somewhere. Raising cattle and sheep, that kind of stuff. I spoke with him on the phone a few months ago."

"What's Mike's last name?"

"Lancaster," Doug says. He pulls out a notepad and starts scribbling down something, then rips off the top sheet and hands it to me. It has Mike's name, phone number, and address in Indiana.

"Thank you," I say, folding the note and putting it in my pants pocket. "I also heard that Officer Stinson had a wife named Samantha. What do you know about her?"

"Shortly after John's murder, Samantha gave birth to their only child, Ryan," Doug says. "She passed away from breast cancer last month, but Ryan still lives somewhere in the area. That's according to Mike."

"Thanks, Doug. I appreciate your help."

He struggles to maintain eye contact with me, uncharacteristically looking sheepishly down at the floor.

I stand up, and Mom puts down her sewing materials, runs over and gives me a warm hug. She squeezes me extra tight.

"You're skin and bones," she says worriedly. "Are you getting enough to eat? Here, do you want some leftovers?" She's already halfway into the kitchen by the time she asks.

"Yeah, that'd be great. Thanks."

A few minutes later, she comes back with several Ziplock baggies full of meats and cheeses from today's sandwiches. I give Mom another hug, shake Doug's hand, then turn to leave.

I get into my car and begin backing out of the driveway. Doug has his arm around Mom's shoulder, and they're both waving goodbye. I rev the engine a few times before leaving, waving goodbye to them as well.

An hour later, I'm back at Brittany's apartment. I swung by my place first in order to drop off the lunch fixings in my refrigerator, feed Hank an early dinner, and freshen up so I'm halfway presentable for my girl. She's offered to make us dinner tonight so that we could stay in and watch a movie on Netflix. I believe she called it "Netflix and Chili," or something like that. I'm not that hip with the new slang in today's modern society. It does sound relaxing, though.

Knocking on her apartment door, I again get a tinge of jealousy over how immaculately clean her apartment building's hallway is. The building also smells nice, like soap or perfume, maybe both. Unlike my building which smells like dirty socks and mold. Brittany opens the door, and my heart skips a beat. She's dressed incredibly ravishing for a night in, wearing a black lace dress, which is practically see through. I follow her inside and shut her apartment door. It would be a shame if her roommate Chester ran off.

She turns back around to face me once the door shuts and wraps her arms around my neck. My hands are still at my sides, and my back has gone as stiff as a board. Soft piano music is playing from a speaker in the living room, and I can see she's activated her remote-controlled fireplace which is set up in the corner of the living room wall. Opposite the fireplace is the back sliding glass door complete with a small deck which looks out at a breathtaking view of the city skyline. Now that I'm more relaxed, the view's even more impressive than the first time I was here. The sun's going down, casting a hazy glow into the apartment.

Brittany takes my hands and places them behind her on the small of her back.

"Dance with me," she says in her deeper, smoky voice.

"Yes, ma'am," I say, and begin to match her step for step. Her choice of music has no beat to speak of, but I'm able to match her rhythm rather quickly.

A few years back, when I was still living with Jess, we agreed to sign up for a dancing class together. It was actually a ton of fun, and I can say with confidence I'm a solid dancer. I learned skills that I'm able to put to good use now with Brittany, this enchanting young woman that I can't stop thinking about. We stare into each other's eyes, and I'm completely mesmerized. Her big brown eyes are like tractor beams, pulling me into the mother ship. She's wearing the same perfume that she wore at work the day she asked me out. The entire scene, and everything she's got going on here has me infatuated like a love-stricken boy, lusting after a girl he's had a secret crush on for years. Our steps are in perfect harmony. Our dance is simple and basic, but it's the dance of two young lovers, learning each other's beat.

Chester sits on the back of the couch, staring at us. I briefly glance over at him, then return my focus back toward the woman of my dreams. Her hands are pressed firmly on my shoulders; mine have migrated higher on her back. For what feels like hours, we enjoy one another's embrace, dancing to the soft classical music she has playing, although when I glance at the clock it's only been fifteen minutes.

The oven timer beeps, and she places her head on my chest. Her hair smells of lilacs, and I can see that she's placed a ribbon in her hair again. She looks back at me, her eyes of dark mascara, her full lips a dark shade of red, and her pouty expression turns into a smile.

"Want to help me dish up?" she asks playfully.

"Of course. I'm looking forward to your homemade chili."

"Chili?"

"Yeah, I thought we were having chili?"

She arches an eyebrow momentarily, then turns to go into the kitchen. The food smells absolutely delicious, and I can hear her slide the baking sheet off the metal oven rack.

"Well, since we had Italian the other night, I figured we could try something different," she says. "I hope you like enchiladas."

My mouth waters. Despite the large lunch that Mom made, I have a healthy appetite for the delicious smelling enchiladas that Brittany has gone through the trouble to make for us.

"I love enchiladas," I say eagerly.

We dish up dinner and eat in the dining room. The blinds are open, and we sit next to each other, overlooking the beautiful skyline as twilight descends upon the city. She's dimmed the lights in the apartment to assist with creating a more relaxed, romantic atmosphere. Throughout dinner, we share stories and laugh frequently at each other's jokes. She has a sense of humor that I haven't found in another woman before. Well, besides Jess. She can make just about anybody laugh.

After dinner, I help her clean up the kitchen area, and she thanks me with a kiss on the cheek. We sit down on the couch together, Chester giving a loud "meow" as he's forced from his perch to find another spot to sit. We share a blanket, and she turns on a movie for us to watch, *Signs,* starring Mel Gibson. My hands are clasped together in my lap under the blanket during the beginning of the film. As the movie gets more intense, with a few jump scares, she playfully grabs my arm, but I keep my hands where they are.

Make a move, dummy, I keep telling myself. Finally, I build up enough nerve to slide my arm up and over her shoulders. She instantly scoots closer and places a hand on top of mine under the blanket. My heart's racing so fast, I feel like it might jump out of my chest and attach itself to her TV screen.

We enjoy the movie together. By the time it's over, I'm too tired to drive home, and ask to stay the night on her couch. She agrees to let me stay the night, and she goes to her room, allowing me to drift off to sleep.

Chapter 15

It's John Stinson's wedding day, and he's more nervous now than any day previously in his life. Even more nervous than when he graduated from the police academy. The black tuxedo and blue necktie looks sharp on him as he examines himself in the bathroom mirror. His best man, Mike, pats him on the back.

"You look very sharp," he says. "If you need to hurl, the can's not too far away."

John rolls his eyes, takes a deep breath, and applies some more gel to his short, military style haircut. He also straightens his mustache, making sure there aren't any whiskers out of alignment.

Samantha and John have been a couple now for almost two years. In that time, he graduated from the Police Academy and joined the Chicago P.D. Samantha graduated from Northwestern University with her degree in education, pursuing her dream of being an elementary school teacher.

A young man peeks his head into the bathroom. "Five minutes. Are you almost ready?"

"Yeah, I'm coming," John says, and leaves the bathroom with Mike following.

Waiting for the ceremony to start, he looks out at the large audience of over four hundred people. About a quarter of them are police officers or have worked with John in some capacity. He can see his two sisters up near the front. The rest of these people, he has no idea who they are. Hopefully they're people that Samantha invited. Of course they are, what a stupid question. Or is it? Why is that a dumb question? Is there security here, or does there need to be security at a venue like this?

He's broken out in a cold sweat. His mind won't stop racing.

The music that he's picked for his walk down the aisle, "Separate Ways" by *Journey*, begins playing over the speakers. Instantly, he regains his composure and confidence. This is why he chose this song, to relax his nerves and sharpen his focus.

He struts down the aisle, one hand clasped across his lower chest, waving to the crowd with his other hand like the Queen. When he makes it up to the front, he hugs his sisters, kissing each of them on the cheek. He takes his position up on the stage. A few coughs can be heard in the audience, some folks shifting around on the old wooden benches. The old man sitting at the organ cracks his knuckles and begins playing the traditional "Bridal Chorus" song.

Emerging at the foot of the aisle, roughly one hundred feet away, Samantha appears with her father next to her, locked arm in arm. They begin their slow walk down the aisle, following the flower girl as she throws flower petals down, seemingly at random. Samantha disengages from her father and makes her way up the stairs where John is waiting for her. They each take their marks, as they were instructed in their three rehearsals leading up to this point.

The preacher, an elderly man with glasses, gives the bride and groom an opportunity to read the vows that they've written.

John clears his throat and begins. "Samantha, even before the day I first spoke to you outside math class at Northwestern, I knew you were the one. Bumping into you, spilling your books all over the place, was the best thing that's ever happened to me. You've shown me how to be a better person, and a better man. Every day I wake up, it's like falling in love all over again being with you. Thank you for being there for me as I chose my career path as a police officer in the great city of Chicago–" several hoots and grunts can be heard from part of the audience "–and thank you for being the one that I cherish and hold dear. I promise to serve and protect you. I promise to always be there for you, until the day I die. I love you."

Samantha wipes a tear from her eye and reads her vows next.

"John, from the day you bumped those textbooks out of my arms, I knew deep down that you would end up being the man I would fall in love with–" a chorus of laughter rises from the audience. "I'm honored to start this journey with you as your spouse, partner, and friend. I promise to always be there for you, through your good days, and the bad, and I will always show you the respect you deserve as my husband. You are my best friend. I will be yours, forever and always."

John's eyes have also begun to water, and he wipes his face with his sleeve. They repeat the vows stated by the preacher, finishing with "I do." John flips the thin veil up from over his wife's eyes, and they meet for a passionate kiss, followed by cheering and clapping from the audience. They take hands, and walk down the steps, down the aisle, and out toward the reception area.

The wedding reception goes late into the night. Alcohol was prohibited from the reception, per John's request, as he didn't want his fellow members of the force drinking in case they got called out for an emergency.

The sound of clinking on glass can be heard, and it's Mike, standing up. "Can I have everyone's attention, please?" He says into the microphone, his voice coming in over the loudspeakers. The fluorescent lights reflect off the top of his balding head. The sober crowd goes quiet immediately. "Thank you. First of all, congratulations to these two love birds. Samantha, you're a lucky woman, but I know you've got your hands full with this guy here, am I right?"

The crowd laughs, some people hoot and holler. "By the way, John, this is a wedding reception, alright? It's nice to have a little bubbly going for your guests. Just a tip for next time. Well, heh, hopefully there's no next time, bud." More chuckles can be heard from the audience, and Samantha busts out laughing. John looks over at her, his eyebrow arched. He begins to laugh as well.

"Hey, sorry about the alcohol-free zone, everyone!" John shouts.

"It's all good, little buddy," Mike says. "Anyway, I just want to say, it was an honor to be your best man. I'm proud to call you my partner. I wish you two the best." Mike raises his glass of sparkling cider. "Drink up!"

Everyone begins clapping. As John surveys the crowd, he sees Doug sitting in the corner with his wife. A short time later, John makes his way down toward their table.

"John, you remember my wife Connie," Doug says. "Look, I'm really happy for you. By the way, I just wanted to let you know that Bradley announced his retirement today, meaning there will be an opening here pretty soon. I recommend you apply for it. You'd make a fine detective."

"Thank you, Doug," John says. "That means a lot."

"Congratulations to the both of you," Connie says sincerely with a warm smile. "You two make a beautiful couple."

"Thank you," John says.

"Are you two planning on being parents?" Connie asks.

"One day, I hope."

"Well, you two will make beautiful children. Isn't that right, dear?" Connie softly elbows Doug, who was staring up at Samantha on stage.

"What's that?" Doug asks, his attention now refocusing on the conversation. "Oh, yes, they'll make great parents."

An awkward moment of silence passes between the three of them.

"Well, you two have a great night," John says, retreating back to the stage to be with Samantha. "Thanks for coming out."

Doug and Connie watch as John walks back toward his beautiful bride.

The dream goes dark, and my eyes open to Brittany staring down at me. I blink repeatedly, trying to shake off the cobwebs from a deep sleep. This is an unusually comfortable couch to sleep on.

"Golly, you sure are a heavy sleeper!" she says, her face directly in mine.

"What time is it?" I ask groggily.

"It's almost noon," she says, giggling. "What, are you just going to sleep all day?"

Chapter 16

On Tuesday after work, I'm sitting in the back of Sweet Loretta's shop with Jess. The room is much better lit today, and on the black table are four green rocks with elastic bands tied around them. Loretta shows us how to use the objects she's created. She takes the elastic string in one hand, slides it over the top of her head, then places the green rock on the front of her forehead, letting the band snap back.

"They're easy to use, comfortable, and won't slide off when you're sleeping," Loretta says, smiling.

"These are wonderful, thank you," Jess says with a tone of relief and grabs one, sliding it over her head and positioning the rock on her forehead as Loretta had shown.

I grab one as well and follow suit. The rock is surprisingly warm against my skin and doesn't weigh much at all.

"Yeah, thank you," I say. "What's in the rock?"

"Magic," she says, then laughs. "It's just something I created for you guys to protect your dreams from X and his treacherous ways. You can refer to them as 'Dream Catchers.'"

"I thought dream catchers were what Native Americans made to put over the bed," I say. "Are these…better? No offense, I'm just curious."

"Yes, these are much more powerful," Loretta says, sliding her Dream Catcher off. "Those work fine in traditional settings, to protect from your mundane nightmare or night terror, what have you. With these, however, I've infused each rock with special ingredients to protect from the most powerful forces trying to invade your mind at night."

I look over at Jess to see if she's buying any of this, and she's staring intently at the woman. I suppose Loretta does deserve the benefit of the doubt. Last time I was in this room, I was sent back through multiple past lives. Perhaps there's some truth to what she's selling.

"What's the history between you and X?" I ask. "When he spoke to me the first time, he knew who you were. Now, you go through the trouble of making us these cool headbands. Which I really appreciate. I do. But something's got you spooked. What is it?"

The woman stares at me and takes a deep breath. "Yes, we do share a history. A long, long history. And it's a long story. I'll save you the time and trouble and tell you this: Do not listen to what X says. He's going to feed your head with lies layered with deceit." She points at the Dream Catchers. "These will protect you, and at this point, knowing what power you possess, your protection is my top priority. You have a mission to accomplish."

"What mission is that?" I ask, leaning forward.

"To solve the murder of your past life. The *who* is equally as important as the *why.* There are bigger forces at work here than you or I. Once we unravel this first string, it's going to open up possibilities beyond your wildest imagination."

"Like what?" Jess asks in a concerned manner. "What's Simon getting involved in?"

"He's already involved. He just doesn't know it yet," Loretta says, then winks at me. "We'll find out more as we progress. But for now, it's important that you wear these when you're sleeping. Take one for each of your friends, Ron and Brittany, since these three are the closest to you emotionally at this stage in this life."

My mind catches on the way she said, 'in this life.' I wonder where I was during this stage of my other lives. Was I already married? Did I have a lot of money? I'm content with where I'm currently at, but I can't help but wonder… what if I had more? What if I already had everything, but I lost it all because of X?

"Thank you again, Loretta," I say, pulling out my wallet. "How much for these?"

"No charge, child," she says dismissively, and sends us on our way.

Jess and I agree to pick up some dinner to take back to Ron's. We spend a half hour deciding and bickering on what Ron would like, then I finally pick up the phone and call Ron to solve our culinary conundrum once and for all. It turns out that Jess is right, as usual.

"I told you it's Taco Tuesday," Jess says, elbowing me in the ribs playfully. "I know you two like the back of my hand. Now, where should we pick up tacos from?"

This question launches us into another five-minute debate before we settle on a local Mexican restaurant, which is voted to have the best taco in town. Jess says she's never tried them before, and my jaw hits the floor.

"Prepare to be amazed!" I proclaim. "I'll pick up the food and meet you over at Ron's."

An hour later, my arms are loaded with sacks of food as I stumble back into my building. I knock on Ron's door, and he lets me in. I disperse our dinner, and we sit down at Ron's small dining room table to eat.

"Man, Brittany made some mean enchiladas the other night, guys," I say. "That girl can cook. By the way, she's looking forward to our camping trip this weekend."

"Me too," Ron says. "I'm looking forward to meeting her."

"Where are we going?" Jess asks, after she finishes swallowing her food. "By the way, great choice on these tacos, Simon. You were right."

Ron and I stand up from the table simultaneously, both of our chairs screeching back on the linoleum, falling on their backs behind us. We get down on our hands and knees, bowing down in her direction.

"She has spoken," Ron says playfully. "She has admitted a man is right about something. All hail Queen Jessica."

"All right, all right, cut it out guys," she says, laughing.

Ron and I pick up our chairs and resume eating.

"I was thinking we'd head on down to Indiana," I say. "There's a neat little town called 'Quakertown' and there's a nice little campground right off the side of Brookville Lake. Their website says we need reservations. How does that sound? I can call them up in the morning and make sure they got a spot available."

Ron and Jess look at one another, then look back at me. "Sounds good!" They both mumble with their mouths full.

It dawns on me how lucky I am to have these two as my longtime best friends. Well, my only friends really. Besides Brittany. I really hope they like her. Having these two meet Brittany for the first time would be like incorporating another fish into Hank's habitat. How would he react? I would never do that to Hank, since I know he likes being an only child like me. But these two meeting Brittany…I just hope they hit it off and we have a fun weekend.

After dinner, we have Ron test out his new Dream Catcher. He balks at the idea of wearing it, but we tell him it's for his own protection. We don't attempt to insult his intelligence with some made up story, like chemicals in the water supply or pollutants in the air. We just both ask that he does this as a favor.

"Hey, alright, I'll do it," Ron says reluctantly. "I mean, it's not that bad. But how long?"

"Give it two weeks for now," I tell him. "After that, I'll let you know."

"Look, if there's something you ain't telling me, just spit it out, alright?" he says, his thick Brooklyn accent coming through. "I really like you guys, I do. But don't hide stuff from me either, okay?"

Jess and I look at each other, and I shake my head. Not yet. Even if I tell him the truth of the whole situation, I doubt he would believe me. It's best that we keep him in the dark, for now.

"Listen, Ron, for the time being, we just need you to trust us," Jess says, gently placing her hand on his shoulder. "Please."

"Alright, whateva," he says, annoyed. "Now that we've got that out of the way, can we start watching the game? They're about to tip off."

We sit and watch the basketball game with Ron. He's put the Dream Catcher into the pocket of his jeans, and it's like he's forgotten all about what Jess and I didn't tell him. We laugh throughout the game, catching up on each other's lives. Ron informs us that he recently lost his job and is now a "free agent." We encourage him that something will come up, and we're here to help him.

After the game ends, we say our goodbyes, and I head across the hall back to my place. I pull up a chair in front of Hank's tank and watch him swim around while I talk on the phone with Brittany for an hour. Afterwards, I look at a map of Indiana on my phone. Mike's ranch is just outside of Quakertown, which is just a bit out of the way from the campground. I'm looking forward to seeing my old friend and partner again after all this time.

Chapter 17

Friday has finally arrived. Weather this week reached the low 70s, bringing more people to the golf course. I was enjoying a moment of peace in the breakroom when Steve walked in, waving at me. I try my best to ignore him with my headphones on. It's still difficult for me to believe that he's actually Tony Alvarez, the man who was presumed murdered, which launched John Stinson's investigation. How can this man live with himself, knowing he faked his own death? He has the audacity to walk around here with a smile on his face, treating me and the other employees so…nice.

It's tough for me to dislike Steve. The man has done so much for me, taking a young man practically off the streets with nothing but the clothes on his back, no work experience and no prospects, giving me a year 'round job to support myself. The current Steve, without the past baggage, is a great man. But knowing what I know now, I don't think I can ever look at him the same. But I don't see how I could possibly confront him about this and not sound insane.

Brittany is her usual chipper, happy self at work, using that higher pitched voice of hers. She's excited for the camping trip tomorrow and will be expecting me to pick her up around ten in the morning. She'll be responsible for bringing the tent and other camping gear, since she's the one with more camping experience than Ron, Jess and I combined. Plus, she's the only one of us that owns a tent. The more I think about it, the more thankful I am that she's coming along, especially considering the rest of us don't have the necessary equipment.

Steve asked me to stay an hour late tonight after close to help clean up, since the increased foot traffic created more of a mess than was anticipated. I'm the last one to leave the building after I've finally finished my assigned tasks.

Walking out to the parking lot after work, I'm looking down at my phone, reading several missed texts from Brittany saying how much she misses me and that she's looking forward to this weekend's adventure. I look up and discover that three men have surrounded my car, each of them wearing black ski masks. One of them is carrying a machete.

"Simon, I presume?" the machete-wielding man asks.

"Who's asking?" I say, reaching for my cell phone.

"I wouldn't do that if I were you," the machete man says threateningly, stepping closer to me and raising the weapon up over his shoulder.

I keep my hand in my pocket and raise my other hand to the sky. "Who are you guys, and what do you want?"

"We're the ones asking questions. Are you, or are you not, Simon Verner?"

"Yes, I'm Simon."

"Great. Now get your hand out of your pocket, and place both hands out in front of you where I can see them."

I comply with Machete Man's demands. He walks behind me and pushes me roughly in the back toward my car. Forcefully grabbing the back of my neck, he slams my head down on the hood and for a moment all I see are stars. One of the men kicks me in the ribs, sending me down to my knees on the pavement. I don't even make a sound as the air from my lungs has vanished. Rolling onto my back and look up at the evening sky, I see the three masked men now standing over me.

I try to speak, to ask these men what they want, but I still can't catch my breath. Another man in the group, incredibly large in size, leans over to pick me up by my shirt collar, and stands me up against the driver's side door of my car, keeping his elbow propped against my chest to keep me upright. There are no witnesses in sight, and my parking spot around the back of the main building is far enough away from the road that no passerby can happen to spot us. I make a mental note to not park back here any longer.

Machete Man approaches me again, a sadistic grin spread across his lips in the hole cut in the ski mask. "My boss wants to speak with you. Are you ready to talk?"

An unexplainable, deep-rooted rage is beginning to boil up within me. A feeling from deep within my mind and soul. The same sort of rage I felt when I saw William Marcini at his restaurant.

I spit in Machete Man's face. His partner, Large Man, punches me in the gut, and I crumple down. I'm immediately hoisted back up to stand on my feet. Machete Man puts a cell on speaker phone and holds it up to my face. The caller ID is a private number, and the voice that comes from the phone is deep and muffled. The caller is using some kind of a voice changer device.

"Hello, Simon," the muffled voice says. "This is X. I would apologize for having my men do this to you, but you can't say you weren't warned. You continue to stick your nose in where it doesn't belong. Tell me, was Loretta the one that made you and your friends the Dream Catchers?"

"Yes," I say hoarsely, still trying to catch my breath. "Look, I've done as you asked. I haven't been investigating John's murder. You've got bad information."

"My sources tell me otherwise."

"Well, your sources are wrong," I say sternly. "I've got no leads, X. I've got nothing. All that I get are the dreams, which I didn't even ask for."

There's a slight pause, and X breathes deeply into the phone. "Do you still want to catch who killed you?"

"I'd be lying if I said I wasn't interested. Look, if you want me to stop, I'll stop. I get the picture."

"Good," X says, satisfied. "I take it by now that you've discovered that your boss, Steve, is Tony Alvarez. Is that right?"

"Yes," I say flatly.

"And who told you that? And don't lie to me, Simon. I'll know."

"I saw him in an old picture. Nobody told me, I found out on my own."

X breathes heavily into the phone again and goes silent for a few moments. "So, you *have* been investigating on your own. Don't lie to me again. What else do you know?"

"I know about Marcini and Chavez," I say. "Look, like I said, I promise not to go back to Marcini's restaurant. I honestly wish I didn't know any of this. It was all so long ago, in another lifetime. It doesn't really matter, at least not to me. Not anymore."

"I don't believe you. This is your last chance. Believe me, I'm not a forgiving person. Consider yourself lucky."

"Why don't you meet me face to face?" I ask. "We can settle this like men."

X laughs into the phone. "See you around, Mr. Verner." The call ends.

The large man propping me up against the car releases his hold of me, and the three of them turn and walk away to their van parked in the darkened corner of the parking lot. The engine starts without any headlights and drives away. The vehicle has no license plates.

I stand against my car, hands shaking, heart racing. If X wants a war, then he'll get a war.

I call Brittany and tell her what's happened, and she invites me to come over. Well, not really "invites" more than insists, and I oblige eagerly.

She greets me with a warm hug. She's once again in a revealing outfit, this one is a vibrant red which shows off a considerable amount of cleavage. I shake my head in disbelief. What an amazing woman I've found. Chester's back on his post on the back of the couch and greets me with his usual "meow."

She cooks us another dinner; this time it's spaghetti and meatballs with red sauce. One of my favorites. We sit and eat at her dining room table overlooking the city skyline again. A thunderstorm has begun to roll in, and lightning flashes behind the skyscrapers.

"I'm glad you called."

"Me too," I say. "Hey, thanks for dinner. It's delicious."

She smiles, nodding her head. We walk over to the couch, and she has me rest my head in her lap as she strokes my hair. I seriously need to get a haircut; my shaggy, curly hair grows more out of control every day. Her delicate hands running through my hair feels so relaxing that I almost don't want to get up. Eventually, at around eleven, I reluctantly go home to feed Hank and get some rest before the long drive tomorrow.

Chapter 18

Blasts of hot yellow and intense blue collide in a symphony of intensity. The two colors flare from the tips of magical staffs, raging toward one another in passionate aggression. Magical energy, particles of molecules taken from the air around them turned into opposing blues and yellows, mashing together and separating. One of the most intense scenes I've ever witnessed. What's causing this battle to ensue? Who's winning?

I can tell I'm dreaming. Violent visions. Not about John, but rather the unknown. Potentially the future. Whether this is my future, or John's future, or another timeline altogether, I can't yet tell. All I can see are these two colors facing off, generating intense heat and bright white sparks.

Hovering over a blurry battlefield, a black hole begins to open at the epicenter of the blue and yellow battle. My body drifts down, traveling through the vacuum of the black hole, dragging me into an alternate dimension. Rivers of hot, molten lava. Volcanoes spouting off streams of orange fire, drifting up into the black clouds above. Large man-sized bats fly around this area of barren rock, gliding between the canyons of hellfire. I soar with them, and land in a large room in front of a throne of human skulls. The Skull Throne. Headless corpses strewn about randomly. A large, monstrous man sits on the throne, chin on fist. This is no man, my subconscious warns me. This is the ancient demon known as Popobowa. He opens his red eyes, causing me to wake instantly.

The next morning, I'm packed and ready to go. I've managed to fit all my clothes and camping necessities into one backpack. Ron, on the other hand, isn't ready when I knock on his door. I sit in his living room for thirty minutes while he gets his gear together, which he's also managed to fit into one backpack, albeit a backpack too full to zip up.

We load up my car and drive over to Brittany's. She's a real girl scout, fitting her clothes and necessities into one backpack, zipped up. Ron admires the city view from her back balcony, then helps me carry down the tent and canopy.

From there, we go to Jess' apartment. Brittany requests to stay in the car, saying she's not comfortable entering a stranger's apartment without meeting them first. Jess opens the door for Ron and me, and she's ready to go.

"Ron, how are the two girls are packed and ready to go faster than you were?" I ask.

"Because I was the first one you picked up, that's why," he says, shrugging his shoulders.

By eleven, we're on the open road. Brittany and Jess agreed to ride in the backseat after Ron had triumphantly called 'shotgun.'

The weather's perfect today with no clouds in sight. Traffic is surprisingly light for a Saturday afternoon, and we enjoy each other's company during the five-hour ride. Along the way we drive through Indianapolis, and take Interstate 74 until we reach highway 44, which we then take east. Brittany and Jess, quiet at the start of the drive, finally formed a conversation and have been talking non-stop for the past half-hour. Deejay Ron, as he insists on being called while in the passenger seat, self-appointed himself the disc jockey for the round trip.

I look in the rearview mirror to see Brittany whispering something in Jess' ear, followed immediately after by a roar of laughter from both of them. Two girls telling secrets in the back of my car. This could be bad news. I'm happy to see the two girls bonding, but at what cost to my already fragile ego and reputation?

"What're you two talking about back there?" I ask cautiously.

"Oh, nothing honey," Brittany says innocently. "We're just talking, you know, being girls." This sends the two of them into a giggling frenzy. I arch my eyebrow and shake my head.

"Deejay Ron, are we nearing our exit?"

"Yeah, we got about another five minutes or so, boss," Ron says, sliding his hand along the dashboard. "Man, I got to tell you, this is such a sick ride. I can't believe you scored this car, man. I still remember when we was rolling past that car lot, and you says 'Ron, that car's got my name on it.' I thought you was full of it, but you really followed through on this one."

"Thanks, man. Yeah, I did get pretty lucky here."

I decide not to tell Ron and Jess about my encounter last night, and thankfully Brittany stays quiet as well. Knowing those two, they would overact, trying desperately to protect me. Jess would insist I contact the police and would eventually contact them herself if I did nothing. Meanwhile, Ron would try and track down the thugs to "talk some sense into them," as he puts it. No, I'll just keep that issue on the back burner right now. I don't want anything to spoil our weekend getaway.

A little while later, we're unloading the car at our designated camping spot. Brittany's already gone to work setting up the tent, with Ron trying his best to keep up with her instructions. Jess and I work on the canopy, which is much easier to set up than the tent, but still a struggle for the two of us. Eventually, we get the canopy upright and secured, and move on to help the other two finish their construction project. Brittany makes the process look so easy, while I just stand and stare blankly at the tent poles in my hands, a dumfounded look on my face. However, within a few minutes, the tent is upright and tied down as well. Unzipping the opening of the tent, Brittany's the first to crawl inside, with me close behind.

"Great view," I say.

The box stated that the tent is meant to sleep eight people, but it clearly must be for children, or Russian gymnasts, because this tent looks like it would be lucky to fit five full-grown adults. Thankfully, it does look roomy enough for the four of us.

I crawl out of the tent, and announce to the three: "Hey, I'm going to drive into town and pick up some beer and stuff. I'll be back in a few minutes."

"Woah, woah, just like that?" Ron asks. "Don't you need some assistance from Deejay Ron?"

"Yeah, stay here and look after the women."

"We can handle ourselves, thanks," Jess says, hands on hips. "But Ron, you can stay with us while Simon makes his beer run. Don't worry, we can protect you."

"Please come back for us." Brittany pleads, causing Jess and Ron to laugh.

I get in the car and load up the GPS directions to Mike's ranch, which is roughly twelve minutes away. On the drive there, the possibilities of what I want to say to Mike and how this whole meeting could end up going run through my head.

Turning off onto a dirt road, I continue for about two miles, passing by nothing but fenced grassland which I can only assume is for grazing. A cloud of dust kicks up from the back of the car, and there's no traffic in sight. I prefer driving on empty roads with nobody around to tailgate me or get in my way. Much more peaceful this way.

I turn right once I see the address that Doug gave me, and park in front of a well-kept, cozy looking one story house complete with a wrap-around screened in porch. A porch swing sits off to one side of the front door, and an American flag hangs limp on the other. Cows stand near the wooden fence leading out into the pasture as I approach the front steps. Taking a deep breath, I open the screen and knock. Footsteps can be heard inside, and the old wooden door opens with a squeak.

The man is an older version of Mike, no doubt about it. He's gone completely bald. His once proud, smiling face is now a tired, rugged scowl.

"Can't you read the sign? No soliciting."

He slams the door in my face. I take another deep breath, clear my throat, and knock on the door again. I can hear him swear on the other side of the door, and it opens back up again.

"You've got five seconds before I shoot." he says gruffly, now holding a rifle in his hand.

I put my arms up, back away from the door and speak quickly. "Mike, my name is Simon Verner. Doug Lewis is my stepdad. I had some questions about your former partner, John Stinson."

He holds the door open, staring at me, and slowly nods his head. "Doug sent you out here, you say? For what, to dredge up the past? Why didn't that sorry son of a bitch come out here himself and talk to me instead of sending his...stepson?"

"Doug's...busy," I say evasively, my hands still up, as he still hasn't let go of the rifle. "We were talking about the unsolved case, and Doug thought it might be a good idea for me to drive out here and talk to you. I drove a long way, sir. Can you please lower your weapon? I come in peace."

After a few tense moments, he places the rifle against the wall by the front door, turns around and walks into his living room, grumbling. I take this as a cue to follow him inside. The living room is surprisingly filthy compared to the well-kept appearance of the outside of the home. The carpet is soiled and stained, with newspapers lying everywhere. An old TV with rabbit ears is propped up on a wooden table in front of a torn-up recliner. Three individual gun cabinets line the far wall, hanging open and filled with an assortment of weapons. Mike disappears into the kitchen, and I stand awkwardly in the living room, stuffing my hands into my jean pockets.

"Shut the damn door!" he calls from the kitchen.

I do as commanded, and Mike emerges from the kitchen with a cup of water.

"Thank you," I say, reaching my hand out.

He takes a drink from the glass, and eyes me narrowly. "For what?"

I clear my throat and withdraw my hand. "Never mind. Anyway, about John; you two were partners on the force for some time, right?"

Mike takes a seat in the recliner, winces, and lets out a grunt. "Yeah, you're a regular detective. You should go apply for a job, I'm sure they could use someone like you. Now can you get to damn the point? I've got a lot to do today."

With no other seats available, I remain standing, hands in pockets.

"I just wanted to know if you knew anything else about John's case. What can you tell me about Tony Alvarez?"

"Oh, you're right, I've been intentionally holding back important evidence after my partner and best friend was murdered," Mike says, raising his voice angrily. "I'm glad you came all the way out here to jog my memory so that case can finally be put to rest. Jesus Christ, kid."

"Look, sir, I mean no offense," I say, taking my hands out of my pockets. "I'm just trying to make the connection between John investigating Alvarez's murder, and the events that led up to his death in that apartment."

Mike slams the glass of water down on the table next to his recliner, shattering glass everywhere. "How in the hell did you know he died in an apartment?"

"It was in the news stories," I say, my voice cracking.

Mike stands up from his chair and approaches me, backing me against the wall. "Don't lie to me, boy. If you know anything about me, you know better than to lie. Who are you, really?"

I swallow and keep reminding myself to breathe. I've clearly struck some kind of a nerve. Either that, or this guy's crazier than an outhouse rat on acid and I shouldn't have followed him inside.

"Like I said, I'm Doug Lewis' stepson. I'm trying to–"

Mike puts his hand around my throat and shoves me against the wall.

Several pictures fall, the glass frames breaking on the floor. Twice in two days I've been threatened and assaulted. I'm becoming quite a big deal lately. The smell of alcohol faintly wafts off his breath as he stares me down.

"Fine, you want the truth, Mike? You're not going to believe me."

"That would be a nice change of pace, Verner. Talk. Fast." He eyes the rifle propped up next to the door. "Next round in that chamber's got your name on it."

"Really, it says 'Simon' on the bullet? Then we both have special powers."

The grip on my throat tightens. His glare could burn a hole through steel.

"Alright, here I go. I'm John Stinson, reincarnated. Now, before you reach for that gun and kill me, I can prove it. I was the best man at your wedding, just as you were the best man at mine. Doug was our boss. You're scared of clowns, you're afraid your second child isn't yours, since you think your wife cheated on you with someone. Not me, of course. And I know about that birthmark, the one you don't think anybody knows about. Look, I know I sound nuts, but it's the truth. I started having dreams a few weeks ago that I was John, and I've learned, over the course of events, that I *am* John. Or, I was, in my past life."

I close my eyes, waiting for him to reach for the gun and fire. Instead, he lets go of my neck. Opening my eyes, I see that he's stepped back a little bit, looking at me in disgust.

"Mike, all I want to know is who killed John. Who killed *me,"* I pat my chest. "But most of all, I want to know why. I think if I solve this case, these dreams can finally stop, and all the other stuff that's going on can end and I can just… I don't know, go back to living a normal life. Please, anything at all will help. I know that Tony Alvarez is still alive."

His intense glare returns, and he steps toward me again, a piece of glass crunching under his boot. "Bullshit," he says. "That bastard drowned in the lake."

"Well, whoever drowned wasn't Alvarez," I say. "He goes by Steve Mason, my boss and owner at Lowland Woods Golf Course. I also know about you and John kidnapping Rafael Chavez. Now, I don't know what happened with Chavez. Not yet. Because I haven't dreamed it yet. But I saw you at that warehouse when we had him tied up in a chair."

Mike continues to stare at me, and he's begun shaking.

"Look, man, I know this is a lot to throw at you. I honestly thought about calling you before coming out here, but I figured you'd just hang up the phone. And I wanted to meet you, face to face."

"I disconnected my phone," he says. "Government was tapping it. Look, kid, I got to admit, you threw a curveball at me today, not gonna lie. And you've got guts, I'll give you that. You have that in common with John. I don't know anything about…reincarnation, or whatever. But from what you just told me… I believe you."

"Great," I say. "That's great, Mike. John really trusted you. When I have these dreams, I can actually *feel* what he felt, and he trusted you with his life."

"I know," he says, briefly looking at the ground, then turns around to sit back in his recliner. "He was one hell of a cop. That Alvarez case ate him up and spit him out. He wouldn't let it go, even to the end. And the thing that really gets me, even to this day, is that his wife was pregnant, and he kept going into that lion's den night after night anyway until he finally met his end."

"Yeah, he was a driven man, for sure," I say, rubbing the back of my head.

"Kid, look, I really got nothing to help you, I'm sorry. I've told the story a thousand times. I was on patrol with John the night he died. We were following a vehicle involved in a recent kidnapping. One of the punks ran out of the car, so I got out to pursue him. John kept on going and apparently went into the building to rescue the kid. As far as the who and the why, I don't know. I don't even know if it was connected to the Alvarez case. But the one thing I can tell you is that Tony Alvarez is dead. This Steve guy must be, I don't know, a doppelganger or something. Chicago's a big city. People are bound to look alike."

"Who do you think killed John?"

He stares ahead blankly at his gun cabinets. "After John died, Doug had me go undercover to burn Marcini's operation from the inside out. But the whole thing crumbled like a house of cards. Doug pulled me out of there. Marcini reached some kind of under the table agreement with the D.A. regarding the Alvarez case. I don't know what came of that. But what I do know is that Marcini's a slippery bastard. My money's on him. Problem is, you'll never see him behind bars. He'll be dead before justice can get through his army of lawyers. The system's screwed up, kid. No thanks to men like William Marcini."

"Well, I saw Marcini the other night at his restaurant," I say.

"Do yourself a favor and stay away from him, if you know what's good for you."

I walk over to Mike's chair and reach out my hand, and he shakes it. A hint of a smile creases his lips. "Look, kid, I'm sorry for…well, for everything."

"Don't worry about it," I say, waving my hand dismissively. "Take care of yourself, Mike. Hey, if you're ever in Chicago, feel free to look me up."

I turn around to leave.

"Wait, Simon, one more thing," Mike says, struggling to stand up. "My memory's slower than shit, but it's coming back to me. I remember Doug talking about a stepson that he kicked out of the house for being a screw up. Was that you?"

"Yeah, that was me."

Mike wraps his arms around me in a bear hug. My arms hang limp at my sides for a few moments before I return the hug. He begins to shake, and I pull back to take a look. Tears are streaming down his face, and he wipes his cheeks with the back of his hand.

"I missed you, John. If that's really you in there, I've missed you."

Chapter 19

Clear, cold-water trickles over the smooth rocks. April twilight has arrived in eastern Indiana, and the smell from a nearby campfire blows through the crisp evening air. Birds are still calling in the red oak, pine and sugar maple trees that call the area home. Bright pink buds are beginning to blossom on the eastern redbuds, and the smell of fresh growth, of renewal, mingles with the campfire smoke. Laughter can be heard in the distance as I sit on a flat rock next to the babbling brook, staring at the water as it runs its course downhill.

Dad used to take me out in the woods when I was a kid, telling me to enjoy the fresh air while I can. He hated living in the city, claiming that the taint of it was wearing off on him, and he wished the three of us could live in a cabin out in the woods. "Off the grid," he used to say. At the time, I had no idea what he was talking about. Now as I sit here, with the smells and sounds of nature enveloping me in the quickly approaching dusk, I understand what he meant. This beats a night living in the city. The constant horns honking, random people shouting, sirens wailing, occasional gunshots, followed by more sirens. It wears on me, knowing so many people are around me, so many of them living in pain, or fear. Sure, there's the occasional laughter from my neighbors as they watch their nightly TV shows. My neighbors above me stomping around like they're a pack of wild elephants. But overall I find it all so…exhausting.

Out here, in the wild, I truly feel more alive than I've felt in a long time. After I'd returned back from my visit with Mike and brought two cases of beer back for the crew as promised, I told everyone I wanted to go for a hike alone. Brittany was the most disappointed of everyone, but I assured her that I'd be back soon. She crossed her arms, giving me a pouting look, sticking out her lower lip.

"You're going to take us all out here and then ditch us twice?" she asked, her arms still crossed.

"I just need to be alone for a bit. Please understand. I'll be back around dusk."

As I'd kissed her on the cheek and turned my back on her, it felt like I was making a big mistake. But now, as I take in all that this wonderful planet truly has to offer, more than the jungle that mankind has built, it feels as if the chains have slid off my shoulders and I can breathe freely. Clean, fresh air, not corrupted by pollution.

A mother deer emerges from the woods, with two small fawns behind her. I turn and gaze at them, and three pairs of eyes return my stare. The mother still has one of her front legs halfway off the ground, hovering between fight or flight mode. I don't move, not wanting to scare them off. My mind wanders back to last Saturday, a week from today, when I was driving in the wooded area behind my mom and Doug's home, and the mother deer with her two children had waited for my car to pass. These deer look so much healthier than those other ones. Man's influence on this region hasn't been as prevalent as back home, with more food ample and available to this family.

A third fawn pokes their head out from the shrubbery, and walks out, unsure of their footing, their legs wobbly. The mother deer nudges her baby to back away from the human invader, but the young one is curious about me. I'm probably the first human this little one has ever laid eyes on. The mom finally stops fighting with her youngest and allows it to approach me, its little steps becoming quicker. After a moment, we're within arms-reach, and it takes another shaky step toward me, nuzzling my hand with its nose.

I'm worried about touching the baby, as I don't want my smell to corrupt the young one, driving its mother away from it and causing her to abandon it in the woods to fend for itself. As much as I want to pet the young fawn, to tell it that I appreciated its effort to come over and say hello, I instead stand up, towering over it. The fawn receives the message and scampers back to its mom, and together all four of them disappear back into the foliage, away from me.

I wipe my hands on the sides of my pants and retrace my steps back to camp, using my cell phone flashlight to find solid footing.

When I arrive back at our camp, I see that the adjacent camping spots are now occupied; travel trailers and pickup trucks take up their spots. Loud music is blaring from another camper a few spots over. It's so noisy, and with the sound of laughter and diesel fumes, I feel like I might as well be back home in the city again.

"Simon!" Ron exclaims, holding a beer bottle in one hand. He stands up shakily and slowly makes his way over to me. Images of the staggering fawn instantly come to mind.

Brittany and Jess giggle next to each other on the wooden picnic table under the canopy. I pat Ron on the back as I walk past him and sit down at the table across from the two girls, prompting Brittany to scramble up, grab a beer from the ice chest, and sit next to me. She places the beer in front of me, going above and beyond by even cracking the lid open.

"Anything for my man," she says, giving me a kiss on the cheek.

"Thanks, sweetie," I say, and take a drink.

Jess just stares at the two of us, then looks off toward the woods taking a big swig from her bottle.

"Don't worry, everyone. I made it back." Ron says, slurring his words, making his way to the table. His shaky steps have gotten worse, and he braces himself against the table for support.

The four of us talk for the next hour, our chatter and laughter growing louder as the night wears on. Brittany remains at my side the entire time, her arm around my torso. Occasionally I peer at her from the side of my vision to see that she's always just staring at me intently. I'm not sure why, but I won't complain. There must be something about this face she likes.

We make our way back to the tent, Ron and Jess staggering into the confines first. I use my phone's flashlight again so everyone can find their appropriate sleeping quadrants. I crawl into my sleeping bag and don't bother to zip it in case Brittany decides she wants to join. Sleep overtakes me instantly.

Chapter 20

John drives the patrol car, with Mike in the passenger seat. The two cops are on afternoon patrol in one of the nicest suburbs of the city. It's been a week since the shootout at the nightclub, and the two of them have decided it's time to make Chavez talk. Every night for the past ten days, the two of them have alternated interrogating Chavez, trying to pry as much information from him as possible. So far, he's proved to be a difficult challenge, not willing to give up any more information on who killed Alvarez.

"Have you heard anything about that detective job opening?" Mike asks.

"No. Have you?" John asks, flipping on the turn signal.

"Nadda," Mike says, sighing. "I mean, you'd think Doug or somebody would've come to a decision by now. I've already had two interviews, and that was over a month ago. There's got to be something up."

John stays silent. He doesn't want to admit to Mike that Doug already told him that he's the favorite to get the job, which is why he was given this assignment. It wouldn't be fair to his friend. For the time being, he needs to lean on Mike to help him squeeze Chavez for whatever information he has on the Alvarez case.

So much for cracking his test case. He's been trying to find Alvarez's killer for months now and has turned up nothing. The entire case feels like a brick wall. But John knows that if he doesn't give up and stays persistent, something will crack.

"By the way, I already fed him this morning," Mike says. "And I gave him some water. He should be good for awhile."

"This whole thing just feels...wrong," John says. "Are you sure we're doing the right thing?"

"Yes, John. This is the *only* thing to do. Doug and I served together in 'Nam. This is how you extract information from the enemy. Just trust me here, alright? I know what I'm doing."

A moment of silence passes between the two of them. John keeps his attention straight ahead on the road. Mike rubs his hands together, his body movements becoming agitated.

"What?" Mike asks. "You do trust me, don't you?"

"Yeah, of course I do," John says, his voice low. "I just…I don't know. We should be going through the courts, trying to go about this the legal way, you know? Not like this. He's not a terrorist for Christ's sake, Mike. And we're not CIA operatives. We're low-level police officers, sworn to serve and protect the people."

"And that's exactly what we're doing. We're serving and protecting the innocent. This guy, Rafael Chavez, he's not innocent. He's a thug with nine priors who deserves to be six feet under. Did you know that he's suspected of not one, but four separate homicides? He's only walking free thanks to our spineless court system, and Marcini's army of lawyers." Mike takes a deep breath, staring intently at John. "We *are* serving and protecting the people. Alvarez deserves justice. His family deserves answers. The courts won't give them answers. They won't give Alvarez justice. Only we can do that."

"I don't know," John says, taking a shaky breath.

"Just suck it up and trust me. I promise, we're so close to breaking this guy, and breaking this case."

Later that evening, John decides to pay Chavez a visit. This time, he comes alone, not telling Mike.

John pulls up to the shipping port, killing his headlights before he enters the parking lot. He walks past row upon row of shipping containers, stacked as many as nine high. Giant forklifts sit stationary, waiting until the morning comes to move the containers from one spot to another. Cargo ships sit off in the distance, with more containers stacked up on their decks. These huge ships will eventually make their way through the St. Lawrence Seaway, a series of locks and canals connecting Lake Michigan to all the other Great Lakes, eventually making their voyage to the Atlantic.

During the day, the Port of Chicago is a bustling hub. The hard-working, blue-collar workers of the city do a great job of making sure this port stays running smoothly. At night, however, John has managed to strike a deal with the evening guards to let him in and give him free access to the place. The head of night security, Kevin, isn't the sharpest tool in the shed, and he easily bought John's story that he needed to use one of the shipping containers to store his guns and ammunition to kill bad guys with.

John walks through the maze of containers until he finds the one he's looking for; an empty, decommissioned container that's been ordered not to be moved. Again, another order that Kevin bought and took to heart.

He feels guilty taking advantage of the gullible security guard, a man who only wants to do his best to help the men in blue. This is just a temporary arrangement, one that will hopefully end tonight.

Slipping his key into the padlock, John opens the metal swinging doors to the container, and turns on his flashlight. He shines the light directly into Chavez's face; he's strapped to a chair, hands tied behind his back and a rag stuffed into his mouth. A metal bucket sits next to the man. His face winces as the light temporarily blinds his eyes, clearly not adjusted to the light.

John removes the rag from Chavez's mouth, keeping the flashlight trained on the other man's eyes.

"Cut it out, you pig," Chavez says annoyingly, looking down at the floor. He spits on John's shoes. "Just kill me and get this over with already."

"'The truth will set you free.'"

"Yeah, you're a real poet," Chavez says, still refusing to make eye contact with John. "I've already told you everything I know."

"Why don't you go ahead and tell me again, Rafael? My memory, it's…a bit fuzzy."

Chavez groans and looks up at the ceiling of the metal container, exposing the full scale of the dragon tattoo around his neck. "I'll say it again real slow for you, sweetheart. Why don't you do us a favor and get a pen and paper. You ready?" Chavez enunciates his next words slowly, like he's speaking with a child or someone hard of hearing. "I don't know who killed Alvarez. I was not there. I was in jail after you arrested me for robbing the jewelry store. You should ask Marcini, like I told you a dozen times already. There, are you satisfied?"

"No," John says, placing his hands on his knees and peering down into Chavez's face. "We've established the fact that you weren't there that night. I'm asking who gave the order to kill Alvarez. I'm asking who among Marcini's men is responsible for his death. I paid Marcini a visit the other night. He had some of his thugs pull a gun on me. Luckily, I got out of there. Something tells me you sent me into a trap."

Chavez scoffs and rolls his eyes. "Man, you a real dumb cop, you know that? How do you think I can send you into a trap, while you've got me tied up in here, huh? Just like you think I killed a guy from jail. Seriously, use your brain, John. Marcini's the one who gave the order. I've already told you this."

John steps back, keeping the flashlight pointed at Chavez. With his free hand, he pulls the pistol out of his holster, pointing it at the other man.

"How do you know my first name?"

"Really, that's what you're upset about?" Chavez says, laughing. "You're so stupid." He beams a wide smile at John, showing off his gold front teeth. "Mike told me your name. He also told me that your wife is expecting. Samantha, is it? John, why are you wasting your time here with me, while your old lady's sitting at home, lonely and pregnant?"

John walks up to Chavez and pistol whips him in the face, sending blood spraying against the side of the container walls. One gold tooth breaks free, clinking down on the ground.

"You don't ever talk about her!" John screams. "Mike didn't tell you that! You're lying!"

"Oh, but he did. How else would I know this? I know even more."

John tackles Chavez, sending the both of them to the floor. The back of the chair shatters on impact, releasing Chavez's rope restraints. Chavez scrambles to his feet, pressing his knee onto John's chest, then punches him in the face with a right hook, followed by a left jab. Right hood, followed by a left hook. Bloodied and battered, John struggles for breath, and reaches over for the pistol lying on the ground next to him as Chavez continues to punch him repeatedly.

"You think you can lock me away?" Chavez roars, grabbing John's head with both hands.

Chavez rolls John over onto his stomach, removing his wallet and car keys from the pockets of his back pants pocket. John can hear the other man going through his wallet.

"Ah, she really is beautiful," Chavez says, throwing a picture of Samantha down on the ground next to John. "Your driver's license is about to expire soon. Too bad you'll be dead by then." Chavez stands up, and kicks John in the ribs. "Looks like I'll be paying your dear old Samantha a visit. She could use a real man in her life. Another one for my collection."

John struggles to his feet as Chavez is turning to walk away. He tackles Chavez from behind, grabbing him around his torso. Echoes of footsteps and grunting bounce off the walls of the shipping container as the two men struggle with one another. After several days of little movement, the strength of Chavez's legs proves no match for John's physicality. Twisting his body around, John shoves the other man hard against the side of the metal wall, causing Chavez's head to bounce violently. His body goes limp and falls to the floor, his head striking the edge of the metal bucket.

Hands on his knees and breathing heavily, John stares at the other man not moving on the ground. He makes his way over to Chavez, standing over his body. It doesn't appear that he's breathing, either. Making sure that his pistol is still within eyesight and out of reach, John gingerly bends down to check Chavez's pulse. Nothing. A growing pool of red begins to form behind Chavez's head. John stands up quickly, placing his hands behind his own head.

"Oh, God," John breathes. "No, no. This isn't happening. This can't be happening!"

His heartbeat quickens, his face hot. After all his time on the force, he's never killed another man.

"Why?!" John yells, punching the hard metal wall. "How could I let this happen? What have I done?" He quickly walks over to his pistol and wallet, picking up both items. Lastly, he picks up the picture of Samantha, kissing it. "I should've listened to you. I should've stayed off this case and been there for you. I'm so sorry."

Tucking the picture into his pocket, he leaves the shipping container, closes the doors and refastens the padlock.

A short time later, he parks his car at a nearby gas station and uses the outside payphone, inserting a quarter. He dials the number, tapping the top of the phone box impatiently. Finally, the line picks up.

"Mike, I need your help. We've got a problem."

When I wake up, my head is throbbing. I remove the Dream Catcher, placing it on top of my sleeping bag. Sunlight illuminates the inside of the tent. I sit up and look around the empty tent, noticing the front flap is unzipped. The others must have already gone outside to start cooking breakfast or something. I crawl through the opening, feeling the cool, damp grass on the ground outside. Standing up, I stretch and feel my back cracking. The air is chilly, but the bright morning sun casts a comforting warmth on my face. Birds are chirping in the nearby trees, excited for the upcoming day. I'm the only person awake yet, it seems, as there's nobody else in sight. They must all be sleeping in after a long night of partying.

A fist slams into my right cheek, sending me down to my knees on the dewy grass. Steam is coming off my breath in the chilly air. I look over to see who dealt the blow, and see Ron glaring at me, breathing deeply, with fists clinched at his sides.

"Stand up, you son of a bitch!" Ron screams. He's taken a boxer's stance now, his fists at the ready in front of his chin. "We know what you did. You seriously thought you could get away with this, huh?"

"What're you talking about, man?" I ask desperately.

"You know exactly what you did!"

He charges at me, tackling me to the ground, pressing his body weight on my chest. With one arm he holds me down, and with the other he begins to punch me in the face. He lands three consecutive solid blows, and I feel my nose gushing blood. On his fourth attempted strike, I block his fist with my forearm, and raise my knees up to knock him off balance. With my other arm, I land a strong punch to his jaw, and he rolls off me. Within moments, I'm on top of him, connecting with repeated punches to the side of his head. My knuckle busts open, blood smearing his cheek. I continue to press my knee on his chest, using both of my arms to pin his wrists to the grass.

"Ron!" I shout. "Ron, talk to me! What happened? I just want to talk. Tell me what happened."

He gives up fighting, his arms sprawled out. He lets out a frustrated groan.

"You marooned us here!" Ron shouts. "You knifed two of the car tires, then you stole our cell phones so we couldn't call for help. You're sick, Simon. You're a sick friend. And now I'm gonna be sick."

Ron rolls his head to the side, vomiting on the grass. I get off him and turn toward where the car is parked. Jess is approaching me now, fury raging in her eyes. She points a finger in my face.

"You're unbelievable. You seriously thought you could get away with this, huh? Is that it?"

I try to reach for Jess' shoulders to calm her down, and she pushes me in the chest. "Don't touch me freak! You don't even remember, do you? Probably because you were so wasted last night."

"Jess, talk to me. Please. Ron's pissed at me too, and I have no idea what happened. All that I remember is going to sleep last night. I literally just woke up."

She crosses her arms, looking off to the side. She can't even bring herself to look at me. This hurts more than Ron's punches.

"You tried to force yourself on me. You tried to crawl into my sleeping bag, under the same tent your girlfriend's in, no less. What's the matter with you? You're…you're sick."

Other campers have begun to emerge from their tents and trailers, staring at us. Some of them begin to murmur with one another. I put my hand up and smile at some of them, which does nothing to deter the glares coming in our direction.

Brittany emerges from the woods. "Sorry guys, I had to tinkle. The restroom was full."

I approach Jess, and she takes a step back. "Jess, did you wear the Dream Catcher last night?"

She looks down at the ground, shaking her head. "I don't remember. I… oh crap." She looks back up at me, a look of embarrassment spread across her face.

"Ron, did you wear yours last night?" I ask.

He looks up at me. "I…I can't remember. Simon, I'm sor–" He rolls back on his side and resumes vomiting.

I approach Brittany, her arms wrapped around herself, shivering. She's wearing Mickey Mouse pajama bottoms and a long sleeve shirt with Goofy on it.

"Hon, did you wear your Dream Catcher last night?" I ask.

"Of course, silly," she says, then takes it out of her pajama pants pocket, smiling. "I wear it every night, just like you told me too."

"What did you dream about?"

"I dreamt…oh, what did I dream?" She places her fist under her chin and looks down at the ground. After a moment, she shrugs her shoulders. "Gosh, I can't really remember. I'm terrible at this game." She giggles. "What's for breakfast? I'm starving!"

I walk back in front of the tent. The audience has all gone back inside of their campers, presumably to catch another few fleeting minutes of sleep. Ron offers to make us all breakfast, and Jess agrees to help. For the rest of the morning, they repeatedly apologize. They explain that their dreams of what they think I had done were so intense and real. I wonder if their excess alcohol consumption last night is what caused their dreams to become so vivid.

The four of us finish eating breakfast under the canopy in complete silence.

Chapter 21

After the Sunday morning mayhem with Ron and Jess, the four of us decided to pack it up early and head home. The car ride back was mostly quiet, with Deejay Ron deciding he no longer wished to sit up front next to the man he got into a fight with that morning. Brittany happily took his place. Jess and Ron both apologized to me several more times in the car, and I kept telling them both that it's alright. Ron had no idea what had gotten into him, while Jess on the other hand had a better understanding of what occurred, hence her silence. She always gets quiet when she understands something that others around her don't, a trait of hers that I've picked up on over the years. I think it may be time to tell Ron my secret as well, but I'm still hesitant. He's not as open-minded as Jess is. She's much more into this kind of stuff.

I had spent the majority of yesterday evening with Brittany, relaxing in her apartment. We ordered some Chinese takeout and enjoyed another Netflix movie. As we cuddled on the couch, it finally dawned on me that I'm so lucky to have her in my life. The first week or so of this relationship had me in a state of shock, as the whole thing just came out of left field for me. It seems like when you're not looking for a relationship, that's when one will jump out and bite you. In a good way. A nice, loving bite.

After work today, Brittany and I head to the shopping mall together. She has me try on some new clothes, including a black leather jacket and skinny jeans. I've never considered wearing these types of clothes before, but she really thinks I look great in them. The clothes aren't on sale, but Brittany says it doesn't matter; these are clothes that I must wear in order to look fashionable in today's society. Personally, I don't care about fashion, as my entire wardrobe consists of a rotation of four outfits at most. When I try to tell this to her, she acts offended, like I've just said something terrible, and begins to pout. She's sticking out her lower lip, crossing her arms, doing everything but stomping her feet, so I give in and spend money on the full priced clothes. The look of satisfaction and happiness on her face makes it totally worth it, even though I really should be saving my money right now, rather than spending it, in order to stay ahead on my car payments. By the time we leave the mall, I have five full shopping bags of new clothes.

When we get back to her apartment, she wants me to change into one of the new outfits. I do as she asks, and she claps with excitement as I twirl around for her. Making sure I keep my eyes closed, she then leads me into the bathroom, where she applies some sort of eye liner on me and sprays some assortment of chemicals in my hair. She leads me back out into her living room area, in front of where I remember a full body mirror to be.

"Okay, you can look now," she says, giddy with excitement as I open my eyes.

The person looking back at me is someone I don't recognize. My once light brown curly hair is now dark black, matching the color of the tight leather jacket. The skinny jeans are of a lighter gray color, a silver chain dangling out of one of the pockets.

"What do you think?" she asks.

"I look totally ridiculous," I say bluntly. "Brittany, this just isn't me." She crosses her arms, then looks away. "Hey, don't be upset. I want you to be happy, but I also want you to like me for who I am, not who you want me to be. Does that make sense?"

She keeps her arms crossed, refusing to look at me. I reach for her arms, but she yanks away. I can feel my cheeks flush, worried that I've upset her. The more I worry, the more I want to make her happy.

"Well, hey, change is hard," I say. "I guess I'll give it a shot, if it means that much to you."

She squeals, wrapping her arms around my neck and we embrace in a passionate kiss. My mind melts, only thinking of one thing: I must make Brittany happy. No matter what.

"I'm only happy if you do what I want," she says, her voice causing my eyes to cross. "You're mine, Simon. Not Jess'. Nobody's but mine."

Later that night, I clean Hank's fish tank, then feed him dinner. I sit in the chair, telling him how happy I am to finally be with the one and only woman in this world who can make me happy. Instead of listening to me, he swims to the back of the tank and hides. Lying down to sleep, only one thought continues to play in my mind. *Brittany. Brittany. Brittany…*

John and Samantha are dressed to the nines as they arrive at the city convention center. Spotlights shine up into the night sky from outside the building, and news crews are parked in front of the building, flashes exploding off their cameras at the front door. Mike's also riding in the back of the vehicle, an open wine bottle in hand.

"God, I hate these things," Mike says, looking out the window.

"But you look so nice!" Samantha says.

"Thanks, darlin'," Mike says, holding the wine bottle out to her. "Want some?"

She places her hand over her stomach. "I better not."

"Yeah, you wouldn't want your kid growing up to be like this lout over here, now would ya?" Mike laughs, pointing at John.

John remains silent as the vehicle comes to a stop. The three of them exit the limo and go inside the convention center. Balloons are hung throughout the building, and a jazz band plays up on stage with only a few people paying attention to them. There's at least three hundred people inside the auditorium, many of them holding glasses of champagne or other liquors, standing around conversing among one another.

"Hey, Charlie!" Mike shouts, waving his hand in the air, and disappears into the crowd of finely dressed people.

"John, how the hell have you been?" a large, burly man approaches with a woman about half his age hanging from his arm.

"George, hey man, long time no see," John says, shaking his hand.

"You're damn right it's been a long time," the man roars with laughter, his double chin shaking. "This is Wendy, my fiancé."

"What are we up to now, four?" John asks, laughing. Wendy glances down at the ground while George lets out another round of laughter, to the relief of John. "This is my wife, Samantha. As you can see, we're expecting."

"Congratulations!" George says boisterously, his jowls quaking.

"How far along?" Wendy asks, her voice soft and delicate. She has to repeat herself louder so that John and Samantha can hear her over the background noise.

"Seven months," Samantha says. Wendy smiles and nods her head, taking a sip of her alcohol.

"John was my finest student back at the Academy," George says, clasping his hand on John's shoulder. "I knew you would make a damn fine cop. You do this city proud."

Shortly later, George guides Wendy away from John in order to find others to mingle with. Looking sheepishly down at the ground, John takes Samantha's hand. He's never been much for social functions such as this, and after the events a few nights ago with Chavez, guilt has wrought him to the core. Several mornings he's woken up, running to the toilet to dry heave, swearing this will be the day he turns in his badge and gun, unable to hide the shame of being a so called "police officer." He was supposed to uphold the law, not break it. Regardless of whether the world is a better place without Rafael Chavez in it.

Telling himself that he did it to protect his family, John sighs heavily.

"What's wrong?" Samantha asks. "Do you see anyone else you recognize?"

He looks his wife in the eyes. "The only person I want to be with tonight is you. Let's just get out of here, what do you say?"

"What? Why?"

Suddenly, a voice comes over the microphone, and the lights dim. Samantha leads John to the closest empty seats at a nearby table.

"Good evening, ladies and gentlemen!" the voice booms into the microphone. "Welcome to the 1986 Chicago Police Recognition Ceremony. On behalf of the fine city of Chicago, we hope you all enjoy our festivities this evening. I'm your host tonight, William Marcini."

The crowd erupts in cheers. John's veins turn to ice, and he stares up at the stage, looking directly at the man responsible for putting him in this situation. A cold-blooded mob boss who should be behind bars. A wolf in sheep's clothing.

The lights come back on, and Samantha leads John to the buffet table. She loads up her plate with delicious looking food, while John picks and chooses, wearily adding bite size portions to his plate.

Later in the evening, as the ceremony continues, John's barely paying attention to what's happening on stage, his elbow propped up on the table, his chin resting on his fist. He plays with a buttered green bean, moving it from one end of the plate to another.

"And the winners are… officers Mike Lancaster and John Stinson!"

Samantha shrieks with excitement, clutching John's arm. Several people begin to pat him on the back, and he stands up, walking up to the stage. He makes his way up the steps, and looks out at the crowd, flashbulbs going off, causing dots to appear in his vision. Flashbacks of his graduation from the Academy come flooding back to him. People call out his name from the audience.

Mike walks up onto the stage from the other side, and the two of them meet in the middle at the microphone. A large certificate is thrust into John's arms, and he looks up to see the smiling face of William Marcini looking down at him.

"Congratulations, Officer Stinson," Marcini says, shaking his hand. He positions his body to block the microphone, looking down at John, his smile gone. "I don't know what you did with Chavez, but I intend to find out. You've made a big mistake crossing me. This isn't over. Now, smile for the cameras."

Marcini puts his smile back on and steps off to the side so that the photographers have a better view of the two men shaking hands, each with a hold on the certificate. Mike also takes a turn shaking hands with Marcini, flashbulbs going off constantly.

Marcini steps up to the microphone. "Seven months ago, these two courageous officers saved a mother and her young baby from imminent danger in a hostile domestic violence situation. John, step on up here and tell everyone how you were able to disarm the aggressor and save the family?"

Marcini steps aside as John walks up to the podium. He taps the microphone, causing a loud "poof" to emanate from the speakers in the auditorium. Perspiring profusely, he unbuttons the top button of his shirt collar, allowing himself to breathe a little easier.

John clears his throat. "Thank you. First of all, I want to thank my wife Samantha, who gives me the strength and motivation to get up in the morning."

The audience erupts in applause, and Samantha stands up, waving at the crowd once the spotlight lands on her. She blows John a kiss.

"Also, none of this would be possible without my partner, Mike," more applause from the crowd, and John waits for it to end. "He's a good friend and has taken me under his wing since I joined the Chicago Police Department.

In regards to the incident we're discussing here; look, it was nothing special. Any of us could've been there and would've done the same as I did. I'm just glad the family is safe."

John closes his eyes, and when he opens them, the crowd has disappeared. Silence deafens the large conference room. Only one man sits at the back of the auditorium, clapping his hands slowly. *Clap. Clap. Clap*. The man stands up, approaching the stage while still clapping.

I'm now in control of John, only it's no longer John. I'm in my own body. The man walks up on stage, and now I'm able to recognize the person as none other than X, with his short brown hair.

"Very good, very good," X says mockingly, hoisting himself up on stage. "What do you think so far, Simon? You were almost as big of a hypocrite in your past life as you are in this one, wouldn't you say?"

I arch my eyebrows and clinch my fists. "He had no other choice. Chavez threatened to come after his wife, I would've done the same thing. Plus, it was an accident, he didn't intentionally kill the guy."

"Of course you would have. You always take the easy way out. By the way, that was no accident. You think someone with as much training as John would've 'accidentally' bashed another man's head into the side of a metal shipping container? You're delusional."

I nod my head. "Fine, whatever you say. What do you want?"

"I just want you to know that I'm watching. I warned you to stop pursuing this case, twice now, yet you keep defying my commands."

"I have no control over what I dream. I'm not pursuing anything."

"Deep down, you can control what you dream. You keep having these visions, these memories, from your past life because buried deep in your subconscious, you want to know who pulled the trigger that night and killed John."

"Keep spinning that narrative. Let's just agree to disagree. You leave me alone, I won't pursue the case when I'm awake, and we both just go our separate ways. Deal?"

X laughs, placing his hand on my shoulder. The auditorium has disappeared, and we're back in the eternal darkness of the Void.

"I can't take that chance. It's frustrating me to no end that I'm unable to control your thoughts. A side effect of my dying wish, sadly. Your gift, it's…

too dangerous. You either learn to control it, or I'll have to deal with you in other ways."

"Keep talking," I say. "All you do is throw empty threats at me, and have your thugs harass me after work. Show yourself in the waking world, and we can talk face to face. Otherwise, I've got nothing else to say to you."

X shakes his head, frowning. "Have it your way."

I wake up three minutes before my alarm is set to go off. Sitting up in bed, I look over to see the Dream Catcher sitting on top of my nightstand.

Chapter 22

After work on Thursday, Brittany and I go to Moretti's for some drinks and pizza. Ron and Jess are already there, and they managed to pick out the nicest booth in the back corner of the restaurant. Ron notices me first, and his eyes practically pop out of his head. Jess stops talking mid-sentence and turns her head, doing a double take when she sees me. I'm wearing another black leather jacket, very similar to the one I wore Monday night. My skinny jeans are a lighter color, and I now have a red bandana tied around the top of my head, my long black hair cascading down to my shoulders.

Brittany grabs my shoulder, whispering into my ear. "They may not like the way you look, baby. Just give them some time to get used to it. If they can't accept the new you, then forget them. I'm here for you."

I nod my head in agreement, and sit down in the booth, scooting over next to Ron. They still haven't said a word, staring at me in what I can only imagine is shock. For several minutes the four of us sit there in silence. Jess eventually picks up the drink menu and pretends to browse the selection of alcohol, while peering suspiciously at me over the top of it. Ron clears his throat several times, tapping his fingers on the table.

Classic rock plays at a moderate level over the speaker system, and the bar is much quieter this evening thanks to the fact that no local basketball game is on TV tonight.

"It looks like you have a new…style," Ron says in a slightly condescending tone. "You look…different."

Brittany rubs my arm reassuringly, helping me build up confidence to strike down my friend's rude behavior.

"If you don't like the way I look, just come out and say it," I say defensively. "You've had the same haircut since ninth grade, Ron."

"Chill, man," Ron says. "I'm not judging you. I'm just…making an observation, that's all."

"He's lying," Brittany whispers into my ear. "He's judging you, and so is the blond. You've outgrown them. Their relationship is an umbilical cord upon your true freedom. Time to sever it."

"What's up with you two?" Jess asks, crossing her arms. She glares at Brittany for an instant, then looks back at me with a softer expression. "Look, if you're trying out a new style, that's fine. It's none of our business. It's a pretty drastic change though. No offense, but you look like Edward Scissorhands."

"He's spreading his wings, Jess," Brittany says, still clutching my arm. "As his friend, I would've thought you'd be more supportive of his decision."

Jess returns her piercing glare back to Brittany. "First off, I wasn't speaking to you, and I know that he can speak for himself. Second off, how dare you come in here and attempt to insinuate that Ron and I are somehow holding him back? Simon's our friend, Brittany. We've known him a lot longer than you have, and we know him much better than you do. Quite frankly, after seeing what's going on here, I think you're a bad influence on him. But I'm not going to tell him what to do. He's free to choose for himself."

"See, there it is," Brittany whispers in my ear again. "She's trying to manipulate you against me. You need to–"

"Why do you keep whispering like that?" Jess asks with one eyebrow arched, leaning forward and placing her arms on the table. She turns her attention to me. "Look, you're my best friend. I'm not going to sit here and watch as this…woman, tries to twist your mind around. You're better than her."

"Don't you speak about her that way!" I shout. Several people in the restaurant stop their conversations and turn to look in our direction. "Let's get out of here." Brittany and I scoot out of the booth and stand up. "You two should be ashamed of yourselves. I finally find someone who loves me for who I am, and instead of being happy for me, you two sit there and judge me. Until you can accept Brittany, then don't bother talking to me."

"Well, when the old Simon comes back, let us know." Jess replies.

"Open your eyes, man," Ron says. "She's twisting you up like a pretzel."

"Shut up!" I yell.

"C'mon baby, let's leave," Brittany grabs my arm, pulling me away from their table.

We leave the restaurant and spend the evening together at her apartment.

The next day at work, several co-workers look at me, then quickly turn their attention elsewhere. Steve walks into the breakroom, and glances over at me, arching one eyebrow. I stare back at him. If he only knew what I knew about him and his deceitful past, he wouldn't dare sit there judging me like that. Like he's better than me.

I hate working at this golf course. The rich, entitled men striking my range picker repeatedly while I'm trying to sweep up the golf balls. The two-faced owner Steve, and all of his little minions that carry out his every command like he's some sort of king. The whole place makes me sick to my stomach. The only reason I've even bothered coming into work this week has been because of Brittany, as she sits there at the front desk, looking at me like I'm a delicious piece of eye candy. My heart explodes and my mind melts when I'm around her. I've never been around a woman so majestic, so beautiful. She enters my every waking thought, and all I can think about are ways to make her happy, and to let her know that I will always do what she needs, whenever she needs it done. I'm her blank canvas, and she is the artist. Just being around her makes me whole and complete, and I can't imagine even taking another waking breath without her by my side.

Ron and Jess are ancient history. Those two liars think that they're better than me, and they're wrong. It's just the opposite. I'm the one who's too good for them. They'll be lost without me, and it's not my problem. Knowing that Brittany's in my corner is all that matters.

Tonight, Brittany's agreed to come over to my place for the first time. I stayed up late cleaning up the apartment last night, making sure the toilet was clean, the sink was cleared of dishes and the floor was swept clean. Hank bobbed around the tank, watching me bob around the apartment, the two of us working up a sweat.

After work, I check twice to make sure no more of X's goons are waiting for me in the shadows of the golf course parking lot. I've parked closer to the road now, rather than in the darkened back lot. Speeding home, I double-check last night's cleaning job, tidying up things as I go. Brittany said she'll be here around seven, and I've agreed to cook.

Cooking is something completely foreign to me, but tonight I'm up to the challenge. Anything I can do to satisfy her. She's cooked me two homemade meals; the least I could do is return the favor. I hope she likes the Simon Special: Macaroni and Cheese with boiled hot dogs.

The doorbell rings. I check the clock on the oven. 6:57. Right on time. This woman is perfect. I give myself a once over in the mirror, straightening my shirt and messing with my black hair. I seriously need to get a haircut. But only if she approves.

Brittany's dressed in jeans and a yellow zipped up hooded sweatshirt, which I'm relieved to see. I hate feeling under dressed. She's also using a wooden cane of some sort, which she props up in the corner by the front door. I decide to not ask her why she needs a walking stick and will allow my Queen to tell me if she wants to.

"Welcome to my humble abode," I say as she strolls past me. "Make yourself comfortable. May I take your jacket, ma'am?"

She giggles and unzips her hoodie, which I throw on the couch. I clap my hands together.

"So, this here's the kitchen," I say, stretching my arms out. "And in here's the bathroom."

She nods her head, smiling. My apartment is about a quarter the size of hers, if that, with a much less impressive view. The more I think about it, my apartment must seem like an outhouse to her. She begins to walk into the bedroom, and I rush over to the oven and flip on the stovetop, where a pot of water is ready to go. I pour a box of macaroni into the pot as well.

"Alright, dinner's cooking," I say excitedly, speed walking back into the bedroom. "I hope you're hungry."

She looks back at me, placing one hand on the bed spread, biting her lower lip.

"I can be hungry," she says in her deeper, smoky voice. "Baby, I can be anything you want me to be."

I gulp and take a deep breath. Moving closer, I wrap my arms around her, pick her up, and throw her down on the bed. I slide across the comforter next to her. She maneuvers around and drops her purse to the ground at the foot of the bed, then positions her body on top of mine, planting several passionate kisses on me. We wrap our arms around one another, kissing each other in blissful romance.

"Be a good boy and lie still," she breathes, pressing down on my chest as she stretches back, reaching down into her purse. "You want to know something that's been itching at me, Simon? How could you possibly think that a woman like me would *ever* be interested in a disgusting, immature boy like you?"

I close my eyes momentarily, and as I open them, she's jabbing a long needle into the side of my neck, squeezing down on the top of the syringe, a satisfied look on her face. Instantly, my limbs go numb. My eyes are still functioning, for now, but I can't move a muscle. She roughly shifts my body on the bed and lays my head down awkwardly on the pillow. She hefts her purse onto the bed, and pulls out a thick rubber band, and another needle. I can't speak. Tears begin to slide down my cheeks, and I want to ask her so many questions. *Why? What have I done wrong?*

She removes the needle from my neck, rolls up my shirt sleeve, ties the rubber band around my upper arm, jabbing the second needle with an empty syringe into my skin. Pulling a couple silver spoons from her purse, she lays them on my nightstand, knocking items over at random. Stepping back toward the dresser, she pulls an old Polaroid camera out of her purse and takes several photos of me. The flash from the camera has me seeing stars for a moment, but I can't blink.

"That's a good boy," she says, now in her sweet and innocent voice. "Simon says 'I'm a strung-out junkie.' Simon says, 'I love heroin more than my friends.'"

She climbs back onto the bed, and lays next to me, staring at me with an intense hatred I've never seen from her before. I'm looking at her out of the corner of my eye, still unable to move or speak.

"Oh, baby, are you crying?" she asks innocently, and drags her fingernail down my cheek. "Now you're really crying. Tears of blood." She removes her bloodstained fingernail, wipes it on her tongue, sending her into uncontrollable fits of laughter, and kisses me on the cheek. When she pulls her head back, her mouth is coated in blood.

"You've always been so slow, Magdoo," she says. "I'll just lay it out plain and simple for you." She proudly places her hand on her chest. "For starters, I'm X."

She gets off the bed and starts walking around the foot of the bed to look out the window, arms crossed behind her back. My entire body is still numb, and the only thing I'm able to control are my eyes. I can move them around, but that's it. I felt no pain when she cut my cheek.

"The human race has grown so much since we were brothers," Brittany says, keeping her gaze out the bedroom window. "With every passing life, their imprint on this planet strengthens. The more their population grows, and their technology advances, the longer their lifespans become, yet deeper the divide between each of them individually grows. I look out this window, Brother, and I see a chasm. I see people that live their lives, but not to the fullest. And worst of all, some of them *hate* it. Isn't that awful? They've been given a great gift. The gift of life, and they waste it. And for what? For money. For power. For respect. When it's all over, what have they really earned? Their soul will just pass into another body, this race will continue to press the limits of the resources given to them by this planet, and they wake up in the next life none the wiser to what they've already squandered countless times before. It makes me so…angry."

She turns away from the window and focuses on me. Where there was once anger and resentment, now there's a look of pity.

"You and I were once brothers, Magdoo. And then, you betrayed me. My name is Mubiru, and for over seventeen thousand years, I've sought revenge for your betrayal. But believe me, this is far from the worst thing I've ever done to you. In nearly every life, not all, but in the majority of the lives you've lived, I've been there to ruin you. To destroy you. And I know that *you* know how your last life ended, as John Stinson. Lying in a pool of his own blood, killed by his own greed and lust for power for trying to solve a crime that he couldn't let go of because of his own selfish pride and ego. And for what? Oh, that's right. For a job promotion. How…how sad."

Brittany gets close to my face, her look now changing back to anger.

"I warned you, but you just wouldn't listen. I cannot…I *will* not allow you to solve the murder of John Stinson. It doesn't matter who killed you in your past life. You needed to leave it alone. But you're so stubborn, you just–"

A forceful knock comes at the front door, and she slinks off the bed, placing her hands on her hips.

"Well, who could that be?" she asks, now putting on a playful southern accent. "Oh Lord, Simon, I didn't realize you was inviting company over. Aren't you just a doll?"

She sniffs a few times, and after a moment, tears begin to roll down her cheeks. She grabs a tissue from her purse, and rushes to the front door. I can hear three voices murmuring in the living room. I recognize Jess' voice, rising a few times.

Moments later, Jess and Ron enter my bedroom.

"Oh my God!" Jess screams, placing her hands over her mouth.

"I know, it's just awful," Brittany sobs, wiping tears from her eyes. "He offered to cook us dinner, but he wasn't answering the door, so I let myself in, and came in here to find him like this. I didn't know what to do. I just got here."

Brittany begins to cry heavily, plunging her face into Ron's chest. He just stares at me, expressionless. He wraps his arms around her in a hug, and escorts her out of the room. Jess approaches my bed, and crouches down on one knee.

"You bastard," she seethes. "I can't believe you'd do this to us. I can't believe you'd do this to yourself." She takes a shaky breath, tears now forming in her beautiful blue eyes. "After my mom and I took you in, after all the hard work you went through to rebuild your life. Why? Why now? Is this because of last night at the restaurant? I'm sorry that happened. I was out of line. If she makes you happy, then that's really all that matters. I just didn't want to see you get hurt. But now…"

She shakes her head, stands up, and leaves the room sobbing. A few minutes later, Brittany returns.

"Sheesh, I thought they'd never leave," she says, giggling. "Those are some true friends you found there. You know, that's always been one of your most admirable qualities. Besides being a backstabbing brother, you've always had the ability to gather good, loyal friends. It's a shame that they'll have to die with you tonight."

Blowing me a kiss, she leaves the bedroom. Glass shatters beyond the door, followed by the sound of gushing water. "Oops," she says from the hallway.

The front door opens, then shuts. I continue to lie in the bed, unable to move.

A little while later, I begin to smell smoke. I've regained feeling in my hands and can nearly bend all my fingers. I keep bending my fingers repeatedly, faster and faster as the smell of smoke grows stronger. The fire alarm begins beeping. I try kicking my feet, and eventually my right foot responds. Thick black smoke has begun to enter the bedroom, setting off the second smoke alarm on the wall opposite the bed.

I keep kicking and punching, using every ounce of strength in my body and in my soul to break free from this drug-induced stasis she put me in. The same thought keeps playing repeatedly in my mind. *Save Jess. Save Ron. Save your friends.*

Minutes later, I'm able to roll off the bed and crash down onto the ground, crawling on the hardwood floor, using my forearms and elbows. I crawl out of the bedroom and into the hallway where my fears are confirmed: she had smashed the fish tank on the way out. I slide broken pieces glass out of the way on the soaking wet hardwood floor.

Hank is lying on his side with one eye open, staring up at the ceiling. I scoop him up into my hands, caressing his limp body. I begin to cry deeply, and a powerful scream escapes me. I kiss his little cheek.

Holding Hank's body in one hand, I continue to crawl across the floor, staying low to avoid the smoke that's filled my apartment. By the time I reach the kitchen, flames have erupted from the stovetop and are licking the ceiling, spreading onto the wooden counter. Whether the fire was caused due to the macaroni being left on the burner, or if Brittany had done something else to instigate the fire, I'm not sure.

Eventually I reach the front door and grab the doorknob with one hand, trying to turn it, but it won't budge. Until my strength returns, it'll take both hands to twist the doorknob and open the door. Holding Hank in both hands, I give him another kiss.

"Goodbye, little buddy," I say, choking back more tears. "You've been so good to me. I'll see you in another life. I promise."

Placing his little orange body on the ground gently, I grab onto the doorknob with both hands to pull myself up. Holding my breath to avoid inhaling smoke, I open the door and stagger across the hall to Ron's apartment. I pound on the door.

"Ron! Jess!" I shout.

Ron opens the door.

"Oh my God! Simon, are you… bro, your apartment! What the hell's going on?"

"We need to get out of here. Now!" I scream motioning for Ron to follow to the stairwell. "Where's Jess?"

"She went back home, saying she needed to be alone."

Walking fast proves to be a challenge, as my leg muscles are still incredibly weak. The smoke has dissipated by the time we reach the end of the hall, and we step aside as a team of firefighters rush up the stairs, the sound of their boots rumbling down the hall toward my apartment.

"Wait!" I yell after them. One of them, an incredibly young man who looks no older than I, stops and turns around. "In apartment 4B, there's an elderly woman named Gladys Stephens," I continue. "Please get her out of there."

He quickly nods his head and yells after his partners. One of them begins pounding on the door until it opens, and the same young firefighter I spoke with leads her after us down the stairwell.

Slowly, we make our way down the stairs, staying far to the side as another team of firefighters rushes past, heading up. By the time we make it outside, five firetrucks are parked outside in front of the building. Water is being sprayed up at my window; flames are spewing out of the building from my apartment windows as well as Gladys'.

Ron and I walk over to a group of firefighters.

"Excuse me, I need to file a police report," I say to one of the men.

Within minutes, a police cruiser arrives on scene, and I give my verbal account of the situation. I explain everything that happened with Brittany. The police officer arches his eyebrow, but I insist that I'm being serious, and that she's a criminal with psychic abilities. He clicks his pen, places the notepad back in his pocket, and assures me that they'll look into it.

"I left my keys and wallet up in my place," I say while frantically checking all of my pockets. Ron's staring down at the sidewalk. "Look, man, I'm really sorry about last night. Brittany had me in a voodoo spell or something, and I acted like a total jerk to you and Jess."

Ron keeps his gaze down. "You really think I've had the same haircut since ninth grade?" he asks quietly.

"Well, yeah, but so what?"

"You do look like a weirdo, though," he says, looking back up at me and laughing.

"Any other time, I would be laughing right with you. But for right now, we need to get out of here. Please tell me you have your car keys?"

He fishes his keys out of his pocket, flashing a relieved smile.

Chapter 23

Ron drives us to Jess' apartment hoping for a place to stay the night. At first sight when she opens the door, I can tell she's been crying. Her eyes are bloodshot. It takes me a few minutes to calm her down and explain the scene that she witnessed was all set up, thanks to Brittany's wickedness. I wasn't on drugs as she tried to make it look like, and I've never used drugs. This causes her to cry again, and Ron and I have to calm her down. Finally, she takes a step back, letting the two of us inside.

When we enter her apartment, she rushes to her closet and gets to work instantly on making up the couch. She tells Ron and I that one of us will need to sleep on the floor, and I volunteer.

Jess' apartment is very cozy, and roughly about the same size as mine is. As mine *was*, I should say. Her entire apartment is hardwood flooring with Persian rugs under each table. The centerpiece of her apartment, a large dining room table made of dark oak, sits just off of the main walkway. Beyond her dining room is the living room, where Ron and I will be staying for the foreseeable future. Ron makes himself comfortable on the couch and is asleep within minutes. Jess and I go back into her bedroom and shut the door, so as not to wake him. Jess sits at the foot of her bed, and I sit in her office chair which she normally uses for the computer.

"Okay, so let me get this straight," Jess begins, brushing her blond hair out of her face. "She drugs you, takes pictures of you to make it look like you just shot up or something, and stages it to…to what? Slander you? Is that why she had you dressing like that and acting like a total ass?"

"I'm not sure what her endgame is here, Jess. But I don't think she was expecting you two to show up."

"What? Yes, she was. She texted me, asking me to bring Ron over for a double date."

I shake my head, staring at the floor. "So, she wanted you two to see me and think I'd used so that you guys would feel guilty about what happened yesterday at the restaurant…and then what?"

"If you had died in that fire, and my last sight of you was... like that… I don't know what I would've done." Jess shakes her head, then looks back up at me sharply. "For the record, I had nothing to feel guilty about at the restaurant. You were acting like a sick simp with no self-respect. I don't know what poison she was filling your little head with, but you needed to be put back in your place."

I nod my head and look her in the eyes. "I'm sorry. You were right. She had my head twisted around." I take a deep, shaky breath. "She killed Hank. She broke his tank open. Poor little guy. He probably suffered. I hate to think about how he went out like that."

The two of us sit in silence for a few moments, staring down at the floor.

"You know, I never liked her," Jess says. "You were too good for her."

"Thanks, Jess," I say. "But that's not the worst of it. She said she was my brother. From an ancient life, over seventeen thousand years ago. And what she says adds up. When we were at Loretta's shop and I had those visions, the first one was of me in an African tribe. I remember my name, Magdoo. And I had this overwhelming feeling of guilt. He had betrayed his brother, Mubiru. And she said this isn't the first life of mine that she, or he, has ruined. We need to call Loretta, but my phone's back at my place."

"Loretta?" Jess says incredulously. "We need to be calling the police. Brittany committed arson, attempted murder, you name it."

"I filed a police report, but the cop didn't really seem to buy my story."

"They can perform a toxicology report on you and find traces of whatever she injected you with."

"And what if they don't? I would've wasted the police's time and put myself on their radar. I'm a man. I highly doubt they'll even conduct a test."

Jess scoffs. "You're so stubborn. And an idiot. Fine, whatever, I'll call her."

She dials Loretta's phone but gets her voicemail instead and leaves a message. Jess also sends a text but isn't confident in Loretta's ability to use her cellphone properly. Jess and I decide to get some sleep since it's well past midnight and agree that we'll figure this out further in the morning. I remind Jess to wear her Dream Catcher.

When I get to the living room, I put Ron's Dream Catcher on his head. Thankfully, Jess still had the object in her backpack from the camping trip; I had left mine behind in the apartment. Laying down on the rug I try to make myself comfortable.

The mall is filled with Christmas shoppers. Holiday music plays over the speakers, and John clutches his wife's hand as they walk into one of the department stores. In his other hand are three large shopping bags from various other stores. Samantha runs over to the perfume counter, and immediately grabs a bottle and spritzes it onto her wrist. She rubs the liquid into her skin, holding her wrist up to John's nose. He takes a sniff, smiles and nods his head.

"This is the one I want," she says with a triumphant smile. "It's called 'Poison.'"

"Okay, dear," he says dryly. "I'll make sure to buy you some poison for your birthday."

"That's why I love you." She stands up on her tiptoes and kisses him on the cheek.

A loud pop nearby, and John grabs Samantha, bringing her down to the ground. He lays over the top of her. "Stay down!" he whispers.

He looks around and discovers that nobody else is concerned. No mass panic, nobody rushing toward the exits, trampling one another. Instead, a couple of women begin laughing near where the loud noise came from. He peeks his head cautiously over the perfume counter and sees three women standing under a large bouquet of oversized red balloons with the word "sale" proudly displayed in white font.

John helps Samantha up from the ground, and she huffs and puffs as she struggles to stand up.

"Our hero," she says sarcastically, clutching her round belly. "I'm sure she appreciates her daddy's protection."

He shakes his head, placing his hands on his hips. With a somber look to his wife, John kisses her on the top of the head.

"I'm sorry."

"When do those counseling sessions start?" she asks, looking up at him with a concerned look on her face.

"Next week," he says, picking up the shopping bags. "By the way, it's going to be a 'he' not a 'she.'"

He takes her hand back into his, and they continue shopping. Darkness wipes across John's vision, and I'm standing in the pitch-black Void.

Mubiru, taking the form of Brittany, approaches me. Her dark hair can barely be seen in the pitch black. She's wearing a black leather jacket with jeans and her arms are crossed over her chest, head slightly tilted.

"It'll take more than that to take me out," I say, stepping closer to her.

"Oh, believe me. If I wanted you dead, you'd be dead. My fun with you is just beginning. My intentions are to thoroughly destroy you. You'll die when I allow it."

She places her hand on my chest and looks up at me; her big brown eyes casting a momentary feeling of doubt into me.

"Just remember that everything that happens next could've all been prevented if you would've simply obeyed. But no, you had to go and try to play the hero again. Your life will never be the same, Simon. Prepare to be tested. I want you to suffer!" she screams abruptly, and pushes me in the chest, sending me plunging down into the empty, bottomless chasm.

I land roughly on my side and look around in confusion. I'm back in Jess' living room. Ron is being lifted off the ground by a large man wearing a black ski mask. Another blow hits my side, and I quickly roll over onto my back to see my old pal, Machete Man, staring down at me. He lifts the machete over his head, and I scramble up, my strength now fully returned, and tackle him around the hips, causing him to drop his weapon. Continuing to drive my legs, I send Machete Man's back through the window in the living room, shattering glass down to the street below. He regains his balance, landing a couple of punches before I have a chance to counter. Crouching low, I tackle him again, driving him down to the ground, and pummel his masked face with my fists repeatedly, rendering him unconscious.

Meanwhile, Ron is being held in an elevated chokehold by Large Man, his feet off the floor. I pick up a nearby glass vase, raise it over my head, and bring it down with all my strength onto the other man's head, spraying shards of glass everywhere.

The man doesn't move an inch. He turns around slowly, keeping one hand firmly pressed against my friend's throat. Ron's legs begin to kick violently, and his eyes roll back in his head. Large Man stares at me through the black ski mask, and grabs for me with his free hand. I reach for his wrist, quickly twist it and hear a loud *crack*. He releases his hold of Ron, clutching his wrist and crying out in pain.

I look down at my hands in amazement. With no combat training, I'm amazed at how effortless and efficient my counterattack was on this man who's nearly twice my size. Ron seizes his throat from behind and drags him down to the ground. I take off the man's ski mask.

"Who are you?" I ask.

He clutches frantically at Ron's hands, unable able to speak. Or breathe, for that matter. I rush over to the machete laying on the floor and return to press the blade against Large Man's throat. Ron lets go of the man who coughs hoarsely, taking several short breaths.

"Check on Jess," I say to Ron, who runs past me. I turn my attention to Large Man, still pressing the blade against the skin of his neck. "Talk."

"We were hired to take you out." Large Man says, still struggling for breath.

"By Brittany, I assume? Or maybe she's using the alias 'X'?"

"I didn't get a name. We don't ask for names of our clients."

Ron emerges from Jess' bedroom. "Simon, you got to see this." I put my hand up in Ron's direction.

"You're the same three that attacked me in the parking lot. Why didn't you kill me then?"

"Our orders were to scare you, not kill you. But out of the blue tonight, we got a call from the client, and they've had a change of heart. They wanted you and your friend Ron taken out. They knew where you two were staying and everything."

"Next time you speak to your client, send them a message from me. Tell them, 'Simon says this isn't over.'"

The man slaps the machete out of my hands. He stands up, brushes past me, and lumbers out of the apartment.

I don't chase after the escaping hit man out of concern for Jess. Ron is still standing in Jess' bedroom doorway, looking worried. When I enter the bedroom, it's empty. She's nowhere to be seen.

Ron and I stare at one another for a few moments.

"What do we do?" Ron asks, his voice shaky.

Neither of us have our cell phones, as we both left them in our apartments during the panic of escaping the fire. Jess' cell phone isn't on her nightstand where she left it; her captor must've taken it with them.

After a brief discussion, Ron agrees to drive back to our building to grab our wallets and cell phones, and I agree to stay behind at the crime scene while he calls the police.

I sit near the front door on the floor, leaving it cracked open for Ron to return. The machete is lying on the floor in front of the fireplace. Its former owner, Machete Man, is lying on the floor as well.

A middle-aged woman appears in the doorway, peeking her head inside. Her eyes open wide when she fully absorbs the scene; me sitting next to an unconscious man, furniture strewn about, and the window broken, the drapes blowing lazily in the breeze.

"Oh my God," she breathes. "I'm calling the cops!"

"No, ma'am, it's not what it looks like!" I say holding my hand up, but it's too late. She's already running down the hall, screaming.

I sigh and relax my muscles, forcing myself to sit still. So still that I can feel blood coursing through my veins. My breathing has begun to slow down, but my heart rate is still elevated from the fight. Chills begin to shake my body to the core, and I hold myself, shivering. Placing my head in my hands, I begin to sob uncontrollably.

Brittany was supposed to be someone I could trust, and someone I loved deeply and admired. Not only did she turn that trust on its head and betray me, but she was also X the entire time. I keep repeating that to myself in my head. *Brittany was X.* And apparently the brother of one of my former lives. He, or I guess "she" now, has a serious axe to grind with me after such a long time. Seventeen thousand years is such a ridiculously long time to vow revenge on someone. I wonder what I did to piss him off so bad. The vision of myself walking back into the cave flashes through my mind, and I remember a feeling of sorrow and guilt, but whatever act of betrayal was done, I don't remember what it was.

And Hank. My poor little buddy. Images flash through my mind of him lying alone and helpless on the hardwood floor, his gills struggling for breath until he eventually succumbs to the cold hands of death. He didn't deserve that.

But now worst of all, Jess has been taken by Brittany's masked thugs, with no witnesses to back up my story besides Ron and he would probably be an unreliable witness in the eyes of the cops. The one cop I spoke with already didn't believe me when I tried to file the initial police report after the fire. Over the past several weeks, as I've become more connected with John, the more my mind has been trained to analyze situations like a police officer.

The more I think about it, from a cop's viewpoint, the more I think this whole scene isn't going to work out well for me. A guy claiming his girlfriend drugged him, then set his apartment on fire, then drives to his friend's house and knocks a man out, breaks her window and the tenant is missing. If I don't go to jail for this, they'll surely think that I've gone insane and will throw me in the loony bin. To top it all off, knowing Marcini's connection with the police, and whatever involvement he and Doug had with Stinson's murder, it becomes clear to me now that I don't want to be involved with the police at all. Perhaps filing a police report was a mistake.

When I was fighting with Large Man, I somehow snapped his wrist. I'm not sure if that was an act of instinct, or something else. Some skill that I had perhaps learned from John, or maybe another life before then. What if I begin to learn skills and languages from my past lives, and they start to emerge slowly over time? And what if that's why Brittany's so crazy? She obviously remembers our relationship as siblings from so long ago; what if she remembers other lives? All of her past lives? That would be enough to drive anybody nuts.

I shake my head. This all sounds so unbelievably insane. The whole belief in reincarnation just seems so unplausible that I would never believe it if someone was telling me this for the first time. Except it's all real, and it's actually happening to me right now. And there's a man behind me, lying unconscious on the floor.

Jess has been kidnapped, and I need to save her. But I can't do that if I'm sitting in a jail cell. Ron would be in as much trouble as me as an accomplice. My breathing starts to quicken again.

I can hear sirens close by, and I approach the broken window, the thin drapes flapping around me. Three cop cars are parked in front of the building with their lights flashing. Cops are exiting the vehicle with their weapons drawn.

The last five years, attempting to rebuild myself from the ground up, keeping a steady job, maintaining good relationships with Jess and Ron, all of it has been set on fire and burned to the ground. Some of it's my own fault, and I accept that. But most of it, I blame Brittany. I've worked so hard to make myself into a better person, into a productive member of society. Through hard work, patience and perseverance, I wanted Doug to accept me, and to be as proud of me as Dad once was. I wanted to be proud of myself. But in the end, none of it even matters now.

Given all that I know, and thinking of all potential outcomes, only one solution comes to my mind now. *Run.*

Chapter 24

With no personal possessions except the clothes on my back, I escape Jess' apartment building, unnoticed by the police. The walk to my old apartment building is roughly two miles, and by the time I show up, five police cars are outside there as well. Ron's car is parked in his usual spot, and as I approach the carport area, making sure to stay low and unseen in the darkened early morning hours, I see a man being led out of the building in handcuffs. Poking my head up for a better view, I see that it's Ron under arrest being taken to one of the squad cars by two officers, one of them reading him his Miranda Rights.

Cursing under my breath, I walk away from the building, keeping out of sight to avoid those cops as well. I scratch my chin, thinking of my next option, or where to go. Mom's house is about fifteen miles away, but it's a pain to get there, if I can even make it there on foot without being spotted by the police.

Brittany's apartment is much closer, and as much as I want to pay her a visit, that'll undoubtedly be a trap. I clinch my fists, anger welling up in my soul as I think of her. She's probably eagerly awaiting my arrival, hoping I come marching up and pound on her apartment door, her goons waiting inside to kill me and feed me to the fishes.

That leaves Loretta as my only remaining option. Which is still a good option. That woman has been in my corner the entire way, and I don't see a reason why she would betray me now. Unless I wronged her in some way in a past life, then I'm totally at a loss.

Sweet Loretta's shop is in a rough part of town. The closer I get, the angrier the streets become. Homeless people are scattered along the empty streets, some of them warming their hands on open flames lit in metal barrels and garbage cans. The temperature has dropped rapidly tonight, and I'm severely underdressed. Remembering my black eyeliner around my eyes and my long black hair in a red bandana, I'm not sure if I'm going to fit in with this crowd of folks, or if I'm making myself an easy target, cruising for a bruising. I take off the bandana, discarding it on the sidewalk.

A man with a long, gray beard walks up to me, his hands outstretched, asking for any spare change. I keep my eyes forward, not making eye contact. A younger woman asks me for a smoke, and I again don't answer, keeping my hands stuffed in my pockets, eyes straight ahead.

Loose papers and trash blow down the street in the direction I'm walking. It's a blustery early morning, and I begin to shiver. Approaching one of the lit barrels, I warm my hands, blowing on them occasionally. Across from me, another young black man approaches the fire, warming his hands as well. He keeps his eyes down, focusing on the fire, concentrating on staying warm. I momentarily glance up at him, seeing that somber, deadpan look upon his young face.

The two of us stand there for several minutes, keeping warm, not saying a word. I begin to think back five years ago, when I was a senior in high school, roughly this kid's age, maybe a bit younger. My girlfriend at the time, Sarah, had just recently broken up with me. There was no reason given, other than she wanted to see someone else. That someone else turned out to be Danny McDuffie, the high school quarterback. He was the Big Man on Campus, and as the B.M.O.C., he must've felt that gave him the right to be the school's bully. He seemed to enjoy shoving me into my locker every chance he got, laughing and high fiving his other intellectually challenged buddies as they walked down the hall together. One day after our breakup, the person he was high fiving after yet another locker shove was none other than Sarah. She looked back, pointing and laughing as my textbooks and papers were strewn about the floor.

For several weeks, I'd become depressed. I was saddened that the girl I liked had gone and turned herself into a bully against me for a reason that was eluding me. Locking myself in my room after school, I would sit and play video games, refusing to come out for dinner. Doug, still with the police force at this time, pounded on my bedroom door one day, commanding me to come out and eat dinner 'like a normal person.'

When I did eventually come out of the bedroom, Doug had grabbed me by the back of my neck, pointing at my chest.

"It's time you started pulling your weight around here," he said to me. "This moping around is a disgrace to this family. Your mom worked hard on dinner and it's time you showed her some respect. It's time you become a man."

After school one day, Danny approached me in the parking lot, thrusting a paper bag into my arms. He asked me to hang onto it for him a couple days, and not to open it.

"Gotta run!" he said, while he literally ran toward his vehicle.

He drove a newer lifted truck, which apparently his dad had bought for him. In my mind, I'd thought that if I did as Danny asked, I'd finally be accepted into his circle of friends, and maybe have another shot with Sarah. I put the paper bag in my backpack, not opening it or peeking inside like he'd asked.

A few more weeks went by. I celebrated my eighteenth birthday with Ron and Jess. Jess' mom had baked a cake and threw me a party at her house, and I blew out the candles, making a birthday wish that would never come true. My birthday was never mentioned at home.

My high school graduation came and went, and I received my diploma in front of a full audience. Except the audience felt empty to me, with Doug and Jill not in attendance.

The paper bag remained in my bedroom, in the top dresser drawer. After I got home one day, Doug greeted me by ramming my head into the drywall of the living room. Jill's protests went unnoticed, as Doug took his belt to me for several minutes. I tried to fight back but was unsuccessful. He was far stronger than me.

Hearing enough of Jill's demands for him to stop, he turned the belt on her, whipping her across the face with the leather. I tackled him from behind, screaming. He immediately outmaneuvered me and struck me several times in the face with his fist, pressing his knee against my chest.

"Stay down!" he yelled and walked over to the dining room table. He came back, throwing the paper bag down on my chest. "After all that your mom and I have given you, just so you can turn around and do this? I want you to get the hell out of this house, and never return. You're a disgrace to me, you're a disgrace to this country, and you're a disappointment to this family."

I stood up, clutching the paper bag. The bottom had been ripped, and inside was a plastic bag full of marijuana.

"Doug, I didn't know what was inside, I swear. Please, just listen to–"

"I don't want to hear another word out of your lying mouth!" Doug screamed and pushed me to the door. "You're an adult now, and since you don't want to act like one here, you can learn to act like one elsewhere."

With only the clothes on my back, I was forcefully thrown out of the house by Doug, landing face first on the front lawn. I could hear Jill inside, screaming uncontrollably. Her screams were quickly silenced.

Too ashamed to ask for anybody's help that night, I walked down to my high school, sleeping on one of the plastic picnic tables in front of the building. The bright morning sun awakened me that morning late in June.

Within the first day, I was incredibly hungry, wishing I could get a warm baked meal from my mom, a meal I knew would be denied. Too embarrassed to ask for money, and in an effort to reduce the amount of energy I was using, I sat still against a brick building for hours, hands at my side.

Two days later, the hunger pains, and the thirst for water, were driving me insane. I began scrounging through dumpsters, feeling elated when I found a half full bottle of water. After taking several eager gulps, I dove back into the dumpster in a desperate search for more nourishment.

Within weeks, my pants were beginning to sag, my last beltloop already proving to be too big for my narrowing hips. I was always a skinny kid growing up, but now I was past the boundaries of skinny. Rib bones could be seen, poking against my skin.

Out of a sense of pride, I refused to go to local homeless shelters for my first month on the streets. Doug's words kept echoing through my mind, and I didn't feel worthy of eating a warm meal; rather that the discarded food left in the trash was all I was good for. As the summer grew warmer, I typically walked around the streets of the city shirtless, tanning easily.

I became my own self-appointed tour guide of the city, seeing areas of town that I'd never been to before. Walking around the base of the Willis Tower, walking under the L Train, looking at the grand reflection in The Bean, strolling around the outside of Wrigley Field, Soldier Field, and all the other sports complexes in the city. I spent that summer memorizing the streets and landmarks.

People would glance at me doubtfully, keeping their eyes straight ahead or down at the ground. Anything to avoid looking at the scraggly, scary looking young man walking shirtless down the sidewalk. Occasionally, people would yell obscenities at me, telling me to get a haircut and take a bath.

"You're gross," a woman said to me while in passing. "Why don't you get a job?"

For a two week stretch, I must've filled out at least a hundred job applications, if not more in all sorts of businesses. Grocery stores, warehouses, gas stations, you name it. I tried and tried to get a job, but as soon as they saw the man handing in the job application, the employee's expression quickly turned sour. More than likely, my application found its way into the infamous 'T' folder. 'T' for trash, that is.

One night, I found an acoustic guitar in a dumpster. Strapping the instrument to my back, I took great care of my newfound possession. For a week in the late summer, I sat alone behind an old brick building, plucking away randomly at the strings, not having a clue of what I was doing, but having fun just the same. An old black man approached me one evening and asked to sit next to me and watch me play. I informed him I have no idea what I'm doing with the instrument, but he's more than welcome to sit with me.

After a few minutes, he asked if he could play as well, and I handed the guitar over to him. With effortless precision, he began playing the guitar so well, better than I could've ever dreamed. He told me his name was Elroy, and he used to play in a small blues band back in the 70's, playing all over the Midwest. His love for the bottle outweighed his love for music, and his family, which is what led him down here on the streets.

"If there was some way that I could go back and change it all, I'd do it in a heartbeat," Elroy said. "There's nothing more important than family."

I informed him of the situation that led me to where I was at, and he shook his head.

"Well, this Doug doesn't sound much like family to me," he said. "Everyone's entitled to their own sets of beliefs and such, but here's what I believe deep down in my soul: We were all put on this planet for a purpose. We're all challenged in certain ways, some more than others; but in the end, it's how you deal with those challenges that makes you who you are."

For the next several weeks, the two of us practiced playing music together. I conceded the acoustic guitar to Elroy, and I played on a makeshift set of drums that we crafted out of materials found in the trash. Eventually, in late September, we took our show public, playing in heavily populated areas of the city with the most foot traffic. We had begun to save up some money throughout the autumn, agreeing to split our earnings evenly. Our hopes were to save up enough so that we could share a small apartment together. Elroy opened a savings account so that we could deposit the money at the end of each night, not having to worry about being robbed while we slept. Some of the money we did spend on buying a tent, as well as coats, hats and gloves to stay warm. Thinking back on it, I would've given anything for one of Mom's knitted scarfs or gloves as winter came.

During the New Year's celebration that year, a group of young men approached the small camp that Elroy and I had built together under the L train. They destroyed our small tent and smashed the guitar against one of the support beams. They kicked holes in my drum set, then ran away laughing into the night.

Elroy wanted to use the remaining money we saved to buy new instruments, so we could keep the show going, and I agreed. Throughout the rest of winter, the two of us kept the music alive, playing in front of small crowds downtown. We had so much fun together, and he taught me to be more positive.

"You were dealt a tough hand, Simon," he said one night as we camped in our tent. "But being angry at the world and wishing ill upon Doug and your mom, it will only make you mean and bitter. Take it from me. When my wife left, I blamed her for years. It built up hatred in my heart. I hated seeing all the rich white folks walking around this town, looking down on me. I hated the bottle in my hands, and I hated the man holding that bottle. But once I learned to let go of the hate, and was able to love myself first and foremost, I was able to spread that love towards others. I can't control what other people do, and the way others see me. All I can control is what *I can* control. You understand?"

I nodded my head, and told him I understood what he was saying, and I'd try to be a better person and learn to respect myself first and foremost.

The next morning, Elroy didn't wake up. The EMTs said he had died peacefully in his sleep. There was no funeral held for him, or a way for others to pay their respects. His last days were spent with me, playing music and trying to survive.

I tried to play my drums solo on the street corners but wasn't able to draw in a big crowd like Elroy did.

One cold, wintry day late in February, Jess and her mom walked by me on the streets. Jess was the first to recognize me, and her mom wrapped me in a hug.

"Jill told me what Doug did to you," Jess' mom said. "She's been worried sick about you. Please, come and stay with us. We have a spare bedroom. We can help until you find a job and another place to stay."

I accepted her offer to come live with them.

As I stand in front of the barrel of fire now, warming my hands with the other young man, I briefly look up at him, hoping that somewhere out there, there's a family that loves him. I hope that he can learn to forgive and love himself, if that's what he's going through, the way I've tried to do for myself.

Chapter 25

I wait outside Sweet Loretta's shop until sunlight creeps up from the east. Eagerly pacing back and forth in front of the building until mid-morning, I eventually give up, deciding that she must not be coming into work today.

The rest of the morning, I meander through the downtown streets, exploring areas that five years ago I had wandered, places that I had once called home. The dumpster where I had found the acoustic guitar, the spot under the L train where Elroy and I had camped and been robbed. Sunshine warms the streets, and myself, as I make my way across town.

Needing to rest my tired feet, I walk inside the lobby of the Willis Tower and sit down on a plush sofa. The building, formerly known as the Sears Tower, was the world's tallest building for twenty-five years. Businessmen walk through the lobby area, glancing over at me with a look of disdain on their faces. While they're probably not the exact same people, they're the same type of people that frequent the Lowland Woods, using my caged range picker as target practice, high fiving one another when they strike the motorized cart.

The expressions on their faces when they look at me match the same feelings I have inside when I look at them. Sure, some of them probably worked hard to get to this point. But I would wager it's a small percentage of them. Most of these men already had a head start in life, with a paid ahead education provided to them, a pair of parents who both cared for them until they were able to land their dream jobs, working for other older businessmen with the same background. It's a cruel cycle, and I know I'll never be able to fit into their exclusive clubs, and for one simple reason only; I don't come from a family of money.

Elroy's voice creeps back into my head, advising me that even these men will have their own trials and tribulations in life. As right as he might be, I would trade my problems for theirs in a heartbeat. At least they have families who care for them. At least they don't have to worry about where their next meal is going to come from. They have a warm bed at night, and they have money, which in turn gives them power to bend and control the system to their will.

A snarl seeps onto my face as one of the men walk past me in a dark suit and tie, carrying a leatherbound briefcase. He quickly looks away, startled by the young man sitting in the lobby staring him down like a mad dog. *Go on, go run to your colleagues and tell them that a scary homeless man is hanging out in the lobby of the building you work at.*

What's gotten into me? I shake my head, saddened and disgusted at these negative thoughts that keep bombarding my mind. This isn't who I am. If anything, I sound jealous. I'm green with envy.

Then, it dawns on me. These feelings I've been experiencing lately began shortly after Brittany started working at the golf course. She's the reason this has all happened. My thoughts about buying that car, the negative thoughts about my job as well these envious thoughts about the businessmen. Over the last five years, I've built myself a steady routine, and a sense of structure in life. Lately, it's like that's all gone out the window, and my mind has been taken hostage by another force. It was Brittany all along, messing with me.

Were my feelings towards Jess also a manifestation of Brittany's manipulation? Did I really want to hold Jess' hand that afternoon in the theater, or was that all part of Brittany's master plan to begin destroying me from the inside out, as Loretta had said X would do?

"Excuse me sir, we need you to leave," a deep voice from behind me says.

I twist around on the sofa and see an armed security guard looking down at me with a determined look on his face.

"I'm just resting my feet for a minute," I say. "I'll be out of here soon."

"Now!" he says, raising his voice.

I stand up, look at him for a moment, then walk toward the doors. He follows me until I'm outside, back onto the noisy, busy streets of downtown. Car horns sound at random, seemingly in annoyance with another person momentarily slowing them down. People are talking into devices connected to their ears, having conversations with people who aren't in front of them. How disconnected we've become as a society.

Thoughts of Brittany rush into my head. Her betrayal and treachery has left me angry and bitter, and I feel like I have no other choice but to deal with the situation personally. I can't wait around for Loretta to show back up at her shop while Jess is missing. Time is running short. I decide to take matters into my own hands and walk to Lowland Woods Golf Course. Brittany will more than likely be working today, as if nothing happened. If anybody knows where Jess has been taken to, Brittany will have the answers.

And as luck would have it, she's the first person I see when I walk through the front door.

"Simon!" she says, her voice set in her sweet, high-pitched tone. "We didn't think you were going to make it in today. I'll call Steve and let him know you're here."

She flashes me a quick smile and picks up the phone. I reach over the counter and put my finger on the hook switch, holding it there while staring at her.

"You two-faced manipulative witch," I say, keeping my voice down so as not to attract too much attention. "Where's Jess?"

"She's safe, for now." A smirk spreads across her face.

"Stop with the games!" I say, my voice level rising. A group of businessmen, just finishing their round of golf for the day and likely heading back to their office, glance over at the counter but keep walking.

"Sir, if you're unhappy with the service provided today, you can always fill out a survey on our website." Brittany keeps her chipper attitude going.

"Enough!" I yell. More people stop their conversations and are looking at us now. "What did you do with Jess? Tell me!"

"Sir, I'm not understanding w-what you–"

I slam my hand on the table. "I swear, I'll jump over this counter and strangle you where you sit!"

Several customers come over now, attempting to drag me away from the counter. Lyle, the old security guard, approaches me as well, grabbing me by my shirt collar. He pages on his walkie-talkie, and a few moments later Steve emerges from the hallway which leads to his office.

"Simon, there you are," Steve says, sounding relieved. "Please, follow me."

Lyle grabs me under the arm and together we follow Steve into his spacious office. The walls, covered in dark mahogany, make the room appear cozy and comfortable. A model sailboat is displayed in a glass case behind Steve's high backed leather chair. He takes his seat, and Lyle forces me to sit in the low wooden chair on the other side of the desk, while he stands behind me, arms crossed over his chest.

Steve folds his hands together and places them on the table, staring at me intently. "I'm very disappointed in you. I just gave you an official warning not that long ago for tardiness, and you had promised me this wouldn't happen again. Now you show up, nearly three in the afternoon, not in proper attire, and you begin to threaten my staff. Brittany's one of my best employees. After everything I've done for you…" he shakes his head. "Please, tell me why I shouldn't fire you?"

"Because I know your real name isn't Steve," I say. "Your name is Tony Alvarez. And in 1985, you faked your own death."

Steve sighs and leans back in his chair. A look of defeat appears on his face, and he's staring past my head, even beyond Lyle. Then he focuses his attention back on me. "That's insane," he mutters. "You're... you don't know what you're talking about."

"Steve, I need your help," I say, leaning forward. "Please, listen to me carefully. Brittany isn't who she says she is. I know about your history with Marcini's crew. I don't know if you got mixed up with the wrong people, or what your past was. But a good man lost his life investigating your murder. He was a police officer who got in over his head trying to track down your killer. Only, he didn't know that your death was staged. There are pieces to the puzzle that I'm missing here. Please, Steve, help me figure out what happened. How did you fake your death? And why?"

Lyle clears his throat behind me, and Steve looks up at him, deep in thought. Then he looks back down at me. "I think I see what's going on here. You're sick. You need help. Brittany told me about–"

"She's lying to you!"

Steve opens his desk drawer and pulls out a photograph, placing it down on the desk and turning it around so I can see it clearly. I'm lying on my back, darkened eyes staring blankly ahead, with a needle sticking out of my arm. She did a great job of taking this picture, setting the stage to make me look that way. In her own way, she's a terrific artist.

"Oh, Jesus, that picture was faked!" I say impatiently. "Brittany injected me with some kind of a toxin or something that paralyzed me. She put that needle and that band around my arm to make me look like a freaking junkie. I've never done drugs. C'mon Steve, you know me!"

He takes a deep breath, shaking his head solemnly. "I know a place in town that you can go. They'll take good care of you and get you clean. Your career here at Lowland Woods is over, but that doesn't mean your life has to be. Let me help you one last time."

"No! You're not listening to me! She burned down my apartment, man! She killed Hank! Then she sent some goons after Ron and me, and they kidnapped Jess. You remember Ron and Jess, right?" I take several deep breaths, trying desperately to regain my composure. "And now my two-faced stepdad is in on it, I don't know how, but I'll find out! And so is William Marcini. Your past is the key to solving this whole case, I just know it. I don't know how, but I'll find out! And she can enter your dreams! Be careful what you dream, she'll make them so real you'll wake up thinking it actually happened. She claims to be my brother in a past life from over seventeen thousand years ago. And…wait, Steve, where are you going?"

Steve has gotten up from his chair and makes his way around the desk, walking to the side of the room and behind me. I turn around in the chair to see where he's going, and Lyle steps aside. Steve opens the two large mahogany doors complete with brass handles. In walk two incredibly large men wearing white cotton shirts and white pants. In between them is Angela holding her notepad. She's wearing a pair of glasses, a tight green blazer and dark dress slacks. Her hair is done up in a tight bun with a pair of chopsticks.

"Simon," she says, placing the notepad down to her side and outstretching her other hand. "Please, come with us. We can help you."

"I'm fine, Angela," I say annoyed, standing up to face her. "Please, you have to listen to me."

"Grab him," she says to the two heavily muscled brutes beside her.

I quickly stand up and bull rush the first one, bumping him off balance. He staggers back into Angela, knocking her down as she shrieks. I run back around the large desk, holding the back of the leather chair. Steve's standing next to Lyle, a hand over his mouth. The second large brute chases me around the desk. He moves to the left, and I move to the right. I continue to mirror his movements, staying on the far side of the large desk, the sailboat model at my back.

"Steve, I know what I said sounds crazy, but you have to believe me," I say urgently. "Please, I need your help." He remains silent and looks down at the ground. "I know that you know I'm telling the truth. The rest of it probably sounds nuts, but I need your help. I need to know who helped you escape Marcini's gang. I need to know who killed Officer John Stinson."

"I don't know who killed him," he says tentatively. "But I bet I know who hired his killer. The same man that helped me disappear."

The beast of a man rushes around the desk, and I sprint around to the other side. Steve is standing right next to me.

"Who?" I ask, desperation coming through my voice.

A jolt of electricity hits my neck, sending me down to the floor instantly. As I lie there looking up at the ceiling, Angela comes into view, a taser in one hand. She looks away from me. "Be gentle with him."

A large pair of hands grab the back of my shoulders and hoist me up. A tight straitjacket is quickly fitted over my head, restricting my arms. My legs are also placed in a pair of tight metal cuffs. I'm being dragged out of the room backwards, my feet sliding across the smooth floor in front of me. They take me out through the back door into the parking lot and both men lift me up, tossing me into the back of a van like a sack of potatoes. Angela climbs in, and squats next to me. The last sight I see before the back doors of the van shut is Steve standing there at the back door, a look of concern spread across his face.

"Sleepy time," Angela says.

I try to talk, but I'm not able to say anything as I feel a sharp prick on the side of my neck. My eyes immediately close.

The blackness of the Void surrounds me, and I know that I'm asleep. But I'm not able to dream of John. Not able to connect the dots. There are so many more questions I have for Steve. I know he was about to tell me what I needed to know. I was so close to this nightmare ending.

Brittany appears in front of me, the blackness of the Void dissipating around her body.

"You've been a naughty, naughty boy," she says jeeringly, pressing her hand on my chest. I grab her wrist, and hold it in front of me, between us.

"You're the one that should be in the back of this van, not me." I say between clinched teeth. "How are you doing this, anyway? Are you in the bathroom, in some sort of a trance?" She snickers. "This isn't funny. Tell me where Jess is."

"Not so fast," she says, yanking her wrist free of my grasp. "You'll see your precious Jess again, in due time. But not until you do something for me first."

"What?"

"You need to solve the mystery," she says, crossing her arms over her chest. "Who killed John Stinson? You tell me who his killer was, and Jess is set free."

"I've been trying to solve this mystery for weeks now," I say. "Can't you at least tell me if she's okay? That she's safe?"

"She's fine," Brittany says, bored. "You're so cute when you're concerned. I think you two were made for one another."

"There's something that's been bugging me about this whole thing," I say. "John Stinson wasn't a bad person. He was a good cop and a loyal husband. Why did he go along with Mike's plan to kidnap Chavez?" Brittany shrugs her shoulders, arms still crossed. "Then, an idea came to me. You're able to enter people's dreams and convince them to do things that they normally wouldn't do in the real world. I bet that you entered Stinson's dreams and made him kidnap Chavez, locking him in that shipping container like so kind of an animal."

She doesn't answer, merely pressing her tongue against the inside of her cheek. We stare at each other in silence. The Void is so quiet, I can hear my own heart beating.

"That confirms my suspicions. Thank you. Somehow, you were close to John. You weren't Mike, Doug or Samantha. You were someone that died a few years before I did." I continue to stare at her, and she shifts her weight from side to side uncomfortably. "Tell me something, Brittany. When you first came to me in the form of X, after I had viewed several of my past lives with Loretta, you were a different man in those visions. Was that one of your past lives, too?"

"Yes," she says, walking away. "I was once Julius Caesar."

I BRIEFLY CLOSE my eyes, and when I open them, I'm lying down in a small room, with white padding lining the walls. The floor is soft and white. I look down, and notice that my arms are crossed, restricted by a straitjacket. I'm inside a padded cell. My worst nightmare has finally come true.

I struggle to my feet, and shuffle to the door with a narrow slit in it, just about four feet off the floor.

"Help!" I yell. "Help me! Please somebody, help me!"

Moments later, I'm led out of the padded cell by the same two large men who dragged me out of Steve's office. They're dressed as orderlies now, and they take me into another room, this one made entirely of concrete. A small metal table in the middle of the room with two chairs sitting on opposite sides. I'm shoved into the nearest chair, and the orderlies leave. I sit in silence for several minutes.

The door opens with a loud buzz, and a large balding man enters the room with a file folder tucked under one arm. Scooting back the other chair on the concrete floor, he takes a seat opposite me at the table. Opening the folder, he looks up and stares blankly at me. Inside the folder are several Polaroid photos. One of them is the same one that Brittany took of me last night. Apparently, she distributed copies of this to everyone in town. I bet my mom has one too. How wonderful.

"Mr. Verner, I'm Detective Erickson. Do you recognize this woman?"

He places down a picture of Brittany. "Yes, that's Brittany. She's – she was my girlfriend. Now ex-girlfriend."

"I see," he says, clicking his pen and writing in a notepad. "And how about this individual?"

He slides another picture across the table. It's a picture of Machete Man, presumably an older picture; his hair is longer, and he appears to be much healthier. Without his mask on, he looks like any regular Joe on the street, nothing special.

"Yes," I say, and clear my throat. "I don't know his real name, but I call him Machete Man. He's assaulted me twice now. My mistake for not filing a police report either time."

"His name is Sean Boykins, and we've been searching for him for quite some time now, Mr. Verner. If you see this individual again, you are to contact the police."

"Look, I know that this is probably the part where I'm supposed to ask for a lawyer, or whatever. I'm just going to be straight up honest with you."

I proceed to tell him the events that have unfolded, from Brittany injecting me with the mysterious substance that temporarily paralyzed me, to my apartment catching on fire. I told him about Hank, to the attack and

Sean being there with two other men, kidnapping Jess. I spare no details and tell him everything I can remember. I don't tell him about the reincarnation situation, as I want him to take me seriously.

"So, Detective Erickson, that's the truth, and I'm being completely honest with you. I'm tired. I'm worried about Jess. I have no idea where she is. Please, help me find her."

Detective Erickson continues to take notes, eventually looking up at me. "Your story checks out," he says. "We picked up Ronald Douglas at his apartment gathering each of your phones and wallets, just as you said. This is an ongoing investigation. I do have one last question in regards to the fire. It appears that you were cooking before the fire started, is that right?"

"Yeah, but I don't see how my macaroni being left on the stovetop could've started that huge fire."

"Grease fires spread quite quickly, Mr. Verner. Unfortunately, your elderly neighbor, Ms. Stephens, now has no place to live."

"Cut the guilt trip, Detective," I say defensively. "I bet Brittany started that fire somehow. I had zero grease on those countertops, they were spotless."

The Detective abruptly closes his folder. "I appreciate your time."

He stands up and heads for the exit.

"Wait, where are you going?" I ask. "Am I free to go?"

"I'm afraid that's not for me to decide. Per the Cook County Department of Corrections, you've been ordered to stay in confinement until the trained and licensed medical staff here determines you're no longer a risk to the public."

"I'm not a risk to the public!" I shout, struggling against my straitjacket. "Brittany's the risk to the public! She's an arsonist, and a liar! You can't trust a word she says, Detective!"

"Unfortunately, that's as much as I'm at liberty to discuss. Good day, Mr. Verner."

With that, the door shuts, and I'm left alone in the room.

"Get back here!" I shout. "I'm not a risk to the public! I'm the only sane one left! Get me out of here!"

Chapter 26

The alarm clock on the nightstand reads 2:30 AM. John reaches over to turn off the alarm. After he finishes buttoning up his uniform shirt, he leans over the queen size mattress they share, and gives Samantha a kiss on the cheek. She's sound asleep, and murmurs something that he can't make out. He smiles softly to himself, comforted with the thought that his wife is dreaming peacefully in their warm bed. They've both worked hard to put a roof over their heads, and to sleep in a warm home in the quiet suburbs. And with a baby on the way, John understands that their lives are about to change forever. He's prepared for the changes to come… or at least he thinks he is. Mike tells him every day what a big responsibility it is to be a father. That the hierarchy of things he finds important in his life will shift. How he'll start thinking more about his family's health and safety more than his own.

It's a lot to take in, but John's prepared himself for this. He's always wanted to be a father, and with the recent announcement that the child is going to be a boy, he's started a list of things he's going to teach his son. Throwing a football, catching a baseball, learning to shoot a gun, watching the Bears, showing his son his favorite movies; the list goes on and on. When his son enters this world, he's going to show him all that life has to offer. All that *he* has to offer. A tear forms in his eye, and he wipes it away as he's still standing over the bed, looking down at Samantha sleeping.

He goes into the kitchen and pours himself a bowl of cereal, drowns it in milk, and sits at the kitchen table. On the table is a bag from one of the stores at the mall. The clock on the oven reads 3:45. He quickly eats the cereal, slurps up the rest of the milk and puts the bowl in the sink quietly. Next, he fastens his utility belt, holster, gun and badge, then lastly grabs the bag before going out the back door. After he finishes locking the door, he hears their neighbor's dog barking. It's a pleasantly warm early morning, and a brief glimpse of daylight is beginning to wash over the darkened night sky from the east.

His car, a maroon sedan, sits in the garage. He had bought it brand new off the lot last year and drove it to Samantha's elementary school to surprise her. She had squealed with excitement, giving John a hug, eager to go for a test drive. John often thinks about how the drive home from the hospital with Ryan in the backseat will go. He's played the scenario in his head over and over. The car is a two-door, so he'll make sure to have the car seat already positioned in the backseat, strapped in and ready for Ryan's maiden voyage.

The car starts up smoothly, and he backs out of the driveway, beginning his drive down to the police station. Traffic is light this early in the morning, which he's always appreciated working this shift.

John walks into the police station, giving his routine morning welcome to Karen at the front desk as he makes his way back toward the locker room where he hangs up his coat and finishes getting ready for his day serving and protecting the fine citizens of Chicago. He takes the item out of the bag he brought from home, and stuffs it into the inside of his coat pocket before anybody sees, then quickly tosses the bag inside his locker and shuts it.

In the hallway, he walks directly toward the office of Sergeant Doug Lewis. He's had a rocky relationship over the years working under him, and he could never quite put his finger on the man. He found Doug to be very unpredictable; somewhat of a loose cannon that could fly off the handle at any given moment, then turn around and be your best friend and buy you a drink the next.

John knocks on Doug's door. No answer. He tries the doorknob, and to his relief, it turns, and the door opens. The office is small, especially for the Sergeant of the precinct. He flicks the light switch next to the door and the fluorescent lights turn on, forcing John to blink a few times to regain his eyesight. He walks around the small desk and pulls out the item from the inside pocket of his coat; a battery-operated tape recorder with a fresh tape ready to go. The first two drawers that John tries to pull open are locked, and John curses softly. He looks around the office and sees a tin Chicago Bears bucket placed on top of a filing cabinet. Bingo. He presses the record button on the tape recorder, and gently places it into the bucket. Briskly walking out of the office, he makes sure to switch off the overhead lights and shut the door behind him.

Doug walks past him in the hallway, and John exchanges morning greetings with him before heading to the cafeteria to make a fresh batch of morning coffee, something he's always done for the entire precinct, earning him popularity among the other officers. They love being able to start their shift off right, with a cup of John's Joe.

Mike greets John, and they sit in the cafeteria for a few moments, exchanging stories about their wives. Being five years John's elder, Mike always gives John some fatherly advice about being a husband, and now a father. It's a morning routine that John has found quite endearing, and he appreciates this time he gets to spend with his partner and best friend.

For the next several hours, the two of them patrol the streets. At eleven, they stop for lunch at a local dive bar called Moretti's and enjoy a nice meal together. The restaurant has always been run down, with questionable characters in and around the building. One day, John hopes that they can revitalize this neighborhood, particularly this restaurant, as he feels it does have some potential to be special. The final few hours of their shift involves the two of them investigating a serious vehicle collision on Interstate 90, where two young women were badly injured. The car had caught on fire, and John selflessly pulled one of the women from the blazing wreckage. The young blond had only received minor burns to her wrist, but she'll survive. Thanks to Officer Stinson.

On the drive back to the station, Mike reminds John that was how Doug's wife Connie had died a couple years ago, in a car accident not too far down the interstate from where they just were. John remembers the days and weeks after the accident happened, and how Doug's demeanor really changed for the worse and became more unpredictable. He felt sorry for the man, but at the same time he was tired of Doug, or 'Sergeant Lewis,' as he insisted on being called now, constantly busting his chops over the smallest things. Day after day, Doug would question him over recent reports, not even giving him the opportunity to explain what happened. John decided it best just to stay away from the man. As far as he knew, Doug didn't have any kids, but if he did, John felt sorry for them. He's an incredibly difficult man to please.

In the locker room after they both change their clothes, Mike invites John out for a beer. John respectfully declines, saying he needs to get back to his wife. Mike says he understands, and the two men go their separate ways.

John knocks on Sergeant Lewis' office door, and again there's no answer. Doug must've already gone home for the night. The lights are still on in the office when he enters, and he heads directly for the Bears tin bucket and grabs the tape recorder inside. The tape appears to have run out a few hours ago. He places the recorder back into his coat pocket and leaves the office, switching off the light again and quietly shutting the door. John turns around to walk down the hall, and almost plows into Doug.

"What're you up to, Stinson?"

John chuckles softly. "Oh hey, Sergeant Lewis, there you are. I was just looking for you in your office, but you weren't in there."

Doug eyes him curiously. "Was there something you needed?"

"Not anymore. It's not important, sir."

"Good. Then would you mind?"

John steps aside to let Doug walk past.

"Actually, Sergeant Lewis, I did have a question. Do you have any updates regarding that detective job opening?"

Doug keeps his hand on the doorknob and turns to look at John. "Yes, Stinson, I do."

John stands there anxiously, clasping his hands together.

"As a matter of fact, you've been on this case for over eight months now. I find your lack of progress into finding even one suspect for Tony Alvarez's killer to be…disappointing. I'm taking you off the case and will assign you a new one. Hopefully you'll have better luck with this new assignment. You'll be hearing from me soon." Doug steps inside his office and slams the door.

John sighs and leaves the police station to go home. He looks forward to spending the evening with his wife.

Forty-five minutes later, John opens the backdoor, and is greeted with the smell of homemade hashbrowns, maple sausage and pancakes. He gives Samantha a big kiss, and she wraps her arms around his neck. They eat dinner together at the kitchen table, then retire to the living room to watch their lineup of evening TV shows on the loveseat. Samantha leans her head on John's shoulder, and he has his arm around her torso.

"Oh, I think he just kicked," she says, giggling. She places his hand on her stomach. "There, did you feel that?"

"I did," he says, smiling.

Just when he thinks that he's caught up with reality, and the realization that his wife is eight months pregnant with their first son, he's always somehow caught off guard again. It's as if he constantly needs to pinch himself to be reminded that he's not dreaming, that this is really happening. He's going to be a father. A new life will enter this world, and they'll be responsible to care for him, nurture him, and watch him grow and develop into his own unique person.

Later, as Samantha is taking her evening shower, John takes the tape recorder down to the basement into his study and listens to it. He fast forwards the tape for thirty minutes before sound can finally be heard through the small speaker. Prepared with notepad and pencil, he listens intently. Random shuffling can be heard. Doug will randomly curse, followed a loud slam on wood, presumably a stack of files on his desk. Then, a loud knocking sound on the office door.

"Come in," Doug says.

The door shuts, and some more shuffling can be heard. Then, a voice that John knows all too well speaks: "I spoke with Daniels last night. He's in. Forty thousand. He wouldn't budge."

"Good."

"I'm going to meet up with him soon to make the exchange. The hit will go down shortly after. He'll plan the details."

"That's fine," Doug says. "Once Stinson is out of the picture, the job is yours. Bill Marcini is paying me a lot to make sure this whole problem just goes away."

"What about Alvarez?"

"Bill and I got that covered," Doug says. "You're going to give him a whole new identity and let him take control of a golf course."

"I bet Marcini will be happy."

"You have no idea," Doug says. "It's all he talks about now. He wants Stinson buried for killing Chavez. It's a good thing you came to me when you did."

"Stinson deserves what's coming to him. He's dug his own grave. Once he's dead, you and I will be able to breathe again. Not to mention we'll both be a lot richer."

"And I'll get what I've always wanted out of this deal," Doug says. "You better make sure this goes through successfully, Mike."

"I won't let you down, boss." Mike says. "You deserve to be happy. Samantha will be a perfect wife for you. Plus, you'll get to be a father like you always wanted. I'm sure she'll take some convincing, but she'll come around to the idea of having you for a husband. She'll need someone to comfort her soon when her husband's gone."

The recording goes quiet, and John stares at the spinning tape for the next several minutes in complete silence. Samantha yells down from the top of the stairs, asking John if he's coming to bed. He tells her he'll be there in a moment. Slowly, he stands up, hands shaking, and presses stop on the tape recorder. He opens the safe, removes the shoebox, and adds this second tape recorder to the box.

Later that night as John lays in bed with his wife, he stares up at the ceiling, unable to sleep.

Chapter 27

The padded cell feels smaller than it did yesterday. And smaller than the day before that. Time has moved by so slowly, yet it feels like I just got here. It's been nearly three weeks since I was thrown in the back of the van at the golf course by Angela and her steroid-infused goons. They still won't let me out of this straitjacket, claiming that I'm a risk to others and to myself. I haven't been able to make a phone call. I have no idea if Jess is alive or dead. The same goes for Ron. Brittany hasn't visited my dreams since the first day I got here.

My dreams have only been about John. One time he took down a gang. Another time he got into a shootout with a local drug cartel and won singlehandedly. The number of heroic actions by John Stinson has me in awe of this man. I'm envious of the life he lived, and I continuously remind myself that it was a life that *I* lived. But on the other hand, I can't take the credit for the deeds and bravery that man showed.

I feel as though my life up until this point has been wasted. Other than picking up golf balls, I contribute very little to this civilization. Yes, I have a job, or at least I did have a job before this mess, and I've stayed out of trouble for these last five years. But compared to John, I'm a nobody. Just another mouth to feed in an ocean of open mouths, taking and taking and giving little back to the machine we call society.

I wish that Brittany would come back to my dreams so I can tell her I solved the mystery of John's death. Mostly so that Jess can be saved, although I have no idea how or when that'll happen. I can't trust Brittany, so her even following through on the promise to release Jess after I've solved the mystery seems unlikely.

Speaking of the mystery, I'm still disappointed that it was Mike who hired the thug to kill John. It takes me days to remember who "Daniels" is, and then one night, during one of my dreams with John, Daniels' name pops up again. Travis Daniels, originally from Louisville, moved to Chicago with his pregnant wife in the winter of 1984. He's the same man that John and Mike took down in the domestic violence call, when John had shot out the sliding glass door and rescued the wife and toddler, earning them the award that night at the banquet. Daniels was apparently released on his own recognizance a few months after his arrest, which explains my initial dream when John and Mike were talking about their frustration with the judicial system.

Now it's beginning to make sense. Doug used his pull in the system to convince the judge, or someone, to let Daniels out early in order to hire him to kill John. A show of ruthless power by Doug. All so that he could be with Samantha and have a child of his own to raise. Instead, he had to settle for my mom and me.

I hate the man. Once I'm out of here, and after I save Jess, he'll be my next order of business. I doubt the man has a shred of guilt, considering he left boxes of evidence pertaining to Stinson's murder in his own garage, so convinced that he was above the law and nobody would suspect him of foul play. That man's actions are unconscionable. He and Mike should be in here, not me.

If my dreams of John had only occurred in order, I feel like this would've all made so much more sense, and I could've put the pieces together faster. The time I've had in this white padded cell has really done me a lot of good. The peace and quiet, the three weeks off work at the golf course. I'm basically on vacation. I start laughing. Angela thinks she's punishing me by locking me away in here, but in reality, she's rewarding me by allowing my mind to be at ease.

The door to my cell opens with a soft metallic squeak and in walks one of Angela's muscular guards, his thick arms crossed over his chest. A bandage strip is stuck over the bridge of his black and blue nose.

"Verner. Lunch time. Then Angela and Dr. Scholinsky want to see you. Follow me."

I roll over on my side, and struggle to my feet. It's amazing how difficult it is to stand up without using your arms, but I've gotten much better at it. The guard still stands at the door with his arms crossed, not wanting to help me up. One of the first times he had tried to get me to my feet, I whipped my head back and got him pretty good in the nose. His temper got the best of him, and he beat me for a solid three minutes until someone came in to get him off of me. I haven't gotten to see myself in the mirror in the past few weeks, but I would imagine I look worse than he does.

Approaching the doorway, the guard steps back to let me pass. I shuffle down the hallway, barefoot. The cold flooring feels refreshing on my feet. At least twenty doors line the hallway on each side. Yelling can be heard in the distance and gets louder as we pass one of the doors. A woman sobbing can be heard behind another door. Narrow slats about four feet off the floor are next to each door, intended for food trays and medications.

I keep telling the staff here that I'm fine, that I'm not a danger to society, and I'd never hurt myself because my only goal is to save Jess. They don't listen to me. Instead, they nod their heads and look away.

The cafeteria is nearly empty, as most of the residents have either gone back to their rooms, or outside to play. They don't allow me outside. These daily trips to the cafeteria are the only times I've been allowed to leave the cell. The guard places his arm underneath mine as we approach the area where food is served. The lunch lady, Ruth, as her name tag claims, looks half asleep, as usual. Her hair is in a fishnet apparatus, and she has reusable latex gloves on her hands.

The guard takes the tray, since my arms are restricted, and holds it out for Ruth as she slaps a pile of slop in one corner, and another pile of goop in the other. I smile at her, but she shakes her head and goes back into the kitchen area.

Together, the guard and I walk to an empty table and take our seats. Same routine, different day. He grabs the spoon, scoops up some of the slop, and holds it in front of my face. I open wide, allowing the spoon to enter my mouth. I take the food, chew it around some, and swallow. It tastes like stale refried beans mixed with cat food. I take each bite slowly and thank the guard when we're done.

Due to my good behavior so far on today's journey, I'm given one hour of play time in the game room. We walk past a woman playing with a baby doll at one of the tables, and she clutches it tightly to her chest as we walk past. At the next table, an older man is talking to himself while playing checkers. He moves the pieces for both colors and starts cursing louder as each move progresses. Finally, I find the game I want to play. Connect 4.

I invite the guard to play with me, and he accepts. He undoes the straps holding my arms together, and I stretch my arms back. This is only the second time my arms have been released during my stay at the asylum, and the feeling of freedom is refreshing. As we play the game, I apologize twice for what I did to his nose and assure him I hold no hard feelings for the severe beating he's given me. The blood in my urine has eased up some over the last couple days. His only response is a rough grunt. I respond by winning the first match.

For the next hour we sit there and play the game. He doesn't say a word, and it appears he's using his entire brain power on defeating me. Which he does, from time to time, but overall, I win the majority of the matches. Once the hour has ended, he secures my arms back in their restricted positions, and leads me down another hallway toward Dr. Scholinsky's office. When we arrive, the good doctor is sitting behind his desk, with Angela sitting across from him.

"Peter, thank you for bringing Mr. Verner in. Will you be so kind as to shut the door?" Dr. Scholinsky asks.

I take a seat next to Angela, not even acknowledging her presence. My eyes remain focused on the ground, trying to decipher the unique pattern on the floor.

"Simon, you're nearing your three-week anniversary here. How are things going for you?"

I look the doctor in the eye. "Wonderful, thank you. I feel like you and the entire staff here have done a tremendous job of treating me. In fact, I believe that I'm ready to go home now."

"That's what we're here to talk about," the doctor says. "Doctor Garry and I have been looking over your history, and your interactions here on site. I feel that you've definitely made some progress."

"You're absolutely right," I say, flashing a bright smile. "'I once was lost, but now I'm found'. I don't know how I could've possibly done it without you. Without the both of you." I look over at Angela, and she immediately shifts her focus away from me and to the floor. "Angela, you've been such a tremendous help to me over the years. Thank you *so* much."

"Hmm, well perhaps I was mistaken," the doctor says. "Your lack of sincerity and condescending attitude here counters what I initially thought. Perhaps you're not ready to leave my care just yet."

I look at him, and all I can see is red. "You narcissistic, two-faced coward," I say, my voice remaining calm. My body, however, is beginning to tremble. "I was drugged, my apartment burned, my fish killed, my best friend kidnapped. You won't even allow me to call my other friend who could be anywhere. And after all of that, you want me to… what? Beg for your forgiveness? How about you cut the act and tell me what it's going to take for me to get out of here. Give me a phone call like I've asked you for every day, and I'll consider not pressing charges against the both of you quacks for maltreatment and false imprisonment!"

My voice is now nearly to a shout. The doctor tries to speak, but I keep going, focusing my attention on Angela. "I trusted you, you know that? I respected you, and you betrayed me. Not as bad as how Brittany betrayed me, mind you. And not as bad as how Mike betrayed me in my past life."

Dr. Scholinsky attempts to interject, but I ignore him and keep going, keeping my attention on Angela. "You were one of the few anchors I had in my life. A life that I was trying to rebuild from ashes after Doug burned my life to the ground, and now you're doing the same thing. The both of you should be ashamed of yourselves. But you won't be. Oh, no. You'll go home tonight in your fancy cars to your big mansions out in some gated community, and you'll have dinner with those you care about, and you'll wake up tomorrow and come back here and do it all over again, because that's your self-appointed purpose. While I'm trapped here like some kind of animal!"

Spittle begins to fly off my lips, and I stand up. "I didn't ask for this! Do you hear me? I didn't ask to have some psychotic woman seduce me, to make me think that I was a somebody for once, only to stab me in the back and toss me aside like a piece of filth like everyone else in my life has. The only two people that have stuck by my side are out there somewhere in serious danger, and I can't do anything about it because you two keep playing God with me. I've worked hard to build my life, and Brittany burned it all down. And you two don't care. You just sit there and keep me here against my will for no reason. I hate the both of you!"

I sit back down, adrenaline shooting through my veins, and begin to laugh uncontrollably. Dr. Scholinsky just stares at me. Angela takes out her notepad and begins writing notes frantically. After a few moments, my laughing eases.

"Angela, do you remember the car accident you had in April 1986?" I ask intently.

She looks at me, a look of confusion on her face.

"Don't worry, I'll jog your memory. You had taken your dad's convertible out for a drive with your friend Kimberly. You were driving too fast on

Interstate 90, and you lost control and crashed into a guardrail. The car caught on fire, and a local police officer pulled up just in time to get the two of you safely out. Your friend suffered some burn injuries, on her right leg, but your right wrist… Angela, why don't you show the kind doctor and I your right wrist?"

Ignoring Dr. Scholinsky's protests, Angela slowly slides the sleeve of her right arm up, revealing severe burn marks on her wrist, scars still not fully healed after all these years, and likely never will be.

"You were much luckier, but this scar here corroborates my story." I look at Dr. Scholinsky. "Do you want to know how I knew she had a burn mark on her right wrist, doctor?"

"Presumably because you were her patient for several years, you probably saw–"

"Wrong answer, Doc. This woman always wears long sleeves. I thought for a while that maybe she was just ultra-modest. You know, maybe she didn't want to share too much skin with us men walking around in the world. But, no, that's not it. You should see how she dresses her legs on Friday nights. It's because she's hiding this scar. Not for the discomfort of others looking at it, but because of the discomfort it brings her every time *she* looks at it. Her guilt, of driving her daddy's car without permission, of her friend nearly being burned alive, haunts her 'til this day. But let me go back to my first question, how did I know that was there? Because I've never seen that mark before in this life."

Angela remains quiet, her eyes focused on her lap. Dr. Scholinsky shrugs his shoulders. "I don't know, Mr. Verner. Tell me, how did you know about that scar?"

"Because I was there," I say, leaning forward. "In my past life, I was the cop that showed up just in time and saved the two girls. I just dreamed about this incident quite recently. It's fresh in my memory, burned into my consciousness, similar to how that scar is forever etched into her skin." I turn to Angela. "The decisions we make have an effect on those around us. Like throwing a rock into a clear lake, our decisions have a ripple effect not only on our current lives, and the current lives of those within our day-to-day sphere, but on our lives that occur *after.* What we do in this life can set up what happens in our next life. And so on. I remember saving your life, Angela. I wish that you could find it within yourself to do the same for me now."

She looks up from the floor toward me, her moist eyes reflecting the glow of the light above. She creases her brow. "You're really Officer John Stinson?"

"Don't give into his nonsense, Dr. Garry," Dr. Scholinsky says dismissively. "The patient is trying to manipulate you based on a wild theory. He had to have seen that scar before."

"Nobody's seen this but me!" she snaps. "I believe him, Todd. And you should too." She takes my hands in hers. "Simon, I'm so sorry. I've made a terrible mistake. I've been having these dreams, incredibly vivid dreams, telling me that you needed to be put somewhere safe for your own protection. A woman came by my house and showed me that terrible picture of you, and she said you're the one that set your apartment on fire. The firefighters can't explain how the fire spread so fast. Their investigation concluded that you set the fire on purpose, potentially out of guilt for being caught using drugs."

"That's all a lie," I say. "I've never done drugs. I would never set my own building on fire. I would've never hurt Hank."

"I know that now. I'm so sorry."

She stands up, turning her attention to the doctor. She says nothing to him and picks up her briefcase, stomping out of the office.

Dr. Scholinsky looks at her as she's leaving, then turns his attention back to me. "Peter, take Verner back to his cell!"

Chapter 28

He folds the letter and stuffs it gently into a plain white envelope, then places the envelope into the same shoebox containing the two cassette tapes he's saving for evidence. Before placing the lid on the top, he clicks his pen and writes "Ryan" on the envelope. He puts the shoebox back in the safe, leaving it on a wooden table inside the newly finished panic room. After some time, he finishes sealing the room in, keeping the safe and what sits inside of it out of sight. When the time's right, he'll be back to grab what he needs.

He smiles softly, then sighs. He's not sure how to proceed with what he knows about Doug and Mike. He knows he'll need more evidence in order to present a solid case before burning his entire career down to the ground. John's been very careful around Mike while on patrol. All trust he's had in the man has obviously been shattered and lost. In the man he once viewed as a brother, all he sees now is a snake and a coward.

Today is the day that he wants to confront Mike about the recording and ask why he would conspire with Doug and Marcini's crew to take him out. The audacity of the man. He knows that John has a baby on the way. But he ultimately knows the timing isn't right. If he lets the cat out of the bag now, he'll never see the endgame to their scheme. So, in the meantime, he'll stay quiet.

When he arrives at the police station, he heads immediately for his locker and prepares for the night out. John's the only person who knows where the tape recorder is. He's the only one who even knows of its existence. As far as Doug and Mike know, he's still oblivious to their cruel intentions, and he means to keep it that way. For now.

However, when Mike passes by in the hallway, John has a change of heart. Mike informs John that Doug wants to see him. He can't let these two get away with this. He has to protect his wife and unborn son, and he'll do anything to make sure no harm comes to them. It's his responsibility to be there for them. Protecting them also means protecting himself. The thought of Samantha being a single mother breaks John's heart. He walks to Doug's office, not greeting anybody in the hallway as he would normally do. The smile he usually wears has been replaced by a stern expression. His brow is lowered, his strides purposeful and direct.

He opens Doug's office door without knocking and walks in, sending the door crashing into the wall. Doug sits back in his chair, crossing his arms.

"Well, come on in, Stinson."

John slams the door behind him and approaches the desk with no intention of sitting down. "You backstabbing coward. You've been in bed with Marcini this entire time? The Alvarez case was… what? A ruse?"

Doug sighs. "John, please take a seat, will ya?"

"No! I want answers, and I want them now!"

"Fine. You want the truth?" Doug sighs deeply. "Tony Alvarez was never killed. The whole thing was staged so that he could escape Marcini's crew and avoid embarrassing his brother, the mayor. He wanted some sort of... freedom, so he faked his own death in order to start a new life of his own. Mike thought it would be a good idea to have you spinning your wheels with Chavez while he swoops in and takes the detective promotion from you. Mike wanted to make you look foolish."

"Wow, you must really think I'm stupid," John says, laughing. "I know for a fact that you're involved in this. And you still are. Marcini wants me taken out, and you're going along with it so you can get a kickback. And you want to get with my wife after I'm dead, too? You sick bastard. I know that you had Daniels released early. I know that you and Mike hired him to take me down. The only thing I'm not sure of is when and where."

Doug sighs, crossing his arms. "What've you been smoking, Stinson? Listen, I know you've been under a lot of pressure, with a baby on the way and everything, but–"

"You'll stop talking if you know what's good for you." John puts his hands on his hips and begins pacing. "You encouraged me to begin investigating the murder, and there was no murder. You and Mike had me chasing my tail to make me look like a damn fool. But I went along with Mike's plan to break Chavez for information he never had, leading to me accidentally killing the man. For the longest time, I wanted Chavez dead. But once he was gone, it was like I could finally see clearly again. Once the fog went away and I saw the result of my actions, I wanted to quit. I wanted to turn myself in! I'm better than that!"

John continues pacing, taking a moment to regain his composure. "So, Mike tells you, then you tell Marcini and the next thing you know, you're giving into that crazy son of a bitch and his wild demands." John stops pacing, and points at Doug. "How much is Marcini paying you to have me hit?"

"You're talking nonsense, John!"

"Quit the bullshit, Doug! Tell me now, or so help me God, I'll go to the media about this. I have a tape recording with you and Mike talking. I have all the evidence I need."

Doug stays silent for a moment, then stands up. "Fine, you want to put all your cards on the table? Chavez was Marcini's right hand man, and nobody's seen him for weeks. You go the media about this, and you'll be up for murder yourself."

"I will burn you and this entire department down. And don't think for one second that I won't."

"You do that, and Samantha will be raising your baby boy by herself," Doug says. "But don't worry, I'll make a great father in your absence."

John reaches over the desk with both arms and grabs Doug by his shirt collar, lifting his body off the ground. Doug's shoes drag across the desk, sliding papers onto the floor and knocking over a coffee cup, spilling coffee everywhere. An uncontrollable rage has taken over John; a temper that he usually can keep in check, now unleashed with a vengeance. Still having a strong grip on Doug's shirt collar, he carries him to the wall and slams him against it, knocking his head against the drywall, eliciting a loud thud.

"You threaten my family, and I'll kill you myself."

"I'm not the one threatening you," Doug's voice begins to crack. "I'm trying to help you here. You're like family. I wouldn't want anything to happen to you or Samantha. I'm talking about Marcini. If this gets to the news, he'll have Samantha killed."

John lifts Doug higher against the wall, now looking up at him. "Then what do you suggest I do here? I'll do *anything* to protect them! You and Mike already ordered my hit. Call it off!"

"I can't! It's too late!"

The office door opens. John looks over his shoulder to see Mike walking in. Mike takes a brief step back, arching an eyebrow at the scene in front of him. Nonetheless, he resumes with what he needs to say.

"John, I need you to come with me. We have a reported kidnapping of a toddler. All units are needed out on the streets as soon as possible."

John continues to look at Mike, then turns his attention back to Doug. "This isn't over." He releases his grip on his shirt collar, and Doug drops to the ground, landing on his side. John steps over him and follows Mike out into the hallway. Together they sprint to their patrol car, and John gets into the driver's seat.

As they exit the parking lot and start driving down the road, Mike advises John that the suspected kidnapper was last seen in a black 1976 sports car, heading east on 63rd in the West Englewood neighborhood. Behind the wheel of the cruiser, John keeps the sirens and lights off, as they don't want the suspects to be spooked and flee or harm the child.

It's 2:45 AM, and the colorful nightlife of Chicago is on full display in the early morning hours. Street walkers can be seen manning their usual posts, scattering at the sight of the cruiser. Neon signs from gun shops, tattoo parlors, and corner dive bars light up the night. The glow creates a reflection off the wet streets and sidewalks. It's been raining steadily for the past few hours, with no sign of it letting up anytime soon.

Mike attempts to start conversations several times to no avail. He asks John why he had Doug in a chokehold, but John remains silent. After multiple failed attempts to get through to his partner, Mike eventually gives up and stays silent, focusing his attention by looking for the vehicle in question. Several false reports come over the police radio. The two officers continue to look earnestly around for the suspect's described vehicle. That type of vehicle on the streets at this time of night should stick out like a sore thumb, John thinks to himself.

After several minutes, the vehicle in question suddenly turns in front of them at a stoplight. They follow from a safe distance. Mike continues to give unwarranted advice on how to catch the criminals. John remains quiet, his attention squarely on the vehicle in front of them.

For fifteen minutes they follow the suspect's vehicle into a very rough neighborhood until it finally speeds up and takes a sharp left turn, followed by a sharp right. John stays within eyesight of the suspect's vehicle and reaches for the radio. Mike slaps his hand aggressively, knocking the radio out of his hand, then bends over to pick it up himself.

"What the hell are you doing?" John demands.

"I could ask you the same thing. What, are you trying to get that kid killed? We call this in, and we'll get twenty cops surrounding them. No, we do this my way. We follow them quietly and rescue the kid ourselves."

"We need to get some backup, Mike. Don't be stupid about this. Call it in."

"No. We do this my way."

John growls and shakes his head. Suddenly, the suspect's vehicle slams on its brakes and a man wearing a black ski mask jumps out of the backseat, sprinting west down a side street. John stops the car, and Mike gets out, pursuing him on foot. The driver of the vehicle peels out and takes off, and John follows, driving past Mike.

One block later, the car stops again, and the driver gets out of the car, running into a tall, rundown looking apartment building. John gets out and pursues on foot.

Oh no, this is it. This is the night he dies.

FLASH

John running up the stairwell.

FLASH

The masked men confronting John in the apartment.

FLASH

John's gun being knocked out of his hands by the door opening.

FLASH

The view of the lit-up basketball court below. Raining outside. The pistol being pressed against his head.

BANG

John opens his eyes, looking around the apartment in a state of shock and confusion. He's still alive. The bullet has intentionally missed John entirely, taking out the window behind him, shattering glass down below.

The man with John's pistol quickly removes his ski mask, unveiling his face. It's Travis Daniels.

"Surprised to see me, John?" Travis says, laughing. "You thought you did a good service having me locked up, didn't ya? Well, surprise! By the way, I was able to get my little boy back from that bitch of an ex-wife. All thanks to your partner, Mike. Man, he's a resourceful bastard."

John, still groggy from being pistol whipped, blinks several times, and

Travis' face sharpens in focus. Behind him, the other man removes his mask. William Marcini.

"You don't have to do this." John says. "I know I screwed up. I've made mistakes, and I'm prepared to own up to what I've done. But it's not too late for you, Travis. Put down the gun and get out of here. Be better than this. Go be a father to your boy."

Travis looks down at the ground for a moment, shaking his head. "It's too late for me. I'm in the thick of it now."

"Just end it already, Travis," Marcini says, annoyed. "He tortured and killed Chavez. He took someone I loved from me. Waste him, and you'll take Chavez's spot in my crew. Let's dump Stinson's sorry ass in the lake before the sun comes up."

"You got it boss."

Daniels points the gun at John's head and pulls the trigger. With that single action, he ends John Stinson's life.

My soul leaves John's body, evaporating from his corpse, and enters another realm of consciousness where no living being has ever been, or will ever be. Traversing past all relative space, through endless colors, through no colors. My soul enters alternate dimensions, parallel universes, beyond all plains of existence, and past the end of known time itself. It travels to the limitless expanse of the bright Beyond, where it spends the next several years until it's born again as Simon Verner.

Darkness

I'm back in my own body, standing in the Void. Brittany walks up to me slowly, a despicable swagger to her stride, still wearing her black leather jacket.

"Looks like that was the end of the line for dear ol' John," Brittany says, frowning. "Too bad. I feel like he had so much more to live for. Tall, dark and handsome. Beautiful wife. Baby on the way. A man in a position of power, to serve and protect one of America's finest cities." She puts her index finger up to her lips. "Let me ask you something, Simon. Do you feel that what happened to John was justified?"

"No. Not at all. He was tricked by men he trusted. He was killed by a madman. Doug, Mike, Marcini, Chavez, Daniels. All of them. They were all morally bankrupt with no purpose."

"What word would you use to describe the way John felt about Mike?"

"Brother," I say. "Mike was like a brother to me. To John, I mean."

"Very good. And what word would you use to describe Mike's actions towards John?"

"Betrayal."

"That's right," Brittany says, walking around behind me. "John was betrayed by his brother. He was stabbed in the back." She pokes her finger roughly into my spine, causing me to jump forward. She steps back in front of me, looking up into my eyes. "Just like me. I was your brother, Magdoo. And you stabbed me in the back."

"I sort of figured that's where you were going with this, Brittany."

"Mubiru. My name is Mubiru."

Brittany's features begin to change, and in the blink of an eye, she's now an incredibly thin black male, ribs poking against his skin and piercings in his lips and ears. I look down and realize I share the same features. Placing my hands on my face, I feel piercings as well. In each of our right hands appear long wooden staffs. A flame of yellow is coming off the end of his staff, while mine has the vibrant color of blue. We're also each wearing a thin piece of cloth around our narrow waists.

Memories begin to wash over me. Memories of my brother, Mubiru. I remember that my name is Magdoo. I remember my father, *our* father, is the tribal Chief Zooberi. I remember our mom, who passed away several seasons ago from unknown causes. The Tribe is starving. The watering hole is drying up. New worries invade my mind, fears of how to survive and protect the Tribe. Danger around every corner. Every howl in the night. The constant strife. The day to day worries of where their next meal will come from. Shelter. Protection. Food. Water. Every breath I take is a blessing from Mwari.

The darkness of the Void begins to wash away into a dry and barren landscape. The wind in the air is warm and carries with it the cackles of nearby hyenas. A herd of them has been circling our camp for days, sensing the weakness and fragility of this tribe of humans.

"I prayed to Mwari to bless us with bountiful hunts," Mubiru says. "We needed water, and a cure for the disease that had been plaguing the Tribe. While I did that, you sat by and did *nothing.* For my selfless acts to save us all, you turned around and tattled on me to the Elders, and to Father, and had me banished!"

"Brother, what you did, praying at the altar of Mwari, that was forbidden!" I say, stepping back from Mubiru. Magdoo's memories are beginning to flood my thoughts. "You knew that, but you did it anyway. You didn't do it for the Tribe, you did it for recognition. Most of all, you did it for Father's approval."

"That's a lie!" Mubiru turns on his heel and throws the staff into dry shrubbery in the distance. "You were always rewarded with Father's approval. Every single time, you were the one that was rewarded, while I was the one that was shunned!"

"Because you were lazy, Brother." I say. "You were always looking for shortcuts. You couldn't stand putting in the hard work that was required. Every day was a battle for survival, and you floated by, twiddling your thumbs while it was *my* thumbs that were bleeding from hard work in the name of the Tribe. If you're looking for an apology, Brother, you've come to the wrong place. I don't regret what I did, turning you into the Elders for sacrilegious practices. I do, however, regret not being a better teacher to you."

"You liar!" Mubiru screams, kicking the hot sand with his bare feet. "How many lifetimes have we spent together, how many times have we met like this, for you to take my knowledge and generosity and spit it back in my face? How many?"

"Brother, if you call these acts throughout our lives to be acts of generosity, then you truly have learned nothing."

He steps toward me, a blank expression on his face. Slowly, his features begin to change. Claw marks appear on his shoulders and torso, bite marks appear on his face, his skin and flesh ripping away and exposing raw tendons and bones beneath. One of his eyeballs begins to droop out of his head, until it detaches and falls to the dirt.

"Look at what you did to me, Brother," he says. "You did this to me. This is all your fault. You did this to me. *You did this to me.*"

The desert landscape fades away until everything around us turns back into a deep, dark black. Mubiru's form shifts back into Brittany instantly, her beautiful features restored without any bite marks, both eyeballs in her head. I'm back in my body as well.

"Do you want to see Jess?" she asks quietly.

I swallow and nod my head. "More than anything."

"Then I'll need you to bring me whatever evidence you have that proves Mike and Doug were involved in John's murder."

"I don't have any evidence."

Brittany frowns. "You're lying again. I've been watching. I know about the tape recorder in the safe down in his basement. Bring it to me."

"Well, I would if I could. But in case you haven't noticed, I'm locked away in an insane asylum. How do you expect me to get the evidence and bring it to you? Wherever it is you are."

"I'm sure you'll find a way," she says, patting my shoulder. "If you want to see Jess again, you'll have to figure this one out, won't you?"

"How do I know she's still alive?"

"I guess you'll just have to trust me." Brittany smiles, then vanishes.

I remain in the Void, waiting to wake up, when another shape appears out of the darkness. She steps closer to me until I can barely begin to make out her features.

"I've missed you, child."

Loretta continues to walk forward until she's directly in front of me, appearing exactly how I remembered her. She's wearing a puffy red blouse and jeans. A blue bandana is tied around her hair, which is blown up into a great afro. Her smile is contagious, and a feeling of relief washes over me. After weeks of being in this facility, to finally see not just a face I recognize, but the face of someone I can trust, brings me pure joy.

"Loretta," I say thankfully, and give her a hug.

"Oh, Simon, we've all missed you so much. Ron's worried sick about you."

"Please tell him where I am. Chicago Mental Health Center. They won't let me leave, Loretta. It's like I'm being kept prisoner. I don't know why! My apartment burned down after Brittany drugged me, and then–"

"I know, child, I know." Loretta says reassuringly, gently placing her hand on my arm. "Don't work yourself up about it. You were framed. The police believe you're the one that set fire to the apartment, then broke into Jess' apartment and shattered her window. You're even the prime suspect of her disappearance, but they have no leads. Ron has a plan to get you out. Just stay patient. You'll see him and Jess again soon."

"Has Ron said anything to my mom, so she knows where I am?"

"I don't know," she says. "Listen, I don't have long. My presence here is already dangerous enough as it is. I just wanted to let you know that we're thinking of you, and we're doing everything we can. I've been working on something special to help you defeat X when you see him again."

"That's great," I say. "But X turned out to be Brittany. Apparently, she was my brother a long, long time ago, in a country far away." I chuckle, and Loretta stares at me, arching up one eyebrow.

"Interesting. I'll need to meditate further on that." Loretta taps her finger to her chin, her eyes looking down at the ground in deep thought. After a moment, she focuses her attention back to me. "I've constructed a device, which I'll refer to as a 'Soul Orb.' The purpose of it is to transfer X's soul out their body. Out of Brittany's body, that is. Her soul will stay trapped in the Orb until I find some way to dispose of it properly." She looks down at the ground, her chin in her hand. "Why? Why could I not sense what body Mubiru was in?"

"Well, I don't think you even met her," I say. "So, let me get this straight. Once I find her, I'm supposed to hold the Soul Bulb up to her and, what, just suck her soul out of her?"

"Orb. Soul Orb. And yes, child. Essentially that's the purpose of it."

"Cool!" I say, smiling.

She shakes her head. "Stripping a human body of its soul is no easy process. It's highly dangerous and has only been done successfully once. Or so I hear."

"How do you come up with these inventions, Loretta?"

She begins to step away from me. "A story for another time. In the meantime, sit tight and we'll get you out of there."

Loretta slowly disappears, and I awake from the dream.

Chapter 29

Alone in solitude, I wait for hours. Hours turn into days. Days turn into weeks. The daily routine is the same. I wake up, wait for breakfast to arrive, and eat breakfast by myself, the food being spoon fed to me by one of the guards. Then, I wait for another few hours until I can walk out with a guard for lunch. Occasionally, there's a meeting with Dr. Scholinsky. Angela has not returned after our last meeting. I hope she's doing alright.

After an hour of playing a board game by myself, I sit and watch TV for a couple more hours until I'm led back to my cell. Where I sit. And wait. And wait. And wait.

The white of my padded cell slowly changes into a milky shade of pale, transforming into elongated puffy clouds shaped like elephants and acrobats, floating gracefully over my head, under my feet, all around until I'm floating with the clouds, prancing with the elephants, laughing with the acrobats, soaring peacefully through a sky of ivory and vanilla. I'm the star of my own show, a hero in my own tale. Everyone loves me. They cheer at whatever performance they see me put on, laugh at whatever joke I tell, cry at my sad stories. Giraffes, gorillas, kangaroos, zebras, tigers all sit around the crackling campfire while I tell them a scary story, filled with horrible treachery, extreme danger, and the hero (myself, of course.) Gasping in fright when something scary happens, they hold each other when the hero is betrayed, they clap when the story is finished, then they get up to leave. I beg them to stay, to come back.

Elroy appears in front of me, holding the guitar, playing the same chords he used to play when we performed together.

"So, Simon, what're you in for?" he asks, giving me a toothless grin.

"I'm not supposed to be here, Elroy. I've been set up by my ex. This whole nightmare just never ends."

"That's what happens when you get stuck with a woman," Elroy says, laughing.

"You want to know the weirdest thing?" I say, leaning forward and whispering to him. "She used to be my brother from a long time ago."

I start laughing, unable to stop, pounding on the table. Laughter turns to screaming and the room around me spinning.

"Would you shut up?" I look over at the man sitting at the table next to mine. He's scowling furiously, shaking his fist. "Shut up!"

I look down at the table, scattered with animal crackers. The box is sitting at the back of the table, not moving. None of the animals are moving. They're all just sitting there, staring at me. Laughing at me. They weren't laughing at my story; they were laughing at me all along.

"Shut up!" I yell at the animal crackers, swiping my arm across the table, sending half of them to their deaths on the cream-colored floor. "All of you! Knock it off!"

The two large men who brought me to this jungle enter the game room, walking toward me with a purpose.

"Shut up!" the other man yells at me. "Get him!"

"You shut up!" I point at him. "You're just like the rest of them! You just want to lock me away while you steal my girl!"

We each stand up and approach one another, swinging our fists. The other man is uncoordinated and misses, flailing at air. A prickling sensation on my neck. My fist also hits nothing but air, and an extreme feeling of fatigue setting in. I'm sprawled out on my stomach now, sniffing the dirty linoleum floor.

One of the men rolls me over onto my back, only it's not a man I'm looking at now, it's Brittany. She still has the syringe in her hands, and squeezes down on the plunger, sending a clear liquid squirting through the needle.

"There's more where that came from," she says, smiling. She erupts into a cackle of evil laughter. "Jess never liked you, you know that? You have the sexual maturity of a teenage boy. You never loved yourself, so you turned to drugs. You're an embarrassment, Simon. Doug was right about you all along."

"You're the devil!" I scream, reaching my arms up, trying to claw at her. "I'm going to suck your soul out, you witch! You demon! Ahh!"

She sprouts an extra set of arms from her side, and all four hands reach down and seize me, grabbing me roughly by the shirt collar. She drags me along the floor back to my cell, continuing to laugh and taunt me.

"Simon says 'I'm crazy.' Simon is where he should've always been. Simon is worthless. Simon is a coward. Simon–"

"You'll regret this!" I scream, beginning to lose my voice. "You don't know who you're messing with! I'm never going to forget this, Brittany! I'll never going to forgive you! I don't care if you're my brother! You're the devil!"

I'm thrown down on the floor, and the restrictive straitjacket is being forced around my torso by her four arms. A second head, which looks like Ron's, sprouts from her shoulders, a look of pity on his face.

"Just stay calm, Simon," he says, keeping his voice down. "Stay calm, I'm here."

"Like you care!" I scream at her second head. Ron's head. "You just wanted Jess for yourself! I'm the one that loved her! I always loved her, but I was too scared to do anything about it because I didn't want to lose you two as friends. Well, I should've told her how I felt. I should've told her what an amazing person she is, and how beautiful she is. That no matter what, I would always be there for her, like she was for me. She's the only one, and I mean the *only* one who has always stuck by me through everything, even since we were kids."

I take a deep breath, then continue, speaking slower. "I saw the way you would look at her. The way you looked at her when I was drugged and paralyzed in my bed, you saw your opportunity and you seized it. You animal! You thought 'hey, Simon's no longer in the picture, so now's my chance.'"

I'm crying now, my words coming out slurred, my eyes getting heavier. Ron's head, still next to Brittany's laughing face, continues to look at me sadly.

"Well, I hope you two are happy together!" I continue. "You two are the only people I've ever cared about, so I'll support you guys. But I'll always wish… I'll always…"

Darkness.

The next morning, I wake up. And I repeat the same routine. And the next day. And the next day.

My dreams have even turned into a monotonous repeat of the same thing. I'm swimming around the fish tank with Hank, eating lunch. He tells me stories of his time in the military, of his ex, of how the country has done him wrong. I sit and listen, awaiting the opportunity to tell him of my hardships, to tell him of my struggles. A time which never comes. He just talks and talks, telling me the same old stories a hundred times, never giving me an opportunity. I look around the fish tank, wishing there was a way out of here, a way to swim out and dive into another tank with less talkative and emotionally unsettled fish. I thought Hank was my friend, and maybe he is, but this one-sided relationship has become too much for me. I need to escape. I need a way out.

One night, as I'm sitting in my cell, staring blankly ahead at the wall, the door to the cell buzzes, and an orderly steps in. I stand up, arms bound, in an act that has become much easier for me now. I'm cognizant of my surroundings now, the feeling in my legs and arms have returned to full strength. I hadn't even realized that my strength was gone until the pain returned.

The orderly stands in front of me, the pale light from the hallway illuminating him from behind. I blink several times to adjust my eyesight, my mind not believing what my eyes see.

"Let's get out of here." Ron says.

Chapter 30

As soon as Ron finishes undoing the straps of my straitjacket, I slide my arms out and wrap them around him in a hug. He hugs me in return.

"There, there," he says, patting my shoulder. "I'm here, buddy. But we need to move."

"How are you even here right now?" I ask, holding him at arm's length. "How did you know where to find me?"

"I'll explain everything later. But we seriously have to move. Now."

I follow Ron out of the cell, shaking the jacket off. The faint glow from the cafeteria ahead casts a dim light on the checkered hallway floor. Screams of terror and cries of pain can be heard from the other patients in their rooms. One of the women weeps loudly in her room, while another man bangs his head against the shatterproof glass of his room.

Ron swipes a badge across a black piece of plastic next to the door at the end of the hall, and the red light turns green. The door opens into the cafeteria, and we walk at a breakneck pace through that room into the game room beyond. There are so many questions I want to ask him, but I know I need to keep my mouth shut until we get out of this place, this prison for the mentally ill… not for me.

We enter another large room; one I haven't been in before. A muted TV is on in one corner, and several couches are situated throughout the room. A refrigerator is humming rhythmically against the nearest wall next to a nice, clean countertop and a sink. After a few moments, it finally dawns on me that this must be the employee break room. My mind is still fuzzy and slow to process my surroundings, like I've just awoken from a long afternoon nap.

I follow Ron to the other side of the break room, and he scans his badge again, opening the door to the sight of a large man with a band aid strip on his nose. Peter, the large and disorderly orderly. His eyes open wide after he turns his attention from Ron to me.

"What do you think you're–"

Ron punches Peter in the windpipe with a quick strike, causing the man to stagger back, clutching his throat. I grab a metal food tray from the countertop, brush past Ron, and swing it like a baseball bat as hard as I can against his face, the metal reverberating violently in my hands, sending Peter to the floor.

I look at Ron with a wide smile on my face, to which he raises his eyebrows. We both step over Peter's unconscious body and enter a darkened hallway. The right side of the hall is one long glass window that looks out into the parking lot. It's nighttime outside, and the moon is full. I sprint toward the exit, eagerly waiting for my friend with his magic badge to swipe me to freedom.

Once outside, a rush of relief takes me, knowing that I'm finally out of that prison. Good riddance. The night air is warm, with no clouds in sight. I stand still, craning my neck up to the starry sky above. An airplane is soaring by, the engines throttling down as they make their descent into O'Hare.

Ron leads me to his car. It's a vehicle that he's always been rough on, yet I've always admired.

"Where's my car?" I ask as I climb into the passenger seat, buckling my seatbelt.

Ron starts the engine and aggressively backs up, then peels out, quickly accelerating once we get on the road.

"I had it towed to my buddy's shop," he says. "Don't worry, it's safe. He's got the keys, too."

"Alright, thanks man," I say, peering out the side window at the passing buildings. A group of a half dozen teenagers walk down the sidewalk, laughing, their pants barely staying up.

"How long was I in there?"

"Almost six weeks," Ron says. "Your mom's been worried sick, but I talked to her. I says 'Mrs. Verner, Simon's my best friend and I swear I'll track him down and get him out.' So that's what I did. I got a job working here. Or should I say 'there.' I guess I'm a free agent once again when it comes to employment."

"Thanks, Ron. For everything."

"Don't mention it." Ron's thick Brooklyn accent has never sounded more endearing to me. "You saved my life when your apartment burned down. Anyways, a couple more things I need to say before I forget. First off, that doctor back there's a straight up criminal and I'm going to see that he pays for what he did to you. He was intentionally prescribing you the wrong medicine, making you all loopy and crazy sounding. I've been confiscating your pills and throwing them away, so if you're wondering why the last couple days seem better, that's why. And second, I couldn't find Jess. After we split up back at her place and those guys took her, I got no leads. Nadda. Zilch. So, I've hired Doug as a P.I. of sorts to track her down."

I nod my head and sigh. "Brittany took her."

"That was my first thought. But I got no proof. When I went to her place to confront her about it, she refused to answer the door. And then, get this, she had me trespassed from her building. Doug tried to look into her, but he says that she's clean."

"That's bull!" I say, raising my voice. "She's dirty. She drugged me to–"

"I know, I know. Man, you've been getting drugged a lot lately. What's up with that?"

He playfully punches me in the shoulder. I just shake my head. As much as I want to tell him I don't find that funny, the truth of the matter is I owe Ron my life. He saved me from being in that place for who knows how much longer, so I'll let his humor slide.

"You'll be happy to know I've been wearing that Dream Catcher," Ron says. "I snuck back into my place about a day after I got out of jail, got my things and grabbed it. I've been crashing over at Jimmy's. He's the one that has your car, by the way. And about me getting arrested, what a joke that was. Some lady at Jess' building saw you sittin' there with some unconscious dude and a freakin' machete on the floor, so she went and called the cops. Somehow, they thought I was involved. Go figure. Well, I mean I know I was there and all, but you know what I'm saying."

We pass by another group of teenagers engaging in a brutal looking fight. One of them gets knocked to the ground and the others start kicking him. As much as I want to ask Ron to stop and pull over so we can help, I think twice as police lights flash from behind, causing the boys to scatter like a flock of birds.

"How did you know where I was?" I ask again.

"Oh man, it's the craziest thing. I had a dream one night, that you was locked away in a mental hospital, and I could see the name of the hospital and everything. And when I woke up, I don't know, I like, had this epic epiphany that I needed to get a job there and bust you out or something. And bro, it worked! Like, what are the chances of that? I should be a psychic or something. I could set up a little stand at the carnival and tell people their fortunes and stuff. I'd make a ton of money. I could even set up a phone number for people to call into. Or, how about…"

I keep looking out the window, my long curly hair pressed against the glass. Thankfully, it's now back to its original color and spongy form after weeks locked away. But the status of my hair, or my looks in general, takes a backseat to the real matter at hand. Jess is out there somewhere, has been for weeks now, alone and afraid. *I'll save you, somehow. I'll find some way to get you out of Brittany's clutches.*

Looking over at Ron, I feel nothing but gratitude for him. As he goes on and on about his psychic abilities and how he plans to profit from them, I take a deep breath and smile. For the first time in my life, I feel a true sense of purpose. And I'm not in it alone. I know that I have a partner through the next stage of this adventure, and no matter what happens, I'm relieved to know that he has my back. And I have his, too.

Once Ron is done talking, I speak up, and tell him everything, starting from the beginning. I tell him about my past life as John, about how Brittany was actually my long-lost brother from thousands of years ago in Africa. All of it. As I dive deep into the story, I don't preface the story by telling him "I know this may sound crazy" or "don't laugh." I just go head-on into it. My faith in him is rewarded by a quiet understanding, and I apologize for not telling him sooner. He tells me not to worry about it, and he would've probably done the same thing in my shoes. I don't tell him that I told Jess and not him, as I'm not sure how he would accept that piece of news.

"Ron, I do have one more question. Did I say anything to you, while you were working at the hospital, about how I felt about Jess?"

"Yeah, man you laid it all out there," he says, laughing. "Don't worry, your secret's safe with me."

Great. So that really did happen. I've been having a tough time trying to distinguish what was fact and what was fiction while in Dr. Scholinsky's care. Well, I'll just have to live with that for now.

After another fifteen minutes, Ron pulls into a dirt driveway. He kills the engine, and we step out of the car. I follow him as he goes around the side of a large garage, which is behind an automotive repair shop. He unlocks the side door, and we step in, bright lights immediately turning on and revealing the inside of a large, pristinely clean garage. Several classic cars, all restored and in perfect mint condition, sit idly, waiting for someone to take them for a drive. There's nine cars total in the garage, the last of which has a gray tarp over the top of it. From the outline beneath the tarp, I recognize the car immediately.

"I'll allow you the honors, Simon."

I look at Ron, smiling. I grab the tarp, aggressively yanking it off to reveal the vehicle beneath. My car. A freshly washed, and apparently polished blue sports car. Trumpets sound from above, two swans soar gracefully above the car, and a chorus of angels gracefully sing. At least, that's what I wished would happen.

Ron passes me the keys, and we get in. The engine fires up, and I clap my hands, letting out a joyful shout. He opens the garage door and I slowly pull forward out of the garage.

While Ron puts his car away in the garage, swapping places with mine, I use his cell phone to call Loretta.

"Hello?" she answers, her voice groggy.

"Sorry to call you so early," I say, looking at the car's clock. 1:14 AM. "It's me, Simon. I'm out free and we need your help, if you're up for it."

"Oh, sweet child," she says, chuckling. "It's good to hear your voice in the real world. You two come by my shop. We've got a soul to capture."

Chapter 31

Ron looks around Sweet Loretta's shop in fascination, making sure to keep his hands in his pockets so as not to accidentally break anything. She leads the two of us into the back of her shop, this time to a door on the right side of the hallway. Inside are tall wooden shelves stuffed full of all sorts of miscellaneous items. I also keep my own hands in my pockets as I peer into a glass jar which contains some sort of eyeballs. Whether they're human or not, I can't tell. Next to the jar is a shrunken head, which causes me to shiver.

Loretta grabs a step stool and climbs up, examining items on the top shelf in the far corner of the room. Ron looks at me and raises an eyebrow, hands still firmly planted in his pockets. I shrug my shoulders.

"Found it!" she exclaims, climbing down the ladder with a black box in one hand.

She places the box down on a small desk in the center of the room. Hieroglyphics of some foreign language appear all over the box in the same green lettering that appeared on the table the night that I was sent into a trance. I shake my head in disbelief. It doesn't feel like that long ago, but apparently, it's been several weeks.

The cube is about nine inches long on each side. It's amazing that she was able to bring this item down with her bare hand, but then I remember those long fingers of hers. She must play the guitar incredibly well.

"So, what's with the mystery box?" Ron asks. "Or are we supposed to whack Brittany over the head with it?"

"Nonsense," she says dismissively. "What's inside the cube is what we're after."

Gently, she places both index fingers, and then both ring fingers on certain areas of the box and holds it firmly. A loud click, followed by a gentle whoosh, and she bends her wrists at an angle away from herself. The cube opens, with some steam coming out from inside. Ron and I gather around behind Loretta to take a look. She takes her hands off the side of the box and reaches inside, her hands shaking slightly, and pulls out a round black ball, roughly the size of a baseball.

"This is the Soul Orb," she says calmly. "This is what we'll use to transfer Brittany's soul out of her body, and it'll be stored in here. That soul is ancient. Just as yours is, Simon. Except while you have done mostly good with the lives you've lived, her soul has done the opposite."

"Loretta, I appreciate all of your help," I say. "But I need you to come clean with me here. I know you two have some kind of history. How?"

"In time, child," she says, placing the ball back inside the box.

"No. Now is the time. I want to know everything. How does she know who you are? As a matter of fact, who are you?" I wave my hand around the room. "All of this stuff, how do you have it? What's your story?"

She sighs as she grabs the lid of the box and puts it back on, preventing any more steam from washing over the table. "I'm a lot older than I look," she says. "For all of the lifetimes you've lived, I have lived but only this one."

"Seriously?" Ron asks. "How old are you, exactly?"

"I've lost count, let's just put it that way," she says, chuckling. "I've seen the human race grow from not being able to communicate with one another to not wanting to communicate with each other. I've seen the rise and fall of empires. I've seen men do awful things to one another in the name of religion or land, and I've also seen the good that people are capable of. I was there when you were born for the first time, Simon. Your mother and I were great friends. Or should I call you Magdoo?" A brief smile stretches across her lips. "Throughout most of your lifetimes, not all, but most, we've found our way to one another until Mubiru ultimately bests you with his evil and treachery. I will see to it that this time is different. We must seal him away in this trap once and for all."

I stare at her disbelievingly, in so much shock I forget to blink my eyes. Or breathe, for that matter. Ron's movement toward the door snaps me back to reality.

"This just gets crazier and crazier," Ron mutters as he leaves the room.

I keep looking at Loretta, then nod my head. "So, you were the Oracle?"

"Still am," she says proudly. "Come on, let's get out of here. Jess needs us."

"Wait. So, you knew that X was Mubiru this whole time? Why did you tell me you didn't know who X was, when I first brought him up?"

"Because I didn't know how you'd react," Loretta says, looking away. "I was afraid you'd get…emotional and do something reckless. That's in your nature. I presumed it to be best if you found out on your own."

"Really?" I ask irritably. "How was the way this turned out any better?"

"We can talk about this another time. Jess needs us."

With that, Loretta turns on her heel with the box holding the Soul Orb tucked underneath one arm. Before leaving the room, she picks up a strange looking wooden walking stick propped against the wall with her free hand. One end, presumably the bottom, is sharply pointed and painted a vibrant blue. The other end of the stick, the handle, is much rounder and has intricate designs carved into it. Most prominently of which is the shape of a head with its eyes closed and a tongue sticking out. The serpent of a great long snake wraps its way along the length of the staff, with the head being the face on the handle, and the pointed blue end being its tail.

Ron agrees to sit in the backseat for once, allowing Loretta to ride shotgun. As I start the engine, I'm hoping she'll compliment my car, but she stays silent. How disappointing.

I drive us to John Stinson's old house, and we park out front. The home looks the same, with just a slightly different coat of paint on it, a new mailbox, and a few new bushes in the front yard. Memories begin to flood into my consciousness. I remember buying this house with Samantha, all those years ago. Our first night, sleeping on the floor, wrapped up in a blanket in each other's arms. I remember watching TV with her in the living room, her home baked meals in the kitchen, me mowing the yard. The laughing, the occasional fighting. I remember how happy I was pulling into the driveway after a rough day on patrol. The house always had a certain smell to it that I could never quite put my finger on, but I would know it as soon as it came to me again.

"So, what's our plan?" I ask.

Ron brought a special kit with him in a small handbag. He holds it up for us to see.

"We break in through the back door, using these," he says proudly. "We just need some way to distract the homeowners." He pulls out his cell phone. "Which is why I'm going to call their cell and pretend to be from the gas company, telling them they need to evacuate."

"How did you find their phone numbers?" I ask suspiciously.

"I have my sources," Ron says, then reluctantly adds: "Google."

"That's all fine and dandy, child, but let me take care of this," Loretta says. "Here's a tip for you, Ron. When you have a Michael Jordan on your team, pass him the ball. You two go on ahead now, and don't worry about a thing. I've got you boys covered."

She gives him a wink and a nod, and Ron reluctantly puts his phone back into his pocket. The two of us get out of the car and walk up the driveway along the side of the house, while Loretta stays back in the car. We stay silent as we open a waist high gate to enter the backyard and approach the back patio. The yard looks a lot better than when I was here last. I was never much for landscape architecture, unlike the current homeowners. I'm glad this lot found someone to bring the most potential out of it.

Fancy lightbulbs are strung around the back patio complete with wooden deck, as opposed to the cement patio we used to have. I step over a dog who is sleeping as we approach the back door. Ron quietly pulls out his tool kit and goes to work picking the lock to the back door while I keep an eye on the sleeping dog.

After about two minutes, the lock clicks and Ron turns the door handle successfully, opening the back door. We creep slowly into the house, our shoes making a ton of noise on the hard linoleum flooring of the kitchen. The interior of the home looks almost identical to how I remember, and that old familiar scent comes back to me, causing more memories of our home to come flooding back to me. Samantha and I dancing in the living room. Our first Christmas with our little tree propped up on a milk crate next to the dining room. Tears begin to cloud my vision, and I wipe my eyes with the back of my hand.

Ron looks at me expectantly with his arms out, motioning me to hurry it up. I lead him down into the basement, toward the spot where the safe was kept behind a layer of drywall. The panic room has been infiltrated; a large hole big enough for a grown man to walk through has been punched into the drywall. A sledgehammer sits on the cement floor off to the side. I step through the fresh opening in the drywall, the wooden workbench still where I left it. The safe, however, is missing. A single piece of paper now rests in its place. I scoop up the paper and read it to myself.

Hi sweetheart. It's me, Brittany. If you're reading this note, you're probably wondering what happened to your dear old treasure chest. Well, I'll give you a hint, because I love stringing you along like the good boy you are. Roses are red, violets are blue. Chester takes a nap where there was once a shoe. Come on over and grab it, and it's yours.

Yours Forever,

XOXO Brittany

PS Jess needs you. I don't know how much longer she's got left. Better hurry!

I crumple the letter in my hands, stuffing it into my pocket. Ron follows me back up the stairs and out the back door.

"Did you find what you were looking for?" Loretta asks when we get back into my car.

"Not yet," I say, buckling my seatbelt and starting the engine. "We have another stop to make."

As soon as I start the engine, bright headlights turn on, shining directly into my car from a few houses down. The vehicle, a black Mercedes, approaches slowly, pulling up alongside my car. The driver, an older man with a receding hairline, rolls down their window, motioning for me to do the same.

"Are you Simon?" the man asks.

"Who's asking?"

"Our boss has a message for you," the man says, poking his head out the window. Now in full view, I recognize the man immediately to be an older version of Travis Daniels.

"Get down!" I yell, shifting the car into drive and pressing my foot down on the accelerator.

Bullets strike my car, causing the backseat driver's side window to shatter, glass raining down on Ron cowering in the backseat. I take an immediate left, remembering the streets of my old neighborhood like the back of my hand. Three pairs of headlights appear behind me now, and I push the gas pedal down further, begging the car to give me more speed. After not being driven for several weeks, the car is initially slow to respond, but after a few moments she's ready to hit top gear. We fly down residential streets at a dangerous rate of speed, with my main goal being to get on the interstate toward Brittany's apartment.

Marcini's men stay relatively close behind; I'm not quite able to shake them. Approaching a red light ahead, I ease off the gas, and lay on my horn, warning other drivers to get out of the way as we speed through the intersection. The three cars behind us don't care about the red light, and they fly through the intersection, nearly striking another vehicle.

More gunshots ring out from behind us, and the back glass shatters. Ron leans onto his side in the back seat, holding his head. I weave through traffic, passing cars like they're standing still, bringing back memories of my first day with the car.

Times seemed so much simpler then; I was just excited to own a car of my own. The dreams of John were just beginning to blossom into the nightmare that my life has now become. My supposed feelings for Jess were taking shape, before Brittany came along and seduced me down a darker path of misery.

"Ron, hand me my staff! Quickly!" Loretta shouts.

He hands her the strange looking walking staff, which was down on the floorboard of the back seat. Taking the staff in her left hand, she unbuckles the seatbelt and leans out the passenger side window, holding the object out of the car. Looking over for a moment, I see a blue beam of energy released from the tip of the staff, directed at the nearest vehicle behind us. The car erupts into a ball of flames, sending pieces of the vehicle flying everywhere.

Loretta sits back down in the seat, placing the staff on her lap. She adjusts her poofy hair nonchalantly, as if this is an everyday occurrence. I take a sharp right turn, which leads me to the interstate on-ramp. It's still early in the morning, and traffic on the freeway is light. I weave in between cars, which honk at me as we pass by.

"What was that?" Ron shouts. "Did you just blow up that car back there? What is that thing?"

"This is a weapon from an ancient time," Loretta says calmly. "We will need it in the battle to come."

Glancing in the rearview mirror, I realize the other two cars have seemingly called off their pursuit. Two motorcycles have now taken their place, their single headlights weaving between cars, quickly gaining ground. I push the pedal to the floor, and the engine responds quickly this time. We surpass 100, then 110 miles per hour. My knuckles turn white from tightly clutching the steering wheel.

One of the motorcycles appears next to me on the driver's side door. The rider reaches for his holster on his right hip, where an Uzi is strapped into.

"Roll down your window, Simon!" Loretta yells.

I push down on the power window switch, the glass sliding down and a heavy gust of wind blowing in my face. Loretta's staff enters my vision, momentarily blocking my ability to see the road. Another burst of blue energy shoots from her weapon, and I can feel an intense wave of heat in front of me. The blue energy strikes the rider just as he's reaching for the Uzi, causing his body to vaporize into a wave of yellow sparks. His motorcycle careens into the median, flipping up into the air and crashing down onto the other side of the highway in the path of oncoming traffic.

"Open the sunroof! Now!"

I comply with Loretta's instructions, and within an instant she's standing up, one foot on the passenger seat, the other on the middle console, bringing her weapon up with her. A flash appears in the review mirror and another blue jet strikes the motorcycle behind us, causing the bike to explode, sending the rider tumbling down onto the pavement, rolling countless times at a high rate of speed.

I continue to speed down the interstate and take the next exit.

Chapter 32

I park the car in front of Brittany's high-rise apartment building. Loretta agrees to wait in the car while Ron and I go in to have a look around for the safe in order to protect the Soul Orb. Ron becomes very talkative as we walk into the building, a telltale sign that he's nervous. I assure him that even though he's trespassed, nobody's going to know he's here as long as we remain discreet. We'll get in, grab the box, and get out, nothing more. He agrees and settles down.

We ride up in the elevator to her floor and step off. Ron gets to work picking the lock of her apartment, and we're in within a couple of minutes. I pat him on the back and shut the door. The apartment is pitch black, and the sound of Chester's meow, presumably from his perch on the couch in the living room welcomes us inside. Ron starts looking around in the living room, throwing couch cushions around indiscriminately. I turn on the light in the entryway, and head for her bedroom to start my search.

Her bed is a total mess, with sheets every which way. A pile of clothes lays in one corner of her room, and random undergarments cover the carpeted floor. I open the top drawer of the nightstand with no luck. Her bedroom closet is incredibly disorganized, but there's no sign of what I'm looking for.

The apartment door opens again, and the sound of footsteps can be heard in the entryway. I shuffle quietly to the bedroom door. Three men, all wearing black suits, tiptoe into the apartment. They're all relatively ugly looking guys, not that I'm one to talk per se. I take a peek into the living room just as one of the men discreetly pulls out a small pocketknife, silently approaching Ron as he's still searching the living room, none the wiser.

"Ron, look out!" I yell, causing him to look up and spin to the side just in time before the man lunges at him with the knife.

Another man sprints in my direction, and I open the bedroom door to let him in. As soon as he steps into the bedroom, I slam the door hard against his side, knocking him off balance. I tackle him into the wall, causing the drywall in the bedroom to crack. I punch him in the face several times, then stand up, grab a discarded tennis shoe off the ground, and yank the shoestring out of it. I wrap the shoestring around my right hand and position myself behind him, bringing it over his head and across his throat. Pulling as hard as I can, he begins slapping his hands against my knees, on the carpet, clawing randomly at air. After about a minute, his body goes limp, and I push him off me.

Standing up, I look at my hands in disbelief. I've never done something like that to somebody before. I feel as if I should be shaking, either with adrenaline or with shame, but neither emotion comes to me. Instead, I feel… neutral. Like I'm in a zone, ready to lock on to my next target and eliminate them. Which is exactly what I do.

Stepping out of the bedroom, I see that Ron has done surprisingly well on his own, two on one. The man with the knife is on the ground, blood gushing from his forehead. He wipes his hand over his brow and stares at his hand in a state of shock. The second man is engaged in a fistfight with Ron and they're exchanging blow after blow, like Ali vs. Frazier.

The knife-wielding man sees me walking into the living room and struggles up to his feet. Chester, still lying on the back of the couch, watches the chaos around him with a bored expression on his face, then yawns. Within two steps, I instinctively pick up Chester by his back with one hand, throwing the cat at the man's face like a football. He screams in terror as Chester, also in a state of panic and screeching, begins clawing and scratching at the man, causing more blood to spray from his face.

I immediately grab a glass vase off the dining room table and smash it over the head of the other man fighting with my friend, knocking him off balance as he staggers past Ron. I sweep his legs from behind, my ankle slicing under both of his feet. He falls backwards into the glass sliding door, causing the door to shatter. Ron and I stare at each other with wide eyes, and fist bump one another as we stare down at the man, with the nighttime view of the city in the distance. Sirens can be heard far off, presumably from where the smoldering remains of the vehicle and motorcycle explosions have occurred.

The sound of a gun clicks, and we stop smiling and slowly turn around. The knife wielder has changed weapons, now pointing a pistol at me. Ron puts his hands up. I follow his lead and put mine up as well. Chester darts out of the living room and into the kitchen, his meowing sounding laborious and wheezy.

"Where is it?" the man asks, trying to catch his breath with his face soaked in blood.

"Where's what?" Ron asks smugly.

He walks over to Ron, and pistol whips him across the face, sending my friend down to the ground, clutching his nose. The man turns his attention to me, aiming the gun at my head.

"What is it you're looking for?" I ask innocently with my hands still raised.

"The safe, moron," he grabs me by the shirt collar, yanking me close. "I was told that it would be here. Now stop wasting my time, tell me where it is, and I promise I'll kill you fast."

His eyes flare at me when I don't answer immediately and he shoves the barrel of the gun into my face.

"Talk!" he screams. He punches me in the gut, sending me down to my knees.

"Did Marcini or Brittany send you?" I ask, trying to gasp for air.

"Marcini. Who's Brittany?"

"Never mind," I say. "Long story."

Two more men enter the apartment. Travis Daniels and William Marcini. My heart skips a beat, seeing two of the men responsible for John's death. The two men that ended my last life.

Marcini is wearing a long black trench coat, and a pair of black leather gloves. Daniels is wearing a matching pair of gloves, and is holding a pistol, complete with silencer in one hand. The two men stride towards us, and Ron begins to regain consciousness.

"Kill him first," Marcini says to Daniels, pointing at Ron.

"Wait, wait!" I yell, keeping my hands raised. "I wouldn't do that if I were you, Mr. Marcini."

He waves one hand up to Daniels, signaling him to stop. Marcini walks toward me, roughly pushing the other man holding the pistol out of his way. Still down on my knees, I look up at the man, the mob boss of one of the biggest crime families in the city, now stooping down to look me in the eyes. He examines me briefly, a look of puzzlement on his face.

"Aren't you the same reporter kid who came into my restaurant a few weeks ago?" he asks.

"That's right," I say confidently.

I've never in my life experienced having a gun in my face as my life hangs in the balance, conversing with mobsters. On any normal day, I'd be shaking uncontrollably, sucking my thumb. Instead, here I am, cool as a cucumber, seemingly unafraid of whatever's about to happen next. Fear is the opposite of what I feel right now. In a strange way I feel…alive. All my senses are clicking, and I'm ready for this confrontation with William Marcini.

I glance past him momentarily at Travis, the man who took me away from the woman I loved and preventing me from raising my son. My nostrils flare, a sense of anger rising in me.

"Tell me, kid, why shouldn't we–"

"Verner. My name is Simon Verner. And if you want to know where the safe is, you'll shut up and listen."

Marcini tilts his head to the side, a smirk on his face. "My, my. You've sure got a pair on you. Good for you. Alright, fine, we'll keep your boyfriend alive, for now. Where exactly is the safe?"

"Do you even know what's in the safe?" I ask. Marcini shakes his head. "Then why do you want it so bad?"

"I…I'm not sure," Marcini says, eyeing the ground for a moment. "I had a dream last night that I was to come here tonight and grab it."

"Boss, can I talk to you for a moment?" Daniels asks, annoyed. He motions for Marcini to come closer.

The man behind Ron and I, who was sent through the sliding glass door, begins to moan, waking up from his nap. The other man with the gun is pacing slowly in the dining room area, his gun now holstered and his hands in his pockets. Marcini puts his ear to Daniels, who is intently speaking with him.

Daniels approaches me now, his weapon drawn. Marcini stands back with arms crossed.

"Stop screwing with us, kid," Daniels says. "Tell me where the safe is, or I put a bullet in your buddy's leg."

He points the pistol at Ron for emphasis. A terrified expression is on Ron's face, and he looks over to me, shaking.

"Tell me, Travis, how did it feel when you pulled the trigger and killed me?" I ask.

"What?"

"You heard me. How did it feel when you ended my life? Not this current life you see now, but my past life. How did you feel when you murdered John Stinson?"

Daniels slowly turns toward me, his hand holding the pistol beginning to shake. Marcini's eyes bulge. The other man has stopped pacing, and he stares at the two of us, waiting for Travis' reply. Daniels rams the muzzle of the pistol's silencer against my forehead, the cool feel of steel between my eyes.

"You…you're full of it," he says, gritting his teeth, a snarl spread across his face. "Boss, give me the word, and I'll end this little maggot right here and now. He's not worth the trouble."

"Go ahead, put me down like a dog, just like you did to me before," I say, squinting my eyes. "That's all you've ever been good for. My wife was pregnant when you murdered me that night. I have far less to lose now. Do it, and you'll never see that safe. Your boss will spend the rest of his days behind bars because Stinson has tape recordings in there that prove Marcini's involvement in his murder. Blood is on his hands."

"Daniels, stand down!" Marcini shouts, his voice slightly shaky.

He turns around to confront Marcini, and I turn to Ron, nodding my head. I quickly stand up, tackling Daniels from behind, knocking the weapon from his hand. Rolling him over, I beat his face repeatedly.

"You took me from my family!" I yell. "I never got a chance to see my son born! He never got to know his father!"

Behind me, Ron has engaged in a fistfight of his own with the former knife-wielding man. Tackling him into the kitchen, Ron slams the guy's head against the dishwasher, causing the door to pop open. Steam rolls out of the dishwasher, and Ron reaches inside, grabs a long steak knife, and slashes violently at the man.

The man who was lying face down on the balcony crawls into the living room, still too woozy to join the fray.

Daniels blocks one of my punches with his elbow and jabs me in the nose. In an instant, he's on top of me, his arm raised over his head, about to bring it down on me. Out of some instinct buried deep down in me, I strike him in the throat, causing his fist to hit the ground next to me. I tuck my knees to my chest, push up with my legs, sending Daniels flying off me. Before he has a chance to regain his balance, I tackle him head on, our momentum carrying us through the empty glass sliding door. Driving him forward with all my strength, I send him over the thin metal railing on the balcony.

Travis Daniels disappears off the balcony, and I look down to watch as he plummets toward the parking lot below. His body crashes through a streetlamp, the sharpened point of the light fixture skewering his back and protruding through his chest. His limbs hang limp.

A gunshot goes off, and I duck down on all fours on the balcony. Marcini's holding a pistol, aimed directly at me. He lets out a frustrated grunt. Just as he's about to pull the trigger again, a blue streak of energy shears through his arm, and the weapon falls to the floor. Another beam of blue light sears through his chest, slicing him in half. His body begins to quickly disintegrate until what was William Marcini is only a pile of smoldering ashes left on the carpeted floor of Brittany's apartment.

Standing in the doorway, the glowing blue staff in her hands, is Loretta. Her eyebrows arched, a look of pure determination on her face. She points the staff at the other man who was fighting with Ron, and he raises his hands toward the ceiling. The other man has crawled over to the couch and is lying still, his arms raised meekly.

Loretta opens a closet door in the entryway, and points inside.

"Is this what ya'll are looking for?"

Ron and I walk over to Loretta. On the floor of the closet is John Stinson's black safe.

Chapter 33

We sit in silence in the car for some time. I drive with no direction in mind, just turning randomly every now and then, until I finally pull over in front of a darkened house in a rough neighborhood.

"You're overthinking this," X says from the backseat, now taking the form of Julius Caesar. "Why don't you just do yourself a favor and drive this nice car of yours into the lake. Just put your foot on the accelerator and end it. Take the witch and your dumb boyfriend with you. It'll do everyone a lot of good."

He begins to laugh, shaking his head. I can see him in the rearview mirror, sitting next to Ron. I close my eyes and tell myself that he's not there. He's not real. Brittany is just astral projecting or something. Just tune him out, he's not there.

"You're never going to find Jess," X continues. "You're a failure. You always have been. I'll give you one final chance to redeem yourself, Brother. I'll give you Jess in exchange for the safe and Ron. You don't need him. You've always been jealous of him. He's better looking than you. Stronger than you. Wouldn't it be nice to finally have him gone so you can have Jess all to yourself?"

I don't respond. My grip on the steering wheel tightens, and my knuckles turn white.

"Sleep on it, Simon. You know this is the only way to save her."

Continuing to remain quiet, I look over at Ron sitting next to X in the backseat. He's staring out the window, seemingly in a state of shock from what just transpired in the apartment. Two men losing their lives. All the violence. All the bloodshed. Something the two of us aren't used to. He risked a lot to break me out of the mental hospital and risked his life just now to help me find the safe, stored safely in the trunk. I'd never sell him out, even as much as I want Jess back safe and sound. I'll find another way. *We* will find another way to save Jess.

"Do you want to know how Magdoo died?" X says mockingly.

"Shut up," I say softly.

Ron and Loretta both look at me, startled.

"He was killed by his own son," X laughs loudly, clapping his hands. "Yeah, that's right. He died, choking on his own blood, by his son's hand. And it was… so *easy* corrupting him."

"I've heard enough," I say.

"We didn't say anything," Ron says, looking around in confusion. "Are we going to go somewhere, or what?"

"You needed the Oracle's help, didn't you?" X leans forward in his seat, now whispering in my ear. "It must be so nice having Mwari assign your soul to the same area where you died last. How…convenient for you. I'm going to raise the stakes, since you have the Oracle on your side now. Let's make this interesting while you ponder my offer. I'm going to give you twenty-four hours to save Jess, or I burn her alive. There's nothing I would like more than to see her silky soft skin melt off those bones." He leans forward and sticks his tongue out, licking my ear.

"I said shut up!" I yell as I turn around, swiping my hand at thin air. Ron's alone in the backseat, and he stares at me with a scared look on his face.

"Are you good, Simon?" Ron asks fearfully.

"I'm fine," I say bluntly, turning the engine back on. "X- Brittany, I mean- was talking to me in the backseat. She's given me twenty-four hours to find Jess." I look over at Loretta and take a deep breath. "I'm so sorry. I appreciate you. I appreciate both of you, I truly do. We can do this. Do you have a place we can crash, Loretta?"

She agrees to let Ron and I stay at her apartment. We make it there in a few minutes, and I realize how easy it is to drive around the city in the early morning with such little traffic. It reminds me of my time going into work early as a police officer. Then reality hits me like a ton of bricks; I was never a cop. That was John.

The thought of my past life blurring with my current life is scary. The way I was able to fight Marcini's men in Brittany's apartment, utilizing skills that I know for a fact I don't possess, tells me that his consciousness, his thoughts, feelings, and perhaps everything he's learned, is now bleeding over into my current life.

Loretta directs me to her apartment building, and I park in her spot, as her car is still at her store.

"I don't think I've ever seen you drive above the speed limit before," Ron says as we get out of the car. "Looks like some time in the slammer got you driving like a whole new man."

We take the stairs up to Loretta's apartment on the second floor. Her building is even more rundown than Ron's and mine was. Loud music can be heard blasting through one of the nearby apartments. Graffiti is coating the stairwell. A woman is sleeping on the landing, and we all step over her body. Loretta waves her hand above the woman's head briefly, and the woman wakes up instantly, her eyes searching her surroundings frantically.

Loretta's apartment is immaculate compared to the rest of the building, although much smaller than mine was. Artwork is hung on the wall, and I instantly recognize the artist. I approach a painting hung above the couch in the small living room. It's a lifelike portrait of Loretta. Large, looping golden earrings hang from both ears, and a soft smile creases her face. Jess has an impeccable eye for painting human faces, on top of her many other areas of art expertise. For some reason, however, I find this particular piece to be my favorite of hers. The attention to detail, from slight blemishes and freckles down to the look of happiness in Loretta's eyes is remarkable.

The same couch in the living room is also a pullout double bed, and that's where I sleep for the night. Ron makes himself comfortable on the floor, despite my repeated protests that he takes the bed.

My thoughts continue to dwell on Jess. I think back to the day the three of us spent at the beach, the same day that I'd first told her of my dreams of John while we were eating ice cream. Only a woman as special as she would listen to me, giving me her full, undivided attention, and not start busting up laughing or patronizing me with false comforting words. Even though she did admit after the fact she didn't fully believe me, just having her sit there and listen meant the world.

I miss her long, blond hair and those bright blue eyes. A man could lose himself in those eyes, like an endless ocean on a sunny day. That smile of hers, which could light up a room and turn my mood from sour to sweet in the blink of an eye… the way that she would laugh at my jokes when she knew I was trying to be funny, and the way she would be serious and quiet when I was trying to tell her something dark and dreary.

I miss you so much, Jess. I'm sorry that I was afraid to tell you how I felt. I'm sorry I never told you how much I love you. I miss you, Jess. I miss you, Jess. I miss…

Her blue eyes open, and she's looking right at me. I'm down on one knee, squeezing her zip tied hands in mine. She blinks several times, as do I. Her once bright blond hair is dirty, with streaks of mud. She's covered in filth.

"Jess, can you hear me?" I ask.

"Simon, is that you? How…how are you doing this?" she asks groggily.

"I'm not sure," I say, looking around.

The room around us is dimly lit, with several pipes and valves all over. Behind Jess is a lit up red 'Exit' sign. A mouse scurries across the floor between my feet. I walk behind Jess to see the sign on the door which reads 'The Palace Theater.'

It takes me a moment, then it comes to me. Gary, Indiana. The Palace Theater, back in its prime, could hold up to three thousand people before it closed in 1972. Several big Broadway style performances were put on here back in its heyday. But now, it's an abandoned, burned-out shell of a building. The crumbling brick walls give way to the exposed pipes and air ducts behind them. I turn around and decipher that we must be in the backstage area. Debris is scattered across the floor, and a gaping hole can be seen in the ceiling above.

I stand in front of Jess, bending down on one knee again, and take her hands in mine. "I'm going to get you out of here. I promise. Please hang on Jess, we're coming for you."

"Is that really you, Simon?" Her voice is hoarse, and her eyes well up with tears.

I put my hand on her cheek, but my hand passes through her skin. I wave my hand several times, unable to physically touch her anymore. I give up, acknowledging the fact that I must be like a ghost now, but at least Jess can see and hear me.

"It's really me," I say, a lump forming in my throat. "How long have you been here?"

"Only for a couple hours. Before this, I was on a boat for several weeks. What happened?"

"After Brittany burned down my apartment, she had some thugs kidnap you," I say. "Have you seen her?"

"Brittany?" she asks, and I nod my head. "Yeah, she was here when they set me up in this chair. I'm…I'm so scared. I'm hungry and I haven't had anything to drink in so long. Please, I need you."

"I'm so sorry this happened. We're going to get you out of here. I promise."

The door opens, and I immediately dart behind a cement column. Brittany walks into the room and looks down at Jess. Then, without warning, she backhands Jess across the face. Bending down to look her in the eyes, Brittany smiles. A wicked, malicious smile.

"Simon has less than twenty-four hours to find you," she says in a mocking tone. "Do you think that coward has what it takes?"

"He isn't a coward," Jess says confidently. "He's going to save me. You'll wish you never crossed him."

I love this woman so much. I'll save you Jess. Just hang on.

As if she could hear my thoughts, Brittany's attention quickly turns to me, and my eyes go wide.

I wake up back in Loretta's living room. She's already awake and has started making breakfast for Ron and me.

"I know where she is!" I exclaim, standing up and running into the kitchen. "She's in Gary. We have to leave. Now!"

"Calm down child," Loretta says reassuringly. "There's no rush. Gary isn't that far of a drive."

"Jess needs our help!" I yell. "We have to–"

I feel like I'm taking a backseat in my own mind. I've lost the ability to control my limbs, and I'm slowly walking over to the table and taking a seat next to Ron. Loretta continues to prepare our meal. My stomach growls as the smell from the kitchen wafts over to our table.

"You need nourishment first," Loretta says sternly. "I promise that we'll save her. But first, we need to fuel our bodies for the battle ahead."

Scrambled eggs, dollar pancakes and bacon. The food is delicious and by far the best meal I've had in a long time. As we sit and eat at her dining room table, I inform the two of them of last night's dream, which Loretta refers to as "Spirit Walking."

I'm now back in full control of my body as I continue to eat breakfast. Taking a mental note, I remind myself not to cross Loretta. Her ability to enter my mind and control me like a puppet is terrifying.

In the improved light of the morning, I take another look around her apartment. It's not nearly as weird as I had imagined her place being, considering how her shop looked. In all honesty, I was convinced she lived in the back of her shop, but it's reassuring to know that she has a nice place to call home that looks relatively normal. Jess' artwork can be found in nearly every room, including the portrait of Loretta in the living room. The piece of art hanging above the toilet is of a similar looking toilet. The one hanging above her bed is of a beach, with waves crashing on a sandy shore.

I hurry while taking a warm shower and getting dressed in a new set of clothes that Loretta happened to have in her apartment. Apparently, they belonged to an ex-boyfriend, and the two of us appear to be roughly the same size; a pair of brown cargo shorts, and a Chicago Bulls jersey with the number twenty-three on the front and back, along with the name "Jordan."

The image of Jess tied up to that chair in the Palace Theater sharpens my mind and brings the importance of our mission into clearer focus. I've been given this gift of seeing through the window of my past life for a reason, and now the reason is beginning to take shape. After we rescue Jess, I will bring the men responsible for covering up John's murder to justice. Doug and Mike must be held accountable.

But first things first. We have to get Jess away from Brittany and bring her to safety. Loretta places the black box containing the Soul Orb in a backpack, as well as a crowbar. She also makes sure that Ron and I are wearing Dream Catchers, which she pulls out of her dresser drawer. She slides one onto her own head as well.

"Alright, remind me why we don't just go buy a gun?" Ron asks. "I mean, more than likely her men will be armed. We don't stand a chance here, Loretta. One bullet to her head and Brittany's out of the picture."

"She's too powerful," I say. "She can astral project herself into another person's mind and alter it however she wants. Last night, I was able to project myself to Jess, but Brittany's so powerful that she could see me. If one of us has a gun, who knows what she would do. We would probably wind up shooting one another, or ourselves, while she just stands there, commanding us with her mind to do it."

"Spirit Walk," Loretta says. "She can Spirit Walk herself into your consciousness. Once she has met you, her soul imprints itself onto yours, or whomever she wishes to manipulate, and she can enter their thoughts, regardless if they're sleeping or awake. Her powers are far greater than I could've ever imagined. She's much stronger than you, Simon. So, to answer your question, Ron, as long as we're wearing these Dream Catchers, she won't know where we are. But as soon as we show our faces in public, we run the risk of her finding us. Right now, we have the element of surprise on our side. We need to take advantage of that."

"Well, that's great and all, but these things can't stop bullets, can they?" Ron adjusts the Dream Catcher on his head. "And if we're wearing these, then how can she enter my consciousness? It's like a condom for my mind, right?"

Loretta gives Ron a harsh glare.

"We aren't taking guns, and that's that," Loretta says. "Listen, I know it sounds like the easy way out. These are made to protect your mind from hers. Also, we need Brittany alive. We can't capture her soul if we shoot her dead. Her soul will just evaporate back into the Beyond, and we'll be back in this same boat two decades from now."

"Whatever you say," Ron says wryly, crossing his arms. "What about the safe? Do we take it with us?"

The three of us look at the small black safe sitting on the floor. Silence hangs over us, as we all contemplate how to handle this situation.

"What do you suggest, Simon?" Loretta asks.

"We take it with us, but leave it in the trunk," I say, then sigh. "We'll have to get Jess out of there before Brittany finds out. But we cannot, under any circumstance, let the contents of what's in that safe fall into the wrong hands again."

A few minutes later, we're in my car heading east on Interstate 90 towards Gary, Indiana. As soon as we enter the once populated city with burned out buildings and graffiti coating the outside of the buildings still left standing, it becomes more apparent how this once thriving industrial American city has slowly turned to rot and decay over the years.

In its heyday, the city's infrastructure was based around one main thing: industry. Once the factories closed, the workers left, leaving behind empty buildings to be looted and ransacked by vandals. Homes were left abandoned, and the factories left to the mercy of time. The Palace Theater, which was once one of the greatest theaters in the country, now sits empty with no shows to draw an audience. Except for today, where Loretta, Ron and I are on our way to save Jess and bring her home safely. And hopefully take down my wicked former brother Mubiru, now disguised as my crazy two-faced ex-girlfriend.

I take the exit off the interstate and turn right on Broadway heading south. The Palace Theater is on the left-hand side of the road. It's a three-story tall brick building with broken glass windows all around it. The front of the building still has the original signage, proudly reading "The Palace Theater." I can tell this building used to be beautiful, even from the outside.

We turn left on 8th Avenue and take another left to enter the alleyway behind the building, which is overgrown with trees and weeds. Trash litters the sides of the alleyway. I pull the car forward several feet to park. Ron takes the backpack, containing the Soul Orb and crowbar, and slings it over his shoulder. Loretta holds her serpent-twined staff with blue painted on one end, which she's now using as a cane.

It's a sunny, warm morning, but clouds can be seen creeping in from a distance. The back of the theater, once boarded up with plywood, now has an opening to crawl through to get inside. I follow Ron as he gently props up the plywood to sneak under, and I do the same, holding it up for Loretta. The inside is dark and damp, with a strong musty smell. Water drips from old, exposed and deteriorated pipes in the crumbling brick wall. The first room appears to be the backstage area where I was with Jess last night in my dream. Sunlight causes a dim glow, seeping through exposed wooden beams above as we walk further into the building; my eyes slowly adjust to the darkness.

I can see the chair Jess was sitting in last night. My heart sinks. This is definitely the right place, but I'm afraid Brittany has moved Jess, that my presence last night spooked her into abandoning the theater for another location.

A woman's scream echoes throughout the building, and Ron and I look at one another. I sprint forward, out of the backstage area, through a darkened hallway, until I'm on the side of the concrete stage to my left. Behind the stage is a large mural of what looks like an old Italian village. Straight ahead, where the audience once sat years ago to enjoy a night of entertainment, now sits a large, empty room with the remnants of theater seats where they once sat until they were ripped up and taken away by looters. There's also a large balcony section, where more seats used to be. The fifty-foot ceiling, painted sky blue, has a large hole in it, flooding the theater with sunlight. Except now, dark clouds are beginning to form, eclipsing the sun.

The entire theater looks like some post-apocalyptic scene after a nuclear bomb has gone off and civilization has begun to fade away. In front of the stage, loose bricks are strewn randomly across the cement floor.

Ron stops next to me, and we both clench our fists. Standing in front of us is Machete Man, a.k.a. Sean Boykins, holding his favorite weapon. Next to him are his two partners. Large Man, holding a baseball bat. The third man is holding a pistol. They've opted to not wear ski masks this time. Standing in front of the three men is Jess. Her hands are tied behind her back with rope and a black hood is over her head. Her dirty, long blond hair falls beneath the hood and over her shoulders. Holding Jess' arm is Brittany.

"Hello, boys," she says, smiling. A staff, similar to Loretta's but with yellow painted on the end, is placed on the ground next to Brittany. It's the same one she brought over when she set fire to my apartment and killed Hank. "Simon, it's been a while. What took you so long?"

Chapter 34

I lean forward, ready to charge at Brittany and push her away from Jess. Adrenaline pumps through my veins, and I can feel my heartbeat beating faster by the second.

"No hard feelings, right?" Brittany raises the pitch of her voice to a sweet and innocent one, then giggles. "Here, I'll make this really easy for you, cutie pie. I'll let Jess go, you let my men take Ron, give me the safe as well as the combination, and we'll be on our way. That's what we agreed upon, after all."

"What's she talking about?" Ron whispers.

"She's lying." I say.

"Am I?" Brittany asks, yanking Jess in front of her. "You promised me, Simon. You said you'd bring Ron here if I'd give you back sweet little Jess." She looks at Ron, narrowing her gaze. "He's the one lying to you, Ron. This was his plan all along, to give you up in exchange for Jess. He values her over you. Always has."

"I wish you guys would've let me bring a gun," Ron whispers to me. Then he turns his attention to Brittany and raises his voice. "He wouldn't do that. And, quite frankly, I don't care what you have to say. You're a liar, and you're insane. Let Jess go, and I promise I'll go easy on you."

"Oh my goodness, I'm so scared," Brittany says, putting her hands up mockingly. "Simon betrays those who he loves. It's in his character. It's in his soul." She pats her chest. "His soul is tainted. You think I'm bad? At least I'm not a scared little coward like he is. In almost every life he's lived, he's betrayed those who he cared about. He sold out his family when he was a slave in Egypt, all for some more drinking water. When he was the Queen of England, she betrayed her own husband to support a rebellion."

Brittany lets go of Jess and approaches Ron and I slowly, keeping her focus directly on me while elevating her voice.

"I could go on and on. But worst of all, thousands of years ago in what is now the country of Zimbabwe, he betrayed his own *brother* by telling the Tribal chief, their own father, that his brother was worshiping a God named

Mwari in solitude. When all his brother was trying to do was to be as good of a hunter as his older brother and provide for the Tribe. But he was too short-sighted to see that. No, no, he only wanted to show, yet again, that he was a better man than his own brother. Better than me!" She takes a shaky breath, rage beginning to consume her. "You had me exiled, sent out into the wilderness to die! I was ripped apart, piece by piece, by ravenous hyenas. But you never came back for me. You didn't care. All you wanted was Father's attention. To be the hero of the Tribe, while your poor, helpless brother died in agony. You are a pathetic, self-righteous coward!"

Thunder crashes directly overhead. The clouds over the theater has darkened the entire auditorium to a dim grey. Brittany's face is directly in front of mine now. She breathes heavily, awaiting my response.

"Do you remember?" she asks softly. "Do you remember any of that? The way you left me to die?"

I match her stare, sighing. "I'd asked you before, several times, not to pray to Mwari alone. It was forbidden. The customs–"

"To hell with the customs!" she screams. "Did the customs tell you to have me exiled, so that I would die alone? Is that what your precious customs and conscience told you?"

"I was wrong," I say, raising my voice. "At the time, I thought that what I was doing was the right thing. But I was wrong. What I did was cruel and unjust. But, Brittany, that happened lifetimes ago. Are you seriously going to hold me accountable for something that was done by another man thousands of years ago? A couple months ago, I had no idea about any of this. If you want an apology, then you got it. I'm sorry for what happened. But that's not me. I have no control or…or ability to change the past. What's done is done. Honestly, it's well past time to move on. You need to let it go. Chasing me down, lifetime after lifetime, and pointing this out to me repeatedly, that's not fair. It's not right. I'm not Magdoo. I'm Simon Verner, born and raised in Chicago, Illinois."

Her glare turns furious, and her nostrils flare. "Is that right? You think that because you're somebody else, that what you did in the past should just be excused? Is that what you're telling me?"

"Yes, it is. I have no control over what those people did. They aren't me."

"They *are* you!" she roars. "You *were* them. You *are* them! You have the same soul!"

"That's complete nonsense. I'm not them. You have no right to persecute me. *I* didn't do those things."

She laughs. "But yet, you go through all of that trouble to solve who killed John Stinson. You found that mystery to be so important, and you chased it down until you solved the crime. You're such a hypocrite!"

"That's different!"

She lets out a frustrated grunt, and marches over to Ron. "Are you hearing this? He's just flat-out not taking any responsibility here. Ron, I'll make you a counteroffer, since Simon is too stupid to take the offer that I gave him." She looks briefly in my direction. "Your offer is rescinded, by the way, Simon. Ron, the deal is that you let me take Simon, and John's safe, and you leave here with Jess. How does that sound?"

He laughs. "Go to hell, Brittany. Just give us Jess, and nobody has to get hurt."

She slaps Ron in the face, turns her back to him, and walks back to her three men.

"Kill them!" she yells.

The man with the pistol raises the weapon from his side, aims it directly at me, and thumbs the safety. An audible click echoes through the theater. Another rumble of thunder occurs overhead. I close my eyes, and my life flashes before me. Dad taking me to the Cubs game, watching basketball with Ron, Jess sitting next to me for the first time when playing baseball, watching TV with Mom, all of the days spent at school learning subjects that went in one ear and out the other. The year I spent homeless, playing music with Elroy. Picking up golf balls in the caged range picker. Watching Hank swim around his nice clean tank. Jess splashing water while swimming in the lake.

A loud bang echoes throughout the theater. I wait for the bullet to take me out, punching my ticket into the next life. I've never been shot before as Simon, but I can only imagine the pain that'll come with it.

But no such pain occurs. I open my eyes to see Brittany's man still standing there, aiming the pistol at me, a look of shocked horror on his face. Blood begins to ooze down from his brow and into his eyes, and he collapses face down on the floor. The other two men and Brittany all jump away from him. I look over to my right. Standing beside Ron is Doug, a faint trail of smoke wafting from the barrel of his pistol. Loretta is standing on the other side of Doug.

Brittany reaches for Jess and yanks her backwards toward the seating area facing the stage.

"Let the girl go!" Doug yells.

Slowly, Brittany does as Doug commands, and walks toward the three of us, her arms raised over her head.

"Don't shoot, Dougie," she says softly. "It's me, sweetheart."

"Stop right there!" he yells, his voice booming. "I said stop where you are!"

Brittany doesn't listen, and keeps walking forward, now within a few paces of us. "Don't you remember who I am, Dougie?"

Doug squints at her, his pistol still raised, aiming at her. "No."

"Let me ask you a question," she says, still slowly walking toward Doug, her arms raised. "What's a retired police sergeant doing out of his jurisdiction, in another state, shooting and killing others?" She stops walking and puts her index finger to her lips, placing her other hand on her hip. "Could it be, maybe, that you were…drawn here? Maybe you had a dream last night that you needed to be here?"

The other two men are still in the auditorium area where hundreds of theater seats used to be. A flash of lightning, followed closely by a loud rumble of thunder, and rain begins to drizzle into the theater from the gaping hole in the roof above. The rain starts slowly, then within seconds is pouring, water gushing down a few yards in front of us.

Doug's hands begin to shake. "I…yes, I did. I had a need to be here today. My dream last night…it compelled me to be here. But why?"

Brittany, now standing directly in front of Doug, puts her hands up to his temples. His eyes roll back in his head, and the pistol falls from his hands, clanking to the floor. Brittany kicks the pistol behind her.

She lets go of his head, and he falls back. Loretta and Ron rush to catch him before his head hits the wooden stage.

"What did you do to him?" Ron demands.

"I opened his mind to accept the truth, which he's been avoiding for quite some time, I'm afraid."

"And what 'truth' would that be?" Loretta asks.

"Silence, Witch," Brittany snaps back. "Wait your turn. I'll get to you in a minute." She gets on her hands and knees, crawling over to Doug. Ron and Loretta get up and step away from her. "Doug and I go way back. Go ahead,

Dougie. Tell them who I am."

"Connie," he says, tears streaming down his face. "Connie, I've missed you. Oh, how I've missed you. I love you. I never got a chance to say goodbye. I never…I…"

Doug's voice trails off and he breaks down into sobs.

"Alright, now I'm lost," Ron says. "Who's Connie?"

"Doug's first wife," I say distractedly, staring down at Brittany who's now holding Doug in her arms. "She passed away in a car accident, several years before he met my mom." I look briefly up at the ceiling, then back at Brittany. "Now it all makes sense. Oh, you sit there and call me sick, but look at you. All of this, just to prevent me from uncovering the truth about his involvement in John's murder. That's what this has all been about, hasn't it?"

She looks up at me, her eyes damp with tears. "Guilty as charged."

"Well, it's not going to stop the truth from coming out," I say. "Mike and Doug are going to answer for what happened."

"Is that so?" Brittany says, stroking Doug's hair. She unwraps her arms from him and lays his head gently on the ground. Standing up, she approaches me yet again. "We'll see about that."

With a quick strike, she punches me in the face, sending me sprawling onto my back. Staring up at the hole in the ceiling, a bright flash of lightning arches across the darkened sky. Brittany stands over me, closes her eyes for a moment, then looks down at me, shaking her head. Slowly, she walks over to her staff that she's laid on the ground next to Jess, picks it up, and points the end at me. I stand up, rolling quickly to my left, avoiding the yellow beam of energy shooting from the end of her staff. I can feel the heat of the energy, like a concentrated column of fire.

"Kill the girl!" she shouts to the two men, who are now standing near the back of the auditorium.

Sprinting full speed toward Jess, I tackle her to the ground, just as a wave of fire comes searing over the top of my head. I pull the black tarp off Jess' head, and she's staring up at me, a bandana wound tightly around her cheeks, gagging her mouth. Taking the bandana out of her mouth, I help Jess to her feet. Her hands are still bound together.

Sean, the machete wielding madman, walks toward us, raising the weapon above his head. I pick up a brick from the floor and throw it at him, striking him in the head, sending the machete flying from his hands, the metal blade clanking onto the cement floor.

The two of us engage in hand-to-hand combat. He attempts a strong hook, which I block with my elbow, striking his chin with my fist. His punches are lightning quick, but I'm able to block nearly every attack of his with ease, several of my punches connecting on his face. His right leg comes up in an attempt to high kick me in the head. With his guard lowered, I seize the opportunity, duck my head, and sweep his left leg, sending him down on the ground. Instantly, I'm on top of him, wrapping my right arm around his throat. I wrestle him in a sleeper hold, and in a few moments he's down for the count, unconscious, but still alive.

Picking up the machete, I lead Jess back toward where Doug's pistol is lying on the floor, just in front of the pool of water forming on the ground. Jess and I crouch behind a cement pillar, out of sight. I use the machete to cut the rope binding Jess' wrists together, setting her arms free.

"Are you hurt?" I ask.

"No, are you?"

I shake my head and squeeze her in a tight hug. We view the carnage developing in the Palace Theater in front of us.

Brittany's involved in a dazzling fight with Loretta. Yellow flames shoot from Brittany's staff and are being blocked by a blue forcefield of some kind from Loretta's own staff, shielding her and Ron. Taking the backpack off, Ron opens it and pulls out the crowbar. He sprints toward Large Man who was approaching from the right, ready to strike Loretta with a loose brick. Ron swings the crowbar at Large Man, but he holds the brick up, blocking the strike. He uses the brick to try and strike Ron, which he blocks with the crowbar. The two of them go back and forth, their battle leading away from Loretta and Brittany's bright scuffle.

"I need something from Ron's backpack," I say, picking up the pistol and handing it to her. "I'll be back."

With the machete in hand, I'm approaching Ron and Large Man, when I'm suddenly tackled from the left, knocking the weapon from my hand and sending me to the ground.

Doug's on top of me in an instant, his hands reaching for my throat.

Chapter 35

My hands stretch upward, fingers clawing at Doug's face as he strengthens his hold on my throat. I fumble around with both hands, and my left hand finds a loose brick. I grab it, striking the side of Doug's head and knock him off me. Dropping the brick, I scramble for the machete, and grab the weapon, holding the blade to Doug's chest.

"What're you doing?" I demand. "Help us fight Brittany and her men. She's out of control."

He has a blank expression on his face, completely devoid of emotion. "I didn't want any of this," he says. "But…Connie's back. I have to do this for her. She means the world to me."

"Connie's dead, Doug, snap out of it! Jill is the woman you love. Think of Jill!"

He looks down at the ground, shaking his head. "I-I don't understand. How is she alive?"

"She's not alive. The woman you loved is gone. She's been gone for years. That crazy woman over there, right now, she's trying to kill us. Please, just stay out of the way. Just stay put. Let us handle this."

He nods his head in agreement and disappears toward the front entrance of the theater.

Ron's still battling with Large Man, the two of them putting aside their weapons, preferring to duke it out in an old-fashioned fist fight instead. Ron's lip is busted open, and a large bruise is beginning to form around his left eye. Hustling over to the backpack on the dirty floor, I get to work on unzipping it, and pull out the black box.

Crouched on one knee with the box containing the Soul Orb in my hands, I take a moment to witness the spectacle around me as the chaos inside the Palace Theater rages on. The two men fighting, matching one another blow for blow. The battle between the two women with their colorful, magical staffs. Violent collisions of yellows and blues, matching the visions I had a few weeks ago. This entire scene is overwhelmingly absurd. I close my eyes briefly, wishing I could go back in time to a few weeks ago, before I was thrown in the padded cell. I wish I could go back to picking up golf balls in my mundane routine, coming home from work and feeding Hank. My life had structure. I didn't see it then, but I can see it now. My life had meaning. I did have a purpose. My desire to be someone else, someone greater, clouded my judgment, allowing Brittany and her manipulations to take me away from my life.

Holding the sides of the box like Loretta showed, it opens. I reach inside and pull out the round, baseball-sized Soul Orb, turning my attention to Loretta and Brittany, still engaged in a duel of elemental powers up by the stage. Yellow flames from Brittany, but the blue shield that Loretta was using moments ago is now a blue beam of energy. The opposing colors collide head on, sending white sparks around the theater randomly, bouncing off the brick walls and ceiling. Both women are intensely focused.

From the direct center of the clash of blue and yellow, a black bubble begins to form. It's very small at first, but gradually begins to grow. As I approach the two of them, both women screaming in a furious rage, sparks bouncing off the eerily black bubble at the point of contact, I shield my eyes.

Sneaking behind Brittany, I activate the Soul Orb by twisting the top and hold it up to her. She screams and drops the staff. Loretta also drops her weapon, collapsing to her knees in exhaustion.

A high-pitched noise comes from the object in my hands, and it begins to get brighter in color, a blinding white, as the object gets incredibly warm in my hands. It feels as if it weighs fifty pounds or more, but I continue to hold the object up, my arms outstretched, the Soul Orb directly against her back. Her body goes limp and begins to levitate off the ground, her arms raising over her head. Suddenly, a strange form in a bluish hue escapes out of her body, like a germ multiplying under the supervision of a microscope. The blue form morphs into a translucent human shape, which comes to a rest standing beside me. I look over to see that the form has the face of Mubiru and is glaring angrily at me, shouting words that I can't hear.

Mubiru reaches out with both hands, and grabs me around the shirt collar, lifting me off the ground. In a state of confusion, I drop the Orb, all brightness leaving it, the high-pitched noise immediately silenced. Mubiru vanishes, and I tumble to the ground. Brittany crashes down on the ground in front of me, but she's quicker to recover than I am. She tackles me head on, sending me to my back, my head bouncing off the concrete. Straddling me, a wide, malicious smile on her face, she punches me in the face repeatedly. Left hand, right hand, left hand. I'm too dazed to defend myself.

"Why do you keep defending them?" Brittany screams, spittle flying off her lips. "You mean nothing to them, Simon. Why do you keep defending these people who mock you and hurt you? You'll never have money. You'll never be noticed."

She stops hitting me for a second, and I take a moment to catch my breath.

"Because they're not all bad," I say. "Humans aren't perfect. They do tend to destroy that which they don't understand, I'll give you that. But even from the lowest of lows, when I was most angry with the world and myself, there was one person, one human, who taught me that this life's worth living for. Elroy was a good man, and he recognized that his flaws are what brought him to that low point in his life. But in the end, he learned to forgive. Most importantly, he was able to forgive himself. Brother, I wish that you could learn to forgive. I wish that you could learn to love."

"And where's Elroy now?"

"He died a few years ago."

"Then you can see him again real soon. You can be with Elroy and your precious little goldfish in whatever form of an afterlife you believe in. We can continue this cycle in another quarter century, like we always have."

She resumes hitting me repeatedly, bloodying my nose. Pain shoots through my face, and I'm powerless to stop her. She's much stronger than I am. She punches me one final time, knocking my head back against the cement.

Instead of waking up in the eternal blackness of the Void, I'm now in a place of eternal bright white.

"Hello, John," a woman's familiar voice says from behind.

I turn around to see Samantha, as beautiful as ever, wearing a white wedding dress. My breath catches, and I rush toward her, enveloping her in a hug. I pick her up, twirling her around.

"Oh, Samantha! I've missed you. I've missed you so much. I'm so sorry that I wasn't there to help you raise Ryan. I should've just dropped that Alvarez case. You were what was important."

"Shh," Samantha says soothingly, placing her fingers over my lips. "It's okay. Once you had your mind set on something, you always had to see it through to the end. I admired that about you."

"Are you… okay? What is this place?"

"This is the Beyond," she says.

The landscape begins to change around us, morphing into a hallway. It takes me a moment, and then I remember what this place is. It's the hallway leading toward our math class when we were students at Northwestern University. This is where I'd bumped into her, causing her to drop those textbooks. The spot where we had officially met for the first time.

"I'd like to think of this as Heaven," she continues. "I'm able to view my best memories here. This is one of my favorites. We were both so young, so inexperienced with the big world around us. Weren't we, John?"

I'm speechless, unable to think of a response. Instead, I wander around the empty University hallway. Even the smell of the school is right, bringing back memories of being a college student, acting like I knew what I was doing when in reality I didn't even have a clue.

"You've probably been wondering why you started having these dreams recently, haven't you?" Samantha says, to which I nod my head. "I was able to send you those visions from here in the Beyond. I wanted you to be able to solve this mystery and hopefully put some closure to your last life."

"So, it was you all along? I don't have superpowers, or whatever? That's a relief."

She chuckles softly. "I wouldn't say that. It still takes a special person with a unique soul to be able to receive messages sent from the Beyond. But what I do believe is that in order for me to have found your soul, and for you to receive my messages, we needed to share something powerful. The most powerful force in the Universe."

"What would that be?"

"Love," Samantha says, looking up at me. "A love so strong, it transcended space and time. I know that our time has passed, but please know that I will always be here for you, John. In your new life as Simon, I hope that you find that true love again."

She wraps her arms around me, and we share one last kiss. "Our time together came to a premature end in our past life. But I believe that sometime in the future, we'll be together again." She sighs into my chest, then looks back up at me. "Can you do something for me when you return back as Simon?"

"Anything."

"After you defeat Brittany, find Ryan. Find our son and let him know that his father loved him."

I feel myself being pulled away from Samantha, and she disappears from me for the last time.

I open my eyes to Brittany continuing to punch me in the face as I lay on the cement floor of the Palace Theater.

"Stop hitting him!" Jess screams.

I look over and see her pointing the pistol at Brittany, who scrambles off of me and grabs her staff. Jess shoots the gun, but misses, the bullet striking the Italian villa painting on the stage. A beam of yellow erupts from the end of Brittany's staff, and Jess spins to the side, barely missing being incinerated. I reach my hand up to try and hit Brittany, but I'm far too weak. She strikes me with the butt end of the staff, and I taste iron in my mouth.

Out of nowhere, Jess' foot connects with Brittany's head, knocking her off balance and sending her staff skittering across the floor. Jess takes on a fighting stance, raises her leg again, and connects with the side of Brittany's head for a second time, sending her face down on the ground.

"Hands off, bitch!" Jess yells.

"Oh, that was a serious mistake," Brittany sneers, wiping blood from her mouth with the back of her hand. Grabbing a handful of cement dust off the floor, she throws it into Jess' eyes. She grabs at her face, screaming, and Brittany tackles her, sending both women to the ground. They exchange body blow after body blow, clawing and scratching one another. I still lay on my back, blinking several times, trying desperately to stand.

Jess gets to her feet first, landing a kick, sending Brittany to the floor again, her black hair covered in cement dust. She growls, trying to stand up.

"Simon, quickly, finish the process!" Loretta shouts, clutching her side with one hand.

I stumble over to the Soul Orb lying on the floor.

Meanwhile, the black bubble that had formed from Brittany and Loretta's elemental duel has now doubled in size and is about five feet tall and equally wide. The inside of the bubble begins to form a picture, turning from a dark black to red. I squint and can see spouts of lava and a dark red canyon wall inside the bubble, like I'm looking through a window. A mountain range of volcanoes can be seen off in the distance, spouting molten lava from their tops. Winged, batlike creatures can be seen flying around the red, barren landscape.

Picking up the Soul Orb off the floor, I hold the object up to Brittany, once more causing her body to go limp. She levitates off the floor, just as before. The high-pitched noise comes from the Orb, and it grows heavy, changing color to a bright white. Brittany begins to scream in agony, looking down at me with an intense fury on her face. No blue men escape her body this time, however.

"This is for Hank!" I shout.

Jess walks up beside me, watching. After a few moments, a small, bright white light escapes Brittany's body and floats harmlessly toward the Orb in my outstretched hands. Her body crashes to the ground. The white light enters the Orb, and the object begins to shake violently in my hands.

"What do I do?" I ask Loretta urgently.

"Twist the top clockwise," she says, sprinting over to me.

She places her hands on top of mine, and together we twist the top of the Orb shut, silencing the noise, and the object goes back to its initial color and weight.

An earthquake shakes the theater, sending loose bricks flying off the walls and falling from the ceiling above. Looking over at the dark red bubble, which has now grown immensely in size, big enough to drive a car through, I see an armored leg appearing through the opening, crunching a brick beneath its boot on the floor. Stepping through the portal is a tall man carrying a staff with fire on the end of it. He has to be at least six and a half feet tall, wearing metal armor from head to toe, and a dark helmet. Scanning the theater, he stops when he sees Loretta. She gasps in terror.

"Oracle," he says, his deep, booming voice shaking the room. "We meet again."

"Popobowa," she breathes, clutching her chest.

Chapter 36

Jess and I look at one another just before Popbowa slams the handle of his staff down on the ground, sending a shockwave rattling throughout the entire building, more debris flying down from the crumbling ceiling and walls. Car alarms can be heard going off outside.

Popobowa turns his attention to me now, studying me closely. He walks over to Brittany's body, picks her up, and carries her back to the portal, throwing her body inside. He remains on our side of the portal, turning back to face me. "One brother cannot live without the other. Your time in this life has come to an end, Magdoo."

He points his staff at me, sending a yellow beam of energy out of the end. A flash of blue comes from my right, hitting Popobowa's yellow light dead on. The flashes of energy collide, sending bright sparks throughout the room, a cacophony of flashing colors crashing against the brick walls and blue ceiling of the theater.

Popobowa turns his attention to Loretta, and the two begin to battle with their magical staffs, sending more sparks flying, mists of blue and yellow dancing around the room, causing the old Palace Theater to shake and quiver violently.

Letting out a frustrated deep yell, he brings his staff back down to his side.

"This isn't over, Oracle," he says menacingly, then turns his attention to me. "You've made a grave mistake today, Magdoo. Your future will prove far more difficult than your past."

Popobowa reaches his hand out, and the Orb jumps out of my hand, soaring through the air. He snatches it with one hand.

"This belongs to me," he says, then steps back through the portal.

The red hue of the portal turns back to black. My feet begin to slide along the floor as I feel myself being pulled toward the black hole, which has now turned into a large vortex. I reach out for something to stop myself from being sucked further into the gravitational pull of the black void, and thankfully grab hold of a loose electrical cable. Loretta's found a steel support on the ground to grab onto. Jess slides over in my direction, and I grab hold of her wrist with my left hand, while clutching onto the cable with my right.

Ron's hanging on for dear life to a small steel support that used to hold a theater seat about twenty feet away from Jess and I, his feet now elevated off the floor.

"Hang on, Ron!" I yell.

Large Man, unable to find anything to grab, is lifted off the floor and flies into the black vortex, screaming. The unconscious body of Sean, the Machete Man, follows closely behind.

Jess clutches my hand and wrist with both of her hands, and I hold onto her with all my strength, while simultaneously grasping the cable which is secured to the ceiling above. Jess' feet lift off the ground, causing her to scream in a state of panic. The vortex now sounds like a jet engine. Thunder clouds appear overhead, causing a bolt of lightning to strike directly in the auditorium.

"I got you, Jess!" I yell. "Don't let go! Hang on!"

Her feet are now above her head, and she's holding my hand incredibly tight with all her strength. I feel my feet being lifted off the floor and my fingers begin to slip off the cable, first my pinkie finger, followed by my ring finger. I scream in frustration, trying desperately to regain my control, until my last fingers lose their grip. I close my eyes.

A pair of hands grab my wrist, and I look up to see Doug, anchoring himself down with a heavy metal cable around his waist. He's leaning backwards in order to position his center of gravity away from me, counterbalancing the strengthening pull of the vortex. The jet engine sound is blasting my eardrums. Loose bricks, including those that have fallen from the walls and ceiling are soaring into the now spinning void of the black hole.

Loretta, using one hand to hold onto the steel support on the floor, her feet flying behind her, reaches down for her staff. It's wedged in between two large concrete blocks, the top end of the stick with the snake's head shaking violently, the suction of gravity trying to take it away. Her long fingers grab the staff, and after a brief struggle, gets it unstuck. She aims her weapon at the vortex, sending a blue beam of light from the staff which strikes her intended target dead-on. After a few moments, the gravitational pull eases up, and

Jess' feet touch the floor, as do mine. The black bubble shrinks in size until it eventually disappears entirely.

"What was that?" Ron asks, his voice squeaking.

The theater has now grown back to being eerily quiet. The ridiculous scene that had unfolded here only moments prior now seems like a distant memory, as if it never happened. Jess and I look at one another, shocked expressions on our faces. Wrapping my arms around Jess, I bring her in for a hug. She begins to weep heavily into my chest. Ron approaches the two of us, and I take one arm and wrap it around him as well. The three of us stand there, holding each other for a few minutes, trying to compose ourselves after the nightmare of whatever just happened.

Breathing heavily, I turn my head to look at Doug standing up on the stage. He's looking back down at me, a concerned crease in his brow.

"So, you finally did it? You figured out what happened to John?" Doug's hands are on his hips, and he's pacing back and forth on the stage. "Son, you can't seriously be considering turning this over to the authorities. It'll ruin me. Everything I've achieved. I fought for this country. I served the community. Think…think of what it would do to Jill. She'd be devastated not having me in her life. She's a fragile woman, Son. Do you really want her to be alone again?"

I let go of my friends and approach the stage, facing Doug, keeping my voice low, nearly a whisper. "Don't you dare bring Mom into this."

"But it's the truth. Jill needs me. And I saved your life! Twice! I didn't have to do that."

"Yes, you did," Loretta says. "Brittany may have been the one to draw you here, but I'm the one who entered your mind and forced you to save Simon and Jess. Your mind is a dark, disturbing place. You would've let your stepson die today. It would've been easier for you if he was out of the picture."

"Just like it was easier for you after John was out of the picture, right Doug?" I ask.

Doug tilts his head in disbelief as I climb up onto the stage.

"I am John reincarnated." I say. "I remember everything. The years working for you on the force, my time with Samantha, the time I spent working on the Alvarez case. All of it."

He collapses down to his knees, an expression of puzzlement on his face, which quickly turns to a look of concern. I crouch down so the two of us are eye level.

"It can't be," he breathes. "That's…that's ridiculous. You belong back in that nut house. You shouldn't even be walking the streets! You're a danger to society. You're a danger to yourself!" He looks around the room, at Jess and Ron. "I feel sorry for you guys, I really do. Having this miserable excuse for a man in your life must be a living hell. He's unstable, you know. Jill and I tried to get him help. He's got a drug problem. His brain isn't fully developed."

Still crouched down in front of Doug, I look the man in the eye. Where there was once the look of a man who couldn't be intimidated, all I see now is a weak, scared man. A man afraid of what comes next.

"You had me killed in one life, and you tried your best to ruin this one. The funny thing is that in both lives, I was trying my best to please you. A goal that I could never achieve." I take a deep breath, then place my hand on his shoulder. "I have just one question for you, Doug. I know that John accidentally killed Chavez, but how did you and Mike get involved? Why did you work with Marcini to have me killed? To have John killed, that is. Why?"

He looks down at the ground, unable to look me in the eyes. "Marcini contacted me one night. Someone tipped him off that Stinson killed Chavez, and he offered me a ton of money to find someone to do the hit. 'An eye for an eye' is what Marcini called it. I knew of an inmate that Mike and John had put away, so I pulled some strings and had Travis Daniels released from prison early. I offered Mike the detective position if he would arrange the time and location for the hit to go down. I was responsible for covering it all up. With me leading the investigation, I was able to hide the evidence and eliminate any leads. It made it so easy for the case to go cold."

I grab Doug by the chin, forcing him to look me in the eyes. "There's something else here. Something you're not telling me. Spit it out."

Doug keeps his attention on me and begins talking faster. "I wanted, no, I *needed* to be with Samantha. She was so…beautiful. After Connie passed away, I developed feelings for Samantha."

"Those feelings had developed before Connie died. I saw the way you looked at Samantha on her wedding night. Admit it."

"John had everything I ever wanted. And when I found out he was going to be a father, I had a need…an impulse, instilled in my mind after a dream I had one night shortly before Connie died, that I needed to find an excuse have John killed so I could raise that child. Only, I never had the chance. I tried to make my move on Samantha after John died, when she was most vulnerable, but she rejected me. She insisted that John would always be Ryan's father, whether he was living or not. Samantha said there was only one man for her heart, and he was taken from her."

I stand up. "You're sick. You covered up your involvement in John's death. And then years later, you kicked me out of the house with only the clothes on my back and with nowhere to go, all over a misunderstanding. You never even gave me a chance. I'm going to return the favor."

I turn my attention to my friends. "Loretta, can you enter his mind again and force him to stay here until the police arrive?"

Loretta nods her head.

I turn back to Doug. "Over the years, I've learned the importance of forgiveness. I've learned what it means to love. It's going to take me time to learn to forgive you. I hope that eventually, in time, I can. That doesn't exclude you from justice, though. You will pay for your involvement in Officer Stinson's death, as well as covering it up. You may have been responsible for upholding the law, but that doesn't mean you're above it."

Chapter 37

I was there to witness Mike's arrest. After a brief standoff with the police, claiming that his land was sovereign territory and he was no longer a citizen of the United States despite the American flag waving in his front yard, he eventually surrendered. He glared at me as his bald head was guided down into the back of the police cruiser. His farm animals all watched from a distance, and I made sure to ask one of the local officers if someone would be able to take care of them so they didn't die of starvation or dehydration now that their owner will be locked in a cage of his own.

Steve, a.k.a. Tony Alvarez, eventually came around to testify against both men. His story was that he wanted to escape the life of crime that he had gotten himself into. Alvarez knew that he would soon be killed by someone within Marcini's crew. He realized he made a mistake joining the Marcini crime family, and needed a way out, so he contacted Mike, who had used to be an old friend of his growing up. Mike helped Alvarez fake his own death, gave him a new identity and convinced everyone that he was killed by someone within the Marcini crime family, his body dumped in the lake, never to be found. Steve later testified that Marcini had roughly a quarter of the Chicago police department under his payroll at the time he changed identities.

The news of the arrests, and the solved cold case of John Stinson's murder, has made national news. As I sit on the living room couch watching the media attempting to tell the story in detail, Mom comes into the living room and sits in her chair. She's been very solemn and quiet ever since the news came out about Doug's involvement in the crime. Whenever she asks me why I was in Indiana with Doug, why I was there when half of the theater apparently collapsed in on itself shortly after we left – which also made the local news – I simply tell Mom I don't remember, to which she nods her head silently. Oddly enough, I haven't seen Mom cry yet. I encouraged her to start seeing Angela, as in my opinion her expertise in the field of psychiatry is unmatched.

After a few nights of staying in a hotel, Jess finally went back to her apartment, although she repeatedly tells me that she no longer feels comfortable staying there after everything that happened the night she was taken. She hates her job, feeling that there's nothing for her in Chicago, and she wants to move out west somewhere.

Ron's still living in his friend's garage. Since getting fired from the mental hospital, he's still looking for a new job. He has several prospects lined up, or so he claims. He offered to stay with Jess to help make her feel safe, which she respectfully declined. My offer to stay with Jess was also denied, but for different reasons, I imagine. If I was to pretend to be Angela, I would say that Jess doesn't want our relationship to move too quickly, which is why she wants me living elsewhere for the time being, and she wouldn't feel comfortable with another man who isn't her boyfriend living with her.

Who knows, I could be way off the mark. Women are a complicated breed to understand sometimes, although I would suspect that women would say the same about men. Venus and Mars, and all of that.

Thankfully, Mom let me stay in the guest bedroom, as I still can't enter my apartment. And at this point, I don't care if I ever move back. There's nothing left for me there except Hank's broken tank and some burnt macaroni. I got my driver's license replaced and a new debit card. What else could a guy need?

I stand up and walk into my temporary bedroom and grab the old, unopened envelope on the nightstand. My heart's racing, and my hand's shaking slightly, but I repeatedly tell myself it's now or never.

"Bye, Mom," I say, giving her a hug in her chair while she knits. I begin to walk toward the front door. "I'll be back soon."

"Drive safe," she says. "Come here so I can take a better look at you."

I take my hand away from the doorknob and turn around. My mom stands up, walks over to me, and wraps her thin arms around me in a warm hug. She steps back and looks up at me, her hands now clutching my wrists.

"I wish your father could see what a fine young man you've grown up to be," she says, her voice shaking. "'Sorry' doesn't begin to do justice to how awful I feel about what happened when Doug kicked you out and I let it happen."

"Mom, it's–"

"Let me finish," she says sternly, then takes a deep breath. "Please. There's a lot I've had on my mind lately, and it's worn on me. You…you're the greatest thing that's ever happened to me. I love you with all my heart, and I always will. But this city…you've outgrown it. I hope that you stretch your wings and go out and do what makes you happy. You're more than welcome to stay here, of course. But if you wanted to leave and get a fresh start, I'd understand." Taking one of her hands away from my wrist, she reaches up and brushes back a curly clump of hair from my brow. "I'm proud of you, Simon. I always have been. I just want you to find happiness and fulfillment in your life."

"Thanks, Mom. I love you, too."

I head out to my car, and drive away.

Flowers have been placed on the various headstones around Acacia Park Cemetery. I walk along the paved path headed toward my father's burial ground. It's been quite awhile since I've been here to pay my respects.

I place a bouquet of flowers in front of his headstone, then stuff my hands into my pockets. For several minutes I stand there, staring down at the cement headstone with his name inscribed on it. No date of birth, or date of death. No message of any kind, per his request. Just his name, Robert Verner.

"You missed quite the show, Dad," I say softly, my chin tilted down. "I met a girl, who turned out to be…it's a long story. But these two women had these magical staffs, one was yellow, the other was blue, and it was…it was really something." I chuckle, itching my eyebrow. The cemetery is incredibly silent. A soft breeze picks up, blowing gently in my face. Clouds begin to part, and the sun shines down. "Ah, there you are. I miss you too, Dad. There's so much I didn't get the chance to ask you. There's so much I didn't get a chance to say. One day, we'll see each other again. I believe it now more than ever."

I kneel down and place my hand on the headstone for a few moments. Then I stand up and continue walking down the path.

A few minutes later, I approach another headstone, roughly the same size as the others around it.

"Hello, John," I say. "We meet at last."

I stare down at the headstone, the words inscribed reading:

John Stinson. October 15, 1955 – April 24, 1986
Loving husband and father to be
Killed in the line of duty
Badge 40092

Standing over the burial grounds of my past life, I'm at a loss to describe the emotions coursing through me. Mostly, it feels creepy. The bones in a box six feet below are actually *mine.* It's the person I used to be. Thoughts, feelings and memories, shared between these two bodies, mine and the one below, begin to feel united as one in a sense. While my soul was once his, and after the last several weeks of his visions that eventually led to the showdown in the Palace Theater, I still feel disconnected from him. After all this time, when I thought that I was him and our memories were shared, ultimately it was just…my imagination. Not to say that what I saw didn't actually happen, but rather the idea that I *was* John. While I still remember the various visions of his memories in my dreams, they're not as vivid as they once were. His memories have begun to fade, drifting away back into the cosmos.

What I'd felt regarding he and I being the same man, was nothing more than my desire to be someone else. My wishful thinking to be someone that wasn't a total failure in the judgmental eyes of society. At least, that's the only logical conclusion that I could come up with. One that Angela and I could potentially agree on, if she was giving her diagnosis of my mental state.

"I'm sorry for what happened to you," I say solemnly. "You seemed like a good man. Not perfect. But really, who is? We finally took down Marcini. Doug and Mike were brought to justice. We finally solved the mystery."

Driving down the highway, all sorts of thoughts flood through my mind. *What will he look like? Does he have a family of his own? Is he happy?* It's a hot summer afternoon, and the need for speed has taken over briefly. I suppress the urge to pass cars like they're standing still; it's not worth it. I'll get there eventually. Turning on the radio, I go with the flow of traffic, tapping my thumbs on the steering wheel and humming. Butterflies are attacking my stomach like they're stuck in a net and sweat begins to dampen my palms. I take a deep breath and try to slow my heart rate.

Ron helped me get the address off the internet. The house is a spacious, two-story home with a short white picket fence outlining the front yard of bright green grass. Shrubbery lines the sides of the yard, with a small island in the middle filled with an assortment of flowers and a small tree. It's an older, quiet neighborhood, with an elderly couple walking down the sidewalk. They wave at me as I park on the street in front of the house.

The doorbell chimes, and I step back onto the spacious cement porch. Rumbling of several footsteps can be heard inside the home, and the door creaks open. A handsome man in his mid-thirties opens the screen door and smiles warmly. He's about six feet tall and has short black hair and brown eyes. My breath catches as a flood of emotions overwhelm me.

"Hello. Can I help you?" he asks, still smiling.

I clear my throat, and take a deep breath, clutching the envelope tightly to my chest. "Hi. My name's Simon Verner. Are you Ryan Stinson?"

His eyebrows furrow momentarily in puzzlement. "Yes, that would be me."

"I know this is out of the blue, but I just wanted to…to give you this," I hand him the aged and yellowed envelope. He takes it, examining it closely. "This was written by me – I mean, this was written by your dad, and he wanted to give this to you one day. I know it was a long time ago, but it would've meant the world to John that you have this."

"Wow…I…." He clears his throat and looks up at me with tears in his eyes. "How did you get this?"

"It's been in police evidence all these years," I say quickly, hoping he'll buy my lie. "It was vital to the investigation."

"Thank you, Simon. This is…" He shakes his head, looking down at the envelope. "I'm glad the police solved that crime. Mom would've been so relieved." He takes a shaky breath. "I wish I could've met him. Even though he wasn't around, I just wanted to do my best in life to make him proud, you know? I would always imagine him up there looking down, wishing the best for my mom and me. He's probably looking down at us with a smile on his face right now. At least, that's what I hope."

"He's closer than you think, and he always has been," I say quietly. "I just think that when we lose the people closest to us in life, they're always right here." I tap my chest.

"I think you're right," Ryan takes a deep breath, looking briefly down at the envelope, then back at me. "Want to come in for some tea?"

"Oh, no thank you. I better get going. It was nice to see you."

A young girl, no more than three years old, runs up behind Ryan. "Daddy, daddy, mommy needs you in the back yard!"

Ryan scoops the young girl up with his free arm, holding her on his hip. He looks at me, nods his head, and gently closes the front door. My breath catches again for a moment, and I walk back to my car.

Later that night, I dream of John one last time.

He's in the kitchen, with a pen in hand, and a blank sheet of paper on the table. His wife is sound asleep in the bedroom, the exhaustion of a day teaching young minds and being eight months pregnant doing her in.

John stares at the paper for what feels like hours, although it's been more like five minutes. There's so much he wants to say to his unborn son. The anticipation of meeting this newcomer to the world is overwhelming him so much that he doesn't know where to begin. He sets his pen to the paper, pressing down, then lifts the pen up and sits back. He stares up at the ceiling, thoughts flowing through his racing mind. The toughest part of any project, he believes, is just finding where to begin. Finally, he puts his pen down on the paper again, and begins to write.

> To my son, Ryan,
>
> As I sit at our kitchen table, trying to find the words to express how I feel, all I can say is I can't wait to finally meet you. We can't wait to finally meet you. Let me start with your mom. She's the most wonderful woman I've ever known, and I know she's going to make a great mother. She has a heart of gold, and she will love you more than anything in this world. She's also a very smart woman, so good luck trying to get a lie past her. If she wasn't a schoolteacher, I bet she would've made a better detective than your old man. Please treat her with respect and love in case I'm not around.

As a police officer, I know this line of work is very dangerous. I do it to serve and protect the innocent. All I've ever wanted to do is help people and do the right thing. I know that you'll grow up to be the same way. Hopefully a better man than me. I can't wait to take you to your first Bulls game and spend Sundays watching the Bears together. In the summer, I hope we can watch the Cubs together. But if you decide to be a White Sox fan, I won't hold that against you.

I can't wait to show you Star Wars and take you down to our favorite spot on the beach. I'll show you how to put up a tent, how to mow the yard, how to bandage a wound on your knee, how to shave. If you're anything like your old man, I bet you'll have girls chasing you home. Don't worry, I'll make sure to do a background check on them, so you'll know they're safe to date. I'm joking.

Anyways, Ryan, I just wanted to write this letter and hope that one day you'll read it and know how much your mom and I will always love you and look out for you. We will do our best to provide for you and keep a roof over your head and food on the table. One day, I hope you'll have a family of your own, living in a big house. Whatever you choose to do with your life, we just want you to be happy. I can't wait to meet you, my son.

Love, Dad

April 24th, 1986

John folds the letter and puts it into the envelope, writes "Ryan" on the outside, and puts it in a shoebox, which he then puts in a small black safe in the basement.

He starts getting ready for work, kisses Samantha on the forehead, and leaves home for the last time.

Several weeks later, Jess is sitting next to me in the passenger seat of my car. Rays of sunlight dance on her hair, and I place my hand on her knee. She puts her hand on mine, and I look over to see her smiling. Her other hand is hanging out the window, her fingers going up and down with the passing breeze.

Mom got back into the dating scene. She said she wouldn't sit in an empty house, knowing that she was married to a "two-faced liar" for so long. She was spending more time out of the house, and apparently, she found another man to start spending her time with. I left Mom a note before I packed up my few personal possessions in a backpack, letting her know that I'll call and keep in touch, but there's nothing else left for me in Chicago.

The trials for Doug and Mike will take years. The last I've heard, they were arguing the merits of the tape recorders. What they couldn't argue, however, was Steve's testimony.

The one loose string to the entire case that I still had trouble wrapping my head around was why Steve decided to stay in Chicago, when he had a chance to be free after faking his death. His only answer was that he loved the city, and he wanted to take over ownership of the Lowland Woods Golf Course.

"Home," Steve had said. "This city is my home. I wouldn't feel right anywhere else. It's like I've lived two lives, but as long as there's one constant in both of them, then I at least have some kind of anchor to fall back to when times get tough. If that makes sense." I told him no, that doesn't really make sense, but I appreciated his explanation, nonetheless.

Jess also agreed to take the jump with me and leave the city behind. There was nothing for her there either, or so she said. She quit the job she hated, sold a bunch of her paintings and other stuff she didn't need, and was ready for a fresh new start with me. I asked her several times if she was sure this was the right decision for her. I'll stay if she wants to, but I would rather drive far away from the city that cut my past life short and had tried to end this one as well. She reassured me that this is what she wants. The feeling of just hitting the road and getting a fresh start somewhere else is what would make her happy. She wants a blank slate.

I couldn't be happier. A blank slate is exactly what I was looking for as well.

"Can you turn up the music?" Ron asks from the back seat.

Yes, Ron wanted to come with us as well. He sold his car and left with only the clothes on his back. Due to his assistance in breaking me out of the mental institution leading to his job termination, this has apparently made him a poor hiring candidate in the Chicago area.

As he requested, I turn the volume up to a song by *Pearl Jam.*

"I like these guys," Ron says "Where'd you say they're from again?"

"Seattle," I say.

"Great, let's go there."

Jess and I look at one another, and we each shrug our shoulders simultaneously. Why not? It's a big world out there, and as we continue on the open road toward the Pacific Northwest, I remind myself how fortunate I am to have these two friends in my life. Why these two would want to head across the country with me after what we've been through is a complete mystery. I suppose they're the best friends a guy like me could ever ask for.

I dream for a brighter future for all mankind. Where Mubiru's soul only saw corruption and hate through tainted eyes, I believe that I can see the best that people have to offer. At least that's my goal. The world isn't a perfect place, and never will be. A lot of people dream for brighter days ahead, no matter how dark it currently is. But I believe that if people dream of coming together, we can learn to listen and communicate. Then, and only then, can we find it within ourselves to set aside our differences and turn those dreams into reality.

Epilogue

Dark mountains surround the Black Palace. The sky is a murky hue of red, reflecting the molten lava ocean that encompasses the land around the Palace grounds beneath. Winged demons fly, going about their daily duties as instructed by their Dark Leader. A procession walks across a bridge over the moat leading into the front gate. Hoisted upon the shoulders of several human slaves is a shrouded golden carriage. The gate opens, and the carriage is brought inside, up a flight of stairs to the Skull Throne.

Those responsible for holding the carriage bend their knees at the same time. A small, gruesome looking individual opens the door to the carriage, giggling uncontrollably, and several other human slaves rush forward at once, piling on top of one another on their hands and knees. They form a makeshift staircase as Popobowa steps out and walks on their backs down to the smooth rock floor which is covered in soot and ash. Holding a young woman's corpse in his arms, he strides over to the Skull Throne and throws her body roughly on the ground, next to a pile of other discarded, decaying bodies. He takes his seat on the throne, one leg up on the arm rest, and places his chin on his fist, a disgusted look on his face.

"Another one for the collection, my Lord?" the giggling man asks.

Popobowa doesn't acknowledge him at first, instead looking at the mountain of bodies on the floor. Several corpses are piled on top of one another, most of which are now decapitated skeletons. The Skull Throne has several of those heads on pikes around the back of it.

"Yes, Zooberi, it appears your son has burned through yet another life. A pretty one, too. Such a shame."

Zooberi begins giggling more frantically, and shuffles over to a wall with human bodies on hooks. He picks one of them up off the hook, and carries it over to the throne, where he gently rests it on the ground at Popobowa's feet.

He sits upright on the throne, bends down to get a better look, then reaches over to pat Zooberi on the head.

"Good work," Popobowa says, standing up.

Another human slave hands the staff of fire to Popobowa, and immediately runs away. A delegation of humans and demons have gathered at the bottom of the stairs, eagerly awaiting new orders from their leader. Far off in the distance, one of the darkened mountains erupts into a spectacular display of fiery lava. A thunderous boom reaches their ears several moments later.

He slams the staff down on the ground. "The Dark Dimension is dying!"

Murmuring can be heard amongst the crowd, and Popobowa waits for them to quiet down.

"I speak the truth. This realm is near its end. But due to a recent and unforeseen glimpse at the living world, I believe the dawn of our time is approaching. There's another world out there, nearly ripe for us to take. Stay patient, and very soon, we will cross over to their reality. When that time comes, I know we'll be ready. And there's nothing that any mortal can do about it. Not even Mwari can stop us!"

The crowd erupts in cheers, fists raised.

A grin spreads across Popobowa's face, and he begins laughing. His war with Mwari and Magdoo is far from over. The time to make his move on the living world has come.

Printed in the USA
CPSIA information can be obtained
at www.ICGtesting.com
LVHW020947181123
764308LV00014B/693